Record Time

More . . .

**St. Martin's Paperbacks Titles
by Beverly Brandt**

True North

Record Time

Room Service

Dream On
Beverly Brandt

St. Martin's Paperbacks

DREAM ON

Copyright © 2004 by Beverly Brandt.
Excerpt from *The Tiara Club* copyright © 2004 by Beverly Brandt.

Cover photo by Herman Estevez

ISBN: 0-312-99484-2

Printed in the United States of America

St. Martin's Paperbacks edition / March 2004

St. Martin's Paperbacks are published by St. Martin's Press, 175 Fifth Avenue, New York, NY 10010.

10 9 8 7 6 5 4 3 2 1

Acknowledgments

First of all, I'd like to acknowledge everyone out there who has a dream of his or her own. It takes courage to pursue your dreams in the face of financial hardship, possible ridicule, and the overwhelming odds against success. To all you dreamers out there, I'd like to say, "Dream on," because without you our world would be a bleak and boring place.

As always, I'd like to thank my insightful and supportive editor at St. Martin's Press, Kim Cardascia. You are the editor of my dreams!

To fellow author Ronn Kaiser, thank you for your timely post on the Novelists, Inc., loop that people dedicated to achieving their dreams have no Plan B. That summed up Bradley's single-minded pursuit of his goal perfectly at a time when I was having difficulty putting it into words.

I'd also like to thank my sister, brother, and father for reading my books and being enthusiastic in your support. Kelley, Brian, and Richard Price—thank you.

And, finally, to my husband, Wes. Thank you for believing in me right from the start.

Dream On

Chapter 1
Reelin' in Reno

"The problem, Bradley, is that I'm Las Vegas and you're . . . well, you're Reno," Robyn Rogers said, her voice strong and assured over the never-ending buzz of cars headed down Second Street on their way toward Harrah's. "I'm bright lights on the marquee, miles of glitz and glamour, the Luxor and the Bellagio all rolled into one. Poor little Reno just can't keep up."

Bradley Nelson used his thumb to tilt his black cowboy hat a little farther back on his head and felt the high desert sun pounding on his forehead through the open window of Robyn's tour bus. The cracked sidewalk next to the bus was deserted except for her driver, who had stepped outside at Robyn's request a few minutes earlier.

"Look, darlin'," Bradley drawled in his best lazy-cowboy voice, "I know you're mad as a wet hen because I asked you to stop here on your way to Vegas, but I promised my mother that I'd drop in and see her when I was in town. It won't take more than an hour."

Robyn turned her catlike green eyes on him, her perfectly smooth blond hair seeming to float in the scorching after-noon breeze. "I'm not a barnyard animal, Bradley, and I don't appreciate being likened to one every time you slip into Roy Rogers mode. This isn't about stopping in Reno.

It's about us. We're just not working anymore. I need a man who's my equal, a man whose career is as successful as my own. This whole country music star wanna-be thing is getting old."

Trying to contain his anger, Bradley watched the bus driver slow to a stop on the hot pavement outside, the soles of his tennis shoes looking as if they were going to melt where he stood. "Well, that's a mighty fine thing for you to say, seeing as how you're a rock star wanna-be yourself—"

"No," Robyn interrupted, standing up to pace the center aisle of the tour bus. "I'm a star already. I'm five years younger than you, and I already have a million-dollar contract from Gamble Records. I'm so far ahead of you, you'll never be able to catch up."

"I didn't realize this was a competition," Bradley said quietly, resisting the urge to add another "darlin'" to the end of his sentence.

"Come on, Bradley, if you were being honest with yourself, you'd admit that you were just using me to get a record contract from my brother-in-law. And it worked. You got your contract, but even that wasn't enough to get you onto the Top 40 charts. Or even the Top 100. That's just the way it goes in show business sometimes. Some artists are destined for greatness, while others . . . well, others just aren't."

"I never used you, not to get a recording contract or for anything else." Bradley barely managed to get the words out between gritted teeth. He had never—not even once—asked Robyn to help him smooth the way with David Gamble, her brother-in-law. For her to accuse him of using her was just plain ridiculous.

"I call things the way I see them," Robyn said, shrugging nonchalantly as if his dreams meant nothing to her. Which, of course, they didn't. And why should they? She was right. She already had the fame and fortune that Bradley was working so hard to achieve. Why should she care if he succeeded or not?

"It's time for me to move on. I want someone who knows about more than just the music business; someone with a little more . . . promise."

Bradley glared at the woman who had so often infuriated him over the past eight months. It took every ounce of will-power he possessed not to toss his hat into the oncoming traffic and holler the truth over the noise from outside. He had plenty of fucking promise, and he knew a hell of a lot more about a hell of a lot more things than she could have guessed. But he didn't say any of that. Instead, he stood up and walked to the door of the bus, tipped his hat to Robyn in the most gentlemanly manner he could muster, turned on his heel, and walked away.

It was all he could do not to look back to see if Robyn had come out of her tour bus to watch him walk away. She had some nerve, accusing him of using her. Hell, if anything it was the other way around. She seemed to love snapping her fingers just to see how long it took him to come running.

He had no idea why he'd put up with her for so long, but he knew for damned sure that he wasn't the one who was going to go crawling back. Let her grovel for a change.

The dry desert air barely stirred as Bradley headed down the block toward the Heart O'Reno Casino, where his mother was currently working as an accountant. On the one occasion his mother had met Robyn, the two women had been cautiously polite, but Bradley could tell that they didn't much care for each other.

So it was just as well that Robyn wasn't hanging around, making Bradley's visit with his mom stilted and uncomfortable. Not to mention that his trip out to Nashville for the Country Music Awards next week could now be made without having to work the layover in around Robyn's touring schedule.

But if he was so eager to see Robyn go, why was he starting to get that panicky feeling in his gut—the one that told him he was letting go of something he shouldn't?

Bradley's steps slowed on the hot pavement. Was he making a mistake by walking away? David Gamble hadn't yet decided whether to renew Bradley's contract. Would Bradley's breakup with Robyn sway David's decision? Bradley could protest all he wanted that he wasn't using Robyn, but he'd be plumb stupid to believe this might not have some impact on his career.

Bradley turned back toward the bus.

"She's already gone, mister."

Bradley looked up, startled by the softly uttered words. A garishly bright neon sign blinked on and off in the window of the Heart O'Reno Drive-Thru Wedding Chapel, which was attached to the similarly named casino where his mother worked. A fake gorilla stood next to the glass front doors, shaking its head at him.

"She's a quick little thing, ain't she?" the gorilla said, then corrected itself. "I mean, isn't she? Isn't she?"

Bradley glanced around to see if anyone else had noticed the talking gorilla, wondering if it was the heat or Robyn's calm dismissal that had driven him insane.

The fake gorilla pulled off its furry head, and Bradley realized it wasn't a gorilla at all—it was a woman wearing a monkey suit. She shook her head as if to clear it, her long brownish-blond ponytail moving from side to side as she did.

"Boy, is it hot in there," she said, setting the gorilla head down beside her on a tiny patch of dried-up grass in front of the wedding chapel.

Shaking his own head at the surreal situation he found himself in, Bradley couldn't help but ask, "Don't you have air-conditioning?"

The woman looked at him with amused blue eyes. "Now, how would we get an air conditioner into this suit? I can barely stand up under the weight of it as it is."

Bradley shook his head, trying to make some sense of this conversation. "No, I meant don't you have air-conditioning in the building where you work?"

"Of course we do. It's not hot in there," she said, gesturing with one fur-covered hand toward the doors behind her. "It's hot in there." At this, she pointed at her chest.

"Oh."

"But I had to get out of *there*," the woman continued, still smiling as she pointed back to the doors, "because the couple using the jungle room were going at it like . . . well, like animals. I figured I'd give them some privacy until they were ready to start the ceremony."

Bradley didn't quite know what to say to that, which was just as well since whatever response he might have come up with would have been interrupted when the doors behind them flew open with a crash of metal against glass. Bradley was astonished to see his mother come flying out the doors with a frantic look on her typically calm face.

Harriet Nelson didn't even pause for a second upon seeing her son standing in the middle of the sidewalk talking to a woman in a gorilla suit. Instead, she yelled, "Follow me. We've got to get out of here," and took off running down the sidewalk.

Bradley hesitated, but only until he saw a man stop just inside the doors behind them to pull a gun out from under his suit jacket. Grabbing the woman's arm, he said, "Come on."

She grabbed the head of her gorilla suit and followed him at a dead run. They'd only gone about half a block when Bradley saw his mother waving at them from inside the motor home she'd so proudly bought two years ago when she'd retired from the IRS. The engine was running, and her foot was poised over the gas pedal.

"Get in," Harriet ordered, already starting to maneuver the behemoth vehicle out into traffic.

Bradley pulled the gorilla woman into the Winnebago behind him just as his mother pulled away from the curb. The woman's foot slipped on the step as his mother jerked into traffic, and the fur went flying. Bradley tripped over the passenger seat and the momentum of the woman in the monkey suit sent him toppling to the carpeted floor of the motor home. The woman landed full on top of him, the gorilla head she was holding in her left hand narrowly missing his head as it slammed to the floor beside him.

"I'm so sorry," the woman said softly, her voice carrying the remnants of a syrupy drawl that made Bradley think of magnolia trees and sweet tea and hot, humid nights full of chirping crickets and promise. He looked up into her pretty blue eyes and almost forgot how they had landed themselves in this position.

"Don't worry about it, darlin'," he said, helping her into a sitting position. "Having a pretty girl fall into my lap is a cause for celebration, not apology." Bradley smiled, expecting the woman to blush or at least smile back at him. Instead, she cocked her head and stared at him with an expression he couldn't read.

"You two better get buckled in," Harriet said from the driver's seat, reminding Bradley that he had no idea what they were doing speeding through the streets of Reno in a Winnebago.

Using the passenger seat to pull himself up off the floor, Bradley stood and held a hand out to the woman on the floor. She took his hand and staggered a bit with the jerky motions of the motor home. Bradley stepped aside and motioned for her to take the passenger seat. Then he turned to his mother and asked, "So, would you like to tell me what this is all about?"

Harriet didn't take her eyes off the road. Her compact body was huddled over the steering wheel, as if it were taking all her weight to keep the vehicle under control. Which it probably was, Bradley thought as his mother responded. "My boss is trying to kill me. That's what this is all about."

"I'm guessing he was the one with the gun?" Bradley asked.

"Yes, that's him."

"And is there any particular reason he's trying to kill you?"

His mother looked up at him then, as if deciding how much of the truth to tell. Then she yelled, "Hold on!"

Bradley clutched the back of the driver's seat as the Winnebago screeched around a corner, banging back down on all its wheels as his mother straightened out the steering wheel.

"Excuse me," the woman in the passenger seat said, as if they were on their way to a tea party instead of barreling through Reno, being chased by his mother's murderous employer. "Where are we going?"

"I don't know," Harriet answered. "I've only lived here for a few months. Do you know where we can hide this RV?"

The woman in the gorilla suit was quiet for a moment. "Yes, I think I have an idea. Take a right up here at the next light."

"Mother," Bradley began, sitting down on the floor with his back braced against the wall.

"Just a minute, dear. I've got my hands full just now," Harriet said as a shot rang out. It shattered the window next to the passenger seat, making the woman in the gorilla suit gasp and throw herself into the tight space on the floor in front of the seat.

"Turn left up ahead on Riverside," Gorilla Girl said, still hunched down on the floor. "There's an RV park about a quarter of a mile up the road. You're going to have to stop at the gate, though."

"Hmm," Harriet said, taking the left turn as fast as she could. Bradley heard the horns of several angry drivers, but didn't poke his head up to see what havoc his mother was wreaking in her wake.

"Maybe . . ." The woman ducked unnecessarily as a second shot came whistling through the already broken passenger-side window.

"Maybe what, dear?" Bradley's mother prodded calmly, as if she dodged bullets every day.

"Maybe we could call ahead and tell the person at the

security gate that our brakes are failing and that we need him to lift the gate for us. If he shuts it behind us, we might just be able to pull this off."

"Good thinking," Harriet said. "Bradley, do you have your cell phone? I can't reach mine."

Bradley looked from his mother to the woman in the gorilla suit and back, feeling as if he'd been pushed off Robyn's tour bus and into some alternate universe. He was riding in a Winnebago with his mother and a gorilla, being shot at by some lunatic. How in the world had this happened?

"Bradley?" his mother asked. "Do you have your cell phone or not?"

Blinking rapidly, Bradley pulled his phone out of his back pocket. "What's the name of this place?" he asked the gorilla.

"Happy Days, I think," the woman answered.

Bradley dialed information and was connected at no additional charge to the Happy Days RV Park in Reno, Nevada. He told the guard at the gate the story the woman had concocted, and was relieved when the man agreed to open the gate for them.

"He said to pull straight through," Bradley told his mother as he hung up his phone. "They have an uphill drive that he says will slow you down."

Harriet nodded and pushed her foot down on the accelerator when the neon sign for the RV park came into view.

"Don't slow down when we get into the park," the woman in the gorilla suit said. "Keep heading toward the river. It's a Friday, so there should be quite a few weekend travelers camped down by the water. If you pull in next to the rest of the motor homes, you might be able to fool your boss."

"Good idea. Roll down your window so he won't see the bullet holes . . . um, I'm sorry. I didn't catch your name," Bradley said.

"Delphine. Delphine Armstrong."

"Pleased to meet you, Delphine. I'm Bradley Nelson and

this is my mother, Harriet," Bradley said politely, despite the strange circumstances.

"Yes, your mother and I met yesterday in the employee lunchroom. It was my first day on the job," Delphine added.

"Oh, well, good," Bradley said. "Look, we need to hide your gorilla suit. I'm not sure if Mom's boss saw you in it or not, but it's better if we don't take that chance."

"Here's the turn. Hold on, everyone," Harriet warned.

Bradley braced himself between the driver's seat and the base of the small dining booth as his mother took the sharp curve. Delphine's gorilla head was not so well braced, however. It flew out of the passenger seat and rolled across the floor, hitting him about mid-thigh.

"Sorry about that," Delphine said once the motor home had straightened out. "I guess I lost my head."

Bradley pushed himself up off the floor, laughing at her lame attempt at humor. "That's all right. Why don't you unzip the rest of your costume and I'll hide it somewhere?" He paused. "You *are* wearing something underneath that monkey suit, aren't you?"

"Yes, of course," Delphine answered, attempting to stand up while the Winnebago swayed from side to side. Holding on to the back of her seat, she awkwardly tugged on the zipper. Bradley put a steadying hand on her fur-padded shoulder, the gorilla head resting between his feet. He helped her peel the heavy suit off as the motor home lumbered toward the river. He still had no idea what sort of trouble his mother was in, but now didn't seem the right time to ask for details. Once his mother's boss was gone, they'd have plenty of time to see what sort of mess Harriet had landed them in.

Bradley tried to be a gentleman while Delphine stripped off her monkey suit. Really, he did. However, he couldn't help but notice the smooth expanse of skin that was exposed when she tugged the suit down over her legs, or the hint of a sturdy white bra that flashed him as she pulled her arm out of the suit, her clean but well-worn T-shirt refusing to remain in place. Finally, she stood in front of him, the metamorphosis complete, and Bradley was surprised to find himself thinking that she was one hell of an attractive woman.

"Aren't you going to hide that?" she asked, startling him out of his appreciative reverie.

"Oh, yes. Sorry," he apologized sheepishly before hauling her costume to the rear of the motor home. The closets in the bedroom were both full of his mother's stuff, so Bradley yanked open the door to the postage-stamp-sized bathroom and dumped the suit into the tiny shower stall. Then he closed the door and headed toward the front of the motor home, just in time to grab the edge of a kitchen counter when his mother spun the Winnebago to a halt alongside several dozen other motor homes.

As soon as the wheels stopped turning, Bradley went to work. "Mom, you need to hide yourself in case your boss comes looking for us. Do you have a screwdriver?"

"Now's not the time for a drink, Bradley," his mother admonished.

"Not *that* kind of screwdriver," Bradley said, rolling his eyes heavenward. God knew he could use a drink after all that had happened to him this morning, but he had more important things to do just now. "I need to get rid of your license plate. Your boss followed us long enough to see your New Jersey plates, and I want to make it at least a little harder for him to find us."

"Oh, well, that's very bright of you, dear. All of my tools are in the storage area below the motor home, but I keep that space locked up tight."

Bradley resisted the urge to sigh. "Okay. What about a knife, then?" he asked, already yanking open drawers.

His mother wafted past him on a cloud of Enjoli perfume, pulled open the top drawer next to the stove, and handed him a butter knife. Then she said, "I'll be in the closet if you need me," turned, and walked away.

"Do you need some help?" Delphine asked, looking more

eager than he would have expected a stranger in this situation to look under the circumstances.

"I don't think so. I'll be back in a minute," Bradley said before heading outside to take care of the license plates.

He walked cautiously around the back of the motor home, looking around at the other campsites, full of brightly colored toys and barbecues and recreational vehicles. He had no idea why his mother had decided to buy an RV when she retired. It was certainly not something they'd ever done when Bradley was growing up back in Jersey. On the contrary, his roots were about as far from roughing it as they could possibly get. The great outdoors was one giant mystery to him . . . but that was his own closely guarded secret. After all, it was hard to pretend to be a good ol' country boy when he knew more about computers than camping.

He crouched down and worked at the screws holding the license plate in place. The second screw stuck a bit, but Bradley soon had it loose. He looked around for a place to stash the thin slab of metal, and ended up burying it under a layer of dust behind the right rear wheel. Then, knowing he couldn't just leave the space empty, he looked around at the other RVs to see if he could find a plate to borrow.

When he saw a motor home with plates on the front as well as the back, he glanced to the left and right to make sure no one was watching and quickly went to work. He had the plate undone and was just standing up when a loud group of kids came around a curve in the road. Bradley nonchalantly stuck the warm license plate into the waistband at the back of his jeans and sidled around the edge of the other motor home. Just before he stepped out of sight, a big black car came roaring up behind the kids and honked its horn. Bradley guessed that the group was mostly teenagers when they refused to get out of the vehicle's way, a tactic that Bradley silently thanked them for, since he figured the driver of the black car was his mother's boss.

Ducking between RVs, Bradley raced to the back of the

Winnebago and slipped the license plate into place. He fumbled with the butter knife, dropping one of the screws into the dirt in his haste. The group of teens was almost to his mother's RV now, and Bradley knew he didn't have much time to waste getting back inside. There were no other adults around, and he didn't want to be hovering around looking suspicious when the black car passed by.

Only, when the kids passed, the black car wasn't following them anymore, Bradley noticed, poking his head around the side of the Winnebago.

"Damn," he muttered. The driver must have parked the car and gone looking for Harriet on foot.

Bradley crouched down, trying to see if he could spot anyone between the motor homes. He spied a set of Italian loafers beside the RV next to them and made his move, racing to the door of his mother's vehicle.

The door flew open just as he reached the bottom step, nearly knocking him backward into the dirt. "Get in," Delphine whispered, grabbing the front of his black T-shirt. "He's right next door."

"I know," Bradley whispered back as he let her pull him inside.

"I'm sorry," Delphine apologized.

"For what?"

"This," she said, then stunned him by yanking her shirt over her head, pushing him up against the stove, and pressing her body against his. Bradley was too shocked to move. Fortunately, Delphine seemed to know what she was doing as she threaded her fingers through his hair and pulled his lips down to meet hers.

The second their lips met, instinct took over. Bradley splayed one hand across the small of Delphine's back, her skin warm and smooth beneath his fingers. He shifted his legs farther apart to settle her comfortably between them and used his other hand to free her hair from its ponytail.

The scent of stale fur was overpowered by the clean smell of whatever shampoo she had used that morning.

Bradley moved his hand down to trace circles in the skin under her ear. When Delphine sighed and pressed closer to him, he sucked gently on her bottom lip, teasing her mouth to open under his. He felt the cool metal of the stove behind him when Delphine pulled his T-shirt from the waistband of his jeans, then felt the heat of her hands on his waist. Pressing his hips to hers, he silently urged her to do more than just tickle the skin of his back.

He blinked when, instead, she pulled back and murmured, "Do you think he's gone?"

"He who?" Bradley asked.

Delphine licked her lips, and Bradley was tempted to kiss her again until she said, "Your mother's boss."

Bradley did his best to act as if he'd just been playing along the whole time. "Oh, right." He looked up, trying not to stare at the swell of Delphine's small but quite adequate breasts. "I don't see anyone outside. But maybe we should give it a few more minutes," he suggested.

"I think we're safe," Harriet called out from the back room, dashing Bradley's hope that he and Delphine could go back to what they had been doing a few seconds ago. "I saw Dickie look through the back windows and move on."

Bradley leaned down and picked up Delphine's shirt from where she had hastily tossed it on the floor. Shielding her from his mother's view, he pulled the garment right side out and gently, but with great reluctance, held it up for her to slip her arms into. When she was all tucked in, he made his way to the back of the motor home and sat on the edge of the bed, propping one black snakeskin cowboy boot up against the faux cedar-paneled wall.

"All right, Mother. What's going on here? And who is this Dickie character?"

Delphine came into the room and slid the curtains closed

before taking a seat on the bed a short distance from Bradley. She looked up and smiled at him, and Bradley found himself smiling back. She was awfully attractive, with her long hair and sparkling eyes and small-town charm, and, in a flash, Bradley realized that Delphine Armstrong fit his image of the perfect country girl—the kind of woman who baked cookies for the local bake sales, went to church every Sunday, and brought casseroles to her sick neighbors.

"Dickie is my boss," Harriet answered, interrupting Bradley's thoughts. "And he was the one who was chasing us. I think he's the one who's deepest into this whole mess." Harriet peered cautiously into the crack between the pink flowered curtains as she spoke.

Bradley raised a hand to push his hat back on his head, but realized it must have fallen off at some point in their wild ride. He looked out of the cramped bedroom, saw his hat wedged up against the side of the passenger seat, and decided to leave it there for the moment. "Deepest into what mess?"

Harriet sat down on the edge of the bed. "The scheme to defraud the taxpayers. My boss Dickie Swanson and his friends are underreporting their income to the United States government. I knew something was wrong the first week I started working at the casino, but it took me a good two months to figure out how they were doing it. They were really pretty smart about it," she added, sounding surprised.

"But that doesn't explain why they were after you," Bradley said, wishing he'd just let Robyn drive straight through to Vegas instead of insisting they stop to visit his mother on their way. Sure, Robyn probably still would have dumped him, but at least he wouldn't be stuck right in the middle of another one of his mother's crazy situations. He supposed this was why he'd always gotten along so well with Robyn's sister, Kylie. Kylie was the only person he knew who could get herself into a mess faster than his mother could. And Bradley had grown up being Harriet's straight man—always ready to lend a hand with her kooky schemes. He had hoped that her retirement from the IRS would settle his mother down, but this latest fiasco proved that hope was as dead as a prize turkey on Thanksgiving morning, Bradley thought, crossing one snakeskin-clad ankle over the other. Since she'd bought this motor home and started driving across the country, taking jobs whenever something in the local want ads struck her fancy, her fiasco ratio was just as high as ever.

Harriet picked up a corner of the bedspread and proceeded to fiddle with the lacy edge. "They're after me because they think I have something of theirs," she said, not meeting her son's gaze.

Bradley raised his eyes heavenward, noting the yellowed water stain on the ceiling. "And why would they think that?"

There was a long silence, which made Bradley uncross his ankles and sit up straighter. "Mother? Why would they think that?"

"Well, because maybe I do," she said. Her lips were set in a stubborn, red-lipsticked line. Bradley knew that face. It was her "I'm right and the rest of the world is wrong" face, the same one she got when she tried to explain why the tax rules made perfect sense if you just thought them through. In all her years as an IRS auditor, she had never once even questioned whether the tax code might be unfair or even the tiniest bit too complicated.

He almost dreaded asking the next question, but he knew he had to. "What do they think you might have?"

Harriet stretched the lacy bedspread out and let it fall back to the mattress. Then she stood up. And sat back down again.

"What do they think you have, Mother?" Bradley asked again. "Poker chips? An extra roll of quarters? A handful of free-drink coupons?" He stood and leaned against the bedroom wall, propping one booted foot up against the cardboard-thin wall. Delphine sat on the edge of the bed, listening intently to their conversation, and Bradley tried to ignore her presence, tried to stay focused on his mother and whatever crazy story she was about to concoct, but it wasn't easy. There was something about Delphine Armstrong that pulled at him, made him want to sit down next to her and tell her all his secrets.

Bradley was so busy thinking about his reaction to Delphine that he almost missed his mother's response.

Almost, but not quite.

And when what she had said sank in, Bradley found himself sliding down the wall. He crouched there on the floor, his boots almost touching the toes of Delphine's tennis shoes. From down here, he could see the stunned expression in her blue eyes—an expression he was certain was mirrored in his own eyes.

"What did you say?" he asked his mother, without turning his head.

Harriet cleared her throat. "I said, they think I took three million dollars that belongs to them."

"Are they right?" Bradley asked, still watching Delphine.

He heard his mother get up and start to pace in the corner of the bedroom. Both he and Delphine turned to look at her when she sighed loudly.

"Yes," Harriet said. "I suppose they are."

Chapter 2
Who's Lying Now?

I've fallen down the rabbit hole. Delphine stared at the pretty, mid-fiftyish woman who had just calmly admitted to stealing more money than Delphine dreamed of seeing in her lifetime.

She knew she should be frightened, but she couldn't help but feel excited at the promise of adventure instead. She hadn't felt this way since . . . well, not since a few months ago when she'd hurriedly packed up her Toyota Camry with everything she owned and left Los Angeles in the middle of the night, one step ahead of an angry boyfriend. There was something exciting about chaos, so much so that she found herself craving the thrill of it when her life fell into too much of a routine.

Nothing about this afternoon could be considered routine, she thought, suppressing a smile.

"I only took the money because I knew they'd find a way to claim bankruptcy if I didn't. That money belongs to the taxpayers," Harriet said from her place near the window.

Delphine couldn't wait to hear more about how this woman, who had seemed so mild-mannered and so maternal when she had first met her in the Heart O'Reno lunchroom, had managed to pull one over on her boss, but the cowboy—Bradley—didn't seem too interested in the how of it all.

Instead, he stood back up and asked, "What the hell are we going to do now?"

"I already have a plan," Harriet answered.

Delphine scooted back on the bed and waited to hear what Bradley's mother had to say. This was so much fun, like being caught up in a 007 movie or something, with bad guys chasing the good guys who were chasing the bad guys with some nefarious plot to rule the world. Her excitement waned a bit when she realized that she would most likely lose her job because of this. After all, she'd only been employed at the wedding chapel for two days. They weren't likely to forgive a new employee taking off for hours in the middle of her shift.

Still, there was nothing she could do about that now. If she lost her job . . . Delphine shrugged. This certainly wouldn't be the first time she'd been fired.

"All right, Mother. Tell me, what's your plan?"

Bradley Nelson crossed his arms and leaned back against the thin bedroom wall. Delphine admired his strong-looking biceps and the smattering of light brown hair that glinted on his forearms. He was slim but not scrawny, with well-defined muscles that didn't scream "bodybuilder" but didn't say "wimp," either. The black cotton T-shirt he wore clung to his skin, showing off a flat stomach that Delphine yearned to touch.

But not while his mother was in the room.

Delphine exhaled slowly and folded her hands in her lap, trying to concentrate on what Harriet was saying.

"I'm going to take the evidence I gathered on Dickie and his friends to my old boss at the IRS," Harriet said. "I know I can trust her. She's incorruptible."

"You have to go all the way to Trenton to find someone you can trust?" Bradley asked with a raise of his eyebrows.

"Maybe not, but I think that would be the safest route to take."

Delphine watched as Harriet parted the bedroom curtains

with her index finger and peered outside, checking once again to see if they were being watched.

"Well, I think the smartest thing for you to do would be to turn whatever you have over to the cops and wash your hands of the whole mess," Bradley said.

Harriet let the curtains fall back into place and leaned toward her son. "We can't trust the cops," she whispered, as it they were in danger of being overheard.

Bradley uncrossed his arms. "That's ridiculous. If you don't want to go to the local police, I'm sure we can hand your evidence over to the FBI."

"I don't know who they have on the payroll at the Bureau. We can't take the chance that we'll give our information to the wrong guy. We could get ourselves killed."

"Mother, you're being paranoid," Bradley said.

"And you're being naïve."

"The police are the good guys, Mom."

"Yeah, and I'm the tooth fairy."

"You *were* the tooth fairy. And Santa Claus and the Easter Bunny, too."

"Don't get smart with me, dear. You know exactly what I meant," Harriet said, straightening the sleeveless blue sweater she was wearing.

Bradley sighed. "Yes, you meant that you think Dickie Swanson and his cohorts—who own a string of third-rate casinos in Reno—have amassed enough money to pay off every law-enforcement official in the country. Well, I just don't buy it. Yeah, these guys make a lot of money. But it would take more than they've got to buy off entire police forces and federal agents. I think we need to go to the authorities."

"*We* don't need to do anything, Bradley. I'm not asking for your help. I know what I need to do and that's that. Now, why don't you go back into town and join that girlfriend of yours. I know you didn't intend to stop in Reno for very long, and I'm sure Ms. Rogers must be getting impatient waiting for you."

Delphine saw Bradley frown, as if he had forgotten all about the woman who had dumped him in front of the wedding chapel. "Robyn already went on to Las Vegas," he said darkly. Delphine noted that he didn't mention anything about the other woman pushing him off her tour bus, but she remained silent as Bradley continued. "Besides, I can't let you do this alone. It's too dangerous."

Harriet shot Delphine a look that she interpreted as "Give me a break!" Delphine gave the other woman a smile and a shrug in response.

"All right, Bradley. If you want to come along, you can. But I think the first order of business is to figure out what to do about Delphine."

Delphine's eyes widened with surprise. "About me? What do you mean?"

"I'm afraid that we may have gotten you in a bit of trouble, dear." Harriet sat down on the bed and crossed her legs, her neat khaki slacks not daring to wrinkle.

She reached over and patted Delphine's hand comfortingly, and Delphine had to force herself not to scoot closer. She'd forgotten how nice it was to be on the receiving end of maternal affection, and—wow—did that comforting hand-pat feel good. Since her own mother had died, Delphine had developed a sort of Mom Meter; an instant reading telling her how likely a woman was to be the type to cut the crusts off her children's PB and Js or stop in the middle of doing laundry to find Scooby-Doo bandages to fix a boo-boo.

When Delphine had met Harriet, her Mom Meter soared off the charts.

"Yes, I'm probably going to find myself out of a job," Delphine agreed, smoothing out the creases in her own jean shorts as she basked in Harriet's concern.

"Oh, dear. I hadn't thought about that. I just meant that Dickie might have recognized you."

"I only started at the wedding chapel two days ago. I've never met the man who was shooting at us."

"But the wedding chapel is part of the casino," Harriet said. "I've seen the books, and the Heart O'Reno Drive-Thru Wedding Chapel is part of Dickie's casino. It's possible that Dickie has seen you around."

"I suppose he might have, but I have to go back. I've got to get my purse."

It was Bradley who answered this time. "Dickie probably wouldn't recognize you. Still, I don't think it would hurt if I went back with you just to make sure it's safe."

Delphine looked up at Harriet's son, who seemed determined to protect everyone around him who was in possession of a vagina. How quaint. She thought about telling him that she'd recovered from much worse situations than this without help from any big, strong men, but before she could protest, Harriet smiled and said, "That's an excellent idea, Bradley. I'll wait here for you to come back. Maybe we can have a nice visit before you have to go back to Seattle. I stocked up on your favorite brand of mac and cheese, and I even made a batch of those pigs in blankets that you used to like so much."

Delphine's mouth started to water. "Did you put cheese in them? I love them that way."

Harriet turned her smile on Delphine. "Yes. I use Velveeta. Would you like one?"

Delphine was afraid her drool was going to flood the Winnebago. "Yes, please. If it's no bother, that is."

"It's no bother at all," Harriet insisted, sliding off the bed and heading up to the kitchen, where she pulled out two small plastic cups and two paper plates and proceeded to make a snack of croissant-covered Lil' Smokies and grape juice for Bradley and Delphine.

Bradley followed Delphine out of the bedroom with a sigh. He ate his pigs in blankets absently while standing at the kitchen counter, washing them down with juice. But not

Delphine. She took her snack to the dining room table, primly putting her paper napkin on her lap and savoring each salty treat by taking the smallest bites she could in order to make them last.

She closed her eyes as she sipped her juice. This was heaven.

Delphine opened her eyes when Bradley's voice interrupted her hot dog and Velveeta–induced trance. "I'm not going back to Seattle," he said. "I was on my way to Nashville for the Country Music Awards. The nominees are going to be announced this week and I know I'm going to be one of them. I've got the tickets and everything."

"That's wonderful, dear. Maybe we can turn this into a road trip. I've never driven through the Southwest before." Then she turned to Delphine and proudly announced, "Bradley is a gifted singer. His talent is amazing. And I'm not just saying that because I'm his mother. He is really good."

Bradley shook his head from side to side in what Delphine took to be a defeated gesture. "Mother, you've just confessed to stealing—"

"I did not steal anything," Harriet interrupted her son. "I merely calculated the back taxes, interest, and penalties on the money Dickie and his friends skimmed from the taxpayers and found a way to pay it back. I have the evidence I need to prove my case, but I wanted to make certain those crooked casino owners didn't find a way to hide all their assets before I could get the proof to our government. It simply isn't right for them not to pay their fair share of the taxes in this country. If everyone did what they're doing, where would we get the money to fund welfare, help students pay for college, build the interstates and transportation systems we need to keep America vibrant, and—"

"I've heard this lecture a million times," Bradley interrupted in turn. "But the fact remains that you're in a heap of trouble. As soon as I get back, we need to decide how to get you and your evidence to New Jersey. For now, though, I think Delphine and I should catch a cab back into town. We passed a tavern a few blocks back. I'll have the taxi meet us there."

Bradley pushed himself away from the kitchen counter and held out a hand to help Delphine up from the booth that surrounded the dining room table. Delphine put her hand in his, allowing herself to feel a thrill of sheer feminine pleasure when his large tanned fingers enveloped her much smaller ones. He pulled her up, not releasing her hand until he turned back to his mother.

"I should be back within half an hour if all goes well. Do me a favor and don't leave the motor home until I get back, okay?"

Harriet nodded, but Delphine had the feeling that the other woman would be slinking around outside the Winnebago the minute they left. Bradley must have been satisfied that his mother was going to stay put, though, because he stepped back toward the bedroom, pulling his cell phone out of his front pocket as he went.

"It was nice to meet you, Delphine," Harriet said. "I hope you're wrong about losing your job."

Delphine shrugged as she cleared her cup and paper plate from the table. "I didn't like it all that much anyway. I was mostly stuck doing a bunch of paperwork. Between that and having to dress up in a different costume depending on which theme room the happy couple chose, it was not what you'd consider a real satisfying job."

"Why did you take it?" Harriet asked.

"It didn't seem so bad when the manager described it to me."

Bradley turned back to the kitchen and announced, "The cab's going to meet us in ten minutes, so we'd better get going."

"Good-bye and good luck," Delphine said, holding out her hand to Harriet.

"Thank you, dear. You, too." Harriet took Delphine's hand, but instead of just shaking it, she pulled Delphine into a warm hug.

Delphine closed her eyes and leaned into Harriet's embrace. God, she missed having a mother. It left such a void in her life, a deep gaping hole that nothing and nobody else could fill.

Harriet pulled back, her warm brown eyes full of maternal concern. "You feel free to come right back here with Bradley if you don't feel it's safe. I just hate the thought that I might have put you in any kind of danger."

Delphine smiled and let her arms drop from around the other woman's shoulders. Harriet Nelson was exactly the kind of mom Delphine had thought her own mother would have been, if she hadn't died. "Thank you. I will."

She stepped away, heading to the bathroom to tug the gorilla costume out of the shower. It seemed heavier in a pile like this than it had when she was wearing it, but there was no way she was going to put it on and go back out into that heat. She'd keel over from heatstroke before they made it half a block down the road.

"Here, let me take that," Bradley insisted, making Delphine rethink her take on that whole "protect those with indoor plumbing" thing. Being taken care of was actually kind of nice, she thought as she handed over the load of fur.

"I'll get the head," she said, not wanting to push his chivalry too far.

"Might be easier if you put it in a bag," Bradley suggested.

"Less conspicuous, too," Delphine agreed, taking the plastic grocery bag that he offered.

She stuffed the head into the bag and followed Bradley back out into the living room of the motor home. He opened the side door and peered out, looking for any sign of his mother's boss.

"The car's gone. Dickie must have given up and gone back to the casino."

"Good," Delphine said, stepping out into the unrelenting sunshine. "Let's get back to Reno and get this over with."

"I heard there was a commotion here at the casino this afternoon," Jim Josephs announced as he took a seat in one of the armchairs across from Dickie Swanson's desk. Dickie watched as Jim's trademark silver hair fell neatly into place, as it always did whenever Jim moved. Dickie often wondered if Jim used hairspray to keep it that way, but decided that some questions were better left unasked.

Dickie's other partner, Gus Palermo, took a seat beside Jim, but didn't say anything. Typical Gus. Silent . . . but deadly, Dickie thought, studying the other men.

This was one of the trickiest situations he'd had to maneuver his way out of in a long time. He couldn't let his partners know about Harriet Nelson's interference with their money-skimming scheme. To them, the accountant's betrayal would be personal, but to Dickie it was just business.

Jim and Gus would first try to discover where Harriet had hidden the three million dollars. Then they'd kill her.

But Dickie didn't care about the money. He was only concerned about two things: where the former IRS auditor was now . . . and how much she knew about his cohorts' and his involvement with Reno's reigning drug kingpin.

"Yes, I had to fire our accountant today," Dickie said now, leaning back in his leather chair as if he were unconcerned about his partners' reactions to the news.

"Oh? Why's that?" Jim asked, smoothing a hand over his already perfect cap of hair.

"She just wasn't working out," Dickie answered.

Gus cocked his head and crossed his beefy arms across his even beefier chest.

"She made a lot of personal calls and took way too many breaks. And she was always asking questions. When I told her she was fired, she refused to leave. I ended up having to chase her out of here."

"I thought you said she'd be perfect when you hired her," Jim said, crossing his legs in a way that would have seemed effeminate on another man. Jim managed to pull it off, though, looking as suave as ever. Dickie felt rumpled in comparison, and tugged on the sleeve of his starched white shirt to straighten out the wrinkles at his elbows.

"She had the same job with the IRS for twenty years. I figured that she'd be a good, reliable drone. You know, do no more and no less than what's asked and don't work a minute past five o'clock. She was just not what I expected, I guess." And if that wasn't the understatement of the year, Dickie didn't know what was.

Both Jim and Gus nodded, apparently satisfied at his explanation. Dickie resisted the urge to breathe a sigh of relief. He wasn't out of danger yet. He didn't know how Harriet had managed to give him the slip back at the RV park, but Dickie had to find a way to ditch his partners and get back there without their knowing what he was up to. The only reason he'd given up earlier and come back to town was because he knew he couldn't miss this previously scheduled meeting with Jim and Gus. To have done so would have seemed suspicious, and the last thing Dickie wanted to do right now was to arouse anyone's suspicions.

He had to find Harriet—fast—and get the money she had taken back into the casino's bank account. Otherwise . . . Well, he didn't want to think what might happen otherwise.

The gun Dickie had tucked into the waistband of his slacks dug into his back, and he almost wished he could just shoot his partners and be done with it. But that wasn't an option. Finding Harriet before she could blow the whistle on them was the only real solution.

It could very well be a matter of life and death.

His, that is.

When he heard a knock on the door, Dickie had to stop

himself from groaning. *Now, what?* Instead, he yelled, "Come in."

The day shift manager of the wedding chapel that was attached to the casino poked her head inside his office. "Mr. Swanson?"

"Yes? I said, come in."

The woman—Dickie couldn't quite remember her name; they had so much turnover in both the casino and the wedding chapel that he had virtually given up bothering to memorize the names of any of his employees—stepped inside his office, keeping one hand on the door as if it were her lifeline to the outside world.

"What is it?" Dickie asked, trying not to sound as impatient as he felt.

The manager cleared her throat. "It's one of our employees, Mr. Swanson."

"Yes?" Dickie asked, a sick feeling in the pit of his stomach. This woman couldn't know about Harriet's embezzlement, could she? If she did, he'd better be prepared to run. Dickie got up from his chair and walked over to a bookshelf near the door. If Gus's reflexes were working properly, there was no way Dickie could escape without being caught. Still, at least he had some chance if the wedding chapel manager said what Dickie was afraid she was going to say.

"She ran off. And she took our gorilla costume with her. Those things are not cheap." The woman sounded indignant, as if the costume had been her own personal property.

"Who ran off?" Jim asked, turning to face the manager.

"Her name is Delphine. She's only been with us for two days. I had no idea she was unhappy, but that doesn't give her the right to steal from us."

This time, Dickie couldn't hold back the relieved sigh that escaped his lips. Thank God. This had nothing to do with Harriet Nelson.

His relief died a sudden death, however, when Gus shot out of his chair, banging his fist on Dickie's desk. "Nobody steals from us," he shouted, his normally tanned skin turning a mottled red.

The wedding chapel manager shrank back, still clutching the door.

At that moment, Dickie had a flash of memory from the chase earlier that day. He'd stopped just inside the wedding chapel doors to pull his gun from his waistband. He pushed open the door and heard Harriet shout, "We've got to get out of here." Then he saw a flash of brown, running away. No, not running away. Running toward Harriet's motor home.

He hadn't been paying attention to anyone but Harriet at the time, had been focused on getting to his car and catching his infuriating former accountant.

Shit. He was so stupid. The woman in the gorilla suit must have been in on Harriet's embezzlement scheme. Of course. Harriet must have used her to smuggle the money out of the casino.

"Get me her address," Gus said. "I'm gonna go after the bitch."

Dickie frowned. No. This was just getting worse. If Gus got a hard-on for this . . . this gorilla woman, he wouldn't stop until he found her. And that meant he'd find Harriet, too. And probably the missing three million dollars.

Unfortunately, the wedding chapel manager had come prepared. She flipped open a manila folder and read off the address that was listed in the employee's personnel record. Then, before Dickie could think of a way to stop him, Gus turned to Jim and said, "Let's go."

As he and Jim left Dickie's office, Gus slapped an open hand on the door, causing the wedding chapel manager to let out a frightened squeal.

"Nobody steals from us. Nobody," Gus repeated, the words seeming to linger in the air until he disappeared from sight.

Chapter 3
Do I or Don't I?

"All I want to do is return this gorilla suit, get my purse, and go home," Delphine said as the cab pulled up in front of the Heart O'Reno Drive-Thru Wedding Chapel.

Beside her, Bradley stopped humming, and Delphine listened absently to the drumbeat of his fingers tapping on the armrest as the taxi came to a halt. She reached for the bag containing the head of the gorilla costume, but Bradley beat her to it.

"I'll go in with you," he insisted, holding her head hostage. He pulled a twenty-dollar bill from his wallet and gave it to the cab driver with an order to wait. The driver put the car into park and leaned back in his seat, apparently content to do just that.

Delphine looped the heavy costume over her arm as she stepped out of the cab and onto the sidewalk. Even though night was approaching, the heat of the pavement seemed to burn through the soles of her worn white Keds.

Bradley held open the swinging door of the wedding chapel, motioning for her to precede him into the welcome air-conditioned atmosphere of the waiting room. Delphine walked across the gray-speckled linoleum floor to the metal desk that had been assigned to her when she'd reported to work yesterday morning. She had been hired to do anything around the chapel that needed doing—answering phones, booking appointments, taking care of the necessary paperwork, selling veils, renting costumes, having cakes delivered . . . whatever the couple involved wanted for their special day. Or special thirty minutes, Delphine thought as she laid the costume on her chair and pulled her purse from the desk drawer. Bradley put the bag with the head on top of the rest of the suit and slid the chair under her desk.

"I'm going to go find the night manager and let him know that I returned the suit," Delphine said.

"I'll wait here. I want to make sure everything's okay," Bradley told her, taking a seat on the edge of her desk. It wobbled a bit under his weight, banging down on one leg.

Delphine shrugged. "Suit yourself."

Bradley watched her walk away, her ponytail swaying in time with her footsteps. Idly, he got up and walked over to a display of wedding paraphernalia lining the wall opposite Delphine's desk. There were a dozen cake-toppers, all of a different sort. A man and a woman in formal wedding attire. A man and a man in formal wedding attire. A set of white porcelain figurines of what looked like two children ready to tie the knot, which Bradley found mildly disturbing. An African-American couple. An Asian couple. A mixed-race couple. A pierced and tattooed couple.

Something for everyone, Bradley thought, moving his attention to a photo album that was hanging by a chain from the display case.

As he flipped open the cover of the album, the front doors were pushed open, letting in a gust of hot air and traffic noise from the street outside. A woman walked in, followed by a man who was about two inches shorter than Bradley. Bradley didn't pay much attention to the couple, figuring they were here to get married. Instead, he moved his attention from the photo album to the array of garter belts on one shelf. Although they looked mighty sexy on those Victoria's

Secret models, he'd never known a real woman who wore hose with garter belts.

But, wow, if he ever found one . . . Bradley had an instant vision of himself kneeling on the floor in front of a set of long, shapely legs, sliding one silken stocking slowly down toward her ankle with nothing like the awkward struggle of removing regular pantyhose.

"I think there may be a picture of Miss Armstrong in our wedding album," Bradley heard the woman say then, startling him out of his fantasy.

At that moment, another woman stepped out into the hallway from one of the rooms in the back of the chapel and headed toward them. She stopped, looking surprised. "Oh, hello, Mr. Swanson. Is there something I can help you with?" she asked.

Bradley's eyes widened with shock. Shit. What was Dickie Swanson doing here?

"I've got everything under control, Angie," the first woman said. "But I think that gentleman over there could use some help."

Bradley swallowed hard. He had to think of a way to get Delphine out of here before his mother's boss saw her. But how?

Think, Bradley, think, he told himself. This guy was dangerous, and if he thought that Delphine was mixed up in his mother's embezzlement scheme, there was no telling what he might do to her.

A door opened down the hallway and Bradley heard soft footfalls coming toward the reception area. He looked over at Dickie Swanson, who was listening intently to something the first woman was saying. They were facing the windows and not the hallway, but Bradley knew they'd look up as soon as Delphine entered the room. He had to do something—fast.

Bradley looked at the array of wedding stuff laid out before him. Reaching out, he grabbed a floppy white hat with a veil sewn on to the brim. He stepped forward just as Delphine entered the reception area, shoved the hat down on her head, and pulled her into his arms. Lifting the veil only slightly, he dropped his lips to hers in the only way he could think of to keep her from talking.

She opened her mouth to him immediately, obviously catching on to his plan. Bradley groaned when she wrapped her tongue around his, sucking him gently under her spell. Her hands slid around his waist and Bradley took a step forward, pressing her back against the wall. She pressed back, rubbing against the instant hard-on he'd managed to achieve when their lips met. Her fingers slipped into the waistband at the back of his jeans, and he felt Delphine urging him closer. He pushed one leg between her knees and it was her turn to groan.

Bradley released her mouth to blaze a trail of kisses along the soft skin of her neck. When his lips touched the sensitive skin just below her ear, she let out a breath that sounded suspiciously like a purr and pressed her hips against his erection, making Bradley wish that this whole scene were for real . . . and that there weren't three other people in the room watching their performance with a good degree of prurient interest.

"You're doing great," he whispered into Delphine's ear.

She slowly opened her eyes then, looking up at him as if in a dream. "Hmm?" she whispered back, her breath tickling his cheek.

Bradley realized then that she had no idea that this had all been a ruse to keep her from being discovered. Shit, shit, and double shit. What was he going to do now? He didn't want to hurt Delphine's feelings, but . . . well, he couldn't let her believe this was for real. Although, he thought, as she rubbed herself against him again, his physical attraction to her was definitely for real. Of that, there could be no doubt.

Taking a small step backward, Bradley raised his hands and cradled Delphine's head in his palms. He lowered his lips to hers again, only this time he stopped just short of kissing her. "Dickie Swanson is right behind us. Play along with me, okay?" he whispered, then kissed her ever so slightly.

When he raised his mouth, Delphine's eyes were open and had lost their dreamy quality. She nodded at him, the move so slight that Bradley was certain nobody else in the room had noticed it. He nodded back, then turned around to face the reception area, doing his best to shield Delphine from view.

The woman who had come into the room from the back hallway grinned at them. "So, I take it you're here to get married? My name is Angie and I'll be happy to do whatever you'd like to make this event as special and unique as your love for each other. Now, let's start with the theme you'd like for your wedding. We have the jungle room, if you're thinking of something untraditional. We also have the ever-popular Viva Las Vegas Room, complete with our own Elvis impersonator, who has taped a number of the King's most heart-wrenching songs that can be played during your ceremony. Then we have the Fantasy Room, where you can choose from any one of our over two dozen costumes. Perhaps you'd like to try the sheik and the harem girl? Or maybe the princess and her slave? Hmm?"

Bradley tried to remain calm. He had no intention of getting married. He'd been careful to maintain his eligible-bachelor status over the years. He knew from firsthand experience that marriage and dreams of stardom didn't mix and there was no way he was going to give up his quest for fame and fortune just yet.

Surely, he could think of a way out of this mess. Bradley was certain that once they were in one of the theme rooms and away from Dickie Swanson, they could make their escape. Until then, he just didn't see another way out.

Bradley pulled his wallet out of the back pocket of his jeans and counted the dwindling number of bills he had left.

He cleared his throat. "What can we get for sixty dollars?"

Angie frowned, obviously disappointed at his meager budget. "The basic, no-frills package," she answered. "That includes your standard ceremony, rice, a complimentary slice of wedding cake for both the bride and the groom, two witnesses, and your wedding certificate framed in a genuine gold-plated picture frame. Do you have your license with you?"

Bradley tried to contain his relief as Angie handed him the perfect excuse to end this farce before it went any further. He made a big show of patting down his pockets before saying, "Dang, I must have forgotten it back at the hotel. I'm sorry, honey," in the most disappointed tone he could muster.

"Oh, that's all right," Angie said cheerfully, dousing his hopes for a quick end to this. "You can just bring the paperwork back here after the ceremony. This happens all the time."

Great.

Bradley looked from Dickie to Delphine and back again. His mother's boss was looking at him intently, as if wondering why he was hesitating. Not wanting to do anything to arouse Dickie's suspicions, Bradley figured they'd continue to go along with this until they saw their chance to escape.

"Great. Let's do it," Bradley said, throwing his arm around Delphine's shoulders and giving her a tight squeeze for show. She looked up at him through her veil but didn't say anything. It took mere minutes for them to fill out the paperwork. Bradley started to sweat when Angie asked for their driver's licenses, worried that the other woman would recognize Delphine's name. It was only when Angie turned to make copies that he scanned the wedding license and saw that Delphine had listed her name as Elizabeth D. Armstrong. So, Delphine must be her middle name, Bradley thought, relieved.

Bradley pushed his way under Delphine's veil and pretended to nibble her ear. "As soon as we get to the chapel, let's make a break for it," he whispered.

Delphine giggled, playing her part as the blushing bride to perfection. She turned to nibble him back, licked his ear, and responded, "There's a window on the right side of the room. As soon as we get there, I'll send Angie back out here to get something . . . maybe one of those garter belts. We can escape while she's gone."

Bradley tried to pay attention to what Delphine was saying, but found himself struggling to concentrate with her tongue in his ear. God, it felt good when she did that. Seemingly unable to stop himself, Bradley turned his head and captured Delphine's lips with his own again. Her mouth was already parted and their tongues teased each other as if they'd been doing this for years. When Delphine gently sucked on his tongue, Bradley felt himself go hard again, and wrapped an arm around her waist to pull her to him. It was only when he heard Dickie start to cough that he regained his senses.

With a somewhat embarrassed laugh, Bradley ended their kiss and let his arm drop away from Delphine's waist. "Sorry, guess I got carried away," he said to Angie, who was studiously avoiding watching them.

"Not a problem. We get that all the time," she said, sliding their driver's licenses across the desk to them. "Now, we'll meet the minister back in room four in just a minute. I only have one hitch. We're a little shorthanded this evening, so I'm going to have to find you another witness."

Bradley looked at Delphine, relieved. It looked as if they weren't going to have to go through with this after all. "Oh, well, then maybe we should just come back later."

"No, I think I have a solution," Angie said. Then, to Bradley's horror, she smiled and turned to Dickie Swanson. "What about it, Mr. Swanson? Would you do the honors and agree to be a witness for the happy couple?"

Delphine reached out to grab Bradley's hand, squeezing his fingers tighter than he would have thought such a delicate-looking woman was capable of. He tried not to grimace, even though he was worried he might never be able to play his guitar again.

When Dickie said he'd be glad to help, Delphine's grip tightened even more.

Angie smiled widely and thanked the casino owner for being such a good sport, and before Bradley could stop her, they were being herded back to a plain room with red carpeting and half a dozen fake ferns surrounding a golden candelabra. The minister came in, directing everyone where to stand, and within minutes, Bradley was being asked to love, honor, and cherish a woman he had known for two hours and forty-three minutes.

Chapter 4
Give Me a Ring Sometime

He asked her first.

When the minister asked if she would love, honor, and cherish Bradley Nelson until "death do us part," Delphine closed her eyes and imagined what it would be like to be part of his family—to have Harriet clucking over their children, bringing them pigs in blankets and grape juice, and letting them sit on her lap while they colored. To have Harriet's warm arms wrapped around them when they scraped a knee or were frightened after a bad dream.

Delphine knew this was wrong. She knew that thinking she could replace her own mother with Bradley's mom would never work.

But for just a moment, she was tempted. And in that moment, she found herself saying the words "I do."

Bradley coughed, a strangled sound way down deep in his throat. Delphine looked at him through her thick veil, saw the bright red flush creeping up his neck as he tried to think of a way out of this.

Delphine drew in a struggling breath. This wasn't right. She couldn't trap Bradley into marriage, no matter how much she liked his mother.

She turned to him then, letting the visions of their happy, well-loved children fade away as she cleared her throat. "Wait a minute," she said, holding her hand up to stop Bradley from answering the minister. "We never talked about children. Do you want to have kids?"

"Yes," Bradley blurted. "I mean, eventually I do. Not right away, though."

The minister turned to Delphine. "And what about you, miss?"

Delphine glared at Bradley. Here she had given him the perfect out and he had been too stunned to take it. Well, she wasn't going to lie to a member of the clergy. "I want children, too."

"Good, then we don't have a problem, do we?"

"Can we get on with this?" Dickie asked, obviously impatient to get back to whatever it was that had brought him to the chapel in the first place.

Bradley raised his hand to his forehead, rubbing his temple as he finally realized what Delphine had been trying to do. *Idiot,* he cursed himself with a mental kick. Now he was going to have to think of something else to stop this farce of a wedding. "Wait," he said, still rubbing his throbbing head. "What about country music? I can't marry a woman who doesn't like country music."

Delphine gave him a look that clearly questioned his intelligence and he even thought he heard her murmur, "Is that the best you can do?" under her breath, but she went along with his ploy, dropping his hand and stepping away from him as if he had just announced that he had leprosy and that she could expect to see body parts dropping off him at any moment now. "Country music? I hate country music," she said. "It's all about drinking and horses and . . . and cowboys."

"And pickup trucks," Bradley added helpfully.

"Exactly. I don't know why we thought this could ever work. Good-bye, Bradley." With that, Delphine swept past Dickie Swanson, her veil fluttering in the wind as she made her dramatic exit.

Bradley shuffled his feet on the well-worn carpet. "Gosh, everyone, I'm really sorry about that," he apologized.

"That's all right," Angie said, sounding more chipper than she should have after just having witnessed the breakup of a relationship. "This sort of thing happens all the time. That's why we collect our fee up front."

"Hmm," Bradley grunted, making his way to the door as nonchalantly as possible.

"So, do you have any plans for the rest of the evening?" Angie asked, following him out into the hall.

Bradley suddenly realized why Angie sounded so cheerful—she'd had lots of dumped-at-the-altar bridegrooms to practice on. "Uh, I think I'll just go back to my hotel and spend the night alone."

"Okay, well, if you change your mind, here's my number." Angie batted her lashes and held out a card, which Bradley took and shoved into his front pocket. Then, with an awkward wave, he headed out of the wedding chapel and into the night.

Delphine had the cab creep up to the end of the block to wait for Bradley. She scrunched down in the seat, her white hat stuffed into the space at her feet.

She tried to avoid looking at the hat. It was too depressing, symbolic of all the things in her life that she wished she could have, but couldn't.

Before she had the time to make herself too unhappy, though, Bradley yanked open the taxi door and slid inside with a hurried order to the driver to get out of there—quick.

Probably one of the reasons I thrive on chaos, Delphine thought, watching Bradley hunker down next to her on the backseat. With all this activity going on, she didn't have time to feel sorry for herself.

"I don't think it's safe for you to stay here in Reno," Bradley said as the cab sped away from the curb. "Why don't you come back to the RV park with me so we can figure out what to do next? I've still got to convince my mother that the best thing to do is to turn the evidence she has over to the police. But first, I think we should get out of town until this all dies down."

Delphine listened to Bradley's deep, soothing voice in the quiet interior of the taxi. She could only imagine what he would sound like up on stage, crooning love songs to thousands of women. A shiver slid down her spine. Oh, yeah. That's exactly what she thought it would be like. "Okay," she agreed, her own voice husky in the darkness surrounding them.

"No, really. I think it would be best if you left town for a while," Bradley insisted.

"I said okay, Bradley."

"Oh." He tilted his hat forward a little and the shadow covered his dark brown eyes from her view. "That's good."

"Can we stop at my apartment first? There are a few things I need."

"Sure. Just give the driver your address," Bradley said.

When they arrived at her somewhat shabby apartment building, Bradley asked the cabbie to wait for them again. Delphine fumbled a bit with her keys as she unlocked the glass door to the lobby of her building. The door squealed open on hinges badly in need of some WD-40, apparently a luxury the landlord couldn't afford on the measly rent he charged his tenants.

An abandoned pile of trash sat in a corner of the lobby, and Delphine didn't even bother to glance its way as she crossed the yellowed linoleum to the elevator. They waited in silence as the elevator made its way down to the lobby. The doors slid open soundlessly and Delphine stepped inside, pressing the button for the third floor. The faint smell of urine had her crinkling her nose with distaste, but she knew the stairwell would have been even worse.

"I'm only living here temporarily while the condo I bought

is being renovated," she said, making sure not to touch the graffitied walls of the elevator.

"Oh?" Bradley asked, tilting his hat up a bit.

"Yes. I decided that I'd rent the cheapest place I could stand to live in. It just doesn't make sense to throw all that money away on rent in addition to the mortgage on my condo. Besides, it's only for a few months."

The elevator stopped on the third floor, and Bradley held the door, motioning for Delphine to precede him into the dingy gray hallway.

"That makes sense," Bradley said as they walked down the hall. "But I wouldn't have thought you could afford both a condo and an apartment with a job like the one you had at the wedding chapel."

Delphine laughed lightly. "Oh, I couldn't. I could barely even afford this dump on what they were paying me. Fortunately, I . . . well, I have a small trust fund. My parents made a bit of money in real estate and they were determined to pass on their good fortune to me and my sisters."

"That was nice of them."

"Yes. We were very lucky." Frowning, Delphine stopped in front of apartment number 313.

Bradley stopped next to her. "What's wrong?" he asked, suddenly alert.

Delphine shook her head. "I don't know. Something just doesn't feel right."

In a move that Delphine had come to expect, Bradley pushed her behind him protectively. "I'll go first, just in case there's trouble."

"What would you do if there was?" she asked, staring at the broad expanse of his back.

He shrugged, then turned to grin at her. "I don't know. Run like hell, I guess."

Delphine grinned back. "That would be my first choice, too."

Slowly, Bradley pushed open the door Delphine had

unlocked. When it stuck, he poked his head inside and looked cautiously around the apartment. Satisfied that no one was lying in wait for them, he pulled his head back and turned to Delphine again. "Let me ask you a question," he said, then paused.

"What?" Delphine asked.

"How would you rate your housekeeping skills? Say, on a scale of one to ten."

"Is ten the highest or lowest?"

"Ten is Martha Stewart. One is the guys from *Animal House*."

"You mean like underwear on the ceiling and dishes that could support new life-forms?"

"Exactly."

"I'd say I'm a seven."

"That's what I was afraid you'd say."

Delphine sighed. "My apartment is trashed, isn't it?"

"That's my guess, yeah."

"Well, let's go in and see if anything can be salvaged."

Five minutes later, Delphine had waded through the shredded cushions, ripped books, and smashed electronics littering her apartment floor and stood staring down at the mess in her bathroom. Toothpaste had been squeezed across the mirror over the sink and globs of it had fallen in tricolor lumps to the counter below. Perfume bottles were smashed in the bathtub, making the small room reek like an overeager sophomore on her first date.

"Did you find your toothbrush?" Bradley asked, having waded through the debris.

Delphine waved in the direction of the toilet and continued surveying the mess glumly. "It's in there."

"Ew."

"Exactly," Delphine agreed. "And all my clothes are ruined, too."

"That sucks."

Delphine was about to agree again with Bradley's

assessment of the situation when she heard a noise from the hallway. "Somebody's coming," she whispered.

"Where can we hide?" Bradley asked, frantically looking around the tiny apartment.

Delphine looked around, too, but there was no place they could go where they wouldn't be discovered. She grabbed Bradley's hand and tugged him after her. "Come on, we'll use the fire escape."

They each grabbed an edge of the window leading outside and tugged as the footsteps outside in the hall got louder. The window jammed about halfway up, far enough for Delphine to escape, but not Bradley. Bradley shooed her out, still straining to get the window unstuck. Delphine slid outside, but instead of starting down the fire escape, she turned around and put both hands under the window.

It slid up just as the handle on the front door rattled, and Bradley dove outside a split second before the door burst open. Delphine pulled him to one side of the metal grating that served as her balcony, just out of sight of the window. The warm bricks of the outside wall of her building heated the back of her thin T-shirt, and Bradley's body heat warmed her front. Her nose was pressed into his chest and she inhaled the clean scent of him as she listened to the latest intruder rattle around inside her apartment.

She lifted her face until her mouth was just inches from Bradley's. "I'm sure that thing isn't going to go quietly," she whispered, motioning to the set of stairs that needed to be lowered down onto her neighbor's balcony in order for them to escape.

"We're going to have to be quick, then," Bradley whispered back.

Delphine nodded. "On the count of three, let's go. One. Two."

"Three," they said simultaneously.

Delphine reached the stairs first, hitting the release lever and groaning inwardly when nothing happened.

"We're going to have to jump down. Follow me," Bradley said. He peeked once into the apartment, then put one booted foot up on the windowsill, propping one hand against the wall to steady himself as he raised his other foot onto the unsteady railing. Slowly, still using the brick wall for balance, he moved his other foot to the railing and crouched down, extending his left leg in search of the bottom rung of the fire escape.

"I can't do that," Delphine whispered, leaning against the rail. "I'll fall."

Bradley's boot found the middle stair and he rested his weight on it while moving his right foot off the railing and onto the steps. He looked up at Delphine, who was glancing from his face to the railing and back. "You can do it, Delphine."

She was shaking her head and backing up toward the wall, as if she'd be safe if only she could remain there. The problem was, she wouldn't be safe. It would only take one glance outside for Dickie or whoever was in her apartment to see them both out here. And once they were spotted, there would be no escape. She had to move, and move now.

Bradley stepped down, braced his feet on the last stair as best he could, and held out both hands. "We can do it together. Come on, I won't let you fall."

He saw Delphine take a deep breath. She looked back toward her apartment, at all her belongings strewn about the floor like someone's garbage. Then she looked at him. She took one step forward. Then another.

Bradley nodded encouragingly. Delphine took the final step that closed the gap between them, and he put his arms around her waist and pulled her against him. "I've got you," he said. "Now, put your hip up on the railing and throw your legs over. I won't let you go. I promise."

Delphine exhaled and did what he'd told her to do.

She sat on the railing, her legs on either side of Bradley's chest. Once again, he had the fleeting thought that the sexual possibilities of this situation were almost too good to pass up. He sighed. If only someone wasn't trying to kill them.

Then he stopped thinking about sex altogether when he saw the barrel of a gun poke through the curtains, followed by a man's head.

Bradley didn't hesitate. Still holding Delphine around the waist, he yanked her off the railing, prepared to jump down to her neighbor's balcony. Unfortunately, the fire escape chose that moment to release, hurtling downward before Bradley had a chance to get a grip on the metal frame.

The stairs jerked to a stop so abruptly that Bradley lost his balance and fell. His back slammed hard against the second-floor neighbor's railing as he and Delphine tumbled off her fire escape and onto the balcony below. His breath whooshed out of his lungs when Delphine landed on top of him, but she recovered immediately. Pushing herself off him, she reached up to release her neighbor's stairs.

She reached out a hand to tug Bradley up, and this time she was the first one over the railing.

"Wait. Stop!" Dickie Swanson yelled from above them.

Bradley scrambled over the neighbor's railing, slid down the steps, and jumped the remaining few feet to the ground. Delphine was already running down the alley, and Bradley took off after her. He heard a shot ring out behind him, but didn't pause to see where the bullet had landed.

He emerged from the alley and almost slammed into the cab he'd paid to wait for them again. Delphine was already sitting in the backseat, holding the door open for him.

"Get in," she urged, shoving aside the white bridal hat she'd left on the seat.

Bradley slid in beside her. "Take us to the Happy Days RV Park," he told the cabbie.

"And hurry," Delphine added, reaching up to grab the seatbelt and buckle herself in.

Bradley did the same, then turned to look at Delphine, who was sitting on the edge of her seat, nearly hopping up and down on the aging springs with excitement. She didn't seem to be concerned that her day had consisted of getting fired, being chased by gun-toting mobsters, and driving around with a multimillion-dollar embezzler. Bradley found that oddly intriguing.

As they emerged onto East Second Street and saw the lights of Harrah's glowing brightly in the early evening sky, Bradley could only shake his head.

What sort of woman was Delphine Armstrong, anyway?

"We've got to get out of here," Bradley announced as he flung open the door of his mother's Winnebago.

Delphine followed him inside, being careful to close and lock the door behind her. "I agree. Dickie Swanson would be sure to recognize us if he saw us again. And I don't think we're going to be able to fool him again with our lovebird act."

Bradley wanted to ask, "Who's acting?" but he managed to stop the words before they escaped his lips. He had never felt such an instant and seemingly uncontrollable urge to kiss a woman as he did with Delphine. The worst part of it was that he knew he should be focusing his attention on getting Robyn back. Robyn fit too well into his vision of life as a successful singer for him to just let her go like that. Robyn knew what the music business was like. She understood the crazy hours, the level of commitment it took to get—and stay—famous. She knew all about intrusive fans, nosy reporters, and the politics of the industry. Not to mention that Robyn was beautiful.

And well connected, a voice inside his head whispered, making Bradley frown.

That had nothing to do with it. Even if Robyn's brother-in-law weren't the head of a record company, Bradley would want her back. He'd gotten signed at Gamble Records based on his own talent as a singer. Robyn's connections hadn't helped him at all.

Yeah, but what if Gamble doesn't renew your contract? that stupid voice whispered again. *Wouldn't it make it harder for David Gamble to drop you if you're dating his wife's sister?*

"Shut up," Bradley muttered under his breath. Yeah, so maybe he had befriended Robyn's sister Kylie because she worked for Gamble Records. And maybe he had hoped that Kylie would bring his demo tape to David Gamble's attention. But that didn't mean he would stoop so low as to date David's sister-in-law just to keep his career on track. He did have some standards, after all.

"Where's your mom?" Delphine asked, interrupting Bradley's thoughts.

Bradley looked around, as if his mother might be hiding in the shadows or crouching in a corner of the small motor home. He peered into the bedroom, but it was empty. Then he knocked on the bathroom door. "Mom, are you in there?"

His question was answered with silence so he pulled the door open. The bathroom too was empty. He looked back at Delphine, who stood in the middle of the motor home, her arms at her sides.

"She's gone," he said, unable to believe that his mother had risked her safety to venture outside the RV.

"Should we go—" Delphine began, only to be interrupted by the rattling of the front door.

"Quick, hide in the broom closet," Bradley whispered, pointing to a door to Delphine's left as he scurried back toward the bedroom.

Delphine opened the closet door, only to find it stuffed full with a broom, a mop, a vacuum cleaner, and several dresses that she assumed belonged to Harriet. She looked around, but didn't see anywhere else to hide, then gulped as the door was flung open. When she saw that it was only Harriet, she stopped clutching her chest and let out a deep sigh of relief.

Harriet hurried up the steps into the motor home and

closed the door tightly behind her. "Is Bradley here?" she asked, sounding rushed.

"Yes. He's back in the bedroom," Delphine answered.

"Good," Harriet said. "We've got to be ready to roll in five minutes."

Bradley stepped out into the hallway, and raised his eyebrows at his mother. "Ready to roll?"

"Yes. While you two were gone, I made friends with some of the other campers. There's one group that's leaving tonight, and we're going with them. It's that whole 'strength in numbers' thing," Harriet said as she made her way to the front of the Winnebago.

Bradley was quiet for a moment. His mother's plan *did* make sense. They had to get out of Reno, and it just might fool Dickie Swanson if they left with a caravan of RVs. "Okay, but you can't drive us out of here. If your boss has his people out looking for you, you'll be easy to spot"

"But they might recognize us from the wedding chapel," Delphine said.

Bradley squeezed his forehead between his thumb and forefinger. "You're right. Damn it. What are we going to do?"

"I have an idea," Delphine said. "But you might not like it."

"What?" Bradley asked, almost afraid to hear her answer.

"Come with me," Delphine said, grabbing his arm and pulling him back toward the bedroom. "Take off your clothes. I'll be right back."

"Delphine, this is no time for—"

She left before he could finish his sentence and returned seconds later with a red dress with tiny white polka dots on it. "Put this on," she ordered, thrusting the garment at him.

"Hurry, Bradley. I told the Boones we'd meet them at the front gate by eight."

Bradley looked at the dress in his hand and groaned. He could not believe what he was about to do, but there didn't seem to be much choice. He couldn't take the chance that Dickie had followed them. He was too easily recognizable as himself, and this getup just might work. The decision made, he pulled his T-shirt up over his head.

Delphine stood back, watching him strip.

With one hand on the snap of his jeans, he asked, "What about my hair?"

"I don't know. Harriet, do you have a scarf or something we could use to cover Bradley's head?"

His mother slowly shook her head while Bradley divested himself of his snakeskin boots and blue jeans. Delphine didn't seem inclined to leave, so he resolutely ignored her as he pulled the thin dress on and tried to pull the edges together, to no avail. A line of tiny white buttons ran from the hem to the neckline, but Bradley couldn't get the fabric to stretch far enough across his chest for the ends to meet. "How the hell am I going to get this thing done up?" he asked, annoyed.

"Here, turn it around," Delphine said, moving to stand in front of him and helping him to pull his arms from the sleeves. "You'll have to wear it backward."

Bradley slipped the dress on again and felt a draft at his back. He looked back over his shoulder and discovered that he was covered about as well as with the typical hospital gown. With a grimace, he clutched the skirt together in the rear. Then he took a deep, calming breath. Yes, he looked foolish, but this ridiculous getup just might get them out of here alive.

"Your hat, Delphine. I could wear the hat you brought back from the wedding chapel. It's white, so it ought to match."

Delphine looked up at him and smiled. "Good thinking. I'll go rip off the veil."

And so it was that Bradley found himself sitting in the driver's seat of his mother's Winnebago sixty seconds later, wearing a red and white polka-dotted dress and a frilly white hat over his thick brown hair. His feet were bare, and the leather seat was cool against his naked back and legs, but he was thankful that they hadn't tried to make him scrunch his feet into the pointy red pumps he had seen on the floor of his mother's closet. It was bad enough as it was.

His mother and Delphine were safely hidden in the bathroom as Bradley drove the lumbering vehicle up to the front gate of the Happy Days RV Park and saw a group of motor homes waiting there. He honked and waved as he approached, then slowed down to let the other vehicles exit the campground in front of him.

As he drove out of the gates, he noticed a well-dressed man standing beside a black Lincoln Towncar. Bradley flashed what he hoped was a coy smile when the man looked his way, then added a friendly wave for good measure.

The man waved back, and Bradley watched in his sideview mirror as Dickie Swanson leaned back against his car and folded his arms across his chest. Then the caravan of RVs pulled out onto the highway, leaving Reno in their dust.

Chapter 5
Four Hundred Miles to Vegas

Four hundred miles to Vegas.

Bradley looked at the road sign and started repeating the phrase to himself until it attached itself to a tune. There was something sad . . . no, *sad* didn't carry enough of an emotional punch. Pining? Melancholy? Sorrowful? Yes, sorrowful was better, painted a more vivid picture in his mind than just plain ol' sad. There was definitely something sorrowful about four hundred miles to Vegas. Now, he just had to find the right story to go with the words.

He pictured a cowboy, on his horse, in the middle of the barren terrain that they were passing through. Maybe his dog was dying? Or his pickup truck? Either one would do, Bradley thought, as he kept the nose of the Winnebago pointed toward the RV in front of him.

"How is it going?"

Bradley blinked, and the picture of the cowboy in his head disappeared. He turned his head slightly to look at the woman sitting in the passenger seat next to him. "Fine. This thing isn't so bad to drive once you get the hang of it."

"You seemed lost there for a minute. What were you thinking about?" Delphine asked, pulling her bare feet up off the floor and tucking them under herself.

"I was writing a song," Bradley confessed with a self-conscious shrug.

"Really? I've never known anyone who wrote songs before. How does it work?"

"I don't know . . . I guess I just get some idea or phrase stuck in my head and I build a story around it."

"How do you know what music to put the words to? I mean, how do you know when you've got it right?"

Bradley laughed. "Well, the good thing about being a songwriter is that there is no one right answer to any of it. Same as being a singer. You just go with what feels best at the time."

Delphine frowned, then stretched out her legs and crossed them in front of her with a yawn. "That sounds really frustrating. I mean, there's got to be a right way, right? That's how you know when you're finished."

"Being an artist just doesn't work like that, I'm afraid. It's not like being a computer programmer, where you write the code to make a little box pop up and say 'Hello, world!' and you know you've got it right when that happens."

"Well, don't you know you've got it right when a song you've written becomes a hit?"

"I suppose that's one way to look at it," Bradley answered slowly. "But does that mean that all the songs that aren't hits are wrong? I think if the song conveys the story the songwriter wanted to get across, then it must have been done right. It's not like in math, where there's one and only one right answer. You could ask ten songwriters to write a song based on one idea, and you'd get ten vastly different versions, and each one of them would be right, according to his or her own vision of the story. Just because one of those ten might be more commercially successful than the others doesn't necessarily make it more right."

Delphine tilted her head. "I guess that makes sense. So, what were you working on?"

Bradley eased the cruise control up another few miles per

hour to keep pace with their traveling companions, then glanced at Delphine. "We passed a road sign a few miles back that said it was four hundred miles to Vegas. I thought that had a ring to it. Kinda sorrowful, you know. Four hundred miles to Vegas."

Delphine let out a long "hmm" and closed her eyes. "Yes," she said after a while, "I see what you mean. It's like Vegas is your goal, but you're so far away that it seems almost hopeless that you're ever going to get there."

"I hadn't thought about it that way," Bradley admitted.

Delphine opened her eyes again and turned to face him. "I remember when I left home for the first time. My dad had given me his old Buick. He loved that car, and I just couldn't say no, even though I wasn't certain it was going to get me to the next town, much less all the way to Tallahassee. I prayed that Buick wouldn't break down because I couldn't wait to get to the city and start my new life there. I loved my family, but I was so excited about having an adventure, you know. But every time I passed one of those road signs telling me how far it was to the next big city, I just sort of held my breath. I just *knew* something bad was going to happen to keep me stuck right where I was."

"And did it?"

"No. I made it to Tallahassee without a hitch." She smiled at him then, a wistful smile that hinted to him that maybe things hadn't turned out quite as she'd planned, despite her lack of car troubles.

"So, what made you decide to leave home in the first place?" Bradley asked, enjoying their late-night conversation.

Delphine turned her head to look out the window. "The usual reasons, I guess. I had a wonderful childhood, but it was time for me to see something of the world." She turned back and smiled at him. "Mama and Daddy didn't want me to go, of course. I was their baby, the last of four girls. I think they would have been happy if I'd stayed with them forever."

"Sounds like a nice family."

"Yes, doesn't it?" Delphine said.

"Do you get back home often?" Bradley asked as his headlights picked out another stretch of dry brush at the side of the road.

"Not as often as I'd like. My parents died a few years ago so it's been tough to see our old house without them in it. I always expect to come into the kitchen and see Mama baking one of her world-famous apple pies or hear Daddy outside on the porch talking with one of the neighbors."

"I'm sorry," Bradley said. "That must be hard. My mom sold our old house after she retired from the IRS. I never missed it much, though. We moved around a lot after she and my father got divorced. I guess I never really thought of anywhere as home."

"That's so sad," Delphine said, reaching out to squeeze his arm. "Whenever I go home . . . well, it's just about the best time ever. My sisters all live on the same street we grew up on. When I go back, they're all fighting over who I visit the most, so I have to be real careful not to favor one sister over the other. Between seeing all my sisters, plus my nieces and nephews, I hardly have any time to catch up with all my old high school friends."

"It must be nice to have such a connection to a community. When you grow up in a big city, I don't think it's quite the same. In a small town, everyone knows everybody else. That must be comforting."

Delphine let go of his arm and sat back in the passenger seat. "I guess I never really thought about it, but I suppose you're right. You always know what to expect from people you've known all your life." Then she smiled. "Maybe that's why I don't have any desire to go back home to live. I love surprises."

Bradley looked over at Delphine. With her blondish-brown hair and blue eyes and small-town charm, she could almost be country music's poster girl, he thought.

"So, where is this paragon of old-fashioned Americana?" he asked, leaning forward to adjust the air conditioner just a bit. In the process, he knocked a pile of papers and books that were sitting on the center console to the ground.

Delphine bent down to pick up the papers, shuffling them a bit.

"Thank you," Bradley said after she put the whole pile back, setting a brightly colored road atlas on top of the stack.

"You're welcome," Delphine answered.

"So, where *are* you from?" Bradley asked again, curious to know where Delphine had grown up.

"Arkansas," she answered. "A small town called Poplar Bluff, a few miles north of Little Rock." Then she yawned before reaching around to the side of her seat and pulling on the lever that made it recline to a more comfortable position for sleeping. "I'm going to get some rest now. Be sure to wake me if you want me to take over the driving."

"Sure thing." Bradley frowned a bit at the abrupt way Delphine had ended their otherwise pleasant conversation. Within minutes, though, her breathing was steady and even, and it was obvious that she had fallen asleep. She must have been exhausted after the events of the day, Bradley thought as he repositioned one of the air conditioner vents so that it would hit him full in the face.

He took his eyes off the back of the motor home ahead of him and glanced at the woman now sleeping in the passenger seat. She had pulled her knees up to her stomach and curled both hands under her chin protectively, as if someone might come by and step on any part of her that wasn't tucked in close to her body. Her hair was still in its ponytail, and Bradley resisted the urge to reach out and let her hair loose. She had nice hair, long and soft and full of blond highlights. He wondered if she always kept it up like she had today.

Then, too tired to think any more about the woman sleeping next to him or the day's crazy events, he let his mind wander back to his song idea.

Four hundred miles to Vegas.

Bradley hummed lightly under his breath, trying to fit the phrase to just the right tune. And this time, instead of picturing a rugged cowboy on his trusty steed, Bradley saw a young woman standing next to her father's well-loved Buick, steam pouring out of the engine. She was wearing a white hat with a veil fluttering in the wind that kicked up from a passing semi. She looked out over the desolate landscape, sorrowful but not defeated, as if she had lived through more then her fair share of disappointments in her life, but was not yet ready to give up her dreams just yet.

The answer to her dreams could be found in Vegas. And Vegas was four hundred miles away.

Delphine was awakened by the loudest screech she had heard since one of the boys in her junior high had been caught hiding in a bathroom stall after PE class to spy on the girls as they showered.

She jerked up out of her seat, only to slide to the floor when she belatedly discovered that one of her legs had fallen asleep and refused to support her. When she looked up to see what the ruckus was all about, she found Harriet standing next to her, beaming down at her with a delighted smile.

Pulling herself up using the armrest, Delphine stood. Harriet held her arms out and stepped forward, engulfing Delphine in the warmest, tightest hug she could recall ever receiving.

"I'm so happy. Bradley just told me that I've gained a daughter," Harriet said, patting Delphine on the back.

Delphine looked at Bradley over Harriet's shoulder, raising her eyebrows questioningly.

Bradley seemed as confused as Delphine. "I was just explaining to my mother what all happened to us yesterday evening before we got back to the RV park," he said.

"Harriet—" Delphine began.

Harriet stepped back, still grinning as if she'd won the lottery. "No, dear, call me 'Mom.' I can't tell you how long I've waited to be able to say that."

Behind his mother's back, Bradley rolled his eyes. "Mother, I'm only thirty-two. Besides, if you had let me finish, I would have told you we managed to escape that mess before it was final."

"Oh. So you're not married?" Harriet asked, sounding disappointed.

Delphine wanted to throw herself back into Harriet's embrace, to tell her that she and Bradley *had* gone through with their wedding ceremony yesterday, and feel that comforting pat on her shoulders that let her know that things would always turn out all right. Most of all, she wanted to have someone to call "Mom" again. Standing in that Winnebago in the middle of the Nevada desert, Delphine wished it were real, wished that she were truly married to Harriet's son . . . and wished that she were really being welcomed into his family. But it wasn't real, and Delphine didn't want Harriet harboring any fantasies that would only disappoint her eventually.

She glanced out the window at the barren earth outside the RV before turning her attention back to Bradley's mother. It looked as if they had stopped at another RV park, this one even more desolate than the one in Reno. "I'm sorry, Harriet, but Bradley's telling the truth. We stopped the ceremony before it was final." Delphine frowned, remembering a small detail she'd learned during her very brief stint at the Heart O'Reno Drive-Thru Wedding Chapel. "But that really doesn't matter. You don't have to go through the ceremony to be legally married. The minister just has to sign the marriage license."

Bradley squinted at her from below the brim of his black hat. "Yeah, thank God for that technicality. If the chapel had been able to provide us with a license, that whole nightmare might have been all too real."

"Well, I didn't realize that marrying me would be so awful," Delphine said, wincing when her voice came out sharper than she had intended. For some reason, she was insulted by the way Bradley kept referring to their almost-marriage as a nightmare and a mess.

"I didn't mean it like that," Bradley said, holding his palms out in a gesture of surrender.

"That's what it sounded like. You know, I have dreams, too. When I get married, I want flowers and bridesmaids. I want all my sisters to be there. I want my nieces and nephews to scatter rose petals down the aisle. I want a white dress, and a real veil, not some stupid plastic hat with netting stapled onto the brim. And I certainly don't want a fiancé who thinks being married to me could be considered a nightmare," Delphine sniffed and brushed away the tears that had gathered in her eyes.

"Oh, dear. I'm sorry I mentioned it," Harriet said, rubbing Delphine's back comfortingly. "But don't worry, you and Bradley can have another ceremony later. I'd be honored if you'd let me help you plan it."

Delphine sniffed again as Bradley dropped his head into his palms. "That would be nice," she said.

"I can't believe this," Bradley said, raising his head. "Delphine and I are not getting married. I've known her for less than twenty-four hours, for God's sake."

Harriet patted her son's arm. "Don't worry. All you need to be responsible for is the honeymoon. Delphine and I will take care of the rest."

"There isn't going to be any honeymoon. We're not getting married," Bradley insisted.

Delphine looked up at Bradley then. He was a handsome man, strong and lean. He also seemed nice, if a bit overprotective. And in that moment, she knew that she didn't want the fantasy to end, at least not yet. Yes, she knew it was a lie. But what was wrong with wanting to live that lie for a few days? Whom would it hurt?

So, instead of continuing to protest, Delphine said, "I think we should go to Niagara Falls for our honeymoon. Wouldn't that be fun?"

Bradley's eyes widened with shock. "Delphine—" he began.

Delphine turned to his mother before he could say anything further. "I'm sure Bradley must be tired from driving all night. I think we should leave him alone so he can get some sleep."

Harriet squeezed Delphine's arm. "That's very considerate of you, dear. There's a coffee shop near the entrance of this RV park. I noticed it when Bradley stopped to get us registered. Why don't we go get a bite to eat and let him rest? Later on, maybe you two can go out and explore Las Vegas. Wouldn't that be fun?"

Delphine smiled at Bradley's mother—no, at the woman who had *almost* become her mother-in-law, she amended. "That sounds like a great idea."

"Now, wait just a cotton-pickin' minute," Bradley sputtered.

Tugging the ponytail ring off her hair, Delphine shook out her long, blond-streaked brown hair. Then she stepped past Harriet and moved to stand in front of Bradley. She tilted her head to look up at him and smiled before reaching out to wrap her arms around his waist. Pressing her nose into his chest, she inhaled the scent of him. Cologne and sweat mingled with the smell of pure man. God, he smelled good.

"It's no wonder you're cranky. You were probably looking forward to a proper wedding night and never got one," she said softly.

"A proper wedding night? What are you talking about, Delphine?"

She looked up and their gazes slammed together. His brown eyes were filled with equal measures of confusion and anger. Delphine reached up and pushed back the black cowboy hat he almost never seemed to be without. Then she winked at him and said, "Oh, I think you know exactly what I'm talking about."

Bradley closed his eyes. "We are *not* getting married, Delphine. This nonsense about a wedding night . . . well, it's nonsense and you know it."

Delphine lifted herself up onto her tiptoes and pressed a light kiss on her almost-husband's lips. "I know. But it sure is fun to pretend, isn't it?" she whispered.

Bradley opened his eyes and looked at her for a silent moment. Delphine felt as if he were looking right through to her soul, but she didn't flinch or look away.

"I think you're crazy," he said quietly, reaching up to pull his hat back down. The brim created a shadow over the upper half of his face, obscuring his eyes from view.

Delphine let her arms drop from around his waist and felt suddenly cold when she stepped away from the heat of Bradley's body. "If you think it's crazy to want something you can never have, then I suppose you're right," she said quietly so that only he could hear. Then she turned to Harriet. "Let's go see about getting some breakfast. I'm starving."

That said, she turned and looped her arm with Harriet's, leading her out of the motor home just as the first rays of morning sunshine kissed the barren desert, turning the once-desolate landscape into a thing of fiery beauty.

Chapter 6
The Heart of the Matter

"You can't blow our whole setup because an accountant and some wedding chapel receptionist flew the coop."

Dickie Swanson glanced at the no-nonsense black-and-white clock on the wall across from his desk and listened to the man on the other end of the phone line as he continued to rant.

He wondered if the seemingly mild-mannered Harriet Nelson knew how much trouble she had caused with her little embezzlement scheme. He also wondered if she knew that she and her accomplice, Delphine Armstrong, would probably die for it.

In the few short months that Harriet had worked for him, Dickie had come to look forward to seeing the attractive widow every day. She always had a bright smile for him whenever they passed in the hall, which Dickie had to admit had been more often than necessary, since he would sometimes step outside his office on some made-up errand when he saw her coming. He couldn't seem to help himself. She was pretty, and she was smart, and she was the first woman he'd been attracted to in a long, long time.

It was too bad she'd turned out to be a thief.

"They flew the coop, as you put it, with over three million dollars," Dickie said into the phone, leaning back and planting his loafers on top of his desk. "If my colleagues here find out, they're gonna be pretty upset. My problem is that I'm not sure if she's got more than just the cash. She may have found out about El Corazon."

"Do you think that's likely? The drug ring's evidence is buried pretty deep."

Dickie crossed his ankles. "I don't know. Nothing would surprise me, though. That woman is damn clever."

"You sound like you admire her."

"I suppose I do. As much as anyone can admire an embezzler, that is. I'd love to know how she managed to slip nearly three million dollars right out from under our security team's collective nose. I've got to tell you, that took some serious *cojones*."

"Well, don't let your feelings cloud your judgment on this. We can't afford for you to take any risks at this point. We're too close to the endgame."

"I know. I'm hopeful that she'll just lie low for a while, long enough for us to finish what we came here to do. I've taken some precautions in case she tries to go to the authorities, but there's no guarantee that word won't get back here to Reno."

"Well, whatever you've done, it had better work. If she exposes us . . ."

"Yeah, you don't have to tell me what the consequences will be," Dickie said, before hanging up the phone. With his feet still propped up on his desk, he reached around and pulled the Glock 9mm from the waistband of his neatly pressed blue dress slacks. He stared at the barrel of the gun. Such an innocent-looking thing, yet so deadly.

He snorted. Much like Harriet Nelson. He had never once suspected that she was up to something. He had been telling the truth earlier when he admitted to admiring her. The balls it had taken for her to skim money from the casino every day while walking past his office and smiling her cheery smile made him want to tip his hat to another pro. Only, he wasn't going to be able to do that if Jim and Gus discovered she'd been fired for more than just a few extra minutes of break time.

When the door to his office swung open and the two men stepped in, the phrase "speak of the devil" flashed across Dickie's mind. He didn't bother to change positions as Jim and Gus entered the room, remaining tilted back in his chair as he waved the other two men into the chairs across from his desk. He hadn't been expecting them, and their appearance made the tiny hairs on the back of his neck stand up.

. Had they discovered Harriet's theft? If so, he was going to have to give the performance of a lifetime while acting as if he knew nothing about it.

"What's up?" he asked, before either of the other men could say anything.

Jim leaned forward, his silver hair never daring to shift as he moved. "Why didn't you tell us you knew Delphine Armstrong?"

Dickie's heels made a loud thunk when he suddenly sat up and put his feet on the floor. "What are you talking about?"

Gus Palermo pushed a piece of paper across Dickie's desk, his dark brown eyes reminding Dickie of a golden retriever's. "This is what we're talking about. You were the witness at the wedding of Miss Armstrong yesterday afternoon. While Gus and I were searching her apartment for the property she stole from us, you were attending her wedding. We want to know what this is all about."

Dickie looked at the form in front of him. Under the bride's name—Elizabeth D. Armstrong—was his signature, bold and unmistakable.

Shit. How could he have been so stupid? He'd been so preoccupied with this whole mess with Harriet, he hadn't even been the slightest bit suspicious at the bride's name. He hadn't even been listening, intent on helping the wedding chapel staff finish the marriage ceremony so he could get back to the reception area and try to find a picture of Harriet's accomplice. But the whole time, said accomplice had been right under his nose.

Dickie chanced a glance at the groom's name and stifled a groan. Bradley Nelson. The last name could not be a coincidence. No way. Obviously, Bradley was a relative of Harriet's.

God, this just kept getting worse. If Jim and Gus put Harriet's and Bradley's names together, they'd certainly be a hell of a lot more suspicious than Dickie himself had been.

"I had no idea," Dickie said, deciding it would be best to stick with the truth in this situation. "I went downstairs with the wedding chapel manager to see if we could find a picture of Delphine so I'd recognize her if I saw her hanging around the Heart O'Reno again. When we got there, a couple was asking about getting married. The chapel was shorthanded and they asked if I'd be a witness. I was just trying to get the couple out of there so I could look through some wedding pictures to see if I could find one of Delphine. It didn't even occur to me that Elizabeth Armstrong and Delphine Armstrong were the same person."

Jim sat back, smoothing his hair unnecessarily. "And the day manager didn't recognize one of her own employees? I find that hard to believe."

Dickie folded his hands on top of his desk and contemplated the other man. "The bride was wearing a veil. I never even saw her face. And she didn't speak while the day shift manager was around. You can go down and ask her yourself."

"Maybe I will."

"Go right ahead," Dickie said, shrugging off his annoyance at the other man. Now was not the time to get out the ruler and see which one of their dicks was bigger. He'd concede that honor to Jim if it meant he'd let this matter drop.

"What about the monkey suit?" Gus asked, cutting through the tension between the other two men.

"We discovered it lying on Delphine's chair when we

searched the chapel after the wedding was over," Dickie answered. "But it never occurred to me that it was the bride-to-be who had returned it."

Jim crossed his legs and regarded him coolly from across the desk. Dickie returned his gaze without blinking. "All right. I believe you," he said, standing up and starting toward the door. He paused at the doorway, then turned back to Dickie. "What was the groom's name, by the way?"

Dickie looked down at the piece of paper Gus had pushed at him. The Heart O'Reno's logo was in one corner, with the words "Ceremony Application Form" emblazoned across the top. Bradley Nelson's name was printed neatly above the line where the word "groom" was typed.

He looked back up at Jim Josephs, a man he'd worked closely with for the last year, and smiled. "Says here he's a fellow by the name of Bradley Newton."

"Hey, mister, your pants are ringing."

Bradley opened his eyes to thin slits, hoping that both the ringing and the childlike voice he heard was just a dream. Unfortunately, judging by the very realistic-looking kid standing right in front of him, he knew he wasn't dreaming.

Opening his eyes the rest of the way, Bradley pushed himself into a sitting position on the too-narrow couch in his mother's motor home. He rubbed his sore neck with one hand and fished his cell phone out from between the seat cushions with the other. The kid, who looked to be about six years old, watched him intently as though she'd never seen anyone answer a cell phone before.

Bradley turned away from the girl's fixated green eyes and pressed the talk button on his phone. "Hello?"

"Bradley, is that you? Did I wake you?"

"Of course not," Bradley answered, as if there were something shameful about being asleep when someone called. "What's up, Hal?"

Bradley propped one bare foot up on the narrow coffee table in front of the couch and combed his fingers through his hair. The little girl who had appeared as if conjured in his sleep clambered up onto the booth surrounding the dining room table and sat looking at him. The heels of her tennis shoes thumped against the hollow wooden side of the booth. He attempted to ignore the insistent *whap-whap-whap* of her heels and turned his attention to his manager's phone call.

"Are you sitting down?" Hal Greenwood asked.

Turning away from the direct gaze of the little girl, Bradley inhaled deeply. This question could mean one of two things: his manager had either really good news or really bad news. Like every up-and-coming musician, Bradley had dreams of getting a call telling him he'd hit the *Billboard* Top 40 list or that one of the national radio stations had added him to their playlist or that one of the major labels wanted to offer him a contract. But, like every up-and-coming musician, he also had nightmares about hearing his option hadn't been picked up or that his next gig was going to be performing at some dive bar in a town nobody had ever heard of or that his next song was flopping like a trout left too long out of water.

Squeezing his eyes shut, Bradley sent up a silent prayer that this was a good-news type of call. He'd worked so hard and sacrificed so much to get where he was—given up six-figure job offers when he'd graduated in the top ten percent of his class from MIT so that he'd have the time to focus on his music career, gone out of his way to make all the right connections in the business, even going so far as to move to Seattle to woo the bigwigs at Gamble Records when it seemed like nothing in Nashville was going to work out.

He'd been out of touch with the business for a couple days. Maybe one of the songs on his album had been picked up by one of the major radio stations. If that happened, his career would get the boost it needed to move ahead. He felt as if he'd been stagnating for so long, waiting for that one thing that would get him moving on the path to stardom.

Maybe he was finally going to get some of the recognition he felt that he deserved.

"Yes, I'm sitting down," he answered.

"I'm afraid I have bad news," Hal said.

Bradley put a hand to his chest, feeling as if his heart had fallen out. The little girl across from him kept kicking the side of the booth, her heels banging the wood in time with the thumping of his pulse. Thump, pound. Thump, pound. Thump, pound. Bradley stood up and walked toward the front of the motor home.

"What is it?" he asked, trying not to dredge up thoughts of all the things Hal could tell him—things that could end his career and crush his dreams of fame and fortune forever.

"Gamble Records passed on your next album."

Bradley took a deep breath and leaned against the back of the passenger seat, staring out the windshield at the row of RVs parked in front of them at the campground where they had stopped this morning after the seemingly endless drive to Las Vegas. Each space had a level concrete pad and amenities such as cable TV, telephone, water, and electric hookups, as well as a sewer connection to take care of the objectionable chore of dumping wastewater. Next to each concrete slab were built-in stone barbecues. The lots were mostly bare of vegetation except for the occasional squat bush. It would be desolate, Bradley thought absently, except for the multitudes of motor homes filled with seemingly happy families that brought life to the place.

"I tried to convince David Gamble that he was making a mistake, but he said with the economy being so tight he just didn't have the budget to take another chance on you. If it's any consolation, he said it was one of the most difficult decisions he's ever had to make."

Bradley rubbed his temple with his free hand. "Why would that be a consolation, Hal? Whether the decision was easy or difficult, the end result is the same. I've been dropped by my record label."

"That's a good point. You always were one to see through to the heart of the matter."

"It's a gift," Bradley said, his voice heavy with sarcasm.

"Don't worry about this, Bradley. It's only a temporary setback. I've got several irons in the fire, and I'm sure at least one will pan out for you soon."

Bradley wondered if his manager might have been able to add one more cliché to his string of assurances. Still, cliché or not, he wanted to believe that Hal had a plan to help keep his career from fizzling out. Hell, he *had* to believe it.

Hal promised to be in touch before he hung up. Bradley remained standing still for another minute longer, until the little girl's thumping intruded on his thoughts.

"Something wrong, mister?" she asked.

"Yes, you're driving me crazy with all that banging," Bradley replied.

"Oh," she acknowledged, but didn't stop. "Do you want to go swimming? My grandpa said we couldn't go swimming without an adult, but he's taking a nap and won't go with us."

Bradley sighed and slipped his cell phone into his back pocket. "Who are you?"

"Mary Elizabeth Boone. My grandpa said I could ask you if you'd come with us."

"Your grandpa doesn't even know me," Bradley protested.

The little girl shrugged. "He likes your mom. So, do you want to go swimming?"

"You're very persistent, aren't you?"

"What's that?"

"Never mind. I'm sorry, but no, I don't want to go swimming. I drove all night and I'm tired. How about I see if my mom will go with you once she gets back from breakfast?"

Mary Elizabeth Boone frowned at him. Then she let out a long-suffering sigh. "I guess so."

"Good. I'll be sure to send her over to your motor home as soon as she gets back." Bradley reached out a hand to help the girl down from the booth, but she hopped off with no assistance from him.

As she exited the RV, Bradley noticed she'd left a trail of dried mud on the otherwise clean carpet. Not wanting to hear a lecture on cleanliness when his mother returned, he opened the front closet and took out the vacuum cleaner that was stored there. He plugged it in to one of the outlets and flipped on the power, but the clumps of dirt stayed put. Patting the zippered compartment that held the collection bag, Bradley realized that it was stretched to the limit.

"Geez, don't you ever change this thing?" he muttered, annoyed.

Then he unzipped the bag . . . and stood staring in shock when a wad of cash fell out onto the carpet. He opened the bag a bit further and more money tumbled out.

When the front door swung open, he turned, still holding the handle of the vacuum cleaner.

His mother entered the motor home first, followed by Delphine, who stopped and stared when she saw the pile of cash lying on the floor.

"Mother, where are the three million dollars you took from Dickie Swanson?" Bradley asked, dreading her answer.

"Somewhere he'd never think to look," Harriet answered calmly, bending down to pick up a fistful of bills.

"Please tell me that it's in a bank somewhere."

"Okay. It's in a bank somewhere."

"Is that the truth?"

"No. But you asked me to say it."

Bradley crouched down and grabbed his mother's wrist, making her stop in the process of stuffing the money back into the vacuum cleaner. "Where's the money?" he asked again.

"I couldn't put it in a bank. That would have been too easy for them to trace. Don't you understand? These people have informants *everywhere*. If I'd opened a bank account and started putting the money there, they would have known about it almost instantly. I had to be smarter than that."

"So you hid it here?" Bradley asked, already knowing the answer.

"Yes," his mother confirmed. "It's all around us. In the walls, in the ceiling, stuffed into my mattress, in the storage bins beneath our feet."

"And in the vacuum cleaner," Bradley added.

Harriet smiled at him then. "Yes. And in the vacuum cleaner. As I said, they'd never think to look for it there."

Chapter 7
Playin' Games with My Heart

"Bradley, I said I was sorry for this morning. I just wanted to . . . to pretend that our marriage was for real for a little while, I guess. I explained it all to your mother at breakfast and she understands."

Ahead of her on the sidewalk, Bradley didn't appear to hear her. Delphine quickened her pace, trotting to keep up with his longer strides as they headed toward the famous Las Vegas strip. It was just after one o'clock in the afternoon, and the desert sun blazed down on them unrelentingly. They were almost alone on the sidewalk, the more sane people either staying indoors during the worst heat of the day or riding in cool, air-conditioned cabs.

"I'm sorry," Delphine said again, reaching out to put a hand on Bradley's arm. "My oldest sister always said that my imagination would be my ruination. I guess she was right. I was just trying to keep on imagining what it would be like to be married, I guess. All my sisters are married, you know."

Bradley stopped abruptly, so abruptly that Delphine stumbled in her haste to stop, too. Bradley put a hand out to stop her from falling, then withdrew from her with a frown.

"Look, Delphine, I accept your apology. It wasn't that important in the first place. I'm not upset about that."

Delphine studied a crack in the sidewalk. Bradley had
been silent and withdrawn ever since she and his mother had
returned from breakfast, and she had assumed it was because
of her act earlier. When he'd announced he was going to
walk into town to run errands, Delphine had insisted on
going with him, hoping she'd be able to coax him out of his
bad mood.

"Then what are you mad about?" she asked.

Bradley was quiet for a moment and when Delphine
looked up at him, she saw that he had a faraway look in his
eyes. "Nothing that you can help me with," he answered
after a moment.

He started walking again, a bit slower this time, for which
Delphine was grateful. It was too hot to be running after
him, trying to keep up. They walked in silence for a while,
interrupted only by the sound of the occasional car passing
them by.

Delphine was surprised when Bradley stopped in front of
a hotel and waited for the automatic doors to whoosh open.
Delphine stepped inside, gaping. The lobby of the hotel was
stunning, with its enormous gold and green and blue and red
glass chandelier taking center stage. An enormous floral
arrangement mirrored the brilliant colors of the ceiling,
while the muted sand-colored marble floor bespoke a less
ostentatious opulence.

She was tempted to stand there for a moment and take it
all in, but Bradley was already halfway across the lobby, so
she hurried to catch up.

They passed a sign announcing a concert by "Country's
Golden Couple—Tim McGraw and Faith Hill" with a "special appearance by Kenny Chesney." The stars' portraits
were splashed over the poster, and Delphine paused to look
at them. They were all attractive, but it was Tim's and Faith's
intensity that made Delphine stop. They looked . . . unhappy,
almost. As if they needed to feel more, hurt more, love more,
in order to convey the emotions of their songs. Without

meaning to, Delphine reached out and touched the photo of "Country's Golden Couple," as if by doing so, she could understand what drove them to make their music.

When Bradley disappeared down a red-carpeted hallway, Delphine dropped her hand and gave the sign one last look. Then she hurried after him. The din from the lobby faded away into near-silence as she turned the corner. Bradley was nearing the end of the hallway where a set of double doors stood. He pulled open one of the doors and turned back to her.

"I'll be right back," he said, implying that she should wait there.

Delphine frowned at the door that closed in her face, but didn't move to open it again. Instead, she leaned back against the wallpapered hall and studied the carpet beneath her feet.

As the seconds turned to minutes, she turned her attention to herself, grimacing down at the rumpled T-shirt that she'd put on yesterday morning before going to work. She needed to buy some new shirts as well as—

"That's ridiculous, Bradley."

Delphine heard the woman's raised voice from inside the room Bradley had just entered. She looked up the hallway and back toward the double doors. She knew this was none of her business, but there was nobody there to stop her from just poking her head inside to see what was going on.

Slowly, so as not to attract attention to herself, Delphine cracked open the metal door at the end of the hall. The room she stepped silently into was enormous, with row upon row of theaterlike seats facing a stage that was crowded with people moving things around and walking from one spot to another. Every sound echoed in the nearly empty auditorium, each scuffle of a foot and whisper of a voice ringing out in the otherwise quiet room.

It took Delphine's eyes a moment to adjust to the gloomy lighting where she was standing, at the end of one row of seats. She heard Bradley's voice to her right and turned toward the sound.

"It's not ridiculous," Bradley was saying. "Ever since you left me, darlin', I've been thinkin' about how right we are together. So let's stop playin' games with our hearts."

Delphine took a step down toward the stage as the woman in front of Bradley gave an inelegant snort. The woman was small-boned, with the kind of blond hair Delphine had always dreamed of having. She wore an emerald-green minidress that perfectly showcased her generous breasts and shapely, if rather short, legs. The petite woman had to crane her neck to look into Bradley's eyes, making Delphine feel like a hulking giant in her own five-foot-seven-inch body.

"Bradley, this is nonsense. I told you yesterday—"

As Delphine watched in shocked horror, Bradley got down on one knee and reached out to take the blonde's hand. She felt as if her heart were being stabbed with a dull kitchen knife when she heard him say softly, "Marry me, Robyn."

When Harriet Nelson answered her cell phone, Dickie could hear the sounds of splashing and kids screeching in the background, and he wondered if she knew that he knew where she was thanks to a mistake her son had made earlier that day. Someone should tell Bradley Nelson that the first rule of being on the lam was to not use plastic of any sort to pay for things—especially not for things that would give the people hunting for you your exact location. Apparently, Bradley was new to this whole fugitive thing, because he had paid their nightly fee at the Wild Wild West RV park in Las Vegas by using his Visa card. Somebody should tell Bradley that mistakes like this could end up getting him killed.

"Hello, Harriet," Dickie said, standing on the hot sidewalk outside the Heart O'Reno casino and squinting in the bright afternoon sun.

"Hello," Harriet said again, more cautiously this time.

"You aren't going to get away with this, you know. The people I work with, they are not the types to just forgive and forget. They've scheduled an audit of the books starting on Monday. They're going to discover that you took the money."

Harriet was silent for a moment. "That money belongs to the taxpayers," she said, her voice full of quiet conviction.

"We're not talking about right and wrong here, Harriet. You may be right, but what good is that going to do when you end up dead? Or your friend Delphine ends up dead." He paused for effect. "Or your son. How are you going to feel about being right when Bradley's throat is cut in some dark alley? Do you think that won't happen? Because I'm telling you, it will. If you go forward with your plan to expose the casino owners, they will not hesitate to punish you and the people you love. And theirs is not the kind of justice you can recover from."

"Don't you see, that's exactly why I have to do it. If I don't have the courage to stand up to you, who will? You'll go on cheating and stealing and threatening people as if nobody can touch you. I've proven that's not true. You're not untouchable. And I'm not giving up, no matter how hard you try to frighten me."

Dickie sighed. "You're being investigated for tax fraud," he announced.

"What?" Harriet screeched.

"Yes, Harriet. Tax fraud. You see, when you have as much money at your disposal as we do, there's no one who can't be bought off. There are now records in your file that prove you were underreporting your income for over a decade. We'll ruin your life. Do you understand?"

Harriet remained silent, so Dickie continued in his calm tone. "All you have to do is turn around, come back to Reno, and give back the money you took. Then drive away. That's all. It's not too late yet. You still have time to fix everything."

"No," Harriet said, sounding shaken. "I have friends—"

"Doesn't matter," Dickie interrupted. "The evidence we

planted is irrefutable. Your friends at the IRS won't be able to help you. Someone once said to me that sometimes the easy way is also the right way. Do what I'm telling you to do, Harriet. It's the right way."

"No," she repeated, her voice stronger this time. "Listening to you is like . . . like listening to the devil. The easy way is not the right way. I know it, and so do you. Good-bye, Dickie."

She hung up, leaving him standing in the middle of the sidewalk listening to dead air. "Good-bye, Harriet," he said to the phone in his hand.

Slowly, he let his arm fall back to his side. It was clear to him what his next move had to be.

Bradley was desperate. For ten long years he had lived the life of a struggling musician. He had worked crappy part-time jobs at Computers "R" Us and in seedy record stores all the way from Nashville to Seattle. He'd played in bars that were such dumps the only pay was half off the drinks he'd consumed between sets. During all that time, he'd never asked his mother for financial help. If he had, he knew what she'd say.

"It's time for you to go out and get a real job."

Those would have been her exact words. He knew it, because he'd heard her say the same thing to his father all those years ago. His dad had dreamed of being a country music star. He'd taken Bradley to Nashville when he was ten years old and they'd spent hours inside the Grand Ole Opry. And when they'd returned home, his parents' fighting got worse than it had been before. And finally, his mother drove his father away. Bradley used to sit in his bedroom with his ear pressed up against the door, listening to his mother tell his father that it was time to give up his dream.

The night Bradley had won his first talent show, his father had walked out on them. Bradley came home from having ice cream with his friends and his dad's car wasn't in the driveway. Dad wasn't sitting on the couch like he always was when Bradley got home, either. His guitar wasn't there, leaning up against the worn green sofa that Grandma Mimi had given them. "Better than giving it to the poor," she'd said. The ashtray on the coffee table wasn't overflowing. There were no beer cans stacked in a pyramid on the floor.

Dad was gone. And it was all his mother's fault for not believing hard enough, or long enough, in her husband's dream.

At least, that's what Bradley had believed at the time. As an adult, he had a more balanced view. He knew how difficult it must have been for his mother, bearing the brunt of the financial burden for their little family, coming home to a mess of cigarette butts and empty beer cans, oftentimes being expected, after working all day, to cook dinner for whichever of his father's similarly unemployed friends happened to drop by for a jam session.

Bradley had vowed not to be a burden to his mother—or anyone, for that matter—while he pursued his dream. But now he didn't have a choice. Gamble Records had dropped him, and Bradley knew that this might very well spell the end of his career. It was hard enough to get a first record contract as a new artist. Getting a second contract when your first album was released to mediocre reviews and lackluster sales was even more difficult. Most artists never recovered.

He couldn't let that happen to him. He had worked too hard to give up now.

He'd spent all morning going over and over his options in his mind, but in the end, it all came down to this. Getting Robyn back was the only way. And not just getting her back in a temporary way, either. Bradley needed his success to *matter* to David Gamble. The only way to do that was to make it personal.

Yes, Bradley knew it was wrong to use Robyn like this, but he remembered reading somewhere that a person bent on success had no Plan B. Well, that was him, all right. He had no Plan B, and his manager's call that morning had driven the last nail in the coffin of Plan A.

He had to do something—something drastic—or everything he'd worked so hard for all his life would be for nothing.

That's why, when Robyn rejected his plea that they get back together as being ridiculous, he knew he had to do the one thing she would never expect.

Bradley kneeled down on one knee and reached out to take Robyn's small hand in his. "Marry me, Robyn," he said, knowing that the future of his dreams lay in her answer.

Robyn's perfectly formed mouth dropped open in shocked disbelief.

Then his own mouth dropped open when he heard a familiar voice from out in the auditorium.

"No. You can't marry her."

Bradley turned toward the voice with a silent groan. "Delphine, stay out of this."

She walked out of the shadows then, looking rumpled and distraught. Her hair was in its usual ponytail and the soles of her ten-dollar shoes made a squeaking sound on the cement as she walked.

Bradley looked back up at Robyn, who was as perfectly turned out as usual. He'd never even seen her with a chip in her nail polish, much less with her hair in disarray or her clothes wrinkled.

He glanced back at Delphine, who was gazing at him with such a look of naked longing that he felt the force of it like a physical blow.

"You can't marry her," she repeated, her blue eyes pleading.

"Who *is* this?" Robyn asked, making it sound as if Delphine were some smelly street urchin begging for leftovers outside a fancy restaurant.

He saw Delphine straighten her shoulders and lock eyes with Robyn. Bradley started shaking his head. "No, Delphine, don't," he pleaded before turning back to Robyn. "She's . . . nobody. Just a friend of my mother's."

Delphine opened her mouth to speak and then closed it again without saying a word. Her gaze shifted to Bradley and their eyes met across the stage in the darkened auditorium. The longing was gone, replaced with sadness. She nodded once and slowly lowered her head.

Then, without saying anything more, she turned and walked away, leaving Bradley standing on the stage, just outside of Robyn's spotlight.

Chapter 8
A Little Fantasy

Delphine stopped outside the gates of the Wild Wild West RV Park with five dollars in her pocket and nowhere else to go. She paused for a moment to wipe the sweat off her neck.

As so often happened, the fantasy world she had built up in her mind bore no semblance to reality. Not that she had expected their near shotgun wedding to mean anything to Bradley—after all, they'd barely known each other for twenty-four hours—but interrupting his marriage proposal to that blonde back there had left Delphine feeling as if he'd somehow betrayed her.

Crazy.

That's what she was. Totally insane to have managed to blow their wild adventure up into something more meaningful in her head. Obviously, Bradley didn't feel anything for her. What had he called her?

A nobody. That's what.

It was painfully obvious that she'd wanted to believe Harriet's philosophy that she and Bradley had been thrown together for a reason.

Yeah, she thought with a snort, walking toward the Winnebago as the sun baked the concrete all around her, it had happened for a reason. And that reason had nothing to do with fate or kismet or karma or whatever. It had happened because she'd been at the wrong place at the wrong time.

How typical.

That pretty much summed up her life. Wrong place. Wrong time. Wrong person.

As she neared the Winnebago, Delphine's steps slowed. She stood there for a moment, looking at the white vehicle with its pink and green accent stripes and thinking to herself that she should turn around and leave right now. She could make a new life for herself in Las Vegas just as well as anywhere else. Even the fact that she had no money didn't worry her. She'd managed to get by before on nothing more than she had now.

She turned to look back toward the gates of the campground. Although it wasn't even close to twilight, the lights were just coming on. On the hotel adjacent to the RV park, a neon cowboy on a bucking bronco moved jerkily forward and back, forward and back. She glanced back toward the Winnebago. There was no future for her there anymore, not now that Bradley was engaged to another woman. Her silly dreams of being part of his life had died a quick and painful death back there on that stage on the Las Vegas strip.

She turned around and started walking back toward the gate.

Behind her, the door to Harriet's motor home opened, and she heard Bradley's mother ask, "Delphine, dear, is that you? Where's Bradley?"

She hesitated for a second, just long enough for Harriet to start down the steps after her. Delphine twisted around to face her almost-mother-in-law and gave the other woman a weak smile. And then, without warning, she started to cry. Great, huge teardrops rolled down her face as she tried to gulp down enough air to breathe.

Harriet hurried down the steps and rushed toward her, throwing her arms around Delphine's shoulders in a motherly hug. "What's wrong?"

"Oh, Harriet," Delphine sobbed, "Bradley's with another woman."

"What?"

"I saw them together. And he—" She hiccupped, drew in a gasping breath, and tried again. "And he—Oh, I just can't say it. It's too awful."

Harriet gave Delphine's shoulders another squeeze before she pulled back. "You can tell me. I know we hardly know each other, but I promise you, I'm here to help. Every couple goes through hard times. Now, come inside and tell me exactly what happened."

Delphine let Harriet guide her inside the Winnebago and took a seat facing the other woman. Bradley's mother smiled kindly at her and patted her hand, making Delphine feel as if she really cared that Delphine was unhappy.

"I think Bradley's in love with another woman," Delphine confessed with a final stuttering breath.

"No," Harriet protested.

"Yes. I think he took up with me on the rebound from her, and now he's regretting his decision."

"Why do you say that?"

Delphine closed her eyes, remembering back to the kiss Bradley had given her in the lobby of the wedding chapel. It had felt real then, with his lips urgent and hot upon hers. She had felt desired at that moment, and she knew—even if Bradley didn't—that she had let their farce of a wedding go on as long as it had because, in truth, she hadn't wanted to stop it.

She had seen Bradley and she'd wanted him, but not just in a sexual way. He had something she didn't, and that's what made him so attractive to her—something even besides his mother, whose maternal nature was feeding an emptiness in Delphine's soul that she had feared would never be filled again.

Bradley had a dream, a purpose, a reason to get up every day and work at what he loved doing. Delphine didn't have that. She wasn't sure she ever had. She stuck with something until the adventure went out of it, and then she moved on to something else, always searching for . . . for what, she didn't know. But Bradley wasn't like her. He kept working toward what he wanted year after year and she found that incredibly admirable. If was as if he had discovered the secret to happiness, and she couldn't let him go until he had shared that secret with her.

Delphine squeezed Harriet's hand. "I don't want to lose him," she said, feeling tears start to trickle down her cheeks again.

The door to the Winnebago banged open, and both Delphine and Harriet jumped as if they'd been shot.

"Well, Harriet, we meet again," the intruder said.

Harriet frowned and let go of Delphine's hand. "You sound like a bad actor in a James Bond movie. You can put the gun down. We're unarmed."

Dickie Swanson stepped inside the Winnebago and pushed the door closed behind him without lowering his Glock. "I don't trust you," he said, looking around the motor home. It was more spacious than he'd have guessed it would be. More luxurious, too. The cabinets were all oak, with Corian-type countertops and polished brass fittings. The whole place was tidy, not surprising since Harriet struck him as a tidy sort of person.

She even looked tidy, with her neatly brushed brown hair held back by a headband and her clothes that didn't dare wrinkle. She wore a camel-colored sleeveless dress, her bare arms tanned and smooth. Her sandals were low-slung and practical, but it was the toe ring she wore on her left foot that surprised him. She didn't strike him as being that daring, but then again, this was the woman who had managed to sneak nearly three million dollars out from under his nose without so much as breaking a sweat.

He moved his attention to the woman sitting across from Harriet in the dining booth. "You must be Miss Armstrong," he said.

She looked as if she'd been crying, and she confirmed his suspicion when she reached a hand up to wipe her eyes. "Yes, that's me."

"So, tell me, were you in on Harriet's scheme from the beginning? I know you hadn't worked at the Heart O'Reno for long, and I must confess that I haven't yet figured out just what role you played in the scam."

"She's just an innocent bystander," Harriet said, sliding to the edge of the banquette, where she swung her legs out from under the dining table and stood up.

"I'd prefer it if you'd sit back down," Dickie said, the gun he'd aimed at Harriet's chest giving the message a bit more forcefully than his words.

Harriet sat back down.

"Now, I need to know where you've put the money." He reached over to the kitchen counter, grabbed a pad of paper that was sitting there, and tossed it Harriet's way. "I want you to write down the names of each of the banks where you've made deposits, along with the account numbers. I also need your mother's maiden name and the personal identification number associated with each account."

He reached into his shirt pocket and pulled out a gold pen. He thwacked it on top of the pad of paper, holding Harriet's gaze. Then, without even so much as blinking his eyes to warn her what he was about to do, he grabbed Delphine by her ponytail, shoved her face down to the tabletop, and put the cold barrel of his pistol against her temple.

"And don't give me your good-versus-evil speech again. If you don't do what I tell you, I'll kill her."

Dickie watched as Harriet's hands started to shake. She picked up the pen and twisted it open. When she started writing, Dickie pressed the gun deeper into Delphine's temple. "And don't try to make up numbers, either. I'm not leaving here before I call to verify the information you've given me. I'm not stupid enough to trust you again."

Harriet stopped writing and looked down at the piece of

paper in front of her. Then she looked up, meeting his gaze. With their eyes locked on each other, she ripped the top sheet of paper from the pad and crumpled it, and Dickie let out a snort that was half disgust and half admiration.

"Um, Mr. Swanson?" Delphine asked, her mouth smooshed against the table.

"What?"

"It's just as effective to shoot me while I'm sitting up. I think we get the picture that you're serious."

Dickie looked down at the woman, unable to believe what she had just said.

"I mean," she continued, "this whole smashing-my-face-into-the-Formica thing was definitely good for effect, don't get me wrong. It's just that I think you made your point."

Dickie was about to concede when the motor home door swung open again. Startled, he took his eyes off Delphine and Harriet for just a moment to see who was making an entrance. It was a mistake he would soon regret.

Bradley came through the door first with his guitar case in one hand and a suitcase in the other. He tripped on the top step as if he were being pushed from behind.

Which he was.

Gus and Jim stepped inside right after Bradley, both of them with guns drawn.

"Gus? Jim? What are you doing here?" Dickie asked.

"You tell us," Gus said.

"You want for me to tell you what *you're* doing here?"

Jim scowled at him. "No. We want you to tell us what *you're* doing here. We suspected you were up to something after seeing your name on that marriage license, so we followed you here from Reno."

"Oh."

"What do you want us to do?" Delphine asked, her head still lying on the table even though Dickie had removed his gun.

"Who the hell are you?" Gus asked.

"Delphine Armstrong. Pleased to meet you," she said, holding out one hand awkwardly.

The man instinctively reached out and took her hand, obviously forgetting that he held a gun in his own hand. Without hesitating, Delphine yanked the gun from the man's fingers, reaching back to slam her elbow into Dickie Swanson's genitals as she did.

"Run!" she yelled, hopping up onto the bench seat as the man whose gun she had stolen lunged at her.

Instead of running, Harriet grabbed the pen Dickie had handed her and jabbed it as hard as she could into the soft flesh between Gus's right thumb and his index finger. He squealed like the proverbial stuck pig and grabbed his wrist with his left hand. Meanwhile, Bradley managed to slam Jim Josephs back against the wall of the Winnebago, but he was having some trouble getting the man to release his gun.

Delphine and Harriet ducked as Jim managed to get a shot off. His wildly flailing arm made aiming impossible and he managed to make things worse when he shot Gus in the foot. Gus screamed while Dickie writhed in agony on the floor.

Delphine stood back and tried to get a clear shot of the man Bradley had pinned against the wall, but Bradley was in the way and she didn't want to take a chance that she might shoot him instead. She gasped when Jim got Bradley's neck in a chokehold. Bradley's face started turning red, and Delphine knew she had to do something. She tossed the gun to Harriet and grabbed Jim's arm and bit down as hard as she could.

"Bitch," Jim screeched. He tried dislodging her by jerking his arm toward her, hard. Delphine's head smacked against the wall and she released her grip as the unmistakably sour taste of blood filled her mouth.

She bit him again, and this time he loosened his hold on Bradley's neck. Then, in a moment that Delphine would recall and cherish for years to come, Bradley turned around and clocked the other man in a perfect punch that would have been worthy of the big screen.

Before Jim hit the carpet, Harriet, Delphine, and Bradley were out of the Winnebago, running as if their lives depended on it.

Delphine heard the heavy tromp of footsteps behind them, but didn't pause to look back.

A shot rang out in the otherwise quiet early evening, and Bradley ducked as the bullet blew a hole through his cowboy hat. Several heads popped out of motor homes, only to be pulled back in when they saw that this was no Vegas sideshow.

The trio ran down a row of RVs and Delphine shouted, "Where are we going?"

Bradley pointed to the hotel up ahead of them. "We can hide there."

Delphine looked toward the hotel, a plain gray building of about twenty stories with nothing spectacular about it except the neon bucking bronco on its side. She glanced over to one side of the hotel, where a huge circus tent was set up. A white banner with red letters was stretched between two tent poles. WILD WILD WEST ADVENTURE SHOW, the sign proclaimed. There was a crowd milling about outside the tent and Delphine almost tripped over her own feet when she changed direction and headed toward the ruckus.

"Come on," she yelled to Bradley and Harriet, who were lagging a bit behind her. "We've got a show to catch."

Chapter 9
Showtime

"Hurry, Harriet, put this on," Delphine urged, holding out a green and purple sequined outfit with giant, peacock-bright tail feathers sewn into the rear.

Harriet took the skimpy one-piece suit and looked at it skeptically. "I can't wear this."

"Chorus girls ready in three!" a beefy man shouted, not even looking twice at the dozens of women in various states of undress.

"Yes you can. Dickie and his thugs would never think to look for us here. They'll be out searching the crowd, not looking for us among the performers." Delphine grabbed a feather headdress and watched another woman pin hers in place before attempting to secure her own. "Ouch," she grumbled as she stuck herself with a hairpin.

She turned around in time to see Harriet shucking off her clothes and nodded approvingly. Then she reached down and slipped a pair of too-big four-inch heels on her feet.

"Here, let me do your hair thingy," she said, as Harriet straightened up and wiggled her breasts to get them settled into the tight costume.

"I look ridiculous," Harriet said.

"Yeah, we all do," Delphine agreed, trying not to poke Harriet as she had done to herself. "I think it's the tail feathers that do it. The rest of the costume isn't that bad."

Harriet wiggled her butt and the fake feathers swept back and forth across the plywood floor of the makeshift dressing room. "You'd never catch a man wearing something so silly."

"Well, you might. He just wouldn't be the type of guy you'd pin any long-term relationship hopes on. Unless you were another man, of course." Delphine stepped back and admired her handiwork. Harriet's headdress listed a bit to the right, but given the circumstances, she hadn't done too badly.

"Okay, ladies, it's show time," Burly Man shouted.

Immediately, all semblance of chaos vanished. The women, dressed in identical feather-laden costumes, lined up from shortest to tallest. Delphine scrambled to find her place in line. Once in place, she took a deep breath and tried flattening out her feet to make sure her shoes wouldn't slip off. Then she smiled at the women to her immediate right and left. The one on the right scowled at her as if she'd committed some unpardonable faux pas, but the one on the left seemed friendly enough.

"Did the temp agency send you over?" the woman asked, sticking her hand down the front of her costume to rearrange her breasts.

Delphine tried to keep her attention focused on the woman's face, but it wasn't easy. "Uh, yes. That's right. The temp agency."

"We get temps every show, it seems. I think it's 'cause of the food. The other shows in town have better chow, so our performers up and quit this one whenever there's an opening at another show. You'd think they'd at least give a couple days' notice. I heard that one of our singers walked out this time. Isn't that rude? I mean, singers are much harder to find than just dancers like us. We're a dime a dozen in this town. Did the agency tell you that you get a free meal after every show? They don't always remember and some of the girls won't tell you this stuff. But not me. I figure it don't take

nothin' away from me to let the new kids in on the deal." The
woman pulled her hand out of her costume, tugged at the top
of it, and smiled at Delphine, her teeth enormous and whiter
than any Delphine had ever seen before. Delphine blinked
back at her, trying to assimilate all the information she'd just
been given. Before she could process it all, though, the
woman straightened her shoulders and said, "Well, looks
like we're on."

"Go, go, go," Mr. Burly said, patting each woman on the
shoulder as she passed by him and through an opening in the
bright blue curtain that shielded them from the arena beyond.

As Delphine moved ahead, she felt herself starting to
panic. What had she been thinking? She had no idea how to
dance in a chorus line. Hell, she could barely even slow-
dance without stepping on her partner's toes.

She clenched her fists at her sides.

Stop it, she told herself. *You can do this. Just pretend
you've been doing it all your life.*

She stumbled a bit when she was pushed out into the
bright spotlight trained on the entrance to the dressing room,
and laughter rolled through audience. "Come on, Delphine,"
she whispered under her breath. "You're a chorus girl. You've
been dancing since before you could walk. You wore tutus
and ballet slippers to your first day of kindergarten. You can
feel the music in your heart and you have to move with it.
It's as natural to you as breathing."

Delphine straightened her shoulders and looked at the
long line of women in front of her. One woman was about
three inches taller than Delphine and there was something
about her that made it seem as if she carried her own spotlight with her. The sequins in her costume seemed to almost
glow. With each step, the feathers sewn into the back of her
costume snapped proudly from one side to the next in time
with the ba-da-bump music that blared out of the sound
system.

Keeping her eyes trained on the other woman, Delphine

attempted to mimic her walk. Toe, hip, slide, wiggle. Roll shoulder, lift chin. Do it again.

After two or three wobbling steps, the magic started happening. Delphine felt the familiar shift in her mind, where fact and fiction ran together. Suddenly, her shoes weren't too big, her costume wasn't too small, and she wasn't some klutz who didn't know how to dance. Suddenly, she *was* a chorus girl, with a dozen glamorous costumes hanging in her closet in the penthouse suite where she entertained her wealthy boyfriends.

Delphine licked her heavily glossed lips and smiled wide for the crowd as the dancers strutted their stuff. The men in the crowd clapped and cheered when they stopped, turned away from the diners, and flipped their tails in the air, revealing fifty-two scantily clad derrieres. With a wiggle and a swish, Delphine let her tail feathers fall and executed a half-turn, linking elbows with the woman to her left as they started in on another routine.

When that was finished, the women spread out into two columns, striking various poses. Delphine waited, her weight on the balls of her feet, to see what they were going to do next.

Her eyes widened with surprise when a man wearing purple leather pants and a filmy green shirt unbuttoned to the waist came riding out into the arena on a white horse. Another man, wearing green pants and a purple shirt, came riding out from the opposite direction on a black horse. The man on the white horse was wearing a black cowboy hat, while the one on the black horse wore a white hat. Delphine thought that was strange, but didn't have much time to think about anything else as the riders sped toward each other. The crowd held its collective breath, waiting to see if the horses would collide. At the last second, the horses veered in opposite directions and began threading through the poised dancers at breakneck speed, like a human slalom course.

Delphine forced herself not to close her eyes as the white

horse galloped toward her. When the rider got close enough for her to see his face, she gasped.

It was Bradley, and he looked as terrified as she felt. He had a death grip on the saddle horn and he was hunched over the horse's neck, as if by staying as close as possible to the animal, he could avoid being tossed off.

If she hadn't been so frightened, she might have found it funny that a man who tried to pass himself off as a cowboy obviously didn't know how to ride a horse.

Bradley looked as if he wanted to say something to her, but his horse raced past her before he could form any words. Delphine watched him gallop away and sent up a silent prayer that they'd all get out of this alive.

The two horses met up again at the front of the stage and the dancers started moving again. They formed two lines and fanned out along the edge of the stage area, then stopped once again as Bradley and his counterpart dismounted. When his feet touched the ground, Bradley staggered, and held on to the horse's saddle as if it were the only thing keeping him from falling to the ground.

Then two little girls in frothy green dresses ran out from the front of the arena and handed Bradley and Green Pants microphones. Delphine saw Bradley look down at the mike as if it were some ancient artifact. Fortunately, his partner felt no such unfamiliarity with the sound equipment, because he jumped right into a rendition of "Thank God I'm a Country Boy."

When the music changed, Delphine guessed it was Bradley's turn to sing because the other man set his microphone down on the ground and nodded, as if challenging Bradley to "beat that."

Delphine stood in the chorus line and cringed as Bradley started to sing over the noisy, chattering crowd of people who were paying more attention to their salads than to the singers. At first, his voice barely rose above the cacophony of conversations and clattering silverware. But then something strange happened. Delphine watched closely as Bradley closed his eyes, squaring his shoulders. It was as if . . . as if he were going through the same process as she had just minutes before—summoning up the belief from somewhere deep within that he could do this.

His voice took on a deeper, stronger quality, commanding the audience to listen. Commanding *her* to listen.

Delphine found herself mesmerized by the sound of his voice as the music swelled in the now-quiet arena. She felt the words slide over her—a man telling the woman he loved that his spirit was there, even though his body was not.

As the words faded into silence, Delphine stood unmoving on the hard-packed dirt and stared at Bradley. Stared at her future. She knew, in that instant, that she had found what she had been unconsciously searching for years to find.

A purpose.

A reason to stick with something after the first thrill of adventure faded. Because she believed in his talent. Because she believed he had the drive necessary to become a star.

And because she wanted to be a part of something. An important part, not just a sitting-on-the-sidelines, waiting-for-things-to-happen part.

As the crowd started clapping and wolf-whistling, Bradley took off his cowboy hat and bowed, letting the brim of his hat scrape the dirt in front of him. Then he righted himself with a grin and a wink to the nearest chorus girl before turning back to Green Pants with an exaggerated raise of one eyebrow—a symbolic "take that."

Delphine pulled her attention away from Bradley when the chorus girls started to parade themselves in front of Green Pants. He looked each of them up and down, as if inspecting them for flaws before deciding which of them to buy at the cattle auction. As she pranced past, Delphine stuck out her chest and gave her tail feathers an extra wiggle.

Green Pants grinned at her and nodded. Then, to her utter

shock and horror, he reached out and pulled her from the lineup.

Oh, God. What had she done now? Had he managed to spot her for the fraud she was?

But instead of stopping the show, he pushed her in front of Bradley. Then he turned back to the chorus line and picked another woman for himself.

Delphine looked at Bradley, whose face was still flushed with pleasure from the audience's applause. And all she could think was, *I want to help make your dreams come true someday.* Then the music started up again and Bradley groaned.

"What?" she whispered, leaning into him.

Bradley surreptitiously covered the microphone. "This song. It's just . . . Oh, never mind."

As Bradley and Green Pants started singing, Delphine looked over at her counterpart to see what was expected of her. The other chorus girl—Green Pants had chosen the taller woman that Delphine had picked out of the crowd earlier to use as her role model—started to walk around the singer, eyeing him up and down just as Green Pants had inspected the women earlier. Delphine's eyes widened when the other woman reached out and squeezed one of Green Pants's butt cheeks. Then she started listening to the words Bradley was singing.

The woman in the song was looking for a sugar daddy, someone to take care of her after a run of tough luck. The potential sugar daddy sounded skeptical, as if he'd been burned by this woman before. So Delphine knew she had to give him something special to take a chance on her again.

With that thought, Delphine turned around to face the audience, her back to Bradley. She lifted her arms up over her head, then brought them down slowly, caressing the sides of her own breasts, then her waist, then her hips as she swayed to the music. She took a step backward, letting her tail feathers swish over the tops of Bradley's cowboy boots as she continued to move her hips back and forth.

Then she turned around and met his eyes. He looked almost pained, but Delphine ignored him. She listened to the words of the song, and in her imagination, Bradley ceased being the man who had just proposed marriage to another woman. Instead, he was the man she wanted—no, needed—to take care of her. Delphine raised her arms and rested them on Bradley's shoulders. She turned her hands toward his neck, letting her fingers rub up and down the sensitive skin from his ears to his collarbone. All the while, she rotated her hips in as suggestive a manner as she could muster.

Of all the women who wanted this man, she was going to be the one he chose.

Delphine slid her fingers into the thick hair at the nape of Bradley's neck and scooted closer. She planted one fuck-me pump between Bradley's snakeskin boots and wrapped her other leg around his waist, grinding against him.

The tone of his singing changed then, becoming edgier and more . . . raw. It was as if he too had been transported into the song. He was the man who wanted to not want her. He wanted to laugh off her attempt to get him back, to toss her back into the street with nothing more than the clothes on her back.

But he couldn't. He *was* her lover. He *was* her man. No matter that she was crawling back to him and begging him to take her back. He would do it, gladly, because she was his.

The last note of the song reverberated in the charged air of the auditorium. The audience seemed captivated by the story playing itself out in front of them.

Bradley lowered the mike from his lips and Delphine let her foot fall from around his waist. The crowd started clapping and cheering, but Delphine felt as if she and Bradley had been enclosed in a soundproof bubble. As the audience applauded and the other dancers made their way off the stage, Bradley dropped his head as if to kiss her.

But whatever he had intended to do was interrupted when a shot rang out.

The audience gasped.

Bradley grabbed Delphine's hand and ran toward the exit, only to stop when he saw one of the men who had been chasing them earlier. He turned around and raced to another exit, but stopped again when Dickie Swanson stepped out of the shadows. He looked to his left and saw the third man coming from the remaining exit, hobbling toward them with murderous intent in his eyes.

Bradley and Delphine backed up until they were in the center of the stage, the three thugs closing in on them.

"What are we going to do?" Delphine asked.

"I don't know."

"I left my gun back in the dressing room," Delphine said.

"I can't imagine how you could have hidden it in that costume."

"Exactly. There's hardly enough room in it for me."

Bradley stole a sideways glance at her. "It looks great. Believe me."

Delphine felt her cheeks go hot. "Thank you."

"You're welcome."

"Maybe you could try whistling for your horse? That always works in the Westerns."

Bradley whistled and the white horse he'd ridden in on perked its ears forward, but didn't move. "It was worth a try," he said.

"All right, you two. I want you to put your hands up in the air and walk real slowly toward the exit," the thug with the thick silver hair said.

Delphine noticed the other one—the one who had introduced himself as Gus right before she'd grabbed his gun and Harriet had stabbed him—had wrapped his hand in a dishtowel and was limping. If he hadn't been intent on killing them, Delphine might have felt sorry for the guy. As it was, he was brandishing another gun (must have brought a backup, she figured) at them and looking as if he'd be happy to shoot them both right here in front of a tent full of witnesses.

A tent full of witnesses.

Delphine gave herself a virtual head-smack. These guys couldn't kill them in front of all these people. Not if they didn't want to spend the rest of their lives wearing orange jumpsuits with little numbers sewn on the chests.

With Bradley still holding her hand, Delphine squeezed his fingers until he looked down at her. She looked from the exit to the white horse that stood pawing the ground at center stage.

He glanced back at the thugs, who had their guns pointed at his and Delphine's backs. Bradley knew what Delphine was trying to say. If they meekly obeyed orders and left the tent with Dickie and his henchmen, they were as good as dead. As long as they stayed onstage, they'd be safe.

The audience was booing and hissing, caught up in the fight between the bad guys and the good guys as Bradley and Delphine marched toward the door. When they were equidistant to the exit and to Bradley's horse, he nodded.

And they were off, racing toward the white horse that stood pawing the dust.

Bradley yelped when he heard a shot being fired from behind them.

Okay, so maybe they'd been wrong about being safe in front of all those witnesses.

They reached the horse at a dead run, and Bradley stuck his foot in the stirrup and vaulted onto the horse's back. He may not have known how to ride a horse, but he certainly knew how to get onto one in a hurry. He reached out a hand to Delphine, who lost a shoe when he yanked her up behind him.

She grabbed him around the waist as they galloped off. Unfortunately, the horse didn't quite know what to do, and Bradley didn't have any idea how to make it change course, either. So, instead of racing to safety, the horse ran the same course it had run earlier, weaving back and forth as if threading a line of nonexistent chorus girls.

The three thugs ran after them, hastily changing direction when the horse turned around and started coming after them.

Bradley figured they hadn't seen the show earlier, so didn't realize they were in the horse's practiced path.

"Grab the reins," Delphine shouted in his ear.

"What?"

"The reins. Grab the reins," she repeated.

Bradley looked at the leather strings that ran along both sides of the horse's neck. The ends of the strings were tied to the saddle horn. Bradley touched one of the strings, then looked back at Delphine questioningly. "These?"

"Yes. You pull on them. To make the horse turn."

"Hmm." Bradley reached out and pulled both of the strings, wondering how the horse knew which way he wanted it to turn as he did so.

The horse jerked to a stop, bouncing a bit on its front legs at the sudden change in its routine. Bradley lost his grip on the reins and started sliding off the saddle. Delphine tried to steady him but had no leverage from where she sat on the horse's rump, holding on to the back of the saddle with all her might to keep from slipping off.

Bradley hit the ground and the air whooshed out of his lungs, leaving him lying in the dust gasping for breath.

The thugs started back toward them, and Delphine didn't waste any time. She pushed herself up and over the back of the saddle and kicked off the one shoe she hadn't lost, grimacing when it hit Bradley in the chest.

"Sorry," she yelled, grabbing the horse's reins and urging it forward with pressure to its ribs. It didn't move.

"Giddyap," she pleaded, pointing the horse's nose toward Dickie and his gang, who had changed direction once again and were gaining on her and Bradley.

"Come on, horse, move it," she begged, but it still didn't budge.

Then she gritted her teeth, smacked the horse on the rear, and hollered, "Yee-haw."

The horse took off as if it had been stung by a bee. It raced toward the thugs, making them dive in all directions to avoid being run over. Delphine gripped the saddle horn with one hand and used the other to try to turn the animal back around.

She got the horse turned to make one more pass, hoping she'd given Bradley enough time to recover his breath. She frowned when she heard the odd sound of a horn honking, but ignored it as she urged the horse forward once again.

"Get up, Bradley," she screamed, looking up just as Dickie Swanson reached Bradley's side.

Dickie grabbed the lapels of Bradley's shirt and hauled him out of the dirt.

Bradley came up swinging, his fist connecting with Dickie's nose. Dickie let him go and Bradley scooted backward to get away from the approaching gunmen.

Delphine shook her head, trying to get the honking sound to stop ringing in her ears. Instead, the noise kept getting louder, as if it were coming closer.

"Come on," she shouted, reaching down to pull Bradley up onto the horse with her. Bradley grabbed her hand and put one foot in the stirrup to haul himself up, but found himself being dragged along when Gus grabbed his other foot. The injured man limped along behind him, trying to keep him from mounting the horse.

Then, from the front of the tent burst a gleaming white Winnebago.

Delphine cursed and leaned on the reins as the vehicle headed directly toward them, horn blasting. But she didn't let go of Bradley's hand.

And neither did Gus let go of Bradley's foot, much to his own dismay when he was dragged right into the path of the oncoming motor home. Gus screamed and let go of Bradley as he hit the chrome bumper on the driver's side of the Winnebago. He fell to the ground and, as Harriet heaved on the steering wheel in an attempt to avoid running over him, the audience went wild.

Amid clapping, cheering, and wolf whistles, Bradley

yanked Delphine from the horse and raced with her to the motor home. He jerked open the door, heaved Delphine, feathers and all, facefirst onto the carpeted floor, leaped up behind her, and yelled, "Go!" to his mother.

And they were off.

Chapter 10
Trust in Me

As Dickie Swanson leaped upon the white horse and chased after Harriet Nelson, he was acutely aware of the irony of the situation. Himself, playing the good guy, chasing the thieves.

The metal horseshoes made a clanking sound on the pavement as he urged the horse to hurry. It raised its head and whinnied, as if delighted to be out in the open air. Maybe it smelled freedom, Dickie thought, wondering if he would recognize the scent if he smelled it. It had been so long since he'd been free. Free of obligations, free of others' expectations, free of the lies and half-truths that made up his life.

Behind him, he heard Jim yell for him to stop, but Dickie pressed the horse to go faster. The sound of Jim cursing faded away as he put more distance between them. Up ahead, he saw the Winnebago come to a stop at the gates of the motor home park. Seconds ticked by as Harriet waited for her chance to pull out onto the busy traffic on Las Vegas Boulevard, seconds that Dickie used to close the gap between them.

He reached out a hand to grab on to the ladder at the back of the RV just as Harriet floored it. Dickie spurred the horse out into the street. Several people honked, but, since this was Vegas and strange things happened here all the time, nobody stopped or paid too much attention as his tired horse trotted down the street in pursuit of the RV. A light ahead of them turned yellow, and Dickie saw his chance to overtake the Winnebago.

He stood up in the stirrups and grabbed for the ladder again, getting a good hold on it just as Harriet must have decided to take her chances on running the light. She hit the gas pedal and Dickie felt himself being jerked up over the horse's neck. His feet were still stuck in the stirrups and he hung on desperately to the metal ladder as the pavement gaped below him, waiting to tear him to shreds if he let go.

Frantically, Dickie jiggled his feet, trying to get them out of the stirrups. Finally, just when he felt his grip start to give way, his feet came loose.

Free at last, his legs slid over the horse's neck and his body whacked against the back of the Winnebago with a painful thud.

Dickie wrapped his right arm around the ladder and pulled his feet up onto the bottom rung, grumbling, "I'm too old for this shit," the entire time. Thus secured in place, he took a minute to wipe the sweat off his forehead. He looked behind him to see the horse still trotting after them, losing ground as Harriet picked up speed.

Then he forgot all about the horse when a blue pickup truck with a camper on it screamed around a corner in front of them, making Harriet slam on her brakes. Dickie grunted as he whacked into the back of the Winnebago again.

When the camper moved into the next lane, Dickie saw that the back door was hanging open and debris was falling out, as if the campers had hurriedly left right in the middle of having dinner or playing a game of cards. He groaned when he saw a woman poke her frightened face out the door, as if trying to figure out what was going on.

Dickie knew exactly what was going on. Jim had commandeered someone's camper . . . with that someone in it.

Shit.

He had to get inside the Winnebago.

The pickup changed lanes in front of them and Jim slammed on the brakes. Harriet swerved into oncoming traffic, braving horns and shouts as she tried to evade the more maneuverable pickup.

Dickie knew he had to do something. Fast.

Keeping one arm looped around the ladder, he started to climb the rungs. Peering over the top of the Winnebago, he could see the brilliant green lights of the MGM and the Stratosphere tower ahead in the distance. The sun had set, but just barely, so there wasn't the full effect of the lights against the night sky. In any event, he hadn't come up here to enjoy the view, Dickie thought as he braced himself once more, scooted closer to the back window of the Winnebago, and slammed his foot against the glass.

He kicked again. And again.

And on the fourth kick, Harriet slammed on her brakes, giving his blow the extra oomph it needed to shatter the glass.

Dickie carefully ran his shoe along the edge of the window to make sure there were no sharp shards left, just waiting to impale him. Then he backed down on the ladder, shoved his head and shoulders through the broken window, and dove headfirst into the surprisingly lumpy mattress in Harriet's bedroom.

Bradley heard the sound of glass breaking over the screeching of brakes as his mother attempted to avoid slamming into the back of the camper in front of them. He looked to the back of the motor home and saw a man's foot plow through the glass.

"Come with me," he said to Delphine, who nodded and unclicked the seatbelt she'd fastened across her chest.

Bradley tried to walk a steady path, but his mother's

erratic driving made that impossible. He smashed into the refrigerator as he rushed drunkenly to the rear of the Winnebago, followed by an equally unsteady Delphine. They made it to the bedroom just as Dickie Swanson dove into the motor home, and Bradley lurched forward one last step and pulled the door closed a split second before Dickie lunged at it from the other side.

Planting his boots on either side of the door, Bradley held on tight as Dickie tried to tug the door open. The door opened a crack and Bradley tugged harder, making it slam shut again. Dickie managed to get the door open again, and Bradley was surprised at the older man's strength. He pulled it closed again after a struggle, feeling the sweat start to trickle down his neck.

He felt a tickle on his arm and turned to find Delphine bowing down, her feather headdress lightly caressing his skin.

"I don't think praying's gonna help," he said.

Delphine leaned down even more, the tickle of feathers raising goose bumps on his arms. Then she straightened up, holding out a strip of flesh-colored nylon. She had ripped off one leg of her pantyhose, but Bradley had no idea what she expected him to do with it.

"What's that for? You planning on robbing a bank next?" Bradley struggled to shut the door again when Dickie pried it open, grunting with the effort it took.

Delphine sighed loud enough for him to hear it. Then she nudged him a bit to get him out of the way of the bathroom door. "No, we can use this to tie the bedroom door closed. Didn't anyone ever do that to you when you were a kid? So you'd be trapped inside and not be able to get out?"

Bradley stumbled a bit when Dickie jerked on the door, his hands starting to lose their grip on the doorknob. "No," he answered. "I didn't live with sadists."

Delphine was busy tying one end of her stocking to the

bathroom doorknob and didn't look up. "Well, I did. Here, let me tie the other end to the bedroom door."

"How are you going to do that? I can't let go."

"Hmm." Delphine stepped back, studying the problem. "Okay, stay right where you are."

She walked behind him and got down on her hands and knees, then crawled under his splayed legs. Then she reached over his thigh and grabbed the other end of her pantyhose and got to work tying off the bedroom door.

The feathers of her headdress were now tickling his chest, laid bare by the cheesy costume he wore, the shirt devoid of buttons and lying open to the waist. Delphine's fingers brushed his as she attempted to get a good knot tied, and Bradley tried to keep his concentration focused solely on the bedroom door.

Her soft blondish-brown hair swept his forearm as she tilted her head.

Bradley studied the knot in the wood of the door.

Her shoulders brushed his crotch.

Bradley noticed a water stain in the veneer of the door.

She turned to smile and tell him she was finished.

Bradley fought back a groan when he realized her mouth was about two inches from his penis, which had gone just about as hard as the door.

Bradley's hands slipped off the doorknob. He licked his lips, stepped back, and rubbed his sweaty palms down the thighs of his saunalike leather pants. "Good, uh, thinking," he said, taking a step back.

Behind Delphine, the bedroom door opened a crack, but not far enough for Dickie to get so much as a finger through. Bradley held out a hand to help Delphine up off the floor. He was careful to keep his distance as she came to her feet. The last thing he wanted her to know was how turned on he was just now.

Hell, it seemed that he was *always* turned on around her,

a condition he put down to a lack of sex between him and Robyn these last few months when she had been away touring. Robyn didn't much like touring, saw it as nothing more than a necessary evil, and she had got downright bitchy with him over the phone before he decided to meet her in Sacramento to join her on the leg to Vegas and then on to Nashville, hoping he could lighten her mood. Of course, he thought now, standing in the cramped hall of his mother's Winnebago trying to hide his erection from Delphine, Robyn had been downright bitchy with him even after he'd joined her in Sacramento.

The Winnebago lurched just then, and Delphine stumbled. Before she could regain her balance, the motor home swerved again, sending her right into Bradley's arms.

So much for hiding his attraction, he thought as he tightened his hold on her so she wouldn't fall. There was no way she couldn't feel him pressing into her, not through that flimsy costume she was wearing. Bradley gave a wry smile. Too bad she wasn't wearing the gorilla suit—she'd never feel anything through that thick fur.

Just then, Dickie pounded on the door with his fist and yelled, "Let me out of here. I'm here to help."

Bradley released Delphine and pushed her behind him as he cautiously moved closer to the bedroom door. "We're not letting you out. Are you nuts?"

"I have a gun. I could blast out of here if I wanted, but I don't want to hurt anyone."

"I don't believe you, Dickie," Bradley said.

There was a rustling sound, and then the unmistakable bang of a gun being fired. More rustling, and then, "Does that convince you? And, by the way, I prefer to be called Richard."

Bradley looked at Delphine, who raised her eyebrows and shrugged. "I'm convinced," she said.

"What do you want, then?"

"Let me out and I'll tell you."

Bradley frowned at the door. Was this a trick? What the hell did Dickie want if not—as had seemed to be his mission this entire time—to kill them?

"Listen, I'm not who you think I am," Dickie said when Bradley remained silent.

Dickie slid something through the crack at the bottom of the door and Bradley snatched it up. It was a business card from a taxidermist in Albuquerque, New Mexico.

"Call the number on this card. Ask for Jorge Ortiz."

"Why should I call a taxidermist in New Mexico?"

Dickie banged a fist on the door. "Do it, damn it! Right now."

Bradley brushed past Delphine, who looked as skeptical as he felt. He rummaged through the suitcase he had brought from Robyn's tour bus earlier, before all hell had broken loose, and found his cell phone. The red message light was blinking, but he didn't take the time to check who had called.

"Hold on," Harriet yelled.

Bradley didn't have time to heed his mother's warning and was thrown against the sink when his mother attempted to make a U-turn in the middle of the busy nighttime traffic. Tires squealed, horns honked, obscenities flew. Somehow, though, she managed to maneuver the vehicle around and point it in the opposite direction from Jim and his stolen camper.

When they were back on all six wheels, Bradley looked down at the business card in his hand and dialed the number shown on the front. The phone was answered on the fourth ring.

"Yes. Uh, hello," Bradley said awkwardly. "Can I speak with Jorge . . . Jorge . . ."

"Ortiz," Delphine prompted.

"Yes, Jorge Ortiz, please," Bradley said into the phone.

"Certainly. Let me connect you."

Bradley jumped when the summons was answered almost immediately by a gruff-voiced man who said only, "Ortiz."

"Mr. Ortiz. I'm calling about Dickie, uh, that is, Richard Swanson."

"And where is Mr. Swanson right now?"

Bradley glanced back at the bedroom door. "He's, uh, locked in the bedroom of my mother's Winnebago."

"Pardon me?" Ortiz asked.

Bradley scratched his head. "Well, we didn't know what else to do with him. He was chasing us and we were afraid that he . . . well, we were afraid that he was going to kill us, to tell the truth."

"What's your name, son?" Ortiz asked in an avuncular manner.

"Bradley Nelson," Bradley responded, then added, "sir."

"Mr. Nelson, you need to let Mr. Swanson out of the bedroom."

"Why should I do that?"

"Because he's one of our best agents."

"He is?"

"Yes, he is."

"And who might you be?" Bradley asked.

"I'm Jorge Ortiz and I run the Albuquerque office of the DEA. That's the Drug Enforcement Agency, in case you didn't know. Richard Swanson has been working undercover in Reno for the last year. Since you're calling, I have to assume his cover has been blown and that you're all in a shitload of danger."

"You got that right," Bradley muttered.

"Excuse me?"

"Nothing." Bradley shook his head as if to clear the confusion that had settled there like a blob of butterscotch pudding. "How do I know that you're telling the truth?" he asked.

"How does anyone know when someone else is telling the truth?" Jorge Ortiz asked philosophically. Then he cleared his throat. "Mr. Nelson, you're just going to have to trust me on this."

"And why should I?" Bradley asked.

"Because if I were lying . . ." Jorge Ortiz paused, then repeated. "If I were lying, Mr. Nelson, you'd already be dead."

Chapter 11
The Chase

"Everyone get buckled in," Dickie—who went by Richard when he wasn't posing as a thieving money launderer—ordered, awkwardly sliding into the driver's seat when Harriet stood up to let him take over. She kept her hands on the steering wheel, her foot on the gas, and her eyes on the side-view mirror as Jim Josephs sped up to overtake them.

Richard fought to find the gas pedal through the tail feathers of Harriet's costume. When he did manage to slide his foot under hers, she had to sit down on his lap to get out from under the steering wheel and let him drive.

The ends of her silky brown hair brushed across his chin, and Richard found himself enjoying the feel of her against him, no matter how unintentional the contact might be.

Harriet slid off his lap and into the passenger seat, while Bradley and Delphine slipped into the dining booth to brace themselves for what promised to be a bumpy ride. Richard looked in the mirror to find that the blue pickup had almost caught up with them. He knew Jim Josephs was not going to give up and just let them go. Jim had a vindictive side—one that Richard had seen firsthand on more than one occasion.

"Why hasn't someone called the police?" Harriet grumbled from the seat next to him.

"This is Vegas. They probably all think this is just part of some show. Besides, I'm just as happy to leave the police out of all this. You never know which ones have been paid off."

As Jim sped up to try to pass them, Richard swerved into the other lane to block him.

"Do you think that poor woman is still in the back of the camper?" Harriet asked, letting her eyes flicker to his face for a moment before turning back to look in the mirror at the traffic behind them.

"Yes," Richard answered grimly. "I have to find a way to stop Jim long enough so that whoever is in the camper can escape." *And I have to do it in such a way as to not get myself and everyone here killed,* he added silently.

"I have a plan," Harriet said, unbuckling her seatbelt. "When I tell you, turn the motor home so that it's blocking both lanes, but do it so that the passenger side is toward the oncoming traffic, all right?"

Richard nodded as Harriet disappeared. Whatever her plan was, he hoped it would work. God knew he hadn't come up with any bright ideas.

He did his best to keep Jim from overtaking them, as Harriet made her way to the back of the Winnebago after briefly rummaging around in the kitchen first. The RV didn't have a rearview mirror so he couldn't see what she was up to, and he was too busy watching the more nimble pickup weave back and forth behind him to take the time to glance back into the bedroom.

When he saw the cloud of white dust billowing out behind them, though, he nodded his approval.

And when Harriet shouted, "Now!" he slammed on the brakes and jerked the steering wheel hard to the right.

The Winnebago's tires screeched in protest at the sudden move and it felt as if they were scuttling sideways like a crab. Richard watched from the shattered passenger-side window to see what would happen next.

The pickup emerged from the billowing cloud of flour with its windshield wipers going full blast. Jim had obviously not factored in the ages-old "flour plus water equals glue" formula, and the sticky mess that covered his windshield only got worse with each pass of the wipers. Fortunately, he had instinctively let his foot up off the accelerator when he encountered the sudden flour storm. Still, he was going fast enough to make Richard glad he'd buckled his own seatbelt when the front bumper of the pickup rammed into the passenger side of the Winnebago, the sound of metal against metal making him flinch.

The pickup hit their front bumper and Richard felt the front end lift a bit and then come back down to the earth with a thud.

Through the cracked passenger window, he saw the now motionless pickup's windshield wipers move again. Then, through a strip of clean windshield, he saw something else: a flash of bright red blood against Jim Josephs's silvery hair.

For a split second, Richard hoped that Jim was dead . . . or at least incapacitated.

That hope died a sudden death when a bullet ripped through the pickup's window, making a pass through Richard's upper arm as it traveled through the motor home. Richard closed his eyes against the burning pain.

Damn, that hurt.

Shocked into action, he didn't even bother to look down to see how much damage the bullet had caused. He didn't have time for that anyway. He had given the campers a chance to get out of the vehicle that Jim had hijacked and that was all he could do for them. It was up to their own survival instincts to keep them safe now. Saving himself moved to the top of his priority list, and he revved up the Winnebago's engine and cranked the RV back into traffic to escape Jim's wrath.

The steering wheel pulled to the right as Richard tried

to get the motor home back into one lane. The frame was probably bent from the collision, but at least the vehicle was drivable.

As Harriet staggered back up to the front of the cab, Richard tossed her a gruff, "Good thinking."

"Thanks. What are we going to do now?"

Richard looked over at her steadily. "Do you want the truth?"

"Yes," Harriet answered, sliding into the passenger seat and ignoring the crumpled front panel that had shrunk her space by a good four inches.

"We're going to kill or be killed."

Harriet nodded, then shocked him when she said, "I vote for option number one."

"Me, too," Richard said. "Me, too."

When the pickup slammed into them for the third time, Bradley braced his feet against the base of the dining table and held tightly to Delphine so she wouldn't slide out of the booth with the force of the impact. The back of the Winnebago skidded toward the Luxor, with its golden obelisk and skyward-looking sphinx, but Dickie or Richard or whatever the hell his name was kept the vehicle on the road, even with the blue pickup truck trying to stop them.

"Hold on," his mother warned, just as the DEA agent made a sharp left turn in front of four lanes of busy traffic.

Delphine slammed against Bradley, her bare arm pressing against the filmy fabric of his shirt as she slipped on her tail feathers.

"Sorry," she apologized, grabbing the edge of the table in an attempt to right herself.

"Don't worry about it," Bradley said, right before his cell phone started ringing.

Who in the world could be calling at a time like this? he wondered. Then he pulled the phone from his back pocket, looked at the incoming number displayed on the screen, and grimaced. He pressed the talk button.

"Robyn, this is a bad time," he said. "Can I call you back later?"

He heard the frown in her voice when she answered, "No. I think we need to talk about this right now. I've given your proposal some thought, and I have an answer for you."

Bradley grunted when Delphine slammed into his side as the Winnebago careened around yet another corner.

"Did you just grunt at me?" Robyn asked, her voice heating up about fifty degrees.

Bradley helped Delphine right herself again before answering, "Yes, but I didn't mean to. Look, I'm sort of, uh, in the middle of something important right now. Are you sure I can't call you back?"

"Are you trying to say that whether we get married or not isn't as important as whatever it is you're doing right now?"

Gripping the back of the dining booth as the pickup hit them from behind, Bradley did his best to keep his cell phone pressed to his ear. "I'm sorry, what did you say?"

"I said," Robyn repeated, enunciating each word clearly, as if he were dim-witted, "don't you think that getting married qualifies as important?"

"Of course I do, it's just—" Bradley stopped, not knowing exactly how to extricate himself from this mess. He began again. "I can explain—"

"Good. Go ahead," Robyn said.

Bradley could imagine her standing onstage, tapping her well-shod toes with irritation while her green eyes shot fire at anyone who dared to glance at her. He let go of the edge of the table to rub his temples, which were suddenly pounding. What could he say? "Robyn, I don't have time to talk because I'm running from a psychopath with my mother, an undercover DEA agent, three million dollars in embezzled funds . . . and a chorus girl whom I almost married yesterday."

He didn't imagine the truth was going to ease Robyn's

temper. He frowned and glanced down at the Formica table-top. The seams where the pink-speckled top met the similarly colored sides were rough, and Bradley absently ran his finger along one edge.

The real truth was, he wasn't sure he really wanted to hear Robyn's answer.

What if she said no? How would he ever get David Gamble to reconsider renewing his contract if Robyn—

Suddenly, it hit him.

Had he really asked Robyn to marry him because she could help his career? After getting the call from his manager that morning, thoughts had run through his mind with a sort of frantic desperation. What should he do next? How could he change Gamble's mind? Was this going to be the death of his dream? No, he'd thought. It couldn't be over. He had worked too hard, sacrificed too much.

Even so, when he'd left the RV park and headed to the hotel where Robyn's next concert was scheduled, he hadn't intended to propose to her. For some reason he hadn't wanted to examine too closely, he simply knew he had to see her again. She was his only hope. His only link to David Gamble.

Proposing to her had just sort of . . . happened.

An act of desperation to ensure his dream wouldn't die.

Bradley looked over at Delphine, who was clutching the table with both hands and doing her best not to stare at him, and he felt his hold on the dream of becoming a country music star start to slip. Had he actually stooped so low as to propose marriage to a woman he didn't love in the hopes of convincing Gamble Records to take another chance on him?

What sort of sick bastard had he become?

He pinched the bridge of his nose between his thumb and forefinger. Then, before Robyn could tell him what her answer was, he said, "I'm sorry, Robyn. I should never have proposed to you. I think we both know that it was a mistake.

I—" Whatever he was going to say was cut off when the Winnebago veered sharply to the left, followed by his mother's loud scream. Bradley looked to the front of the motor home to see his mother frantically fighting with her seatbelt. Richard Swanson was slumped over the steering wheel . . . and they were heading straight for the Eiffel Tower outside the Paris Hotel.

"I've got to go, Robyn. I'll call you back," Bradley said hastily, before tossing his phone onto the table and pushing himself out of the bench seat.

"Grab the wheel, Mom," Bradley shouted as the Winnebago jumped the curb on Las Vegas Boulevard South.

"I'm trying," Harriet said, attempting to move Richard's heavy shoulders off the steering wheel.

Bradley grabbed Richard's right arm and lifted it, trying to place his shoulder under the other man's armpit to get some leverage. It wasn't easy in the confined space, but Bradley managed to half drag, half carry the DEA agent away. He laid Richard on the floor between the two front seats and slid into the driver's seat, slamming his foot down on the accelerator and tugging the steering wheel to the left as people on the sidewalk ducked and ran for cover. The Winnebago's front bumper clipped one of the steel girders of the Eiffel Tower before Bradley managed to get the motor home back out onto the street.

"Now what?" he muttered, not expecting anyone to answer.

From the floor, Richard groaned. "Albuquerque," he said groggily.

"What?"

"Get to Albuquerque. Don't stop. It's the only way."

Bradley looked down at the other man and saw his eyes close. He also saw the bright red stain oozing into the carpet from Richard's left arm. They needed to get Richard to a hospital, not to Albuquerque.

He flinched and whipped his head around when he heard

a bullet rip through the window in the dining room. "Are you all right?" he asked Delphine.

She peeked out at him from under the dining room table, her blue and green feathered headdress shaking. "Yes. I'm fine."

"Could you help my mother get Richard to the back and try to stop his bleeding?" Then he looked out the side window, gritted his teeth when the blue pickup came into view, and added, "I'm going to get rid of this son of a bitch, once and for all."

Delphine crawled out from under the table and headed toward Richard's head. "I'll get this end," she told Harriet, who bent down to pick up the DEA agent's feet.

Bradley sped toward the next intersection. They had to get on the open road and away from all the traffic clogging the streets of Las Vegas. The heavy traffic gave Jim Josephs an advantage over the less maneuverable motor home. Once they got onto the highway, they might have a chance.

With single-minded determination, Bradley wove between cars and trucks with the pickup on his tail. Soon, he was headed east on Sahara, ignoring the double yellow line to pass cars that were blocking his way. One thing he discovered was that the right of way had nothing over being confronted with a vehicle five times one's size. Honda Accords and Dodge Caravans leaped out of the way after seeing him pull into their lane. Even giant Chevy Suburbans and Ford Expeditions let him pass. Soon, they were speeding toward the highway with the blue pickup on their tail.

He hit the highway going sixty miles an hour and waited to make his move.

Although traffic was fairly heavy, he moved the Winnebago into the left lane, knowing he was going to piss off a dozen faster vehicles that would be forced to pass using what was supposed to be the slow lane. But, looking out at the desert surrounding them, Bradley knew he had to position himself correctly or innocent people would be hurt. If he played his cards right, Jim would wait until the traffic was lighter, and then try to pass him on the right. That's when Bradley would make his move.

Bradley slowed down to a steady fifty miles an hour. As the traffic behind him gave up waiting for him to move despite their annoyed honking and began going around him, Bradley tightened his grip on the steering wheel and waited for his chance.

At long last, the cars behind him had all sped past, the last one's taillights fading into the darkness like the red eyes of some wild animal retreating into the wilderness.

Finally, they were alone with their enemy.

From the passenger-side mirror, Bradley saw the headlights of the pickup truck glide smoothly into the right lane. He waited. And waited. And waited, until he could see the moonlight shining off Jim's cap of silver hair.

Then he made his move, cranking hard on the steering wheel as he attempted to push the truck off the road. From behind him, he heard a cabinet door bang open, and then heard a soft gasp and a thud, but he couldn't afford to take his eyes off the side mirror. If Jim slowed down and got behind him, or sped up and got in front of him, the chase might continue forever.

He had to end it. Now.

Bradley pushed the blue pickup to the edge of the road. As Jim pressed the accelerator, his tires spun on the loose gravel. The nose of the truck edged past the Winnebago and Bradley leaned on the gas, all his attention focused on this race. The motor home edged ahead, and Bradley gave another sharp tug on the steering wheel, trying to make Jim lose control of his vehicle.

Suddenly, as if his wish had made it come true, Bradley saw the pickup hit a spot of soft earth just past the shoulder of the road. The desert seemed to grab hold of the vehicle, clutching the tire that had landed on its precious soil and spinning the truck around in the dirt. Bradley slowed, not foolish enough to speed off and assume that his enemy was no longer a threat.

He watched as the pickup's brake lights flashed on and off as Jim tried to get the vehicle back under control. Then the truck must have fallen into a gully, because it suddenly disappeared from sight.

If they'd been in Roswell, New Mexico, Bradley might have believed the vehicle had been abducted by aliens. Since Nevada was a state where the tricks were usually of a man-made variety, he was willing to bet the truck had fallen into an irrigation ditch instead. In any event, he was satisfied that, even if Jim was unharmed, it would take him at least an hour to get the truck out of whatever it had fallen into. By then, Bradley planned to be across the border in Arizona.

With that thought, he turned to see how his mother and Delphine were doing with Richard . . . only to find Delphine lying in a crumpled heap on the floor next to the couch.

"Delphine? Are you okay?" he asked, squinting to see her in the darkness.

When she didn't respond, Bradley quickly moved over to the shoulder and slowed the Winnebago to a stop. He jumped from the driver's seat and stepped back into the living area of the motor home, crouching down next to Delphine's unmoving form.

Reaching out, he put a hand on her shoulder and gently rolled her over. Then he swept the soft hair away from her face. He'd never noticed how smooth her skin was before, even though he'd been close enough to count her eyelashes on several occasions. He ran the back of his hand across her cheek, just to see if her skin was as soft as he thought it would be.

Her eyes were closed and her breathing shallow, and Bradley didn't know what to do. He was certainly no medical expert, and he worried that if he moved her any more than he already had, it would just make things worse.

"Delphine, are you all right?" he asked again, his face just inches from hers as he listened to her steady breathing.

Her eyelids fluttered like those of a baby bird trying to open its eyes for the first time. And then she was looking up at him with a drowsy stare, as if she'd just awoken from a leisurely nap. She reached up with one hand and caressed the side of his face, her fingers sliding from the hair at his temples, across his cheek, under his chin, and down his neck. She stopped at his collarbone, even though the shirt he wore gave her full access all the way down to the waistband of his leather pants.

"Bradley?" she murmured, her breath warm against his lips.

"Yes, Delphine, what is it?"

"I think I may have broken a rib," she said, just before her eyes rolled back in her head and she fainted once again.

Richard lay on the lumpy mattress in the back of the Winnebago, sliding in and out of consciousness. Snippets of memories of the past year played in his head like one of those artsy movies that he never seemed to understand. Him as a bad guy. Him as a good guy. Leading yet another double life, trying in vain to break up yet another drug ring.

God, when had this all become so complicated? He didn't remember it being so hard in the early days. Or maybe he had just been younger, so all the details of who was telling what lie to whom was easier to keep track of in his more youthful, more nimble brain.

Or maybe it had been easier because Evelyn had been with him then. Beautiful, vivacious Evelyn, who lived life to its very fullest until, in one cocaine-soaked moment, she decided to end it all just as grandly as she lived it, leaving him a note and telling him that she was going to lose herself forever in the bat-infested caves of the Carlsbad Caverns. Her body had never been recovered, and Richard had never found another woman in all the years since her death to give his heart to. He sometimes feared that he had nothing left to give, that whatever capacity for love he had come into this world with had been taken away by his lovely wife's death.

Richard found himself staring at the lacy pink bedspread covering him, frowning as he tried to recall where he was. This wasn't his current home, the eight-thousand-square-foot monstrosity where he lived, doing his best to fit the image of a successful—and incredibly wealthy—casino owner. Evelyn would have loved that house, in all its garish magnificence. She had always wanted the best and, even though he hadn't been able to provide it for her, she told him that she had faith in him. She said she knew that when the time came for him to make the tough choices about how he was going to provide for his family, he'd make the right one.

She had been completely, utterly wrong. And Richard knew that the choice he had made had pushed his wife over the edge into a depression from which she never recovered.

Richard felt the familiar pressure behind his eyes and closed them, welcoming the darkness that threatened to swallow him.

He had loved his wife.

But in the end, he had killed her.

Chapter 12
Leaving You in the Dust

"I can take a turn driving," Delphine said, trying not to grimace as she shifted positions in the passenger seat.

"Are you sure?" Bradley asked.

He hovered over her as if she might collapse at any minute, and Delphine fought the urge to roll her eyes heavenward at his protectiveness. "I'd rather do that than take care of Richard. The sight of blood makes me queasy," she said, closing her eyes when a wave of pain hit her as she reached out to turn the air-conditioner vent away from her face.

They had stopped at a gas station just outside of Kingman, Arizona, a little over two hours after leaving Jim in the proverbial dust outside of Las Vegas, so that they could fill the tank and switch drivers so Bradley could get some rest.

"I'm going to get a snack from the vending machines. Can I get you something?" Bradley asked, pushing open the driver's-side door.

Delphine looked at him and giggled. "You're not going like that, are you?"

Bradley looked down at the purple pants and see-through green shirt he was wearing and pulled the door closed behind him. "Thanks for the reminder. I guess I forgot how ridiculous I look in this getup."

He put a hand up on the top of the seat and pulled himself

into a standing position. Then he stretched his arms toward the ceiling, and Delphine sat back and watched the show. Under the filmy green shirt, Bradley's muscles flexed and relaxed. He had nice broad shoulders—not Hulk-like but still strong and solid. And his butt, which was clearly outlined in the tight leather pants, was just like a man's butt should be, a little bit rounded and not totally nonexistent like some guys' were. She was tempted to reach out and squeeze him, just to see if he was as firm as she thought he would be. He had tennis-player legs, with thick, muscular thighs that made Delphine think of what those legs would look like wrapped around her.

He turned around then and caught her ogling him, but Delphine quickly pasted an innocent look on her face and smiled. "By the way," she said, blinking up at him as if she had not just been thinking of what he would look like lying naked on top of her. "Do you have a shirt I could borrow? This costume is a bit itchy and I don't really think tail feathers are my thing."

Bradley squinted at her, obviously not certain that her innocence was real. After a moment, he shrugged as if to say it didn't matter either way. "I'm sure I can find you something."

He rooted around in the suitcase he'd tossed inside the motor home just before Jim and Gus had come bursting through the door, and came up with a faded white T-shirt with the slogan WHEN LOVE FINDS YOU on the back. A stack of promotional copies of his first and only CD tipped over, and Bradley neatly arranged them again before handing the shirt to Delphine.

Delphine took the shirt and looked at the picture on the front of a man wearing cowboy boots and jeans with one foot propped up on a red truck. Exactly what one would expect of a country star, she thought.

"Who is this?" she asked, pointing to the picture on the front of the T-shirt.

"Vince Gill. I went to his concert back in 1995. It was a great show. He did over an hour's worth of encores. Patty Loveless opened for him."

Delphine cocked her head and looked up at him. "You really love country music, don't you?"

Bradley continued riffling through the clothes in his suit-case. "I want to be a star."

Delphine frowned as he pulled out a pair of blue jeans that had faded so much they were the color of a cloudless summer sky. "That's not what I asked. I asked if you loved the music."

"Of course I do. Why would I be in the business if I didn't?"

Without waiting for her to answer, Bradley pulled another T-shirt out of his suitcase and turned, heading back toward the bathroom. Delphine watched him go, idly continuing to admire his rear view while she pondered his last question.

"As suspected, Dickie Swanson is a traitor. He's headed east on Interstate 40 toward an unknown destination. Await your instructions."

The e-mail message had been sent from a public-access Internet terminal in Las Vegas and was signed by longtime associates Gus Palermo and Jim Josephs. The message had been sent to an address that could not be traced back to Reno's reigning drug kingpin—or queenpin, as the case might be.

Evie Smith narrowed her eyes at the computer screen on her desk and wrapped her tongue around the end of the pen she was holding. She'd broken herself of the habit of nail biting years ago, but couldn't seem to get over the urge to be fidgeting with something at all times. An oral fixation. That's what her shrink had called it when she'd still believed that going to therapy might save her from herself.

She laughed a short and humorless laugh. That had been a long time ago. Now she realized that all those years lying on some man's couch would have been better spent lying underneath some man on his couch. At least then she would have gotten some pleasure from the encounter, rather than simply uncovering more and more pain.

That's the thing shrinks didn't realize, she thought, still nibbling on the end of the pen. Unearthed pain had the ability to hurt you more than the stuff you left buried. Unfortunately, that had been a lesson she'd had to learn on her own. Everyone else had kept hoping that with every dark secret she revealed she'd somehow, miraculously, get better. Instead, it was as if each cloaked secret she held tight to her breast helped protect her from harm. As each layer was peeled away, she became more and more exposed to the raw pain she had experienced growing up. It became more real, more hurtful, and more damaging than when she'd kept it all buried inside.

And so, to escape the pain, she'd found solace in drugs. At first, just getting drunk had been enough. But with every visit to the psychiatrist's office, she needed more and more alcohol to dull the pain. Soon, she could no longer hide her addiction—especially not from her husband, who had made a career out of hunting down those whose livelihoods depended on others' substance abuse.

She'd been Evelyn Swanson back then, a troubled young housewife whose husband had a promising career in the DEA. She knew her alcoholism was hurting him both personally and professionally, and when the solution came to her, it was surprisingly ironic. With drugs, she could hide the evidence of her addiction so much easier than with alcohol. There would be no empty bottles to hide, no scent of whiskey on her breath to give her away. And, even better, her husband had files on all the local drug dealers, which made it incredibly easy for her to arrange her drug buys.

For several years, she'd played the happy homemaker,

and Richard had never even suspected she was using drugs to get through her everyday life. She proclaimed herself to be cured, quit going to the shrink, and all the evidence of her alcoholism vanished as if by magic. She had devised the perfect plan and, indeed, for years it worked like a charm.

Every morning after Richard left for work, Evelyn would take two Valium and a Vicodan and tidy up their small house in a daze of drug-induced numbness. Then, while she was still coherent, she'd prepare their dinner, even going so far as to set the table.

And then, right around noon, she'd pop another round of V and V, strip down to a pair of high heels and a lacy teddy, and wait for her first customer to appear. Prostituting herself was something that she hadn't even thought twice about. She needed money, money that Richard wouldn't notice was missing when she spent it on drugs. To her, having a man (and the occasional woman or two) poke things into her various body openings was nothing more than that. They poked at her, she moaned and groaned and pretended to be overcome with passion, and they came and it was over. And for nothing more than a few hours and a set of sheets that needed to be cleaned ever other day or so, she was paid enough to keep herself in painkillers for months.

Only after a while, the painkillers made her feel dull and listless. One night, at a party one of Richard's social-climbing coworkers was hosting, Evelyn discovered cocaine and a whole new world opened to her. Cocaine made her feel alive again, only alive in a way that she had never felt before. She became fast friends with the couple, saw what a wonderful life they were building for themselves. And she wondered . . . why were she and Richard struggling so hard to make ends meet when this couple—with their daily drug habit, their brand-new three-thousand-square-foot house, and their matching convertibles—had it so well?

So she asked Richard one night. Why were they so poor? And Richard had told her that his colleague was suspected of being a dirty agent, but that nobody had any hard evidence on the man. Evelyn wanted to tell him then, "You're just as smart as Bill is, Richard. You find a way to do it, too. I want a nice house. I want a new car. I want to bury my nose in white powder every day and never worry again about not getting enough."

But she didn't say it to him. Not for another six months. For that half a year, she continued to sleep with strangers to pay for her habit—only it was different now. With cocaine, she couldn't hide. The things they did to her . . . now she felt every touch, every violation of her body a thousandfold. But she couldn't go back to Valium. She loved the cocaine high too much to give it up.

When Richard caught her snorting the first time, she knew it was going to change their relationship. She asked him then what she hadn't been able to ask before.

Make the right choice, Richard.

I need more.

More. More. More.

He had looked at her as if she'd asked him to murder someone. Then he had told her he had to go to work. Before he left, he wrote down a phone number and slid it across the dining room table at her, and Evelyn laughed a bit hysterically when she realized he was giving her the number of another shrink.

Didn't he know this was how it had all started? Her first psychiatrist had opened Pandora's box and she couldn't get the demons back inside, not without the help of her drugs.

When she found out the next day that Richard had left the night before to arrest their friend Bill for accepting bribes, selling drugs, and stealing evidence, she knew it was over. Richard would never change.

But *she* could.

Evie looked at her own reflection in the silver frame of the only photo she kept on her desk. She looked nothing like Evelyn Swanson had. She'd dyed her red hair a muted blond, nothing so garish as platinum or honey blond for her. She wore gray-tinted contact lenses to hide her brown eyes. She'd had extensive plastic surgery to change the shape of her eyes and her nose. She'd even had breast-reduction surgery.

Even her own husband wouldn't recognize her. She had proven that time and again, playing her role as the wealthy widow of one of Nevada's high rollers with such ease. She'd waltzed in and out of the casinos, shaking hands and drinking cocktails with all the owners—including the so-called Dickie Swanson, who she knew was not the person he was pretending to be—and he never once took her aside and said, "You resemble someone I used to know." Instead, he treated her carefully and politely, dismissing her as the nobody wife of someone who used to be important.

Evie rolled the pen around on her tongue. How amazingly easy it was to fake one's own death and miraculously come back to life as someone completely different.

The real miracle, though, was how her life had turned out. As the wife of a DEA agent, she knew all the major players in the drug game. She had seen the map Richard had hung in his office, with colored pins to mark the major drug-trafficking areas. Ten years ago, she had noticed that Reno was conspicuously bare of pins.

For months before she had faked her own suicide, she had laid the foundation for her new life. She made appointments, she made connections, she made plans. And when the time was right, she set the stage for her own death.

If anyone had looked into the suspicious nature of her suicide, they might have noticed something odd. The day after Evelyn Swanson supposedly killed herself, a sixty-year-old man in a neighboring state was bludgeoned to death in his sleep. The crime scene was particularly gruesome and most of the details were not made public.

And Evelyn Swanson had taken the first step in becoming a new woman.

Little did she know that killing her father—a man who

had repeatedly raped, beaten, and sodomized her while she was growing up—would prove to be all the therapy she would need to finally kick her drug addiction.

Now, Evie Smith, clean and sober for almost a decade, picked up the silver picture frame and gently rubbed her thumb over her husband's face. Richard Swanson had been the only man who had ever really loved her. That's why, although she could have—and probably *should* have—had him killed on more than one occasion, she had given the order that he was not to be harmed.

She set the picture frame next to her computer and looked from Richard's smiling face to the e-mail she had received and back again. She hastily typed a note to Jim and Gus to do whatever was necessary to keep tabs on her husband. They might not know where Richard was headed, but she did. He was going back to New Mexico, back to the DEA. She told Jim and Gus to fly to Albuquerque. In the last line of her message, she ordered them to report back to her every day, including sending her pictures of what Richard was up to, and then told them that under no circumstances was Richard to be harmed.

During all the years since her death, Richard had remained true to her. He'd never remarried, never so much as dated for any length of time as far as she could tell—and she'd had him tailed enough to know.

As long as her husband still loved her, she would never let anyone hurt him.

Chapter 13
Lonely Time

Four o'clock in the morning was such a lonely time.

Delphine leaned her elbow on the armrest of the driver's seat and rested her head in her hand. The interstate was empty, the sky the darkest shade of black, and the terrain around them bleak. The entire earth felt devoid of life, as if Delphine were the only creature feeling and breathing and wondering if anyone felt as alone as she did at this moment.

In the seat next to her, Bradley mumbled something in his sleep and stirred briefly before resuming his light snoring.

Delphine turned her attention back to the deserted road and cranked up the volume of the CD player to keep herself from getting drowsy. She was going to have to wake up Bradley soon to relieve her, but he had seemed so exhausted earlier that she wanted to let him sleep as long as possible.

Tim McGraw's voice came over the headphones she was wearing, and Delphine found herself listening for the story in the song. She'd always liked that about music—it was probably why she wasn't a big fan of classical music. No words, no story, and, for her, no passion.

Tim sang about a family being torn apart by the wife's anger and disappointment over the way her life had turned out. As Delphine listened to the words, she put herself in the husband's head as he sadly packed his things to leave. She felt his own anger at being made to feel responsible for his wife's disillusionment, as if it were his job to make life meet her expectations.

"What a sad song," she murmured, pressing the button on the CD player to flip to a different album.

As the CDs shuffled, Delphine tried to look at Tim's song from the wife's point of view but found it difficult. She, herself, had learned very young that life was full of bitter disappointments. Blaming someone else or expecting another person to fix things for you . . . well, that was just stupid. Getting angry was even more stupid because that hot red emotion only served to overwhelm logic and make it even more difficult to get what you really wanted.

No, the only thing that had ever really worked for her was lying, although Delphine preferred to think of it as role-playing. Much like pretending to be a chorus girl in Vegas by letting herself believe that she really *was* a chorus girl. She'd found it amazingly easy to fit into a role simply by immersing herself in how she believed a person in that situation would act or feel.

And what role are you playing now? a voice inside her asked, sounding as skeptical as these voices typically did.

Now that was a question, Delphine thought, watching the WELCOME TO NEW MEXICO sign go by. She closed her eyes for a second and yawned. She wasn't going to be able to make it much longer. Her eyelids felt as if someone were pulling them down, trying to cover her eyes. But she had no intention of arriving in Albuquerque in the back of an ambulance so she opened her eyes and glanced back over at Bradley. She smiled softly at the way he slept with his arms and legs sprawled out around him. He looked younger without the cowboy hat he seemed to almost never be without.

She thought about the way he had looked at her when she'd finished her dance at the Wild Wild West Show, as if he had been mesmerized by her performance. And he had been aroused. She'd felt his erection pressing against her thigh when she'd wrapped her leg around him for her grand finale. He may have proposed to another woman, but he was not unaffected by her. Delphine knew that for certain. Whenever they were together, she felt that sort of awareness that happens when two people are attracted to each other.

"I wonder if you feel the same thing when you're around her," Delphine whispered, breaking the silence inside the motor home.

"Did you say something?" Bradley asked, stretching out his arms as he slowly sat up in the seat next to her.

Delphine coughed and ripped the headphones off her ears. "I was just . . . uh, singing along to the CD."

Bradley rubbed his eyes sleepily. "Oh. Are you ready for me to take over driving?"

"Whenever you're ready," Delphine said.

"All right. Just let me go check on my mother and then I'll switch with you."

Bradley walked to the back of the motor home and found his mother on her bed, sleeping in a sitting position next to Richard Swanson. It was strange to see his mother with a man, even though Richard was unconscious and his mother was sleeping fully clothed on top of the pink bedspread. Bradley hadn't seen his mother with another man since the day his father left. He knew that she had dated, but it had never lasted long enough or become serious enough for her to bring the man home to meet her son.

She must be lonely.

Bradley hadn't given it much thought before, preferring to believe, as most people did about their parents, that his mother didn't need sexual companionship. That was totally ridiculous, of course. His mother, at fifty-six, was still very attractive. She had the trim figure of someone who worked out several days a week, and she always made a point of dressing neatly and professionally—no sloppy sweats or oversized T-shirts for her. She religiously dyed her graying hair the same dark brown shade as when she was younger.

She slept with one hand on Richard's good arm, as if by doing so, she could tell if his condition worsened, even as she slept.

Bradley shook his head and turned back toward the front of the Winnebago. There was more to his mother's relationship with Richard Swanson than she let on. But for now, he figured, it was really none of his business.

Delphine eased the motor home onto the shoulder of the road and left the motor running. As she stepped out of the driver's seat, Bradley realized that she was wearing the Vince Gill T-shirt he had loaned her ... and not much else. The shirt caught her at mid-thigh, but still left an awful lot of creamy white skin exposed.

As he slid into the newly vacated driver's seat, he watched her sit down in the passenger seat. The T-shirt rode up almost to the top of her thighs now. There was no way he could concentrate on the road with that distraction sitting so close at hand. He got back up from the driver's seat and found his suitcase. He didn't know why he hadn't thought to loan her some pants before. He supposed he just hadn't thought about it.

Freudian slip, a sarcastic voice in his head whispered.

"Oh, shut up," he grumbled.

He pulled out a pair of gray sweatpants that had a drawstring at the waist and handed them to Delphine. "Here, you can borrow these."

"Thanks," she said, uncrossing her legs and giving him a brief glimpse of plain white panties. She shook the sweats out and slid them up her legs, pulling them up and under her borrowed T-shirt.

Bradley stood over her, frowning. That one tiny flash of her panties had been seared into his brain, as if by a white-hot brand. For some reason, he'd found that tantalizing sight incredibly sexy.

Man, he needed to get laid if a glimpse of some woman's underwear got him panting.

No, not just any woman's underwear, that sarcastic voice whispered. It was the sight of *Delphine*'s underwear that had him thinking like a teenager whose only sexual experience involved *Playboy* magazine and his own palm. Bradley was beginning to think that if he didn't have some sort of release soon—whether self-inflicted or not—he might be in danger of exploding the next time Delphine bumped into him, which happened surprisingly often in the confines of the Winnebago.

He put his foot down on the accelerator and guided the motor home back onto the interstate while Delphine reclined in the passenger seat. She curled her knees up onto the seat, put her hands under her head, and closed her eyes. Then, sounding as if she were just seconds from drifting off, she asked, "Why do you want to be a country music star?"

Bradley's lips curved into a dry smile. "Doesn't everyone want to be rich and famous?" he asked back.

"No," she answered sleepily. "Some people just want quiet lives surrounded by people who love them."

"Lives of quiet desperation," Bradley said absently as he switched lanes to pass a slow-moving semi.

"Seems to me they're no more desperate than you, putting off happiness until you become a star."

Bradley looked over to find Delphine's blue eyes studying him carefully, as if he were a sort of science experiment gone awry. "I'm not putting off happiness. As a matter of fact, I'm doing everything I can to achieve it." *Everything including asking a woman you don't love to marry you,* the sarcastic voice added. Bradley grimaced at the thought. He had never imagined he'd become so desperate for success that he'd do something as calculating as that. Even the fact that he truly hadn't realized what he was doing at the time he proposed to Robyn was no consolation. He'd never imagined that he'd sink so low in his quest for success, and the idea that he had left him feeling slightly sick to his stomach.

"And are you happy?" Delphine asked, making him swallow down the acid he felt rising in his throat.

"I was happy when Gamble Records signed me," Bradley said. "It was the best day of my life. Even though the money was crap, it was the first step in achieving my dream."

"And now?"

Bradley took a deep breath and looked out over the desolate, predawn landscape. "The Country Music Awards are coming up next week and I feel certain that I'm going to get a nomination in the new male vocalist category. That would make me happy."

"Why?"

"These awards are very influential in the industry. Getting nominated almost guarantees that I'll get picked up by a major label. By next week, David Gamble and his indie record label will regret not offering me another contract."

"What makes you think you'll get nominated?"

"I don't know. I just feel it. I've made some great contacts this year and my first album got some good reviews. I was even featured in an article in *Country Weekly* magazine. It just . . . it *has* to happen. It's not possible that I'd have one album out and then . . ." He paused, putting his hands up in the air as if to make his point. "And then nothing."

Delphine continued watching him, her intense scrutiny making him want to squirm in his seat. Finally, he couldn't take it anymore. "Why do you keep looking at me like that?" he asked.

She opened her mouth as if to say something, then took a deep breath and closed it again. Finally, she said, "You never say anything about the music itself. Doesn't that matter to you?"

Bradley scratched a spot on the back of his head and looked around for his hat. "Of course it does. But everyone knows these awards shows are all about the politics. There are lots of great musicians out there whose careers never go anywhere because they think it's the music that's most important. I know better. I watched my dad kill himself to make great music. He thought that alone would make him a star. Since I was a kid, that was all he ever talked about."

"Did he ever make it?"

Frowning, Bradley turned to look out the window as the sun's rays turned the top of a dull brown hill a brilliant pink color. "No. He gave up too soon."

"Why'd he give up?" Delphine asked.

Bradley turned around to face her, his shadowed brown eyes meeting her clear blue ones. "Do you want the truth?"

Delphine nodded, curling one hand under her cheek as she did so.

Bradley glanced back at the bedroom, making sure his mother was still sleeping soundly. "My mother drove him to quit. Every day, she would come home from work and he'd be out on the covered patio with his friends. They were all musicians, too. Our house was always littered with instruments. That's why Mom hired some guy to enclose our patio one day. She had him put up one of those corrugated plastic roofs, the kind where it seems you can hear every drop of rain falling on it like nails being dropped on tin. After that project was done, she practically banished my dad and his friends out there."

"How long did this go on?"

"At least since I was in kindergarten, because I remember coming home on the bus at lunchtime and getting Dad out of bed to make me something to eat. He and his friends stayed up late writing songs and practicing. That was one of the reasons Mom made them move out to the patio. She said that other people had real lives and had to get up early. It never bothered me, though. I guess I was just used to it since I'd fallen asleep to them playing every night since I was born."

"Didn't your mom know that your dad wanted to be a singer when she married him?" Delphine asked, her eyes closing and then opening abruptly like one who was trying her best not to drift off to sleep.

"Yeah, she did, but I guess the reality wasn't quite as glamorous as she'd thought. I mean, the truth is that there are very few people who make it in the music business. Most of us have 'real' jobs that pay the bills while we're trying to hit it big."

"Did your dad? Have a job, I mean?"

Bradley flexed his fingers on the steering wheel and shifted to a more comfortable position in his seat. "No. He was focused entirely on making his music. That's what I meant earlier when I said that I saw firsthand that the music itself wasn't enough. If my dad had moved to Nashville or L.A. before he had given up on his dream, he would have made it. I know he would have. He . . . well, I guess he let me and my mom get in the way of his success. Mom wouldn't move, and Dad waited too long to leave us. By the time they got so sick of each other that they couldn't even stand to live in the same house together, it was too late. It wasn't six months after my dad left us that he was killed in an accident. He hit a telephone pole going fifty miles an hour. Mom and I never talked about it, but I'm not so sure it was an accident."

Delphine didn't say anything for so long that Bradley thought she must have fallen asleep. He glanced over at her and her eyes were closed, her breathing shallow. Figures. This was the closest he'd ever come to telling someone about his father's death, and she'd fallen asleep.

Just as well, he figured. He hated the pitying looks he got whenever someone found out that his mother had driven his father to his death.

Just then, Delphine reached out across the space that was separating them and laid her hand on his thigh. "I'm sorry," she said simply, giving his leg a comforting squeeze. Then she started to withdraw her hand, as if unsure whether the contact would be welcome.

Before she could pull away, Bradley reached down and covered her hand with his, trapping her fingers against the warmth of his thigh. He looked over at her, but her eyes were still closed.

Without thinking about what he was doing, Bradley raised her hand and turned it palm up. Then he lowered his mouth to kiss the tender flesh just above her thumb, closed her fingers around the kiss, and guided her hand back to its nest under her cheek. She nuzzled his hand, turning her face into him and pressing down as if to keep him there. She looked at him then, her blue eyes soft and sleepy and filled with sadness.

"Thank you," Bradley whispered, caressing her cheek with the hand she'd trapped underneath her.

She nuzzled him once more, then let him go. She didn't say anything more as she let her eyelids drop one last time, and in no time at all, she had drifted off to sleep.

Chapter 14

Right or Wrong?

Richard Swanson opened his eyes to find a nicely rounded set of breasts blocking his view.

Too bad every day didn't start out this way, he thought.

He didn't say anything, decided he didn't want to have this pleasant experience come to an end any sooner than necessary. When Harriet sat back on her knees and saw that he had been gaping at her cleavage, she rolled her eyes and shook her head.

"It appears that you're feeling better," she said.

Richard gave her a weak smile, taking a mental inventory of his body parts. "Well, I'm not dead. Though my arm hurts like a son of a bitch."

"Yes, I'm sorry about that. I didn't have anything stronger than Tylenol to give you."

Richard scooted up against the headboard of the bed, realizing with some discomfort that he wasn't wearing anything but his boxer shorts—which meant that Harriet had probably stripped him. Not that he minded being stripped by an attractive woman, but hell, he usually liked to be conscious when it happened.

He looked over at the neat bandage on his arm and lifted his right hand to remove the adhesive tape and inspect the damage. Harriet reached out and stopped him, saying grumpily, "Don't touch that. I just changed it."

"I wanted to see how my arm is healing."

"It doesn't seem to be infected but I'm no expert on gun-shot wounds," Harriet said, leaning back against the head-board beside Richard and crossing her legs. "So, now that you're awake, would you fill me in on what's going on here? Bradley said you're some sort of drug enforcement agent? Why were you skimming money from a casino in Reno? And why have you been chasing us?"

Richard's gaze slid sideways to the woman sitting on the bed next to him. She'd changed out of her chorus girl cos-tume and into a pair of silky red pajamas. With her dark hair, dark eyes, and tanned skin, she looked exotic, like some-thing out of a magazine where women lounged around all day drinking mai tais and listening to the wind rustle through palm trees. He had a sudden vision of himself slid-ing the red silk off her shoulders and laying her down in the white sand, covering her body with his while the ocean pounded away.

He lifted his right leg under the covers then to hide his growing erection, and forced his mind back to business. He had known from the start that letting his attraction to Harriet Nelson get to him was a mistake.

"Yes, I'm an agent with the DEA. I've worked for them since I graduated from college over twenty years ago. I've been undercover in Reno for about a year now as casino owner Dickie Swanson."

Harriet's gaze didn't waver as she asked, "Why did you start stealing? Was the temptation too great? I mean, I saw the amount of cash that flowed through the books every day. It must have been too much for you to resist."

Richard snorted and shook his head. "I did it to get closer to Jim and Gus, who had been laundering money for El Corazon—he's the leader of Reno's drug ring—for years. My mission was to find out the identity of El Corazon, but nobody seems to know who he is. Every time we think we're getting close to him, an informant mysteriously disappears or a supplier is murdered. This guy knows what he's doing. He doesn't plan to get caught."

"I still don't understand," Harriet said, tugging at the hem of her pajama top, which only served to tighten the fabric across her breasts.

Richard turned his head and studied the small pink flowers threaded through the wallpaper in the bedroom. This was obviously a woman's domain, full of frills and flowers and lace. He found himself wondering if Harriet had ever slept with a man here. Then he grinned. Well, she had slept with *him* here in her pink, feminine cocoon. Although that hadn't exactly been what he'd meant.

He cleared his throat and tried to pull his mind away from what he figured had to be pain-induced lust and back to business. But it wasn't easy.

"Let me start at the beginning," he said, folding his arms across his bare chest. "About eight years ago, my team in the DEA noticed a marked increase in drug activity in the Reno area. In addition to the typical minor possessions charges, we were starting to see some major shipments being intercepted. We also saw a pattern that we had come to associate with the start-up of a well-organized drug ring: many of the existing dealers were turning up dead, not to mention that certain cops were suddenly being reassigned to narcotics—a sure sign that someone with a lot of money was paying off local law enforcement to get corruptible cops on the narc squad. We sent in a couple of agents over the years, but nobody managed to get close enough to discover El Corazon's identity.

"Then, about eighteen months ago, one of the former owners of the Heart O'Reno Casino came to us to say he was being pressured to launder El Corazon's drug money, and my boss saw his chance for us to infiltrate the drug ring. We made arrangements to buy out the former casino owner and make it seem as if he had quietly retired to Palm Beach. I took over and have been running the casino ever since.

Because of my role in the community, I've been able to help identify and catch some major drug buyers, dealers, and suppliers, but finding El Corazon hasn't been as easy as I'd hoped."

"You do know about the money laundering, then?" Harriet asked.

Richard nodded. "Yes. Every day, ten percent of our total take is added to the cash we've collected that day. The money runs through our books and gets deposited into our bank accounts, only to disappear into untraceable offshore accounts.

"We're taxed on the money, of course, which is why Jim and Gus decided to start skimming some cash off the top, thus underreporting their income to the IRS. El Corazon is forcing them to launder his money, without leaving any extra for taxes. That got the owners pretty pissed off, but they couldn't do anything about it."

"Why didn't someone just go talk to this drug kingpin person? I mean, he's got to understand that you all have businesses to run, too."

Richard tried not to laugh at Harriet's naïve view of the world. "Well," he said, his mouth tugging up at one corner, "one reason is that nobody knows who this 'drug kingpin person' is. Another reason is that we've all seen what happens to people who cross him. People have been brutally murdered, their businesses destroyed. Sometimes, he even goes after people's families. Nobody wants to risk that, so they just keep paying."

"Hmm," Harriet said with a frown. "That sucks."

Richard did laugh this time. "Yeah, it does."

"So you came after me because you were afraid this drug kingpin would find out why I took the money and would come after you and your friends?" Harriet asked, still puzzled.

Uncrossing his arms, Richard pulled the frilly blanket up to his waist to cover the waistband of his boxers. Then he turned and looked Harriet straight in the eyes.

"No," he said. "First of all, Jim and Gus are not my friends. They're thieves and money launderers. Secondly, I came after you because I was afraid that Jim and Gus would discover you'd taken three million dollars from them and they'd hunt you down and kill you. I had no way to replace the money you'd taken, and I couldn't risk telling you who I really was because you just never know if they've bugged your office, tapped your phones, or gotten to someone who will rat you out."

Harriet's eyes widened. "You mean you blew your cover for me?"

Richard reached up and scratched behind his right ear. "Well, that wasn't my intent. I had hoped I'd be able to convince you to tell me where the money was so I could put it back before Jim and Gus discovered it was missing. But they must have gotten suspicious because they followed me to Vegas."

Harriet put a hand on his arm, her bright red fingernails looking like drops of blood on his skin. "I'm so sorry. I'm . . . God, I'm such a fool. My husband used to say that my self-righteous attitude would prove to be my downfall one day. I guess he was right."

"He did?" Richard asked, pulling the blanket up to cover his stomach. He felt suddenly self-conscious, sitting there virtually naked with Harriet looking on.

"Yes. He's been gone for years, but he always hated the way I see things. Black or white, that's the way it is for me. And when I think I'm right . . ." Harriet shook her head, self-disgust evident in her every word. "Well, when I think I'm right, nobody can reason with me. I'm such an idiot."

It was Richard's turn to frown. He let the blanket slip down his stomach as he turned to face Harriet. "You're not an idiot. And thank God there are people in this world who are willing to act when they see an injustice. As far as I'm concerned, Harriet, there are too few people like you and too many like El Corazon—people who think they're above the law, who only do what's right for themselves without caring about anyone else."

"But I've put you in danger. And I've dragged Bradley and Delphine into my mess, too. And for what? I was just so . . . so angry that the majority of people work hard and pay their taxes and . . . and always do the right thing, only they end up broke and living off Social Security and worrying about every penny they spend. When I saw all the money that was being hidden from the government and I calculated just one year's worth of unpaid taxes, it made me so mad that I had to figure out a way to give that money back to the taxpayers."

Richard laid an arm across the top of the headboard and turned toward Harriet. "How did you do it, by the way? You were searched every time you left the office. How did you manage to get so much cash through security?"

Harriet's lips twitched despite herself. "It wasn't easy. I knew I had to get it done before the next monthly audit, so I took a little bit every day."

"You had to take more than a little bit—to get to three million dollars in less than one month, you had to take a hundred thousand every day."

Harriet shrugged somewhat sheepishly. "Yes, I did. Fortunately, we had some high rollers who didn't play with quarters. If I'd had to take the money that way, it just wouldn't have been so easy."

"But you'd have found a way, wouldn't you?"

Harriet blinked, then looked straight into his eyes. "Yes, I would have."

Richard reached out and squeezed her shoulder. "Good for you."

"I think you're crazy for still believing that I did the right thing."

He grinned at that. "Harriet, do you know how often I see people trying to do the right thing in my line of business?"

She shook her head.

"Never. I have spent the better part of my life with drug

pushers and addicts, murderers and rapists, money launderers and thieves. You've just given me back my faith in humankind."

And with that, he leaned forward and kissed her right on the mouth, pulling her to him with his good arm. Harriet seemed surprised at first, but after a moment, she leaned into him, parting her lips under his. Richard groaned and realized he was doing a rotten job of keeping his professional distance, but he still didn't pull back for a good long while.

When he finally pulled away, he did so with regret. "You still haven't told me how you managed to slip all that cash by security," he said.

Harriet gave him a half-smile as she scooted back against the headboard. "I put it in my tea. Every morning and every afternoon during my coffee breaks, I lined a mug with the largest bills I could find, slipped a teabag in the center, and filled the cup with hot water. Then I went through security. They never stopped me. I guess they thought I was leaving to have a cigarette or something. Instead, I took my tea to the Winnebago, rinsed out the cash, hung it up in the bathroom to dry, and made myself a new cup of tea. I always came back with the same cup, so they never got suspicious."

"Ingenious."

"Thank you. Still, I must have done something wrong because you found out. When I saw you coming toward me that afternoon as I was coming back from my break, I knew you had discovered the truth."

"Yes, I meant to ask how you knew to run that day. What gave me away?"

Harriet studied him for a moment, making him feel like a bug under a high-powered microscope. After a while, she answered, "There was something in your eyes. I can't explain it. I just looked at you and . . . I knew."

Richard laughed humorlessly. So much for his superior undercover skills. Being able to hide what you were thinking was of supreme importance in his line of work. If he'd lost that ability then he really should consider retiring.

Just then, the Winnebago slowed to a stop. Richard drew back one flowered curtain and saw that they'd stopped outside the address he'd given Harriet's son that morning when he'd regained consciousness. He looked at the familiar drab gray building where he'd been stationed for years before going undercover. Evelyn's suicide had driven him to undercover work. He couldn't stand the sympathetic glances and the way conversations would come to a halt when he entered a room. Such a cruel irony, he knew they were saying. One of our top agents, and his wife was a hopeless drug addict.

Richard's fists clenched on top of the lacy coverlet as he remembered the anger and helplessness he'd felt back then. Of all the people he couldn't save, why had his beautiful, headstrong Evelyn succumbed to the lure of cocaine's siren song?

Looking back now, he realized that he had never really understood his wife. They'd married young—when they were both just shy of their twenty-first birthdays. She had been so alive back then. Her name was on the top of everyone's guest lists back when they were in college. Hell, even after college, she had always been the life of every party. Richard knew it was that totally uninhibited lust she carried with her—lust for life, for knowledge, for him—that drew him in. Evelyn had tasted what the world had to offer and she wanted it all. She did everything full-out. The first time they met, they'd ended up having explosive sex in the front of his Chevy with all the windows rolled down in front of her dormitory. Richard had halfheartedly tried to convince her that they should go somewhere more private, but Evelyn had laughed wildly, unzipped his pants, and impaled herself on his enthusiastic erection before he could voice more than an obligatory protest.

She'd screamed when she came that night.

Richard would never forget the sound of that scream

rending the quiet night. She'd laughed when the lights in the dorm rooms above came on. Richard had barely stopped shuddering with the force of his own climax, but he knew they had to get out of there. He laughed too as they sped away. He'd never met a woman before who screamed during sex or who didn't seem to care if he saw her naked. Most of the girls he had dated had been just that. Girls. Girls who were self-conscious about their bodies and who had been raised to believe that in order to get a man to marry them, they had to pretend they didn't want sex. But Evelyn was different. She danced naked on the hood of his car later that night. And she taught him more about sex during the next two months than he'd learned in all of his previous twenty years. And she never once mentioned marriage.

It had been he who was smitten, and for whatever reason, when he had asked Evelyn to marry him just three short months after they met, she said yes. Richard could only assume it was his stability that drew her, proving without a doubt that opposites certainly did attract. He and Evelyn could not have been more different—a fact he learned very quickly after they were declared husband and wife.

"Are you all right?"

Richard nearly jumped when he felt a warm hand covering his own. He blinked and turned his head to see Harriet watching him with her dark eyes, dark eyes that seemed to read him a bit too well.

He turned away. "Yes, I'm fine. Now, if you'll bring me my clothes, we can go find my boss and get this over with."

Harriet remained motionless on the bed for a long moment. Then she squeezed his hand with surprising strength before sliding off the bed. She walked to the closet and brought out a neatly folded pile of clothes and laid them down near his feet.

"Okay, then. Let's get this over with," she said, nodding at him briefly before turning to walk out of the room, closing the door gently behind her.

Chapter 15

Free for Life

"I still can't believe you put the money in your mattress," Bradley said, shaking his head.

"I figured it was such an obvious place that nobody would ever look for it there."

"I think we should drop the whole subject," Richard said. "The money and your mother's evidence against the casino owners are safely in the custody of the U.S. government, so it doesn't really matter where she was hiding the cash."

"I agree. And since both Mr. Ortiz and Richard are certain that we weren't followed to Albuquerque, I think we should go out and enjoy ourselves. After all, we've been cooped up in the motor home for days."

Bradley looked over at Delphine, who had seemed out of sorts ever since he'd woken her that morning when they arrived at the Albuquerque office of the DEA. They'd spent hours providing details of their journey to Richard's boss, Jorge Ortiz, with only a short break to wash down the dry, tasteless sandwiches that had been brought in for them with lukewarm sodas.

It must have been a trying day for her, having to relive the ordeal she'd been unwittingly sucked into three days ago. Bradley rose and walked over to stand behind the passenger seat, which Delphine had swiveled toward the living/dining area of the Winnebago.

While they'd been gone that day, Richard had arranged for an RV repairman to come by and fix the various dents, dings, and broken windows the motor home had suffered since they'd left Reno.

Too bad he hadn't arranged for similar treatments for the people riding in the motor home, Bradley thought ruefully. They all seemed a bit on edge this afternoon, having been dismissed by Mr. Ortiz to get some rest before having to come back in the next day and repeat their stories to a larger audience of DEA and IRS personnel.

Bradley leaned his elbows on the back of Delphine's chair and laid his hands on her shoulders, rubbing them gently in an attempt to help her relax. "Don't worry," he said quietly while Richard and his mother started talking about investigative procedure. "I'm sure the DEA will let you go tomorrow. Then you'll be free to get back to your life."

He felt Delphine's shoulders stiffen under his fingers, but her voice was pleasant when she said, "Yes, that will be nice, won't it?"

Narrowing his eyes, Bradley turned Delphine to face him. "Okay, you've been grumpy all day. What's wrong?"

Delphine frowned and looked out the newly repaired passenger-side window. "I don't know. Maybe I . . ." Her voice trailed off. Then she pushed open the door and slipped past him. She hopped down on the pavement and, without turning around, said, "I need to get some air."

She started walking away from the Winnebago at a fast clip.

"We'll be back," Bradley hastily said to his mother and Richard before he jumped down to the sidewalk and trotted off after Delphine. He caught up with her in three long strides, ignoring the sour look she shot him as he easily kept pace with her.

They walked in silence for several minutes, the oppressively hot air around them stirred occasionally by a welcome gust of wind. When Bradley saw a sign for Old Town, he reached down and took Delphine's hand to tug her with him to Albuquerque's historic district. If she wasn't going to talk to him, at least they could enjoy some of the sights of the old Western town.

They walked past several shops and turned when Bradley saw a gold-colored church to his left. The occasional tourist passed them on the sidewalk, but traffic here was much lighter than on busy Central Avenue. The setting sun struck the adobe church, turning dull brown walls to gold and earthen brown to a fiery copper. Bradley stopped in the opening of the wall surrounding the church and peered into the courtyard to admire the beautiful, simple structure.

He squeezed Delphine's hand. "Pretty, isn't it?"

Delphine nodded, remaining silent.

Bradley kept hold of Delphine's hand as he crossed the street, leading her to a bench in a dusty park surrounded by a thin line of trees. He sat, pulling her down next to him. "All right, spill," he ordered.

Delphine took a deep breath and let it out loudly. Then she turned to him and blurted, "I don't have anywhere to go."

Bradley frowned. "What do you mean?"

Delphine tugged her hand out of his grasp and turned away from him. "I mean, I can't go back to Reno. It's too dangerous. But I hadn't planned on having to move again so soon, either. I'll be free to leave tomorrow, but I don't know where I'm going to go."

"I hadn't thought of that," Bradley admitted.

Delphine kept her eyes trained on the gazebo in the center of the small park. She hadn't meant to sound quite so pathetic, but the idea of leaving Bradley and his mother had been bothering her all day. The truth was, she liked the idea that she might somehow be able to help Bradley become a star. When the thought had occurred to her back at the Wild

Wild West Show in Las Vegas, she had sensed that maybe she could do something important, be someone important.

But that, she knew, was nothing but a pipe dream. She had no record company contacts, no country-music-star relatives, no knowledge whatsoever of the music business . . .

Or did she?

Delphine narrowed her eyes on a sickly looking blade of grass that braved the brutal heat of the sun to poke up through the cobblestone pathway. Just because she didn't know anything about the music industry right now didn't mean she couldn't learn. Hell, she'd made a life out of learning new things and adapting to different environments. If she could make a difference in his career, Bradley might see her as more than just a nobody. And that, she realized, made her want it even more.

"You could always go back to your family for a while," Bradley said, interrupting her thoughts.

"What?" Delphine asked, squinting at that plucky blade of grass as a herd of tourists clattered across the cobblestone path.

"You could go back and stay with your sisters. Just until you decide what to do next, I mean. I'll bet you love going home since your hometown is so nice and all. What's the name of it again? Something 'Hollow'?"

The tourists passed, crushing the blade of grass beneath their feet. That's what you get for trying to thrive in a hostile environment, Delphine thought, shaking her head. She cleared her throat and looked back at Bradley. "Um, no, it's Bluff. Pine Bluff. Best little town in Missouri."

Bradley frowned. "Missouri? I thought you said you grew up in Arkansas."

Delphine blinked once. Then again. Then she smiled. "Yes, I did, didn't I? I was born in Missouri, but we moved to Arkansas when I was just a baby. Sorry."

"Hmm," Bradley said, still frowning. "And I thought the name of the town was Poplar Bluff?"

"Wow, you really are a good listener, aren't you?" Delphine said with a smile. "That's right. The name of the town *is* Poplar Bluff now. When we first moved there, though, it was Pine Bluff. Then one of the town council members pointed out that the trees the town had been named for were really poplars and not pines, so he got it into his head that the name should be changed. It was the biggest controversy the town's ever seen. In the end, the people voted to change the name. So *now* it's Poplar Bluff. But when I was little, it was Pine Bluff."

Bradley started to say something more, but was interrupted when the sound of a single gunshot exploded into the quiet evening.

The air whooshed out of Delphine's lungs when Bradley threw her down onto the hard-packed earth and dove on top of her with a shouted, "Stay down!" Delphine would have asked him if she had a choice, but couldn't manage to suck in a breath with his heavy weight crushing her to the ground.

Another gunshot rang out, sounding closer than the first.

"Jim and Gus must have found us," Bradley whispered, his breath tickling her ear. "We've got to make a run for it."

The scrubby brown grass that grew in the park scratched her cheek when Delphine nodded. Bradley eased up a bit and she was finally able to draw in a breath again as two men came running out of one of the streets that dead-ended into the courtyard, brandishing pistols. The setting sun glinted off the silver barrels of their guns, and Bradley didn't waste any time hauling Delphine to her feet. He pushed her ahead of him toward an alley that ran between two single-story buildings. The vendors selling turquoise and silver jewelry outside the buildings looked up at the commotion, but didn't duck inside to hide as Delphine had thought they would.

She didn't pause to think about it, however, as more gunshots were fired from the courtyard behind her. Instead, with Bradley on her heels, she slipped into an open doorway marked "Employees Only" and found herself inside a storeroom cluttered with women's clothing in varying stages of readiness to be taken out onto the sales floor.

When the front door of the storeroom opened, Delphine grabbed Bradley's hand and pulled him into a crouch. Had Jim and Gus found them already?

As quietly as she could, she scrabbled backward, trying to stay hidden by the racks of halfway-unpacked clothing. When she found a rack that was almost completely full of clothes, she motioned for Bradley to slip in the center. Bradley looked at her as if she'd lost her mind, but he did as she indicated when the footsteps of whoever had entered the storeroom came closer.

Just as a pair of worn brown boots came into view, Delphine slipped between the hanging clothes behind Bradley. They stood huddled together in the center of the circular rack of sequin-covered dresses, trying to stay as still as possible.

Suddenly, the rack moved.

Delphine stifled a gasp of surprise and almost tripped over Bradley's feet as they attempted to stay hidden in the midst of the clothing. The wheels of the rack squeaked as it was pushed along the carpeted floor and the dresses danced gaily as they rolled along, their plastic hangers clicking together as they slid across the bar at the top of the rack.

They passed through an open door and the noise level increased dramatically. Delphine surmised from the ratio of female voices to male that they had been rolled out into the showroom of a women's clothing store. But why would Jim and Gus do that? If they wanted to kill her and Bradley, they would have done it back in the storeroom where there wouldn't be any witnesses.

The rack rolled to a stop and the dresses swayed once more before settling into place.

Delphine hazarded a peek between two denim jumpers, parting the material carefully with her index fingers to see an older man wearing a pair of blue jeans and a brown and white checked Western-style shirt with a black bolo tie fussing with the clothes on the rack next to where they were standing. He lifted one blouse off the rack and slid it behind another one, shaking out the material so it would hang just right. Then he turned back to the rack of dresses, making Delphine drop her hands and take a hasty step backward, landing right on top of Bradley's left foot. She looked over her shoulder and shrugged apologetically while Bradley cringed in silent pain.

Western Shirt Guy shook out the dresses that Delphine had touched (her meddling had obviously ruined his presentation), then he gave the rack one final shake and walked away.

Delphine's thighs were beginning to ache from crouching to stay hidden. She looked down at the floor and decided to give her legs a rest since there was plenty of room for her to sit at Bradley's feet. Awkwardly, she lowered herself down onto the carpet, crossing her legs yoga-style in the cramped space. When she looked around, she realized that she'd made a grave logistical error, since her face was just about level with Bradley's crotch.

This wouldn't do at all. She couldn't sit here staring at the bulge in Bradley's well-worn blue jeans and wondering if that impressive-sized lump was for real. Before she could stand up, though, Western Shirt Guy came back and started pushing the rack again.

Delphine was tempted to shout, "Oh, for God's sake, just leave it where it is!" but, instead, she hastily crab-walked forward a few inches when the dresses hit her back, finding herself face to crotch with Bradley when the rack stopped moving again.

And then, because she'd been agonizing all day about what she could do to make Bradley want to keep her around long enough so she could help his career, Delphine was suddenly hit with inspiration. She would be a fool to let an opportunity like this pass her by. So she shifted positions, putting her weight forward on her knees as she reached up and slid her palms over the smooth denim covering Bradley's thighs. Slowly, her hands moved upward, her fingers stopping on either side of his crotch as her thumbs caressed the base of his penis.

"Delphine," Bradley whispered in a tortured voice.

She looked up to see that he was watching her with half-closed eyes. She touched him again and he pressed against her hands, whether involuntarily or not, Delphine didn't know. What she did know was that she didn't have much time to make her plan work, and she was going to make the most of it.

Besides, he was damn cute and she wanted to show him, in the best way she knew how, that she was attracted to him.

With that thought, she ran her fingers down the length of his now-erect penis, smiling with feminine pleasure when he groaned just loud enough for her to hear. It was as if the shoppers just a few feet away had ceased to exist. They were locked in their own private cocoon, sheltered here in the middle of their own world.

Perhaps it was the threat of discovery or the leftover adrenaline from hearing the gunshots back in the courtyard, but Delphine was beyond caring about anything but what she was doing. Slowly, she unbuttoned the top button of Bradley's jeans and slid the silver zipper down inch by interminable inch. He watched her the entire time, his shoulders bent to keep out of sight.

Delphine fumbled a bit to free his erection, but when she did, she noted with satisfaction that the bulge she'd seen hadn't been exaggerated. He wasn't frighteningly enormous, but she doubted anyone had ever complained about his equipment, either. She looked up at Bradley as she took him into her mouth, letting her tongue glide around the head of his penis as she sucked him in and let him slide back out.

His skin was so soft, like velvet over hard steel. Delphine moved her hands around to cup his hips, reveling in the feel of his taut muscles. There was nothing, in her estimation, like a guy with a great ass, and Bradley ranked right up there with the finest she'd ever seen. She squeezed, pressing his hips toward her and taking his penis back into her mouth.

"Delphine." Bradley groaned her name again as she teased him with her tongue.

"Do you want me to stop?" she whispered, nipping him gently.

Bradley reached out and buried his hands in her hair, his fingers caressing her scalp. "Are you crazy?" he asked.

Delphine laughed low in her throat. No, she certainly wasn't crazy.

She slid the tip of his penis into her mouth again, slowly letting him slip inside her until she had taken all of him that she could. Then she pulled back just as slowly. She repeated the movement again, only this time she felt Bradley's hips tense when she'd taken him in, as if he were holding himself back from thrusting into her. He slid out, then in again, quicker this time. Delphine moved her hands to his thighs, caressing him through the fabric of his jeans. He had taken over the pace now, sliding in and out of her mouth, but still holding back.

Delphine could feel the pressure building and building inside him, in the rock-hard feel of his thighs, the urgent thrusting of his hips. He was groaning almost silently now, straining with the effort to keep quiet. He pushed into her once again, and Delphine slid her tongue along him right before he tensed and stiffened. Then he hurriedly pulled out of her mouth.

"You didn't have to—" Delphine began to protest.

"Shh," Bradley said, pushing her head against his thigh.

Delphine wrapped her arms around him then, resting her cheek against the soft fabric of his jeans. Always the gentleman, she thought with a smile.

The real world came back with the clatter of plastic hangers being slid across the metal bar of the rack. Bradley hurriedly tucked in all his parts and zipped up his pants, and

Delphine gasped as a woman's face appeared in the gap between the dresses she had just pushed aside. Without thinking, Delphine grabbed the dresses from the other side and tugged them back together.

Delphine heard the other woman's surprised intake of breath and tugged on Bradley's pants leg. "We've got to get out of here," she said, peering out into the shop to see if Jim and Gus were anywhere near. When she didn't see anything besides women's shoes, she crawled out from the middle of the rack, waving for Bradley to follow her.

Bradley felt they'd be a little less conspicuous if they didn't crawl out of the store, so instead of following Delphine, he parted the section of dresses in front of him and stepped out into the shop. He tipped his hat to the surprised-looking woman whose hand was still on the hanger of the dress she had selected from the rack, and then turned to help Delphine up off the floor.

Delphine dusted off the knees of his borrowed sweatpants, smiling at the shop's customers the whole time. One thing about Delphine, Bradley thought, she sure knew how to put on a show. With a hand under her elbow, Bradley guided her toward the front door. Then, with his fingers wrapped around the doorknob, he stopped, his attention arrested by a sepia-toned poster hanging in the window.

"WANTED: DEAD OR ALIVE," the heading read. Bradley scanned the rest of the poster.

Then he started laughing. Soon, there were tears in his eyes and an ache in his stomach and he still couldn't stop laughing.

Delphine looked at him as if the heat—or maybe the mind-numbing blow job she'd just given him—had addled his brain. "What's so funny?" she asked.

Bradley pointed to the poster and wiped the tears from his eyes, still trying to catch his breath. Delphine pushed him out of the way so she could read the smaller print under the headline. Pretty soon, she was shaking her head and chuckling.

"So," she said, leading him out into the sunshine, "Jim and Gus weren't chasing us after all."

"Nope."

"There's a group that reenacts a Wild West gunfight every Sunday evening at this time. Right out there in the square where we were sitting. That's why the shopkeepers and the tourists didn't run away. They knew it was all just an act."

"Yep."

"And we were never in danger."

"Nope," Bradley said again, wiping another tear from his eye.

"Well, I *suppose* that's a good thing," Delphine said, sounding more than a little put out.

Bradley grinned and stopped in the middle of the street, grabbing the back of Delphine's T-shirt and pulling her to him. He wrapped his arms around her stomach and pushed her silky hair off the nape of her neck with his chin. Then he planted a row of kisses down the smooth column of skin he had exposed. "Delphine, what am I going to do with you?" he asked softly, inhaling the clean scent of her. She was complicating his life. If he were smart, he would be trying to figure out a way to send her home to her sisters so he could get back to focusing on his career. When she was around, he found himself thinking way too much about kissing her and touching her, and, hell, even just sitting around talking to her made him feel good. But that was the problem. She was too much of a distraction. When he'd been with Robyn, he'd never had trouble staying focused on his music. Robyn understood that business always came first. Delphine . . . well, Delphine was a great kisser and she was warm and soft in all the right places, but she had nothing to do with his music career. Hell, she didn't even seem to understand what it was that drove him to want to become a star.

Delphine turned in his arms, looking up at him with guarded eyes. "Let me come to Nashville with you. I . . . I didn't want to say anything about this before, but . . ." Her voice trailed off.

Bradley gave her a faint smile. There was no way he could be around her for the next week while they continued on to Nashville. His inability to resist Delphine today in the dress shop only confirmed his worst fears—he was incurably attracted to her. If they were together for five more days, or even one more day for that matter, Bradley knew they would end up having sex. Not that he had anything against sex in general, or even sex with Delphine in particular, but he knew that she would want it to be more than that, and he couldn't give her more. He was too focused on making his career a success to devote any time or energy to a relationship.

Bradley turned his attention back to Delphine. "But what, darlin'?" he asked, retreating into his finest cowboy impression. He'd carefully refined what he thought of as his "aw, shucks" persona over the years, dropping the *g* from the end of his words, using farm animals in as many sayings as he could, and, most of all, not letting on that he was a kid from Trenton, New Jersey, who had loved tinkering with computers almost as much as he loved his music.

In country music, as with most other professions where people were in the public eye, image was everything. That's why he never mentioned his degree in computer science, the degree he'd gotten at MIT—one of the most prestigious universities in the world. The last thing he wanted was an image as the geek of country music. He'd lived through enough years in junior high and high school of being treated like a two-headed freak to ever want to go through that again.

"Faith Hill is my cousin," Delphine blurted, causing him to stumble on a cracked cobblestone. "We were like this when we were kids." She held up her hand to show two fingers intertwined.

Bradley gaped at her. "You know Faith Hill?"

His mind started to race. Faith Hill was a giant in the

country music industry. She and her husband, Tim McGraw, probably laid claim to over half of the awards at the Country Music Awards show every year. If Bradley had that sort of backing behind him, nothing could stop him from becoming a star.

"When did you last talk to her? Are you still close? Why didn't you mention this before?" Bradley asked, the questions coming in rapid succession.

Delphine shrugged. "We haven't seen each other since high school, but I'm sure she'd be happy to meet with me if I came to Nashville. I didn't say anything before because I guess I wanted you to like me for myself, not for my country music connections. I'm sure you know what that's like— having people use you for who you know."

She blinked up at him, her blue eyes so clear and trusting that Bradley instantly felt like a heel. Damn, hadn't he learned his lesson yet? He couldn't go around using people for what they could do for his career.

"I'm sorry, Delphine, but I couldn't ask you to talk to your cousin on my behalf. It just wouldn't be right," he said, trying to ignore the voice inside his head that kept repeating, *She actually grew up with Faith Hill.*

Delphine stopped in the middle of the street and smiled. "But Bradley, you didn't ask me to do it. I offered because I want to help. I think you have a lot of talent and . . ."

She hesitated and Bradley reached out and took one of her soft hands in his. "And what, Delphine?" he asked.

Her fingers laced between his as she answered, "And I want to help make you a star."

Bradley's fingers tightened around hers convulsively. This was just what he needed to get his stalled career moving again. God, how could he be so lucky? Was he being a fool to take the help she so eagerly offered, or would he be even more of a fool to turn her down?

He thought about it for a long, hard moment, finally coming to the conclusion that—unlike his proposal to Robyn earlier, which could have produced disastrous results for them both—accepting Delphine's offer to put in a good word for him posed no risk to either of them.

Bradley began walking again, pulling Delphine close with an arm around her shoulder. "Well, darlin'," he said, "it looks like you and me are goin' to Music City."

Chapter 16
Learn to Love

Monday morning dawned clear and bright, and Delphine found herself greeting the newly risen sun with a smile. Tomorrow, they were going to leave for Nashville, and Bradley wanted her to come along. It had turned out just as she had hoped.

Yawning, Delphine stretched out her arms and rolled over in the pull-out couch in the living room of the Winnebago to find Bradley sitting in the passenger seat watching her. She blinked at him and smiled sleepily.

"Good morning," she said, sitting up and disentangling her bare legs from the sheets.

Bradley grunted and kept watching her, as if she were some sort of exotic animal and not a half-naked woman who had just woken up ten feet away from him.

Delphine reached up and patted her hair. "What? Is my hair a mess?"

Bradley shook his head. "No," he said, his voice low and husky. "I just had the most incredible dream."

Delphine licked her lips and stretched out against the back of the couch, letting the T-shirt Bradley had loaned her yesterday ride up dangerously high on her thighs. "You did?"

Bradley stood up then, his bare chest smooth and tan in the soft light of morning. He was wearing his jeans and nothing else that she could see. His feet were bare, his toes long and thick. He had nice feet, she thought, realizing she had never paid much attention to a man's toes before.

"You were in it," Bradley said, stalking toward the couch, a purposeful light in his eyes.

"I was?" Delphine asked, smiling like a cat who was just about to get fed a nice bowl of cream.

Bradley put one jeans-clad knee on the couch next to her hip, looming over her. He was so close that Delphine could count the dark hairs on his chest. She slid her hands up the taut muscles of his abdomen and made lazy circles around his flat nipples.

He scooted her over toward the center of the couch, putting his other knee up against the side of her hip, straddling her. He fisted his hands in her hair, gently tugging back to raise her face to his.

"Yeah, you were. And do you want to know what we were doing?" he asked, not waiting for her to answer as he lowered his mouth to hers.

Delphine felt as if she were being devoured. There was no other way to describe it. Bradley's tongue wrapped around hers, their mouths hot and wet and hungry. Bradley scooted closer, pressing her back against the couch, and Delphine could feel his erection prodding her in the stomach. He broke off the kiss, but only so he could rain a moist trail of kisses down her neck before he came back up and took her mouth again.

Delphine felt heat pool between her legs and moaned deep in her throat, frustrated that Bradley's weight on her thighs prevented her from moving against him. She ran her hands down his chest and around his tightly muscled bare back. His skin was hot and silky beneath her fingers and she slowly trailed her hands downward, burying her fingers under the waistband of his jeans. She teased his sensitive skin, wishing he'd move so she could get better access to that nice, firm butt of his.

Bradley lifted his head and started an assault on the skin just below her ear. Delphine's hips jerked involuntarily when he ran his tongue just under her earlobe and Bradley whispered, "Ah, you like that," just before doing it again.

Delphine's eyelids felt heavy, as if she were being drugged with pleasure. She heard herself make a noise that sounded suspiciously like a purr, and wondered if that sound had really come from her throat. She couldn't recall ever purring during sex before.

"I want you so badly right now that I ache," Bradley said softly, his breath hot and urgent in her ear. "I woke up dreaming that I was inside you."

He ran his hands down her arms, making her shudder. Delphine almost felt like whimpering for him to stop teasing her and take her right now. "Is your mother a light sleeper?" she asked, eyeing the still-closed bedroom door.

"I don't really care at the moment," Bradley answered, pushing his hands up under her T-shirt.

Delphine felt every muscle inside her clench when his hands stopped just under her breasts. She ached for him to touch her, but she knew that if they didn't stop now they would both be past caring about propriety in about ten more seconds.

"Don't," she said, the word ripped from her throat.

"I have to," Bradley said, tenderly reaching up with his thumbs to abrade her nipples.

Delphine laid her head back on the couch and moaned with pleasure. She raised her hips, frantically trying to rub up against him. She feared she would climax at his first touch, but she was beyond caring.

Bradley laughed then, a husky, sexy laugh that told her that he knew she was dangerously close to the edge.

Delphine narrowed her eyes and squinted at him. Laugh at her, would he? Well, she'd teach him. She reached down between their bodies and cupped him, rubbing up and down with her fingers and reveling in the feel of the hard length of him pressed against the soft fabric of his jeans. She wiggled out from underneath him, pushing him back so she could straddle him. She felt him hard against the silky nylon of her panties and gave herself the pleasure of rubbing against his erection until she was about to scream with frustration. So much for showing him, she thought, almost panting with need.

Bradley slid his hands up her thighs, teasing her as his fingers got closer and closer to the center of her desire. Impatient, Delphine stopped waiting for him to give her what she wanted and thrust her hips forward so that he was touching her where she most wanted to be touched.

Bradley laughed again. "Impatient, are you?"

Delphine moaned her answer, pushing up against his fingers as the pressure built up inside her. And built. And built. Until she was ready to come apart.

"Do you have a condom?" she asked, trying to stave off her orgasm.

"Let go, Delphine. This is what I woke up dreaming about," Bradley said, sliding the guitar-string-roughened pad of his index finger into her wet heat.

Delphine wanted to wait for him but she couldn't. Not with him touching her like this. He flicked his thumb across her throbbing clitoris and she felt her mind go black. She forgot about everything except the pleasure of the moment, the cool air wafting over her heated skin, the feel of Bradley's worn jeans on the insides of her thighs, the sight of him watching her with satisfaction as she moaned his name and came apart in his hands.

When it was all over, she felt herself go limp, her body morphing into his as if they had become one.

Bradley straightened her panties and tugged her borrowed T-shirt down so she was modestly covered. Then, to Delphine's stunned surprise, he moved on top of the blankets ("So as not to shock my mother if she wakes up before us," he said), slid one arm under her shoulders, and pulled her close.

He lightly kissed her forehead before pulling back to look at her, smiling at the puzzled look on her face.

"Think of it as payback for yesterday," he said. And with that, he gave her one final grin, closed his eyes, and fell fast asleep.

"This is the hose you want to use for your black water. Now, be sure you don't get it mixed up with the intake hose for your drinking water. That is one mistake you don't ever want to make." The motor home rental service's customer care representative grinned and shook his head as he stowed the hoses back in the closet of the Jayco. Then he turned to a panel of switches and gauges and started explaining all about amps versus volts, water pumps, DOT and ASME LP gas containers, engine power, shore power, coach power, generators—

"Just give us the damn keys," Jim Josephs growled, his normally perfect cap of silver hair a bit mussed from shaking his head in frustration.

The rental company rep frowned. "It's important that you understand how your motor home works. If you don't, you could get into some real trouble out there."

Gus grabbed the keys from the man's clipboard and shoved a wad of cash under his nose, backing him toward the front door with one intimidating step after another. "We got what it takes to fix any problem we might run into. Now get out."

"But, but—" the man sputtered.

"Don't worry, we're sufficiently intelligent to be able to handle this," Jim assured the man, right before Gus nudged him out of the motor home and slammed the door in his face.

"Let's get out of here," Gus said.

"I don't think it was necessary to browbeat the man like that," Jim said.

Gus scowled at him and limped to the passenger seat, his foot still sore from where Jim had shot him. His hand ached from the stab wound Harriet had inflicted on him, and he was tired. To top it all off, Jim was mincing around the Jayco, opening all the cupboards and closet doors and sniffing as if to test the motor home's cleanliness.

He didn't have time for this shit.

"Get in the fucking driver's seat and get this thing out of here," he ordered, slamming his good hand against the dashboard and making Jim jump and bump his head on a cabinet door.

Jim came to the front of the motor home, rubbing his head. "There's no need to get grouchy with me. It's not my fault we're stuck trailing after Dickie."

Gus looked out the window at the barren mountain rising up out of the desert. "I know. But I hate this roughing-it crap and I ain't thrilled about running errands for El Corazon, either. It pisses me off that we gotta launder money for the asshole and now he treats us like we're his fucking employees, too. I wish somebody would just kill the bastard."

"I agree, but wishing won't get us out of this mess. We have to get close to Dickie, and the only way I can think of to do that is to do as the Romans are doing, so to speak."

"Yeah, I guess you're right," Gus agreed, sounding glum but resigned to his fate.

Jim only nodded as he put the key in the ignition and started the motor home's engine. Then he waved to the sullen-looking rental company rep, who gripped his clipboard in both hands and refused to wave back.

"Now that she's turned over the money, do you think Harriet is safe?" Richard Swanson asked, watching his boss's obsidian eyes carefully. Jorge sometimes had the habit of telling Richard what he wanted to hear. And in this case, he wanted to hear that Harriet would be safe.

Jorge tapped the end of his pen on his metal government-issue desk and studied his subordinate. "No," he said after a while. "I think that she's underestimating the danger. I think Jim Josephs and Gus Palermo will keep coming after her because they will take it personally that she discovered their scheme and had the nerve to steal from them."

"She thinks their anger will be directed at the IRS, and not her personally," Richard said, leaning forward in the chair across from Jorge.

Jorge was already shaking his head, the pen tapping a staccato rhythm on his desk. "She's wrong. They'll take her actions personally, just as they'll see your defection as a personal insult against them. Unfortunately, we can't offer Mrs. Nelson official protection. If she knew El Corazon's identity, I might be able to pull some strings. But as it is . . ." Jorge shrugged, leaving the words unspoken.

Richard knew what his boss wouldn't say. Harriet wasn't valuable enough for them to protect. She knew about the casino owners' tax evasion, but that was hardly the sort of thing that made prosecutors' hearts go pitty-pat. Tax evasion was nothing compared to a high-profile drug bust.

"How long do I have before my next assignment?" Richard asked, laying his hands on his boss's desk.

Jorge narrowed his eyes at Richard. "I can give you a few weeks. Why?"

"Because I need some time to convince Harriet that she's in danger. I don't know what I can do besides teaching her to use the typical precautions, but I can't just let her go like this."

"You've been trying to protect this woman all along," Jorge said, his normally calm voice taking on an edge of anger. "You blew your cover going after her, which I'm willing to overlook because of your stellar record—"

"And because you knew we weren't getting anywhere," Richard interrupted dryly. Jorge would never overlook a rookie mistake like the one Richard had made to go after

Harriet if he truly thought they were close to discovering the identity of Reno's drug kingpin. The truth was, they were no closer to wrapping up the El Corazon case than they had been a year ago. Richard's flight had no more botched the operation than Harriet's meddling had. It was a dead case and both he and Jorge knew it.

Jorge stopped tapping his pen on the desk. "I was going to pull you at the end of next month," he surprised Richard by admitting.

"What?"

His boss shrugged. "As you said, we weren't getting anywhere. I was going to kill the op next month anyway."

Richard shook his head with disgust. "Then why are we having this conversation?"

"Because what you did wasn't right. You were getting bored in Reno. That's why you took such a chance."

Richard considered telling his boss the truth—that he had taken the risk of running after Harriet Nelson for a much more personal reason. During the months Harriet had worked for him, he had come to admire her. He had even begun to look forward to seeing her arrive at the office every morning, smiling and laughing with the security guards. And now, knowing that the whole time she had been sneaking dirty money out past those very same men she joked with every day?

God, he could learn to love a woman like that.

And he planned to do everything in his power to keep her safe until he did.

Chapter 17
I Do

"Hey, Mom, can I borrow your computer for a while?" Bradley yelled through the door of the bathroom. He took her muffled reply to mean yes and unzipped the black laptop bag that had come with the computer he'd bought her last year for Christmas.

He was in a good mood. There was no doubt about it.

He'd awakened first thing this morning with a hard-on that could have chiseled slate and, although he hadn't had his own desire satisfied, watching Delphine come had been the next best thing. Then they'd slept together for another hour, her long legs intertwined with his, and when he'd woken again, he'd reveled in the feel of her warm hands curled against his chest.

He used to think that Robyn was every man's dream. She was a tiger in the bedroom, not shy at all about telling him exactly what to do to please her. And she hated cuddling after sex. When they were finished, she was ready to move on to the next thing. But for some reason, Bradley had always felt a bit empty after having sex with Robyn.

The computer in front of him beeped, dragging Bradley back to reality—a reality that had more to do with his stalled career than sex.

With any luck, his manager was already busy making

calls to other record companies, trying to put a spin on why Bradley's first album hadn't sold as well as they'd hoped, and to see if anyone else would take a chance and pick him up. Bradley knew it wasn't going to be easy, but, hell, that's why he paid Hal twenty percent of his own meager earnings. His manager's job wasn't *supposed* to be easy.

Bradley connected his mother's computer to the Internet and logged on to his Web mail account to check his e-mail. Before he could see how many new e-mails he had, his electronic calendar popped up a reminder.

Today was the day the Country Music Awards nomination calls were to go out.

Bradley's stomach clenched. This was the first year he was eligible for an award. Getting a nomination would almost guarantee his future success. Virtually every new artist who got nominated in the past decade had gone on to become wildly successful. He didn't even need to win the award for best new male vocalist. Just getting a nomination would be the shot in the arm his career needed.

With a humorless smile, Bradley sat back and stared unseeingly at the computer screen. Gamble Records would be sorry for dropping him, then. He'd have no problem getting signed by MCA or Warner Brothers or one of the other major labels if he got the nomination.

And why shouldn't he get nominated? He was every bit as talented as anyone else. God knew, he'd sacrificed as much or more than anyone else.

Bradley slid out of the dining booth and went up to the front of the Winnebago to make sure his cell phone was powered up. He didn't know if the awards show people would call him directly or if they'd try to contact him through Hal, but either way, he didn't want to miss the call because his phone was dead. He brought the phone with him back to the dining room and set it down next to the computer.

His e-mail was full of the usual offers of penis-enlargement and miracle weight-loss products. Bradley had to admit to a certain smug satisfaction as he deleted the former. "Don't need more than I've got, thank you," he muttered.

He waded through the rest of his mail, admittedly distracted by the cell phone lying silently next to him.

He read a message from a fan, one of the few he had received since his album had been released. The woman said she'd really enjoyed his latest CD (as if there were others, Bradley thought with a snort), and was looking forward to his next release.

"That makes two of us," he said, glancing back over at the phone as he hit the reply button. He always answered his fan mail. He even planned to set aside an hour every day when he got famous to make sure he had time to send personal replies to his fans. It was the least he could do, he figured, to pay back the people who had made him famous. He knew how much it had meant to him when, as a boy, he'd written to Willie Nelson and received a personal reply, encouraging him to live his dream. He wanted to do the same for some other kid someday.

Bradley sighed.

Someday. That seemed to be the word of the moment. But he was getting tired of waiting for "someday" to get here. He wanted things to start happening for him *now.*

He picked up his phone and pressed the talk button, just to make sure he was getting a dial tone.

He was.

He set the phone back down again and composed a reply to his new fan. He thanked her for taking the time to write, and told her that he was glad to know that she'd enjoyed his album. He said he was hopeful that he'd have news on a second release soon, and that he'd be sure to let her know when he did. Then he signed the mail and hit send.

The rest of his in box was the usual mix of greetings from friends, e-coupons and promotions from various record stores, and questions of no urgency from his webmaster about updates to his fan site.

Bradley was looking over at his phone, tempted to test the dial tone again, when the front door banged open.

Delphine stuck her head inside. "Sorry about that," she said. "My hands are full." She hefted two plastic bags up and laid them on the carpet, then climbed up the steps and into the Winnebago and closed the door behind her.

"What time are we leaving?" she asked after she had stowed the bags in the closet.

Bradley closed the lid of his mother's laptop. "Richard asked us to wait until tomorrow. He has some time off and wants to come with us, but he needs to get some things in order first."

"And your mother agreed? I thought she was convinced that we weren't in any danger."

"She is convinced that we're safe. But I think she likes Richard, so that's why she agreed to let him come along."

Delphine laughed. "Really?"

Bradley put his arm on the top of the dining booth and smiled back at Delphine. "Yeah. The good news is, he seems equally smitten with her."

Delphine walked over and slid into the booth next to him. Bradley felt the warmth of her thigh touching his and had to force himself not to put his arm around her shoulders and pull her even closer. He wondered then if she had discovered some sort of magic lust potion that made him want to touch her whenever she was near. It was like some sort of voodoo drug thing.

"Does it upset you? Seeing your mother with another man, I mean?" Delphine asked.

Bradley pulled off his cowboy hat and scratched the back of his head. "No. She and my dad split up so long ago. Besides, it's not like I feel that she owed him a lifetime of devotion. After my dad died, my mom did her best to provide a stable home for me. She never brought a parade of guys home to meet me. Hell, I don't even think she dated at all until I went off to college. She and my dad were really wrong for each other, but that doesn't mean that she doesn't deserve to find happiness with somebody else. She was— is—a good mother."

Delphine started to say something, but was interrupted by the sound of someone sniffling behind her. Bradley heard it, too, and they both craned their heads toward the back of the RV at the same time to find his mother standing just outside the bathroom door wearing a flowered robe with a towel wrapped around her head. She was crying.

"What's wrong?" Delphine asked, jumping up from the dining room table to give Harriet a comforting hug.

"Nothing." Harriet sniffled. "I just heard that my son thinks I'm a good mother and it, well, it made me cry."

Bradley stuffed the cowboy hat back on his head. "Oh, Mom, you know I love you and I think you're the best mom a guy could have. You don't interfere in my life, you never try to set me up with your friends' daughters, and, above all, you've never once asked me when I'm going to settle down and give you some grandkids."

"That's what you think makes me a good mom?" Harriet asked, wiping her eyes with the end of the belt of her robe.

"No. But I knew it would make you stop crying." Bradley grinned at his mother and got up to give her a hug. Then he kissed her loudly on the cheek and said, "I think you're a good mother for too many reasons to list. You taught me the importance of a good work ethic. You always have time to listen to me. Even after Dad left, you were never bitter, never said bad things about him even though I know it was hard on you with him gone. You taught me to stand up for what's right, even if the consequences for doing so were hard to take."

His mother smiled up at him and patted his cheeks. "Well, I'm sorry that I got you and Delphine caught up in this mess with me. I was only trying to practice what I preach and do the right thing. It certainly hasn't turned out like I'd planned."

Bradley gave his mother a final squeeze and stepped back. "It's definitely been one of our more interesting visits," he acknowledged.

Harriet dabbed at the last of the moisture under her eyes and glanced from her son to Delphine and back again. Then she shot Bradley a mischievous grin. "Yes, but you know, now that you mention it, I would like to know when you plan to start on those grandchildren."

Delphine tilted her head and looked at Bradley, waiting for him to frown and tell her to mind her own business. But he didn't. Instead, he just laughed good-naturedly and shook his head as his mother excused herself to go get dressed.

"What are they doing now?" Gus asked, squinting across the street as if that would help him to see inside the bar where Dickie and Harriet had gone with Harriet's son and that wedding-chapel employee.

"Nothing. Sitting at a table having a drink. Like I wish I was doing instead of standing here in these bushes," Jim answered, lowering the binoculars from his eyes.

"This is boring. I don't know how cops do it, sitting around all night spying on people."

Jim grimaced as the scrubby bush at his back scratched him through his shirt. "I agree. I say we go back to the RV and wait for them to come back. After all, they're parked right next to us. They can't go anywhere without us hearing them."

"Good, then let's go. I got a bottle of whiskey waiting for me."

Jim blinked at him and Gus silently dared him to say something about not being able to drink on this mission. If he did, Gus was going to lay him out, right there on the sidewalk. He'd been stabbed and shot at, and he'd be goddamned if he'd deny himself a little Southern Comfort for his troubles.

Fortunately for Jim, he kept his mouth closed in a tight-lipped line as he motioned for Gus to exit the bushes in front of him.

"I stopped by a record store this afternoon," Delphine said, leaning close to Bradley to be heard over the noisy crowd in the bar. He had taken a shower right before they had gone out to meet Richard for dinner at a local Mexican restaurant, and he smelled good. Really good. Like soap and clean skin and spicy cologne and man. Delphine fought the urge to lick him. He did that to her, made her want to run her tongue all up and down him as if he were her own personal Mansicle.

Bradley turned to look at her, his eyes colliding with hers in the two inches between them. "Whew, is it hot in here or is it just you?" he asked, grinning.

Delphine smiled a wicked sort of smile and scooted forward on the hard wooden chair until her bottom was just barely balanced on the edge. Their noses were almost touching now, Bradley's lips just inches from hers. "Oh, I don't know. I think you're pretty hot, too."

She reached out and rested her palms on his thighs, not touching him intimately—his mother was sitting a few feet away, after all—but definitely touching him suggestively. Then she ran her tongue over her bottom lip, lowering her eyelids a bit. "You know what I was thinking just now?" she asked.

Bradley put a hand behind her head and pulled her forward. He kissed her soundly on the mouth before pushing her back onto the chair. "Don't tell me," he said. "You'll just get me all aroused and I don't see any clothing racks that we can make use of in here."

Delphine sat back, still a little befuddled by his kiss.

"So, you were telling me about the record store you were in this afternoon," Bradley said, taking a sip of the beer that he'd ordered. He leaned back and stretched his legs. He was sitting facing Delphine, with one leg on the outside of her seat as if he were shielding her from the crowd.

On her errand-running this afternoon, Delphine had stopped in at a secondhand store in search of some clothes. While she didn't mind borrowing Bradley's sweats and T-shirts, she hadn't wanted that to be her only option. She'd found a pair of well-worn jeans and some cute strappy white sandals. Her real find, though, had been the filmy blouse she'd discovered among the racks of T-shirts. It was white scattered with blue orchids and cut low in the front, to accentuate her adequate-sized breasts. It was also the tiniest bit see-through if someone were really looking.

She hoped Bradley was really looking.

She leaned forward to pick up her seabreeze, making sure her knee rubbed up against Bradley's thigh. "Yes, I passed a record store today while I was shopping and I went in to look for your CD, but it wasn't there. Isn't that great? They're sold out."

There was a loud scraping noise as Bradley sat back in his chair. He turned abruptly away from her, facing the crowded dance floor of the bar instead. "I doubt they're sold out. They probably never stocked my record to begin with," he said.

Stupid, stupid, stupid, Delphine mentally chided herself, giving herself a virtual head-smack. "I'm sorry. I just assumed . . ."

"Yeah, well, that's how it's *supposed* to work. You get bought by a record label, produce an album, and they get behind you and make sure you're getting good distribution and airplay on the radio stations."

Delphine ran her fingers through the condensation on her glass. The bar had windows that were propped open to the warm night air, giving patrons a view of the lighted courtyard outside. Half a dozen ceiling fans circled lazily overhead, not doing much to cool the place down. It wasn't unpleasantly hot, though. Just a bit still.

She laid a hand on Bradley's forearm. "Isn't that what happened for you, too?" she asked.

Bradley laughed mockingly and raised his bottle to take a long drink of the amber liquid inside. "Not exactly. Look, I'd rather not talk about it tonight, okay? Let's just enjoy ourselves."

Delphine was happy to let the subject drop. She had thought she was giving him good news, not poking at what was obviously an open wound. "Hey, they're doing karaoke," she announced. "Why don't you get up there and show them how a professional does it?"

Bradley set the condensation-slick beer bottle back on the heavy wooden table and turned to smile at her. "Maybe we could sing a duet?" he suggested.

Delphine chuckled. "You do not want to hear me sing."

Bradley stood up and pulled out her chair, holding out a hand to help her up, whether she wanted to get up or not. "Everybody sounds terrible at these things. Now, are you coming under your own steam or do I have to carry you?"

Delphine's eyes widened with shock. "You wouldn't," she protested.

Bradley shot her a devilish grin. "Oh, yes, darlin', I would."

"You couldn't. I'm too heavy." Delphine pressed her spine into the back of her chair and wrapped her arms around her middle. Then she squealed when Bradley leaned down, stuck his shoulder into her stomach, and lifted her, butt first, into the air.

"Put me down," she hissed into the back of his dark blue flowered Hawaiian shirt.

In response, he patted her rear end as people in the bar clapped and cheered.

"I'll get you for this," she said, wanting to kick him but afraid she'd lose her new sandals if she moved her feet too much.

Bradley stopped at the side of the stage in front of the bar.

"This little lady wants to sing a duet with me," he announced to the guy running the karaoke machine.

The guy poked his head around Bradley to look at Delphine. "What song did you have in mind?"

Delphine growled at him, starting to feel light-headed from being upside down.

With his big warm hand still resting on her butt, Bradley suggested, "How about 'When I Said I Do' by Clint Black and Lisa Hartman Black?"

"Yeah, I've got that," the guy said. "You two can go next."

Bradley squatted down until Delphine felt the heels of her sandals touch the floor. She was tempted to duck under Bradley's arm and make a run for it, but his body was blocking her. Besides, he was smiling down at her with such amusement that she really didn't want to get away from him anyway.

And then it hit her.

She never wanted to get away from him.

Not just because she believed he had talent, but because she loved him. He was ambitious and funny. He smiled a lot. She liked that. He wasn't angry all the time, even though things didn't seem to be going quite as he'd planned. And he was just so damn nice.

She remembered the way he was that morning, interested only in giving her pleasure and then pulling her into his arms afterward. He wasn't rude or mean and he was kind to his mother.

And she loved him.

Delphine closed her eyes and put a hand to her forehead, feeling dizzy with the realization that she had fallen for someone who was only keeping her around because he thought she might be able to help his career. *And there you have it,* she thought, reaching out a hand to steady herself on the wall beside her. The fatal flaw in their relationship. All she had ever wanted was for someone to love her, but Bradley would have left her here in New Mexico if she hadn't told him about having a relative in the country music business.

She was setting herself up for heartbreak, and she knew it.

"Are you all right, Delphine?" Bradley asked, laying a hand on her shoulder. "You look a little green."

Delphine opened her eyes and saw the concern in Bradley's brown eyes. She gave him a weak smile. "Yes, I'm fine. Just not used to being carried around like a sack of potatoes, I guess."

"Good, cuz it looks like we're on." He grinned and turned her around, pushing her up the stairs.

All Delphine could think of as they took their places on the stage was that she had to find some way of making Bradley fall in love with her before they reached Nashville. She took a deep breath as the music started playing. She could do it.

She had to.

Chapter 18
Better or Worse

Bradley seated himself on a stool, facing Delphine. He held the microphone down between his knees as he used his thumb and forefinger to pull his hat lower on his forehead. The brim cast a shadow across the top of his face, hiding his eyes from the crowd. Delphine perched nervously on her stool, as if dreading what was about to happen, but Bradley momentarily tuned her out. Instead, he focused on the energy of the crowd, letting it enter him with each deep breath he took. He closed his eyes, hearing every note of the introduction of the song, feeling it touch him like a lover's fingers.

And then there was nothing else. Just him and the song.

No disappointing past. No frustrating present. No uncertain future.

No fear.

He opened his eyes and looked at Delphine. Ignoring the TV screen with the words of the song rolling across it, Bradley lifted the microphone to his lips and began to sing.

" 'These times are troubled and these times are good, and they're always gonna be'."

That's the way marriage was. Good and bad. Better and worse. Sometimes at the same time, depending on which one was doing the thinking.

Delphine joined in, her voice trembling at first. Bradley

got up from his stool and walked across the stage to stand in front of her. Then he got down on one knee, raising his face to her and singing to her, and her alone. She sang the words with him, her voice getting stronger with every note, telling him that when she had said "I do" back in Reno, she had truly meant it to be forever.

The last note faded away, but the words seemed to hang in the air as Bradley remained there on the floor, looking up at Delphine. She reached out then, still holding her microphone, and laid her hands on either side of his face, her fingers caressing his cheeks.

Then she lowered her lips to his, the top of her head pushing his hat back on his head as their tongues tangled together.

And the crowd went wild, hooting and whistling and stomping their feet.

Delphine lifted her head and Bradley, still lost in the moment, laid his head against her stomach, not wanting to let her go.

Finally, he pushed himself up off the floor, and, grabbing Delphine's hand, he turned toward the crowd and took a bow. Then he nudged Delphine forward, as if showing her off. The applause got louder.

He pulled her into his arms and gave her a big stage kiss for the audience, took another bow, and then led her out of the spotlight.

"God, I love doing that," he said, as he motioned for her to precede him down the stairs.

"Wait a minute," the guy running the karaoke machine said, stopping them at the bottom of the stairs. "What are your names? I want to introduce you to the audience."

Bradley tipped his hat to the other man. "Bradley Nelson and Delphine Armstrong, at your service," he said.

Delphine looked down at the floor, then back up at him, a sadness in her eyes that he had never seen there before. "If I hadn't lied about not liking country music, I might be Delphine Nelson by now," she mumbled. Then, without waiting for his reply, she headed back to their table, her hips swaying in the tight-fitting jeans she had worn that night.

He had no idea why she was so upset . . . but man, did she have a nice ass, Bradley thought, talking off his hat to run a hand through his hair.

"Female trouble, huh?" the karaoke guy asked, as if he were intimately associated with the phenomenon.

"Yeah," Bradley said, putting his hat back on. "It seems that way."

The guy shook his head. "I've given up trying to understand them. Well, do you want to go back up and sing? If it's any consolation, the crowd seems to like you."

Delphine had her back turned to him and appeared to be talking to his mother. Bradley shrugged and turned back toward the stage.

"I guess I might as well. Doesn't look like I have an appreciative audience waiting for me back at my table."

"Don't those idiots know that they shouldn't run their generator all night?" Harriet groused, stumbling out of her bedroom at two o'clock in the morning. Bradley and Delphine were curled up on the pull-out couch, with Bradley on top of the blankets as if letting his mother see him sleeping with a woman was simply not acceptable.

She shook her head, supposing that she should be grateful he wasn't like her friend Barbara's son, who had used his mother's digital camera to take pornographic pictures of himself and his girlfriend having sex on Barbara's brand-new leather couch and then was so stupid that he downloaded the pictures to a file on her computer and labeled the file, "DO NOT OPEN." Right. As if that weren't taunting someone to look inside.

Yes, Harriet was glad that her son at least had the decency to care about what his mother might think.

She rubbed her eyes and tiptoed through the living room.

She hadn't come out here to spy on Bradley and Delphine. No, she had come to tell their neighbor in the RV park to turn off his generator. Not only was it loud and smelly, it was also dangerous to keep it running all night.

Harriet pulled open the door of the Winnebago, tugging her robe more tightly around her.

Then she gasped.

She could hear the alarms going off in the Jayco parked next to them. She turned back around and shook Bradley out of his sleep.

"What? What?" he asked groggily.

"Our neighbor's carbon monoxide alarms are going off. You've got to help me get them out of there."

Bradley bolted upright in bed. His bare feet hit the floor a second later. He didn't pause to pull on his boots, bounding down the stairs with his mother right behind him.

Just as they reached the front door of the Jayco, it was thrown open from inside. Then it was pulled shut again and Bradley could hear the muffled shouts of a man coming from inside.

He pounded on the door. "You need to get out of there," he shouted.

There was more noise from inside and some clattering. Bradley tried to open the door but it had been locked from the inside.

Were these people trying to kill themselves?

Bradley motioned for his mother to try the driver's-side door. It opened easily and she stuck her head inside. "You're being poisoned with carbon monoxide," she yelled into the darkened interior. "You've got to come out and turn off your generator and all your appliances."

"We're fine. We're on our way out," a nasal-voiced man yelled back.

"Are you sure you're all okay?" Harriet asked.

"Yes, we're fine," the man shouted. "Could you just go

away? We're . . . uh, we're nudists and we're, um, naked, and we'd rather not come outside until you go away."

Harriet pulled her head out of the Jayco and rolled her eyes as Bradley stepped away from the front door, shaking his head.

"All right, we're leaving," Harriet called into the gloom one last time. "But in the future, remember that it's not safe to run your generator all night." With that warning, she closed the door.

Bradley threw his arm across his mother's shoulders as they walked away from their neighbor's motor home. Behind them, the Jayco's front door opened and they could hear people coughing, but neither of them turned around.

"There sure are some weird people in this world," Bradley said, opening the door to the Winnebago and holding out a hand to help his mother up into the motor home.

"Yes, Bradley, there sure are," Harriet agreed, shaking her head as she made her way back to her bedroom for the night.

Maybe all the award nomination calls hadn't gone out yesterday.

That was Bradley's first thought when he woke up the next morning. His second thought was that there sure were some strange people in these campgrounds. And his third thought was how much more comfortable it was to be sleeping in a bed instead of trying to get a good night's rest in the reclining driver's seat, as he had been doing the past three nights.

He opened his eyes to find Delphine still asleep beside him. By the end of last night, she'd warmed back up to him and had offered to let him have half of the sofa bed—just as long as he stayed on top of the covers. For a girl who had given him a blow job in the middle of a crowded clothing store, she seemed awfully concerned about what his mother might think if she saw them in bed together. He appreciated her attitude, however, not really wanting to shock his mother, either.

Bradley pushed a lock of silky hair behind Delphine's ear, remembering the hurt he'd seen in her eyes when he'd introduced them to the karaoke guy. He didn't understand her, that was for sure.

He rolled on to his back then, grimacing when something hard dug into his shoulder. As quietly as possible, he reached behind his back and pulled out the offending object. It was a book. A big book, with the title *This Business of Music* emblazoned across the top.

Bradley flipped to the end of the book. It ran 698 pages, including the index.

Delphine had marked her place in the hardback with the book's jacket. She'd made it to page 28 last night before falling asleep. He flipped back a page to see what the topic was.

"Centralized Manufacture—Exclusivity," the subheading read.

Bradley started reading about exports and American licensors and tariff barriers.

His eyes started to glaze over about halfway into it. It wasn't that he didn't understand the business jargon, it just wasn't particularly interesting to him. He figured it was his job to make music and perform that music and to be well read enough on industry issues not to come across as a complete ignoramus. But as for understanding everything about foreign sales, distribution, and performing rights organizations . . . well, that was the kind of stuff he figured he paid his manager to know about.

Delphine yawned and opened her eyes. She saw him thumbing through her book and said, "Oh, I'm sorry. I must have dropped that last night."

Bradley slid the jacket back in place to mark her spot and handed her the book. "Where did you get this?" he asked.

"A used book store. That's one of the errands I ran yesterday afternoon." Delphine sat up, smoothing his Vince Gill T-shirt over her stomach as she did so.

Bradley stretched out beside her, put his hands under his head, and crossed his ankles. The sweatpants he was wearing were making him hot, but at least they were more comfortable than sleeping in his jeans. "Why did you buy a book on the music business?"

Delphine looked at him, and then looked away. "I think a wife should know something about the business her husband is in, don't you?"

Bradley sighed and looked up at the ceiling of the Winnebago. "Delphine—" he began.

She looked back at him and grinned before he could say anything more. "Yeah, I know. Despite your mother's wishes, we're not getting married. I was just trying to get a rise out of you."

He moved with lightning speed, reaching out to grab the front of the T-shirt he had loaned her and pulling her on top of him. The ends of her hair swept across his naked chest, tickling his nipples. Her blue eyes were full of mischief and surprise. She squirmed against him, trying to regain her balance, but succeeded only in arousing him.

She rubbed her hips against his and laughed. "I guess it worked. I definitely got a rise out of you."

Bradley moved his hands to cup her bottom, holding her in place against him. "Yeah, you do seem to have a knack for that," he agreed.

They heard the bedroom door start to open and Delphine squealed, sliding off him in a way that didn't much help to ease his erection. She stood up quickly, tugging the bottom of his T-shirt down below her green silk panties while Bradley sat up and crooked a leg to hide his own state of arousal from his mother.

"I'm just going to, uh, grab a quick shower," Delphine

squeaked out as Harriet sleepily wandered out into the kitchen to make a pot of coffee.

Delphine's announcement didn't help Bradley at all, because now all he could think about was Delphine, wet and naked, standing under the spray of water from the shower. She bent down to grab some things off the floor, giving Bradley another tantalizing shot of green silk-clad ass. Then she hurriedly disappeared into the safety of the bathroom.

"You know," his mother began, taking a bag of coffee grounds from the freezer where she stored them to keep them fresh, "there's room enough for two in that shower."

Bradley felt his mouth drop open like the character in some Saturday-morning cartoon as he stared as his mother's back. "Mother, tell me you didn't just say what I think you did."

Harriet calmly measured water into the coffee carafe and poured it into the reservoir before turning the machine on. Then she turned to her son, leaning back against the counter and regarding him levelly. "Bradley, do you think I'm blind? Every time you and Delphine are in the same room, the temperature's about fifty degrees hotter. I'm surprised things haven't started melting yet," she added dryly.

Bradley cleared his throat, feeling his cheeks go hot under his mother's scrutiny.

"You kids didn't invent sex, you know. It's not like this is some new fad that I've never been exposed to before. You might even be surprised to hear that I've done it myself a time or two."

Bradley started coughing at that and put his hands in the air in protest. "No, please, don't say anything more. I'd love to see you find happiness with another man. I said it yesterday and I meant it. But that doesn't mean I want to hear the details."

His mother rolled her eyes heavenward at that. "Oh, for heaven's sake, Bradley. Don't be such a prude."

"I am *not* a prude," Bradley said, remembering exactly

how unprudish he had been two days before, having oral sex with a woman in public in broad daylight. Maybe he should tell his mother about that little episode. Maybe then she wouldn't accuse him of being a prude.

Bradley shuddered.

Or, maybe he shouldn't.

He stood up, all thoughts of desire having died a quick death as soon as his mother started talking about sex. "Look, Mom, there are just some topics I think we shouldn't discuss. This is one of them. Yes, it's true that Delphine and I . . . um, like each other. But that doesn't mean we can't control ourselves. We're adults, after all."

"Yes, and healthy adults have active sex lives. That's all I'm saying."

Bradley put his head in his hands and groaned. Why wouldn't his mother just let the subject drop?

"Delphine seems like a nice girl and the two of you are obviously attracted to one another. So, as long as you practice safe sex, I think you should go for it. Or is that saying out of date?" His mother frowned, pursing her lips as if trying to remember the last time she'd heard the phrase.

Bradley felt as if his head were about to explode and gripped it harder.

"Besides, I think couples should have adventurous love lives. It helps to keep your relationship fresh. Would you like some coffee?"

Backing up until he ran into the sofa bed, Bradley looked at his mother as if she had just morphed into a werewolf. They had always had a good relationship, but they had never talked about sex. Well, except for that one time when he was in junior high school and his mother had explained about condoms—which he already knew all about thanks to his friend Zack, whose parents worked late all the time and had quite a collection of pornography that they never thought to keep locked away from their teenaged son and his horny friends.

He was saved from any more sexual advice from his

mother when someone banged on the front door of the motor home.

Bradley nearly tripped over the bed in his haste to see who was at the door.

Delphine sat on the couch, reading the section about the role of an artist's business manager for the third time. She scribbled several notes on the pad of paper she'd picked up at the drugstore back in Albuquerque and tried to ignore Bradley, who had been staring out the window and scowling ever since they'd gotten back on the road two hours ago.

Richard had taken over the driving this morning, and Harriet sat in the passenger seat, talking quietly to Richard above the hum of the Winnebago's engine.

"If we pass another herd of cows, I'm going to scream," Bradley said sourly, thumping his fist down loudly on the dining room table.

Delphine slipped her thumb between the pages to mark her place in the book and looked up to see Harriet and Richard exchanging glances before turning their attention to Bradley. "Isn't it a herd of *cattle*?" she asked.

"Then why are they called 'cowboys' and not 'cattle-boys'?" Bradley asked, sounding as peevish as a bored four-year-old.

"Why don't you get something to read, dear?" his mother suggested.

Bradley scowled at his mother instead of at the passing landscape. "You don't have anything to read around here besides the revised tax codes."

Harriet shrugged and looked at Richard as if to say, "What's wrong with that?"

"Is something wrong?" Delphine asked. "You've been acting strange all afternoon."

"Yes, something's wrong. I can't get my damn manager on the phone. I pay this asshole twenty cents out of every lousy dollar I make and the bastard won't return my calls. When we get to Nashville, I swear I'm going to walk right into his office and fire him. He doesn't deserve me."

Delphine kept watching him. "Why are you trying to get in touch with him? Is something going on?"

Bradley stood up and paced restlessly from one end of the small living room to the other, coming to a stop in front of her. Then he let out a frustrated sigh and plopped down on the couch next to her, making Delphine scramble to keep her notebook from falling off her lap.

"Yeah," Bradley admitted, slouching down into the couch and sliding his booted feet out in front of him. "I told you about the big awards show coming up next week? Well, the finalists were supposed to get calls yesterday."

Delphine closed her book and set it on the side table on top of her notebook. Then she slouched down on the couch, mirroring Bradley's position. Reaching out, she grabbed one of his hands in hers, rubbing her soft fingers against his guitar-string-roughened ones. "You didn't get a call, did you?" she asked softly.

She felt his shoulders sag but didn't turn to look at him.

"No, I didn't. I was hoping they called my manager instead. You know, thinking that's how they'd do it, not call the artist directly but go through his manager?"

"You could be right."

Bradley sighed. "Yeah, but I could be wrong, too."

Delphine squeezed Bradley's hand. She didn't know what else to do. She knew all about being disappointed, and there was nothing anyone could do—no matter how well intentioned they were—to make you feel better.

"I really need this, Delphine," Bradley said quietly, as if he were admitting to some sort of dark secret.

"Why?" she asked, tilting her head so she could see his handsome face out of the corner of her eye.

His lips tightened and she was tempted to raise her fingers to his mouth and touch him, but she didn't. "My career is . . ." he began, then stopped, shaking his head. "Well, it's just not going the way it should. You've seen for yourself that my first album isn't in any of the stores. I can't get anyone to pick up my next recording contract with the sort of numbers I've got on my first record. I would have been better off if Gamble hadn't picked me up in the first place."

"How would this award help?" Delphine asked.

"If I got nominated for an award, it would prove to Gamble—prove to everyone in the industry—that I'm not some second-rate singer. I'd get national airplay on the radio. Gamble Records would make sure my records are out in the stores. It would change everything."

"What happens if you didn't get nominated?"

Bradley closed his eyes briefly before opening them again. "I don't know. I've been working this dream for over ten years now. I gave up a promising career in high tech after graduating from college. When all my classmates were making millions, I was making demo tapes and working part-time as a sales clerk in a computer store for minimum wage. I can't keep doing this forever. Sometimes I feel like, like . . ." He stopped, frowning.

"Like what?" Delphine asked, turning to face him.

Bradley's eyes met hers. "Like a loser. Sometimes I feel like such a loser because I've got nothing. Do you know that my best friend from college owns a house in Silicon Valley that's worth over eight million dollars, and another one in Aspen worth about the same? He has all the toys you could ever want. Boats, skis, cars. His kids go to the best schools, and his wife . . . God, his wife has enough jewelry to open her own store. And the worst of it is, he's a nice guy. His wife is wonderful. Even his fucking kids are great." Bradley grimaced.

"But that sort of success doesn't happen to very many people," Delphine protested. "There's nothing to say that if you had stuck it out in computers that you would have been in the same boat as your friend."

Bradley laughed a cold sort of laugh that sent a chill up Delphine's spine. "He built his company off an idea we came up with together at MIT. When we graduated, he wanted me to be a partner in the company he started to take our idea to market." Bradley laughed again.. "I was such an arrogant asshole that I told him I was going to make more money as a country music star than he'd ever see in the computer business."

Delphine didn't know what to say, so she remained silent as Bradley continued. "If I don't get this nomination, I don't know what I'm going to do."

He pulled his cowboy hat down over his face, shading his eyes from her view. Delphine's brow furrowed as she frowned, her mind racing.

What had he said earlier? That he was going to fire his manager because the man didn't deserve him. Suddenly, Delphine's frown cleared. Bradley might not realize it, but he had just revealed how she could make him fall in love with her.

The old saying was that the way to a man's heart was through his stomach, but that was not the case with Bradley. The way to Bradley's heart was through his music career, and if she could somehow help to make him a star, she'd be willing to bet it wouldn't take much more to get him to fall for her.

With a sudden burst of resolve, Delphine let go of Bradley's hand and went back to her book. As she buried herself in the technicalities of mechanical rights, tour support, and royalty clauses, her mind raced.

Delphine was determined to make an impact on Bradley's career by the time they reached Nashville.

For better or worse.

Chapter 19
New Beginnings

Richard flicked the pink curtains of the bedroom window open just a crack and looked out over the sparse smattering of vehicles behind them on the interstate. No suspicious-looking armored tanks or gun-wielding thugs appeared to be following them as they crossed the New Mexico border into Texas, but he hardly would have expected Jim and Gus to make their presence so obvious. He let the curtains fall back into place and walked to the kitchen to get a glass of water.

"Let me know if you want me to take over the driving," he said to Bradley, who was humming to himself and tapping his fingers on the steering wheel as he drove.

Bradley nodded distractedly, and Richard wondered if Harriet's son always made up songs in his head while he drove. In the passenger seat, Delphine was equally immersed in her own world, with her nose buried in a thick book.

Richard turned back to Harriet, who was studying her laptop as if she were trying to solve one of life's greatest mysteries.

"You see, this is how I figured out that something was wrong," Harriet said, pointing to a spot on her computer screen.

Richard leaned over her shoulder and squinted at the

jumble of numbers on her laptop. "Well, yes, I can see how it would just leap right out at you," he said dryly.

Harriet turned and looked at him above the rims of her reading glasses and Richard grinned, waiting to be scolded. But instead of giving him a lecture, she just rolled her eyes and laughed. "Okay, so maybe it's not so clear from where you're standing. Here, why don't you sit down and I'll explain it to you?" She scooted over and patted the bench seat next to her, and Richard knew that she was flirting with him, but sat down next to her anyway.

It was kind of nice to be flirted with, he decided as Harriet's breasts brushed against his arm when she reached out to grab a pencil. He found it a little hard to concentrate on her figures when he was otherwise occupied concentrating on her . . . er, figure.

"This column shows the income from the slot machines. A customer comes in, puts his quarter in the machine, and the program registers the income. When the machine pays out, it does so in quarters. Not nickels, not dimes, not pennies. Just quarters."

Richard shook his head, to clear it more than anything else. "Uh-huh. It's all crystal clear to me now."

Harriet sighed. "Let me make this easier for you to understand. Let's pretend that a specific machine had only one customer put only one quarter in it all day long. At the end of the day, that quarter would be collected and brought to the cash room. Then your drug kingpin comes in and adds his ten percent. That quarter would now be twenty-five cents plus two and half cents. That's rounded to twenty-eight cents, because, of course, there's no such thing as half a cent. So then the money goes to you, and you've arranged it so that ten percent gets taken off the top and funneled into a secret bank account or your magic sock drawer—"

"Or my mattress," Richard interrupted, raising his eyebrows.

"Exactly," Harriet agreed with a smile. "Or your mattress.

You take two-point-eight cents off the top. Maybe you even round it to three cents. The books are now back to twenty-five cents in, twenty-five cents out, and everything's a-okay, right?"

"Right," Richard said.

"Okay, so say it's the next day, and now we have a customer who puts one dollar into that slot machine. The drug ring adds ten percent, so we're at a dollar and ten cents, then you take your ten percent off a dollar ten, which is eleven cents, and . . . oops, now we're down to ninety-nine cents. That just can't happen in what's supposed to be a closed system. There's no combination of quarters, dimes, and nickels that will get you to ninety-nine cents. Or anything else, for that matter, that doesn't end in a zero or a five. And none of our machines took pennies, so I knew then that something was wrong. When I asked my predecessor about the discrepancy, she said it was just rounding. I've always found that when the math doesn't work like it should, there's something going on. And it's never rounding."

Richard sat staring at the attractive brunette sitting next to him. God, he loved smart women.

He frowned for just a second, thinking about Evelyn. She had been smart, too, but in a different way from Harriet.

Street-smart. That's what Evelyn had been. Street-smart, and street-worn. Her intelligence had always had an edge to it, although Richard knew that she'd needed that edge to survive the harsh upbringing she had only hinted to him about.

If Evelyn had discovered the casino owners' scam, she would never have tried to take the evidence to the authorities. Hell, she probably would have found a way to take another fifteen percent for herself.

And, unlike Harriet, she would *never* have been caught.

Not because she was necessarily smarter than Harriet, but because she would have expected the worst to happen and would have planned for it. She'd have blackmailed them all into silence or bought them off. She may even have slept with at least one of them to get him on her side. Richard had known a lot more about Evelyn's sexual escapades than he had ever let on.

He drew in a deep breath. Evelyn had been the love of his youth and he had given her everything within his reach to try to make her happy, but she had always wanted more. In some ways, he blamed himself for her suicide—he knew he couldn't be the man she wanted him to be, but he couldn't walk away from her, either.

Maybe if he had left, it would have forced her to get treatment. Maybe if he had been strong enough to walk away, she wouldn't have felt so desperate to escape a life she hated.

But maybe his wife's problems were not all his to solve, either. If she had been so unhappy with him, so miserable with her middle-class life, maybe she should have been the one to leave.

Richard let out a heavy breath and felt a piece of the guilt he'd been carrying around for a decade ease out of his chest.

Yes, Evelyn had been the love of his youth—a love that was filled with lust and excitement and a careless disregard for the future that came with being young. But he was older now, and more cautious, more aware of how everything he did impacted the life of another human being.

Evelyn had made the choice to stay forever young and careless.

Now it was his turn to choose.

And he chose happiness.

Delphine sat down at a picnic table at a rest area a few miles west of Amarillo and looked around to make sure nobody was watching her. Turning her back to the Winnebago, she flipped open Bradley's cell phone and dialed information. She asked the operator to connect her to Gamble Records in Seattle while a hot breeze sent a ripple through the tall grass at her feet. The air outside the motor home was heavy and dry. Summer in the Southwest—when the unrelenting sunshine was broken only by violent lightning storms and torrential downpours that soaked the earth and immediately evaporated afterward.

"Good morning. Gamble Records," a polite voice answered after Delphine was patched through via the operator.

"Hello. My name is Delphine Armstrong and I'm the assistant to Bradley Nelson's manager. I'd like the name and phone number of the local promotion manager assigned to the Oklahoma City and Little Rock markets, please."

Delphine held the cell phone to her ear and looked at the notes she'd jotted down earlier to make sure she was using the correct terminology. She held her breath, waiting for the woman on the other end of the line to call her bluff.

"I'm sorry," the woman began, making a bead of sweat appear on Delphine's upper lip. She just *knew* the woman was going to check her records and discover that Delphine was not, in fact, an employee of Bradley's manager. "But we don't have an LPM in that area," the woman continued.

Delphine let out the breath she'd been holding. "Oh. Well, then, could you give me the names of the program directors for the top country stations in these cities? Mr. Nelson is planning a tour, and I'd like to let the local radio stations know that he's available for interviews."

"Certainly. Hold on and I'll look up that information."

Delphine thanked the woman and waited, pen poised, during a short silence. When the woman came back on the line, Delphine wrote down names and call letters and phone numbers. Then she asked whom to contact about making certain that Bradley's album was in the local record stores. The woman asked her to hold, and Delphine expected her to come back with another set of contact numbers. Instead, the phone was picked up by a man who sounded as if he didn't much appreciate the interruption.

"Klein here," the man very nearly barked into the phone.

"Um, yes, my name is Delphine Armstrong and I'm the assistant to the manager of one of your artists. Bradley Nelson?" she said, not intending to make it sound like a question.

"Yeah?"

Delphine heard the impatience in the man's voice and straightened her shoulders. She refused to let herself be intimidated by this guy. *Act like you know what you're doing and nobody will question you,* she reminded herself silently. "Mr. Nelson is going to be doing a tour through Oklahoma and Arkansas, and then plans to go on to Nashville to attend the Country Music Awards show next week. He'll be doing radio interviews and some live appearances, and I'd like to make sure that his CDs are available in the markets where he'll be stopping. Are you the correct person to handle this?"

"That's me," Mr. Klein answered, sounding a bit less hostile than before.

"Good. Can I give you the information on our tour dates?"

"Yes, go ahead. This was for Bradley Nelson, right?"

"Yes, sir. Mr. Nelson will be in Oklahoma City tomorrow morning. He's been booked for radio interviews on—" She glanced down at the information the receptionist had given her a minute before and read off the call letters for two of the stations. "He'll be in Little Rock the next day, and I'm hopeful that we'll be able to arrange similar radio appearances there, and also in Memphis and Nashville later in the week."

"You're not giving me much notice here," Mr. Klein complained.

"I know, and I'm very sorry about that. Mr. Nelson let us know about this tour several months in advance, but we—I mean, I—I dropped the ball. My baby got sick with pneumonia right after Mr. Nelson sent me his schedule and, with all the hospital stays and late nights and all that, I just forgot all about it. And now . . . now I could lose my job because of it. I know it's short notice, and I apologize for the inconvenience. I would really, really appreciate it if you could help. I'll do anything you need me to do—I'll even run the CDs around to the record stores if you'll overnight them to me at the Oklahoma City post office. Just give me a list of what stores to hit and who I need to talk to. I'll do anything."

Mr. Klein grunted. "No, that won't be necessary. Gamble Records has sales staff in the area who can take care of it. Why don't you give me a number where I can reach you, though, in case there's a problem."

Delphine rattled off Bradley's cell phone number and thanked Mr. Klein for being so helpful.

He grunted again and then said, "By the way, I hope your baby's better. Is it a boy or a girl?"

Delphine blinked at the notepad in front of her. Hmm. Did she want to have a boy or a girl? "A boy," she said. "He's eleven months old and he's the best baby ever. He hardly ever cries, even when he's sick."

"I've got one that age, too," Mr. Klein admitted. "A baby girl named Lily. But my little girl, she's a screamer. Got her daddy's temper, I'm afraid."

Delphine smiled and turned to a blank page in her note-book. Balancing the notebook on her lap, she wrote, "Gam-ble Records Sales Manager. Mr. Klein. Eleven-month-old girl. Lily." At the top of the sheet, she wrote "Contacts" and underlined it twice.

"Well, you enjoy your little girl, Mr. Klein. I really appre-ciate your help." With that, Delphine hung up, still smiling. Then she flipped back to the page where she'd written the radio station contacts, dialed another number, and waited for the phone to be answered.

It looked as if her new career were off to a flying start.

Chapter 20

Cut to the Quick

"I'm sorry, Bradley. You didn't make the cut."

Bradley felt the words like a punch to the gut. "No!" he wanted to scream. He wanted, no he *needed,* this nomination. Without it . . . God, he didn't want to think what was going to happen without it.

"Are you sure?" he asked, trying to keep the anger and desperation out of his voice. He took his cowboy hat off and laid it on the bumper of the Winnebago. The west Oklahoma sunshine was just too hot, and it seemed as if the black hat absorbed the heat and increased it tenfold. Gasoline fumes stung his nostrils as Richard filled up the Winnebago's tank, surrounded by several other travelers doing the same thing. Bradley ignored them all, staring straight ahead at the seldom-used vacuum and water pumps as his manager answered.

"I've got the list of nominees right here in front of me," Hal Greenwood said.

"Who made it for debut male vocalist?" Bradley asked, pinching his forehead between his thumb and his forefinger.

Hal read off the names of the five men deemed to be the most talented in that category. Bradley snorted loudly when the last name was read off. Hell, he thought, make that four men and one boy. They'd chosen a fucking kid over him—a fucking kid who hadn't even been alive when Bradley gave up everything to try to become a star. Bradley felt fury welling up in his chest, the hot flames of it burning like bile as it climbed up his throat.

"What sort of idiots vote for this award?" he asked, unable to contain his anger. "Two of those guys don't even sing country music. They're like the goddamn boy bands of pop music with their slick dance moves and repetitive lyrics. And Bobby Gorman? For God's sake, the kid's what? Seven years old? Eight? I mean, that's two guys out of five who actually have some fucking talent."

"Bradley—" Hal tried to interrupt.

"No, I mean it. What the hell kind of business is this that real talent isn't recognized? I could understand if all these guys were better than me, but they aren't. This is all about politics. These guys are on the list because they're at better record labels than I am or they have connections that I don't. This has nothing to do with talent."

"Bradley—" Hal tried again.

"I tell you, I am about fucking ready to fucking give up," Bradley said, pounding his fist against the Winnebago for emphasis. His anger grew inside him like a giant-fanged worm, slimy and ugly and devouring everything in its path, leaving nothing inside him except a gorged maggot of envy.

"I hate this *fucking* business," he said, his teeth clenched tightly, as if to keep the worm safely inside himself, leaving it to grow and fester in the darkness.

"You're going to hate it even worse when you hear what I have to say," Hal said quietly, finally getting through the green fog of Bradley's anger.

Bradley frowned into the phone and leaned against the Winnebago's bumper, putting a hand on his hat. "What do you mean?" he asked, hating the cautious, half-frightened tone in his own voice. Anger was a much easier emotion for him to deal with. It came more naturally and ran its own course. Fear was another matter altogether.

"I have to resign as your manager. You're a very hard

worker, Bradley, and I think that could take you far in this business, but I don't have the time to devote to you right now. One of my clients has gone platinum this year, and she needs more of my attention than she did when I signed you a year ago. It's not fair of me to keep you on when I can't give you what you need. If Gamble had picked up your next album, or if you had made the nominee list . . . well, then I might have been able to keep you on. But with things the way they are now, I would have to spend too much time just trying to get you back to where you were a year ago. I know you already know this, but it's worse to have an artist with bad sales numbers than to have one with no numbers at all."

Bradley couldn't believe what he was hearing. The irony that he had been ready to fire Hal just yesterday was not lost on him as he sat on the hot metal bumper and stared at the dusty ground between his booted feet.

He felt as though Hal's words were the sword that killed the envy inside him. Only they had slaughtered everything else within him as well—his ambition, his drive, his single-minded determination to succeed where his father had not—it was all gone, leaving him hollow.

Bradley was surprised that his legs were still strong enough to support him. He had a sudden vision of himself lying atop the dying prickly brown grass, having the dusty earth blow over him, filling his eyes and his ears and his mouth with dirt.

Or maybe it was just his dreams that were being buried in the unforgiving ground.

He felt tears prickling at the backs of his eyes and hastily wiped the back of his hand across them and took a deep breath. He was not some sissy kid who was going to cry at every disappointment. Hell, he'd leave that to little Bobby Gorman.

But . . . damn, this hurt.

"I'm sorry, Bradley. I've got another call coming in and I've got to go. I wish you the best in your career," Hal said.

And then he hung up, leaving Bradley with his cell phone still pressed to his ear, the sound of the empty dial tone ringing in his head.

"I really appreciate your seeing me on such short notice," Delphine said, making a point of squishing her breasts together to create the illusion of cleavage as she leaned forward to take the proffered hand of the program director of Oklahoma City's premier country radio station.

"We're always glad to meet the musicians and their representatives when they come to town. I'm just sorry we didn't have any time to interview Mr. Nelson this week. With the National Cowboy Hall of Fame hosting their anniversary show this week, we already have some of the biggest country music legends here. Willie Nelson and George Strait. Vince Gill. Leann Womack and Jo Dee Messina. I've heard that Tim and Faith are here, too, but we couldn't get hold of either of their publicists to arrange interviews. Still, it's been a busy week."

"Faith Hill is here?"

"Yes," the program director said, making Delphine's heart plummet to her stomach.

It'll be fine, she told herself. Surely the Hall of Fame was large enough that they could avoid running into a big star like Faith Hill. Delphine had thought she'd been lucky to get Bradley a half-hour gig at the Hall of Fame that afternoon. She hadn't realized that there was a big event going on. That explained why the event coordinator had said something about a last-minute cancellation before she'd happily agreed to let Bradley perform.

"I'll have to admit that I've never actually heard anything by Mr. Nelson," the program director said, interrupting Delphine's thoughts.

Delphine smiled at the man and pulled a CD that she had pilfered from Bradley's stock out of her purse. "I brought this along just in case you hadn't. I'd be delighted if you'd take it."

She held out the CD, repeating her cleavage squish. "I really think we're going to have hits with tracks one, four, and seven," she said.

The man took the CD, glancing first at the cover and then at the back. "Thanks. Now, is there anything else I can do for you? You got to meet our morning drive-time deejays, right? And my assistant gave you the station tour?"

Delphine kept her smile pasted on her face she pondered his question. She didn't know what else to ask for. What she really wanted was for this man to listen to Bradley's album and agree to add it to the station's playlist, but he had seemed uninterested in the CD she'd just handed him. "Yes, thank you. Your assistant was very helpful. Um, you wouldn't happen to be free this afternoon, would you?"

Surprise flashed across the man's face, but he covered it quickly. "Actually, no. I'm not . . . er, I'm married."

Delphine laughed. "Oh, no. That's not what I meant. Bradley's going to be playing at the Hall of Fame at four o'clock this afternoon. I was just wondering if you might have time to stop by and hear him."

The program director looked relieved. "Yes, actually, I had already planned to be there for this evening's events. I'll be sure to stop by and give him a listen."

"Thank you. It was a pleasure meeting you." Delphine put her hand out, forgoing the breast squeeze this time.

They shook hands and then Delphine left the station, stepping out into the hot summer sunshine. She felt the heat wash over her as though she were going through a carwash without a car. Ah, humidity, she thought, realizing how different Oklahoma City was from Reno. Reno had the dry heat that everyone in the southwest seemed so pleased about—as if a dry one hundred degrees was any more bearable than a wet hundred degrees. One hundred degrees was damn hot, and that was all there was to it.

Delphine lifted the hair off the nape of her neck and

wished she'd brought her ponytail band with her. She knew, though, that she looked more professional with her hair down around her shoulders, so she'd braved the heat with it down.

Of course, the heat hadn't been so bad when she'd set out early this morning to make the rounds of the country music stations—none of which had been able to squeeze Bradley in for an interview.

Now it was almost one o'clock and her stomach was already grumbling and she had a half-hour walk back to the RV park where Harriet had parked the Winnebago. Still, it was worth it if it meant that Bradley might start getting some airplay.

She set off down the scorching sidewalk, trying to ignore the way the straps of her sandals were digging into her toes and the dribbles of sweat that were sliding down her back.

Sometimes you just had to suffer to get what you wanted for the people you loved.

"Did you happen to run across any clues about who might be running the drug ring?" Richard asked, leaning back against the kitchen counter as he waited for two slices of bread to pop up out of the toaster.

Harriet kept staring at the screen of her laptop as if she were looking into a crystal ball. "No. I can see where the extra ten percent got added to every day's take, but I can't figure out how they knew how much to send over. They always added ten percent. Now, how did they know how much that would be? They had to have access to your sales numbers somehow."

"But how? We tracked every outgoing telephone call and e-mail for months trying to find out who was funneling information to the drug traffickers. We followed up every lead, and they were all dead ends."

Harriet frowned at her computer. "I don't know, Richard. I

can't tell from this information what was going on. But . . ." She looked up at him, her voice trailing off.

"But what?" Richard asked.

When the toast popped up, he neatly layered three strips of bacon over the golden-brown bread, then added lettuce, tomato, and mayonnaise to make the sandwich complete. He cut it diagonally into two symmetrical triangles, put both halves on a plate, and slid it in front of Harriet with a paper napkin.

One thing he had learned about this woman in the past few days was, brilliant as she might be, her cooking sucked.

Her pantry was full of canned spaghetti—how disgusting was that?—boxed macaroni and cheese, and creamed corn. It was as if the Winnebago had been stuck in a time warp from twenty years ago—back when she'd been raising a ten-year-old who would only eat bland, salty, slimy food.

But he was going to change that.

No grown woman should eat food cooked by Chef Boyardee.

The front door banged open just then, and Harriet's son stepped in, looking flushed.

"You forgot your sunscreen, dear," Harriet said, absently looking up from her work.

Bradley only grunted in response, making Richard think that something more than the intense sunshine was bothering the other man.

"Would you like a BLT?" Richard asked, turning to put two more pieces of bread in the toaster.

"No, thank you. I'm not hungry," Bradley said. He reached into the fridge instead and pulled out a beer, twisting off the cap and draining nearly the entire thing in one huge gulp.

Richard raised his eyebrows at the semidesperate look in Bradley's eyes, but he didn't say anything, even when Bradley cracked open another beer and drank it almost as quickly as the first.

"You know," Harriet said, looking over at Richard,

"Bradley might be able to help us here. I copied several of the programs we used to reconcile our books before I, uh, left on my last day. Bradley might be able to look at the code behind the programs and tell us if he sees anything suspicious."

Richard saw Bradley look sharply at his mother. His face was mottled with angry red splotches, and unless Richard's guess was way off the mark, he figured Bradley was pretty pissed off about something or other.

"Why don't I make you a sandwich," Richard suggested, smoothly stepping in front of Bradley and blocking the younger man's view of his mother.

Bradley looked at him with eyes full of a bitterness Richard hadn't seen in the younger man before. "Sure. Why don't you do that? In the meantime, I'll go use my talents to help my mother. You know, Dickie, she always encouraged me to stick with computers. That way, when I finally outgrew this whole country music bullshit, I'd have a real skill to fall back on."

"I prefer to be called Richard," Richard said calmly. "And I'd be willing to bet that even Elvis's parents said the same thing to him before he hit it big. Now, whatever's going on with you, I don't think it's right for you to take it out on your mother. If you need some time to be alone, why don't you just go back outside and take a long walk around the block?"

They stood there, shoulder to shoulder, staring at each other like prize bulls fighting over the same tiny piece of earth.

Neither one of them moved when the front door banged open again.

"Hi, guys, what's up?" Delphine asked, her high-heeled sandals clattering on the metal steps leading into the motor home. Then, without waiting for an answer, she continued, "Boy, is it hot out there. What did we ever do without air-conditioning?"

Bradley frowned and glanced toward Delphine, breaking

eye contact with Richard. Before Delphine could close the door behind her, he grabbed her arm and said, "Let's go."

Richard heard her sputter. "But I was going to get some lunch."

"We'll get something to eat later. I want to get down to the Hall of Fame. Now."

Delphine sighed loudly. "Okay, but we still have over an hour before you need to get there and start setting up. I don't know why you're in such a hurry."

Bradley yanked two more beers out of the fridge and bent down to pick up his guitar case on the way out. At the door, he turned to look back at Richard, who was still standing protectively in front of Harriet.

"You know, Richard," Bradley said, emphasizing the last word, "I'll bet Elvis's parents never encouraged him to have a Plan B because they never doubted that he'd be successful. It must have been nice for him to know when he was out there giving everything he had to the music and to his fans that he had people at home who believed in him. There are others with the same dream who are not quite as fortunate."

And with that, Bradley stepped outside, closing the door behind him with a decidedly angry click.

Chapter 21
Because I Believe

"So, would you like to tell me what that was all about?" Richard asked, turning to Harriet, who suddenly seemed smaller and more fragile than she had a few minutes before.

Richard slipped into the booth and pushed Harriet's uneaten sandwich away from the edge of the table. Then he scooted closer, closed the top of her laptop, put an arm around her shoulders, and pulled her to his side.

He reached out with his left hand and lifted her chin so that he could look into her pretty brown eyes, which were rapidly filling with tears. Rather than telling her not to cry or trying to tell her that everything would be all right, he leaned down and kissed the trail of tears that rolled down her face.

Harriet leaned into him, but didn't explode into the noisy sobs he had expected. Instead, she cried quietly for several minutes before drawing in a shuddering breath and raising a hand to dry her eyes.

"Bradley's father wanted to be a country-western music star," she said. "We met back in my senior year of college, in an accounting class. I was the teacher's aide, and Tom was just a freshman who was struggling to grasp the basics of T-accounts. I thought he was cute and, of course, I was too blinded by that to realize how incompatible we were. He had no head for business." She shook her own very practical head, whether in disgust with herself or her late husband, Richard wasn't sure. He didn't ask, just kept stroking her bare arm and waiting for her to tell him her story at her own pace.

"We ended up getting married two days after I graduated. Tom said he was going to go back to school the next fall, but he never did. I got a job as a low-level flunky in the local office of the IRS and Tom stayed home all day writing music." She paused, then laughed without humor and added, "For the first two years, at least."

"What happened then?" Richard asked, encouraging her to continue.

"I had Bradley, and it was as if Tom knew that he could use the baby as his excuse to stay home forever. I had thought Tom was ambitious, but now I began to wonder. I mean, it was nice that I could afford to support us on what I earned. And I suppose if the roles had been reversed, nobody would have thought anything of it. Especially not thirty-some years ago."

"But you resented it?" Richard probed.

Harriet's shoulders rose and fell as she took a deep breath and let it out. "I didn't resent it, exactly." She stopped talking for a minute. Then she looked up at Richard and said apologetically, "Okay, yes, I suppose I resented it. Not because I minded working. I didn't. I knew from the beginning that I wasn't cut out to be a full-time mom. And I wouldn't even have minded that Tom wasn't successful as a singer. I guess . . ."

"Yes? You guess what?"

"I guess I just expected him to try harder. I mean, everyone knows that there's a tiny number of artists—whether it be painters or musicians or writers—who ever make a living with their art. But still, I wanted him to at least be working at it." Harriet grimaced. "I would come home from work and there would be empty beer cans everywhere. Sometimes Tom and his friends would even stack them in front of the door so I'd knock them over when I came home. As if it were some big joke. 'Ha-ha. Harriet knocked over the cans again.' It was like living in a fraternity house, only I was twenty-five years old with a baby and a husband who acted like he was twelve."

Richard rubbed Harriet's shoulder and let silence linger in the cool air of the Winnebago. "I understand," he said after a while, his voice sounding rusty, as if it were a metal pipe left for too long out in the rain. He had never discussed his relationship with Evelyn with another person, let alone another woman, and he was finding it difficult to speak now. He doubted he'd ever share some of the horrific secrets he had kept for so long. But he had finally realized that he was not betraying his first wife by sharing how it had felt for him to be the only sane one in the madness that had been their lives together. "My first wife—" He stopped and cleared his throat, and then began again. "My first wife had a good heart, but she wanted too much without wanting to work for it. She wanted things the easy way. I often thought that if she ever put her mind to it, she could run the world. She was so smart." And so broken, he added silently.

"That's how I felt about Tom, too. He could have made something of himself, if only he'd stopped expecting it to come easy. But playing with the baby and drinking beer with his friends and pretending that he was working toward his dream by strumming his guitar every now and then through-out the day . . . well, that just wasn't going to get him any-where and I knew it."

Harriet turned to face him, her eyes clear and bright in the sunlight shining in through the open curtains. "Bradley was right. I stopped believing in Tom, and I let it ruin our mar-riage. I was so angry and disappointed, looking ahead and seeing that I was going to be the only one supporting our lit-tle family for the rest of my life. And Tom wanted more kids," she said, with a hopeless sort of laugh. "When I refused, he called me a heartless bitch."

Richard squeezed his eyes shut, wondering why the people who were supposed to love one another the most were
the ones who, instead, tore each other apart.

"I would have loved to give Bradley a brother or sister,"
Harriet said, sounding wistful. "I just didn't want to keep
adding to our family, knowing that I had to be our children's
sole supporter. It was hard enough to feed a family of three
on what I made. I couldn't see how I would manage with
four or five of us. I was working as hard as I could and getting promoted as often as possible, and it still was barely
enough."

"When did it end?" Richard asked, opening his eyes to
the sunshine again.

"Long before Tom actually left," Harriet answered with a
mocking laugh. "Bradley thinks I drove his father out, but
that's not true. By the time Tom left, we were living separate
lives. I had come to terms with the fact that Tom and I were
finished, and actually, he was a wonderful father to Bradley
and it was nice having him around. He never minded
Bradley hanging out with him and his friends, and he took
him on vacation to Nashville and taught him to play the guitar. He was a good father."

Just not a good husband. That's what she didn't say, and
Richard didn't need to say it aloud, either.

"Why did Tom leave? What finally pushed him over the
edge?"

Harriet looked at him and her eyes grew bright with
unshed tears.

Richard shook his head, frowning. "You don't have to tell
me. It's all right."

Harriet blinked several times and managed to hold back
the tears. "No, it's just . . . I've kept it inside for so long."

Richard reached out and tenderly smoothed a lock of
Harriet's hair behind her ear. All these untold secrets, all
these unspoken words, all these unshed tears. Sometimes he
wondered if his life was more about what was held closely

to his heart than what he let others hear and see. "I won't judge you. Whatever your secret is. Whatever you may have done, I care about you for the woman you are now."

Harriet took a deep breath. "That's just it. It wasn't me, but I let Bradley think it was for so long. At first, I didn't want him to know because I knew how much it would hurt him. He adored his father. And then, after his father died so suddenly in a car accident, I felt it would be wrong to tell him the truth."

Richard waited patiently for Harriet to tell him the secret she had kept locked within herself for so long.

She looked at him with steady brown eyes that belied the pain she might be feeling at the stirred-up memories. "When Bradley was twelve years old, he won the church talent contest," she announced, making Richard wonder if the truth was just too painful for her to tell. But then she continued. "Tom left us because he couldn't stand the thought that his son might succeed where he, himself, had failed."

"He was jealous of his own son?" Richard asked, frowning.

"Yes. Bradley never knew, and I'll never tell him."

"How did you find out?"

Harriet closed her eyes and twin tears rolled down her face. Richard slid his thumbs under her eyes and wiped away the tears. "Bradley went out with some friends that night after the talent show. He was so excited because the prize was one hundred dollars. He was going to treat his friends to ice-cream cones at Baskin-Robbins, and put the rest of the money away for a new guitar. One thing about Bradley, he was always very focused on his music.

"Anyway, Tom had come with us to the talent show because Bradley had asked him to. Afterward, the two of us drove home in silence. When we got home, Tom said that Bradley hadn't deserved to win. He said that our son, whom he had raised and cared for for twelve years, had no talent and then he . . ." Harriet blinked again, letting loose a new flow of tears. "Then he took Bradley's guitar out of the back-seat of the car and he smashed it against the porch. Over and over and over again, he hit it until it had splintered into a thousand pieces. It was everywhere. In the flower beds. In the lawn. I found pieces of it in the house months later."

"What did you do?"

"I told him to get out. Bradley was Tom's biggest fan. It would have crushed him to know what his father really thought."

"Maybe that wasn't what he really thought. Maybe he just said that out of frustration because he knew what he had always wanted so much was never going to happen," Richard suggested, trying to give the other man the benefit of the doubt.

"I know he didn't really mean it. But that he had allowed his dream to become so sick and twisted and pathetic that he would lash out at the one person left in the world who still believed in him . . . that was just unacceptable to me. I may not understand how Bradley feels about music or his ambition to become a star, but I love my son and I refused to stand by and let his own father destroy him. I hoped that maybe if Tom weren't living with Bradley, didn't have to hear about his successes every day, he could come to terms with his own failure." Harriet closed her eyes. "The sad thing is, he wasn't even a failure. He'd never even tried hard enough for that. What he was, was . . . nothing. He was nothing. He sat on the couch and drank beer with his friends and pretended that he wanted more out of life, but he didn't. Not really. Not enough to work for it."

"What did you do about the guitar?" Richard asked.

"The guitar?" Harriet asked, opening her eyes.

"The one Tom smashed?"

"Oh. I was out on my hands and knees picking up splinters from the driveway when Bradley got home that night. There was too much of it still left when he got back. I tried to clean it all up, but I couldn't do it fast enough." Two more tears rolled down her cheeks and dripped from her chin onto her chest. "I told him that I had accidentally run over his guitar. I said that I had taken it out of the car when his dad and I got home and that we'd had a fight and his dad left. I said I had gotten in the car to go after his father, and that's when I ran over his guitar. I'll never forget how he looked at me then. It was as if I had killed his dog or something. But he wasn't angry. He just seemed so . . . so disappointed in me. As if I had let him down. And it hurt me so much to keep it all inside, but it would have hurt worse to tell him the truth."

She was crying openly now, and Richard gathered her in his arms and rocked her back and forth, whispering soothing words into her hair.

And as a sudden, uncharacteristic wave of anger washed over him, Richard began to wish that Tom Nelson were still alive. Because if he were, Richard would have liked to demonstrate—in a very physical sense—exactly what an asshole he thought the other man had been.

Delphine stood in the back of the Special Events Center of the Hall of Fame and listened to the man she loved go through the motions of singing the lead song on his first album.

He was not the same man who had gotten down on one knee and sung a duet with her two nights ago at the bar in Albuquerque. *That* man had cared about the words he sang. *That* man had made her believe in him.

This man knew all the right moves, played all the right notes, and sang all the right words, but he wasn't feeling any of it. And the audience wasn't buying it.

Leaning against the yellow plastic wall of the tent, Delphine winced as a baby down in the first few rows of seats started to cry. She heard Bradley's voice falter, his eyes darting around the crowd to find the source of the distraction. Then, two teenage boys near the back started laughing and a couple in the middle section got up and noisily made their way out of their seats. Bradley kept singing, and then threw himself into the end of the song with a flourish.

The applause was polite but unenthusiastic.

Several more people got up to leave, and Delphine saw Bradley's eyes follow them as they left through the exit doors.

He began another song—one about a lonely cowboy on a trail ride far from home—and Delphine cringed at the absolute lack of emotion in his voice. He could have been singing about persistent mildew or a new brand of diapers for all the enthusiasm he displayed.

When a man walked into the room, Delphine looked up and nearly groaned aloud. *Oh, no, not now.*

It was the program director from the radio station she had visited that afternoon.

He stopped just inside the shadows of the overhang at the entrance to the room, leaning against the wall like Delphine was doing herself. After no more than two minutes, he turned to leave.

Delphine raced after him.

"Wait," she called, once they were outside the room.

The program director turned, two spots of red on his cheeks, as if he were embarrassed to have been caught running away. "Oh. Miss Armstrong. Nice to see you again."

"Thank you," Delphine said, slowing to a stop next to the man. "Do you have a bit more time? I could introduce you to Bradley after this song."

The man hesitated and Delphine found herself crossing her fingers at her sides. Please, she prayed, please let me be the only one who noticed that Bradley's performance wasn't his best. Maybe the program director had just stepped out to go to the men's room. Maybe he'd had every intention of coming back to listen to the end of Bradley's act.

His words crushed the hopes she was harboring. "No, that won't be necessary. I think I heard enough of Mr. Nelson's act to know why he isn't getting any airplay." He fished the

CD she had given him earlier out of the pocket of his suit jacket and handed it back to her. "He won't be getting any on my station, either. I'm sorry."

Delphine reluctantly took the CD. "Couldn't you give him another chance? He's . . . he's not himself today." That, at least, was the truth. She had never seen Bradley so angry and uptight, like one of those old-fashioned barrels of gunpowder in the cartoons, just sitting on the set waiting to blow.

The man looked at her for a long moment. "I'm going to tell you something that you may or may not want to pass on to your client. Professional musicians—the kind who are headed for stardom, at least—never let the audience know how they're feeling. When they get up there on stage, it stops being about themselves and becomes all about the music. Until your Mr. Nelson can figure out a way to remove himself from the process, he'll never make it beyond this stage of his career. Now, if you'll excuse me, I have things to do."

With that, the program director nodded at her and walked away, leaving Delphine staring at his retreating back.

"I hate fucking cowboys," Bradley said, walking past a framed lariat in the hallway leading to the dressing rooms that had been set aside for the bigger-name stars performing at tonight's show.

"Oh, I don't know. I don't mind it so much except for the spurs. They can leave bruises if you're not careful."

Bradley shot Delphine a look that could have melted wax. In Antarctica.

"Sorry." Delphine shrugged, trying not to sigh.

Bradley stopped in the middle of the hallway and spun to face her. "I don't care about any of this crap. Ropin' and ridin' and 'get along little doggie'? It's all bullshit. I'm from New Jersey. Nobody there rides horses or herds cattle. I don't care about the prairie or rodeo clowns or ranches or any of it. I don't know why I ever thought country music was for me. It's all about things I don't give a shit about."

Delphine frowned, her eyes narrowing on Bradley. He stood in front of her wearing his usual costume: black snake-skin boots, black jeans, black T-shirt, and black cowboy hat. He had a belt on today with a big silver buckle embellished with intricate detailing. Dressing up for his performance, Delphine figured.

For someone who professed to hate all things country, he sure had the costume down pat.

"Have you listened to any country music lately?" she asked.

"Of course I have," Bradley answered, angrily pushing his hat back on his head. "That's all I ever do. Listen to country music. Play country music. Write country music. My whole damn life revolves around country music, and it's all a giant lie. My whole life is a lie."

Delphine wanted to tell him that everybody she knew lived a life of lies, but she didn't. Instead, she grabbed Bradley's arm when he started walking away. "All of that so-called crap is not what country music is all about. It's about heartache and loss. Love and family."

"Yeah, and truth, justice, and the American way, too," Bradley added sarcastically.

"Yes, those things, too. What about the song we sang together in Albuquerque? That had nothing to do with horses or cows or any of that. It was a love song between two married people. And what about some of the others that you like? 'Angry All the Time' by Tim McGraw. That's about a man wondering why his wife has changed, and why she can't go back to being the woman he married. 'How Do You Like Me Now?' by Toby Keith. A musician comes back to his hometown and rubs his success in the face of the cheer-leader who made fun of him in high school. 'The Good Stuff' by Kenny Chesney, about a guy who has a fight with his girlfriend and turns to alcohol and the bartender who tells him that's not what's important. 'I'm Already There' by Lonestar. A man has to travel for his job and he misses his wife and kids, but tells them a part of him is always there for them.

"There's nothing in these songs that a guy from Jersey can't understand, Bradley. You have life experiences that mean something and are just as important as those of other musicians. And they aren't singing about cattle drives, either. They're singing about real life. *Their* real lives."

Bradley pounded his fist on the wall, making Delphine jump. "Well, that's the key, isn't it? They have real lives to sing about. I have had nothing but minimum-wage jobs that I'm way overqualified for and a singing career that's so dead, rigor mortis has already set in. Do you really think people want to hear me sing about that? About what a loser I am? Because that, Delphine, is the only thing I really know about. Being a failure. Hardly what you want to listen to on your drive into work, huh?"

With that, Bradley shook off her hand and pushed past her.

Delphine grabbed the back of his T-shirt in an attempt to make him stop and hear her out. "You're not a failure, Bradley. I think you have a lot of talent. If you'd just stop trying to act like some cowpoke from Texas and show the world who you really are, you could do it. I know you could."

Bradley turned to her then, his eyes narrowed and full of the anger of broken dreams. "Don't you get it, Delphine? If I'm not this person"—he spread his arms—"then I'm nothing. I don't have a backup personality to change into. I've bet it all on this one. I'm either Bradley Nelson, up-and-coming country music star, or I'm no one."

"Then *be* Bradley Nelson, up-and-coming country music star. But stop trying to be Bradley Nelson, cowboy. Or Bradley Nelson, guy from a small Midwestern town. Be yourself. That's good enough. *You're* good enough."

Bradley stepped closer, his teeth clenched with anger. "But I'm not good enough. Don't you understand? I wasn't good enough to get a second record contract. I wasn't good enough to get nominated for a country music award. And I damn sure wasn't good enough to hold on to my manager. I wasn't even good enough for a guy I wanted to fire," he said with an angry snort.

Delphine closed her eyes, her heart aching for him. So that's what he was so upset about. "I'm sorry," she said softly, the words echoing in the emptiness of the hallway.

"Yeah, well, so am I." He took off his hat, and his anger seemed to leave his body, as if his hat had been holding it inside him. He took a step backward, giving her a bit of space. "I don't know where to go from here, Delphine. My career is over."

"No it isn't," Delphine said fiercely. "I can help you. When we get to Nashville, I'll contact my cousin Faith. Besides, I know a thing or two about the music business—"

"What? From reading those books?" Bradley interrupted, shaking his head skeptically.

"No. I was . . . uh, I worked with a manager for a year or so in Los Angeles. The guy handled rock stars mostly. He was a bit nuts—had a Czech supermodel girlfriend and half a dozen dachshunds—but he was an effective manager. I got those books just to brush up on the things I might have forgotten since I quit the business."

"You really know how to be a manager?" Bradley asked.

"I got you this gig, didn't I?" Delphine asked, not really answering the question.

"Yeah, you did. Why don't you talk to Faith while we're here in Oklahoma? I mean, she and Tim are here. They're going to be performing in a few hours."

"I don't want to bother her. I know how much she hates to travel, especially if her kids aren't here with her. I think it would be better to get her at home, where she's more comfortable and relaxed. That way, she'll be more inclined to pull some strings for us."

Bradley nodded as if her argument made sense to him

and Delphine let out a relieved breath. He may have stopped believing in himself, but she hadn't. And she wanted nothing more than the chance to help him show the world how talented he really was. She could do it. She knew she could, if only he'd have some faith in her and give her some time to make a difference. She wasn't going to give up on him, even though he was ready to give up on himself.

The thought made her so hopeful that she raised herself up on her tiptoes and kissed Bradley on the mouth, a friendly kiss full of promise for the future. Only, when she started to pull away, Bradley put an arm around her waist and held her there. With his free hand, he pushed a lock of hair behind her ear, his fingers curving under her chin to lift her gaze up to meet his.

"Why are you doing this, Delphine? Why are you helping me?"

Because I love you, Delphine thought, but didn't say the words aloud. That would only frighten him away. "I'm doing it, Bradley, because I believe in you."

Chapter 22
To Tell the Truth

Bradley had woken up the next morning with Delphine's words echoing in his ears.

"I believe in you," she had said. Of course, David Gamble had believed in him once, too. So had Hal Greenwood. And Robyn Rogers. Even hard-as-nails, skeptical Robyn had believed in him at one point.

He'd proven them all wrong.

So why, when Delphine had looked up at him, her blue eyes full of trust and hope, had he started to believe once again that maybe, just maybe, he could do it? Was he just kidding himself?

Well, maybe he was, but if he gave up now, he'd never find out if he had what it took to be a star. With Delphine's help, he could give it another try. She seemed to know what she was doing and her familial relationship to one of country music's top stars didn't hurt, either.

From his seat at the dining room table, Bradley looked over at Delphine, who was sitting on the couch with his phone pressed to her ear, nodding occasionally and scribbling notes on the pad of paper she had balanced in her lap. As if feeling his gaze on her, she looked up and smiled, her teeth small and white and even. Bradley was struck by how pretty she was. Not flashy or glamorous like Robyn, but more quietly attractive—the kind of woman who got prettier the more you got to know her.

Delphine hung up the phone, stretched out her arms, and then announced, "Okay, I've got you a gig tonight at the Little Rock Bar in Little Rock. It doesn't pay anything, but the morning deejay I talked with at one of the radio stations said that some of the people involved in the local music scene are known to drop in from time to time. I'm sure this won't make your career skyrocket into stardom, but maybe we can get some momentum going before we hit Nashville. I'm going to have a much harder time booking you once we get to Music City."

"That's great," Bradley said. Delphine had booked him for more performances during the last week than he'd had in the past six months.

"I'd like to go over the songs you plan to sing. Try to pick ones that mean something to you. No cowboys or lonely prairie songs, all right?"

Bradley grinned. "You got it, boss." He was enjoying the personal attention of his new manager. As a matter of fact, he thought as Delphine stood up and stretched, her low-cut blue and white striped shirt sliding up to expose the expanse of creamy skin above the waistband of her jeans, he wouldn't mind getting even a bit more personal with his new manager.

When she walked past him, presumably to get another cup of coffee since she held her empty coffee mug in her hand, Bradley reached out and put an arm around her waist to stop her. He slid his legs out of the booth and planted one booted foot on each side of her legs, trapping her between them.

She turned to face him, setting her mug on the table. To his surprise, rather than pulling away and telling him to leave her alone since she was busy, she stepped closer and put her arms around his neck. Her chest was just inches from his mouth, and Bradley was tempted to kiss each one of her small, round breasts in turn. Instead, he closed his eyes and buried his nose in the valley between her breasts, inhaling the scent of laundry detergent and soap and woman.

When the door to his mother's bedroom was pulled open, Delphine tried to back out of his embrace, but Bradley wouldn't let her go. He did lift his face out of her chest, however, as Richard stepped into the hallway, followed by his mother.

"Lucky bastard," Bradley muttered, seeing the look of satisfaction on the other man's face. If only he and Delphine had some privacy . . .

His mother looked embarrassed as she headed toward the coffeepot—fully dressed even though Bradley knew she hadn't yet taken a shower.

"Good morning," he said, feeling a bit awkward about the fight he'd initiated yesterday in addition to the fact that he knew what his mother and Richard had been up to this morning.

"Morning," Harriet mumbled.

"Beautiful day, isn't it?" Richard asked, shooting Bradley a look of warning.

"Yes, it is. Mom, can we go outside and talk for a minute? There's something I need to say to you."

Bradley watched his mother pour herself a cup of strong black coffee. She turned to him, squared her shoulders, and nodded. Bradley gave Delphine's waist a squeeze before standing up and sidestepping her. He walked to the front door and held it open, indicating that his mother should go ahead of him out into the warm Oklahoma morning.

When they were outside in the bright sunshine, Bradley turned to find his mother was about to say something. He held up one hand. "No, wait. Let me go first." He paused for a moment, hitching his fingers in his belt loops when he realized he wasn't wearing his cowboy hat and didn't have anything else to fidget with.

"I'm sorry about yesterday. I know that you supported

Dad and his dream for as long as you could. I also know that you encouraged me to get a degree because you didn't want me to be in the same position Dad was, of having to make his wife support him while he made a go of it, because he wasn't qualified to do anything else. That was the practical thing to do, and I know it was the right thing to do."

Harriet carefully set her coffee mug down on the top step of the motor home, trying to remain calm. Her face felt as hot as the coffee in her cup, and she took a deep breath to try to cool down. For some reason, though, she couldn't seem to get back her usual inner calm. For twenty years, she had let herself be cast in the role of the bad guy, and she was tired of it.

Yes, she had been the mature one who enforced bedtimes and nutritious food guidelines and rules about homework while her husband had hung out in bars at night, pretending to be serious about his career in music so that he could continue mooching off her long after it was time that he grew up.

And *she* was the one who taken the blame for his failure—all because she hadn't wanted to hurt her son and knock his father off the pedestal Bradley had put Tom on all those years ago.

Well, she'd had about enough of it.

No, as a matter of fact, she'd had *more* than enough of it.

"Bradley," she said softly, filled with a deadly calm, "it's time you and I talked about your father. I don't know where you got the impression that I was holding him back from becoming a success, but wherever you got it, it's wrong. Your dad started out with some talent, but he was lazy. He never finished anything. He pretended to write songs all day, but not one was ever completed. He formed bands with his friends and they played at several of the local bars, but they never made a demo tape, and never tried to do anything more than perform in the bars around our neighborhood. You seem to think that I stopped your father from moving to

Nashville or L.A. or wherever he needed to go to make things happen for him in his music career, but that's not true. I would have moved anywhere. There are IRS offices almost everywhere in the country, and I could have transferred to any one of them.

"The truth is, your father never wanted to go. He didn't have the guts to do it. He was too afraid that he would fail, and that fear kept him from trying. That's the part that I couldn't stand. Your father was a coward, a coward who found it easier to blame me—and he blamed you, too—for his lack of success.

"And as for encouraging you to go to college? That wasn't because I wanted you to have something else to fall back on. I just wanted to make sure that you had what it took to set a goal and go after it without having anyone supporting you or pushing you or making you do it. You could have dropped out of school anytime. And you could have majored in anything you were interested in. You may choose to remember it differently, but I didn't force you to go to MIT, and I didn't force you to major in computer science. Those were your decisions and you stuck with them, and, yes, I was very proud of you for doing so. But just because I was proud of you doesn't mean that that's the only thing you could have done that would have met with my approval.

"It was you who got the scholarships, and you who passed the tests, and you who graduated with honors, and I was happy to see you do it because I knew then that you were not afraid to meet a challenge head-on, like your father was. That's why I was so proud of you. It had nothing to do with where you went to school or what your major was.

"You can say that I should have believed in you just because I loved you. But I loved your father, too, and I believed in him and he let me down because he didn't believe in himself. Pretty soon, I stopped believing, too. I wanted to make sure that didn't happen with you."

Bradley stood out in the bright morning sun, blinking at his mother. She picked up her coffee cup and took a sip, her gaze steady on his.

He opened his mouth and closed it again, doing his best dying-trout impression. Then he shook his head to clear it.

"Wow. That was quite a lot of baggage you had stored up inside," he observed.

His mother nodded and took another drink of her coffee. "Yes, wasn't it?" Then she let out a deep breath. "It feels good to have said it."

"Mom?"

"What?" she asked, sounding a bit afraid that he might ask her to bare even more of her soul.

"I love you."

At that, she started crying, big fat tears rolling down her face and splashing in her coffee. Bradley took the cup from her hands and enfolded her in a bear hug, resting his chin on top of her head.

"Why did you cover for Dad for so long?" he asked.

She kept her face pressed to his white T-shirt. "You looked up to him so much. I didn't want to shatter your illusions."

"Mom, I was twelve when Dad left. Do you think I didn't notice that all he did all day was drink and hang out with his friends?"

She looked up at him then and frowned. "You noticed that?"

"Of course. I did think that we were the reason he didn't go to Nashville to try to make it in country music, but I knew he didn't have the drive necessary to be successful. I think that's why I've tried so hard to make it. I guess . . . I guess I wanted to prove that if he'd worked harder, he would have been able to succeed. I'm not so sure anymore. He could have done everything I've done and still ended up a failure, Mom."

She reached up and brushed a lock of hair off his forehead. "You're not a failure, dear."

Bradley snorted. "Yeah, well, I'm not a success, either. I'm not ready to give up yet, though. Delphine has some great connections and she says she knows exactly what to do to get my career moving again. I'm beginning to believe that if anyone can help me, she's the one."

He smiled down at his mom, expecting her to smile back. He was surprised when her mouth turned down in a small frown instead.

"What's wrong? I thought you liked Delphine," Bradley said.

Harriet stepped back, patting his arm absently. "I do. I just—" She stopped and shook her head. "It's nothing. If Delphine says that she can help, I'm sure she's telling the truth."

"Of course she's telling the truth." It was Bradley's turn to frown. "Why would you say something like that?"

His mother picked up her cup of coffee and took a long drink of the now-cooled liquid. "I didn't mean anything by it. It's just a phrase. Now, I need to go in and take a shower so we can get moving. By the way, Richard offered to drive today because I have a favor to ask of you."

Bradley stopped with his hand on the front door of the motor home. "Oh?"

"Yes. I know you chose guitars over computers a long time ago, but I'd like to see if we can put that expensive education of yours to the test. I have an idea of how we might find the identity of the drug kingpin in Reno, but I need your help. If you don't mind, that is."

Bradley shook his head. "Naw, I don't mind. I need to put together a list of songs for Delphine, but after that, I'm all yours."

"Good," his mother said, following him up the stairs. "Let's get moving."

. . .

"Okay, I see how the reconciliation program accounts for the money coming in and going out again, but I don't see how it signals to anyone how much to add every day," Bradley said, staring at the computer screen in front of him.

"That's what we can't find, either. We know that the drug kingpin added ten percent of our daily take to our cash every day, but how does he know how much to send over? How does he know what our daily take is going to be? We certainly didn't call and tell him," Harriet said, sitting back in the booth surrounding the dining room table and sighing with frustration.

"Why didn't you just trace his couriers?" Bradley asked.

"We did, but we could never find the source. It's as if the drug kingpin is a ghost," Richard answered from the driver's seat. "He never left a trail."

"Hmm." Bradley frowned. There had to be a trail. No one could keep track of so much money coming and going without leaving a trail. "Was there some sort of computer that tracked the incoming cash from all the different slot machines?"

"Yes. That's how the central cash department knew if the amount the collectors brought was off or not. As you can imagine, with such a cash-heavy business, the potential for embezzlement is quite high—"

"Just ask your mother," Richard interrupted with a laugh.

"I did not embezzle any money, Richard. I just took what rightfully belonged to the taxpayers." Harriet sniffed and turned back to Bradley. "Anyway, as I was saying, the cash collectors roll a steel cart around the gambling floor and retrieve the cash from each slot machine. When they bring the cart back to central cash, the manager has a printout from the main computer that tells her which machines have been emptied and how much cash should be in each cart. The money has to be reconciled before the cash collector can go home after his or her shift.

"The books were closed twice a day, at seven A.M. and again at three-thirty P.M. so that I could make bank deposits. Each day, between the time the money left central cash and made it upstairs to my office, El Corazon's agents would come to add their ten percent. It was as if they were sitting outside waiting for the central cash manager to finish her reconciliation so they'd know how much to bring."

"Maybe they were," Bradley said, narrowing his eyes as he thought about the flow of cash.

"We already checked that out," Richard said as he changed lanes to pass a tractor-trailer rig. "There were no phone calls in or out of the cash collection center, and we even put one of our own agents in that position for a time just to be sure. There was no contact with anyone outside about the amount of each day's take."

"Well, no, maybe not quite so overtly," Bradley suggested. "But there are other ways of communicating besides using the telephone."

"We checked everything. Land lines, cell phones, e-mail, Internet connections. We couldn't find a thing."

"Just because you couldn't find it doesn't mean it's not there," Bradley murmured.

"That's what I thought," Harriet agreed. "We must have missed something."

"You wouldn't happen to have a copy of the cash collection program, would you?" Bradley asked.

His mother smiled and pointed to one of the icons on her desktop. "Yes, of course I do. I couldn't figure anything out from looking at it. But, then again, *I* don't have a computer science degree from MIT."

"You have a degree from MIT?" Richard asked, whipping around to look at Bradley. The motor home jerked a bit and a car behind them honked.

"Yeah," Bradley admitted, as if it were something to be ashamed about. "Okay, give me some time and I'll take a look at this."

"It's all yours." Harriet slipped out of the booth and walked up to the passenger seat of the motor home, buckling herself in next to Richard to await their next move.

"They're pulling in to another RV park," Gus Palermo all but groaned.

"Not again. I can't take another night in this motor home. I don't care about El Corazon anymore. I need room service. I need a hot bath. I need to get out of here," Jim whimpered. "We've been cooped up in this thing since Albuquerque. I'm afraid to turn on a light in case it sets off another alarm. I've been peeing at McDonald's for three days. And you snore."

"Pull yourself together," Gus ordered. "I'm tired of hiding out in this thing, too, but we can't let it get to us. We have a job to do. Now, it can't be that complicated. You've seen the sorts of people who inhabit these RV parks—none of them look like brain surgeons. It can't be that hard to get this thing up and running like it should."

"We should have listened to what the rental agent was telling us. That was your fault. You were too impatient."

"Me? I wasn't the only one who wanted to get on the road. As I recall, you weren't listening to the guy's instructions, either."

"All right. Fine. We were both at fault. But I can't stand another night of eating uncooked hot dogs and potato chips. And I desperately need to take a shower. We have to get our stove and water working, at the very minimum." Jim stopped to pay the twenty-five-dollar nightly fee at the RV park's front gate. He took the instruction sheet the gate guard handed him, paying particular attention to the notes about water and electricity. There was no way he was spending another night trapped in the dark shell of their rented motor home. Tonight, he was going to have a hot shower, a hot meal, and enough light so that he wasn't forced to sit in darkness after the sun went down, praying for sleep to come while the campers all around them played music, watched TV, and read by the soft lights in their vehicles.

If those bozos could figure out how to make things work, I can, too, Jim vowed, pulling the Jayco onto a flat slab of concrete and malevolently eyeing the outlet panel next to them.

Chapter 23
Once More, with Feeling

The dingy bar was lit by a few dim track lights that might have been considered trendy a decade ago, but were now too small and too dusty to add much to the décor. The place was filled with heavy wooden tables and vinyl-covered green stools with faux brass tacks. In front of the tiny stage was a hardwood dance floor with darkened scuffs that told a story of happier times long gone. At nine o'clock in the evening—the beginning of prime bar-hopping time—the Little Rock Bar in Little Rock, Arkansas, was half-empty, and the current patrons looked as if they hadn't seen the light of day in quite some time.

Bradley's eyes met Delphine's in the dim light and she smiled halfheartedly. "I'm sure business will pick up as the night wears on."

Bradley looked at her from under the brim of his cowboy hat.

Delphine licked her lips. "Let me just find the manager and tell him you're here."

As Delphine walked away, Bradley sighed, thinking what a waste of time this was. He had hoped he was past having to perform in this sort of place, and the smell of stale beer and urine brought back the bad memories of his early career, when every night had been spent in dives like this.

A group of men—almost boys, really—wearing beat-up cowboy boots, checked Western shirts, and nearly identical worn blue jeans sat at a table near him, pouring themselves frequent drinks from two giant pitchers of beer. A waitress came by and unloaded another two pitchers on the table, pausing to bump one of the guys in the shoulder with her rear.

Great. A room full of music lovers.

"The manager says you can get set up whenever you're ready," Delphine said, patting his arm encouragingly.

"I think this is a mistake."

Delphine kept her smile pasted on her face. "No it isn't. You'll do fine. No, you'll do better than fine. You'll do so great that you'll knock their boots off."

Bradley shook his head, looking around the room. The male-to-female ratio was about twenty-to-one, and the majority of his fans were of the female variety. Seems a number of them were just as attracted to his firm abs as to his voice. He hoped this wasn't the kind of bar where these guys would be checking him out in that way, but, hell, he'd probably be better off if it was. "I'm going to bomb here, Delphine. As a performer, you get a sense about this kind of thing. It's like you can smell the imminent failure in the air. I know this scent. It ain't the first time I've smelled it."

" 'Isn't,' not 'ain't,' " Delphine corrected absently.

"Whatever."

Delphine grabbed his arm and pulled him past the long, scarred bar and into a darkened hallway that ran alongside the stage. She pushed him back into the corner, standing in front of him as if to block his exit—a moot point since there was an emergency exit door right behind him. "I want you to get up there and perform as if this were the Grand Ole Opry. Every performance you make should be like that. You owe it to these people—no, you owe it to yourself—to give it all you've got every single time. Go out there and feel the songs. Stop thinking about all you've sacrificed and all the success you should have and give the audience what they deserve. Give them everything you've got."

Bradley set his guitar case down on the floor, trying not to think about what manner of debris he was exposing it to. "That was a great speech," he said. "Very inspirational. You should tape it. Maybe you could sell it on the Internet."

Delphine frowned and leaned up against the wall. "Okay, so maybe I can't motivate you to pretend this is anything other than what it is. But hey, what else would you be doing tonight? Playing cribbage with your mom and Richard? I got the impression that they were both pretty glad to see us go."

Bradley grinned. "Yeah, it's a good thing Mom got new shocks on the Winnebago last year. I think she and Richard are definitely putting them to the test."

Delphine rolled her eyes. "I don't want to think about it."

"Really? I've been giving it a lot of thought lately."

"What? You've been thinking about your mom and Richard having—"

"Ugh, no." Bradley interrupted. "I didn't mean them. I mean *it*. Sex. I've been giving sex a lot of thought lately. With you," he added, just in case he was being unclear.

Delphine looked down at the floor and swallowed, then looked back up at him. "You have?"

Bradley stepped in front of her and placed his arms on her shoulders. "Yes, I have." He took a step closer, pushing her back against the wall. "I've been thinking about doing this." He kissed the soft skin under her left ear. "And this." He trailed a row of kisses down her neck.

"And what else?" Delphine asked, putting her arms around his waist to draw him closer.

Bradley slipped his hands under her shirt at the back, running his fingers up the taut skin and expecting to find the strap of her bra. "You're not wearing a bra," he groaned into her hair when he encountered no resistance.

"In case you hadn't noticed, I don't really need one," Delphine said dryly.

"I'm a guy. Of course I noticed," Bradley replied just as dryly. He let his fingers slip down to her waist. "And I think you're sized just right."

Delphine giggled—she couldn't help herself—and reached around to cup Bradley's crotch. "I think you're sized just right, too."

Bradley rocked his hips forward, taking full advantage of the contact. "I think I'd much rather give my performance right here. Just for you. I promise to give it everything I've got. What do you say, boss?"

Delphine stroked him, making him go hard. He reached up and cupped the back of her head with one hand, keeping her still while his mouth captured hers.

As if she had any intention of going anywhere.

Even when she heard the *clomp-clomp* of heavy boots coming down the hall, she was tempted to stay just as she was, letting Bradley devour her with his hot mouth on hers, his stomach pressed to hers as she teased him into full arousal. It was Bradley who pulled away first.

With a whispered, "We're gonna finish this later," he stepped back, looking her over with a hot sweep of his eyes.

"You promise?" Delphine asked, tugging at the hem of her blouse to make sure she was decent.

Bradley picked up his guitar case and started up the stairs to the stage. "You can bet on it," she heard him say, just as the bar's manager came into view, obviously coming to see where the night's talent had disappeared to.

He was doing it again.

Delphine squinted up at the darkened stage. Bradley was singing the words to the songs he had chosen, but he wasn't feeling them. He was, she decided, treating this performance as if it were a job. And that was a problem.

Because when he sang as if it were a job and not a passion, nobody cared enough to listen.

She looked around the bar, at all the people whose conversations had only become louder when Bradley started singing. They should have quieted, with every ear focused on the man on stage. If Bradley let that passion out from wherever he had locked it away inside himself, they would all become silent.

She knew it, because she had heard it. That night in Albuquerque. And at the Wild Wild West Show in Vegas. He sang to her and every voice faded away because he was singing from his heart and not his head.

Yesterday, he had lost his confidence as well as his manager, and Delphine knew she had to do whatever she could to help him get it back.

Passion was the key. She had felt it coming off him in waves back in New Mexico. Whenever they had touched, it was as if they were in danger of lighting themselves on fire. But now that explosive heat was gone. Even their encounter in the hallway half an hour ago had been lacking in real passion—at least on his part.

Delphine looked up at the stage, watching as Bradley strummed his guitar with strong, sure fingers. The next song in the set was one he'd told her he'd written himself. Delphine had read the words on the insert of his CD and knew it was a song about that rush you get when you first meet someone you think you could fall in love with. It was a song every person in that bar could relate to.

It was a song *she* related to, because every time Bradley touched her she felt her heart flutter in her chest. She felt her insides go hot and soft and wet, and every nerve in her body seemed to tighten, waiting for the slide of his tongue across her skin or the feel of his mouth on hers.

It was a song meant to be sung with passion and, even knowing she was probably about to make a total ass of herself, she knew she had to do something to make him sing it with all the feeling the words deserved.

Leaving her drink on the bar, she stepped to the edge of

the empty dance floor. As Bradley finished his song to a smattering of applause, Delphine sent up a silent prayer for courage.

"You can do this. Pretend until it becomes true," she told herself.

She felt a sudden calm deep within her as the first notes of the next song rang out in the loud room. Delphine stepped onto the dance floor and stood motionless for several seconds, letting the words wash over her. Then, ignoring the frown she heard in Bradley's voice, she closed her eyes and raised her arms above her head. She felt cool air caressing the naked skin at her waist as her shirt rode up, but she didn't tug it down. Instead, she swayed her hips to the music, running her hand down her arm like a lover's touch.

Someone from the surrounding tables let out a loud wolf whistle and clapped, but Delphine ignored him. She let her hands slide down to her shoulders, then pushed her fingers through the hair at her temples and turned her head as if to receive a passion-filled kiss.

When she turned back toward the stage, she opened her eyes to find Bradley watching her intently. His voice had gone a notch deeper, huskier than before.

He continued to sing, and Delphine kept one hand fisted in her hair while she slid the other down her chest to her stomach, making lazy circles on her abdomen.

Suddenly, she felt someone—a very male someone—touch her from behind. She felt the stranger put his hands on her waist, rubbing his erect self against her hips. Bradley started forward, but Delphine shook her head. She turned around and put her hands on the man's shoulders. He was one of the young-looking cowboys who had been sitting and drinking beer with his friends when she had ventured out onto the dance floor.

Delphine stepped back until the man was at arm's length. Then, with a smile, she pushed him away, turning back to Bradley instead.

And then it happened.

Bradley started singing to her as if he really meant the words. Not just the words of passion, but the words of love, as well. They rang so true and so clear that for just a moment Delphine really believed he meant it.

Then he stopped singing and dropped his guitar, leaping off the stage when the man Delphine had pushed away a moment ago came back for seconds.

Delphine squealed with surprise when she felt the man's hands on her breasts. She had been so focused on Bradley that she hadn't seen the other man coming in time to get out of the way. Unfortunately, he grabbed one of the slim straps of her shirt just as she jerked back to get out of the way of his groping hands.

The shock of air-conditioned air on her bare skin followed the unmistakable sound of fabric ripping.

Right before Bradley tackled him, the other man looked from Delphine's shocked face to the shirt he'd torn off her, and Delphine wasn't sure which of them was more horrified.

Bradley landed on top of the man with a primal roar of fury. Delphine was glad she didn't have any of those pesky notions about nonviolence as she watched Bradley crack the other man's head against the hardwood floor while she kept her breasts covered with her hands.

Whether the younger man had meant to rip her shirt off or not, he obviously needed to be taught a lesson in manners.

Unfortunately, young men in need of etiquette training rarely traveled alone, and this young man was no different. With several battle cries, his friends leaped up to join the fracas.

Delphine yelled a warning and would have laughed at Bradley's loudly muttered, "Oh, shit," if the situation hadn't been so dire.

"Run!" she shouted, grabbing Bradley's guitar off the stage and turning it upside down to shield herself as she dashed past Bradley and headed toward the emergency exit.

She pushed the lever that cautioned that an alarm would sound if she were to open the door, but was met only with silence and a smelly back alley.

Bradley came out of the door just seconds behind her and pointed toward the entrance of the alley. "Get out of here," he ordered, stopping to push on the Dumpster beside the door. Delphine looked down at her naked chest, then back up at Bradley, who had barely budged the trash bin. She set his guitar down on the pavement and went to stand beside him, pushing against the warm metal with all her strength.

The back door came open just as the Dumpster started rolling, and Delphine heard the surprised screeching as the men tried to get back inside before they were squashed between the garbage bin and the wall.

Bradley turned and tugged off his T-shirt. "Put this on and follow me. Fast," he added. Then he stooped down, picked up his guitar, and took off toward the entrance of the alley.

Delphine hit the pavement beside Bradley, tugging his T-shirt on as she ran. It was warm and way too big for her, but it smelled like him and Delphine found herself breathing in his scent as she ran.

They made it to the entrance of the alley and headed away from the bar. Bradley grabbed her hand, as if that would help her run faster, and said, "They're gonna come around the front in four, three, two—"

The pack of young men burst from the bar and out into the warm night as if on cue.

Bradley cursed as if he hadn't expected to see them.

Delphine closed her eyes momentarily, trying to recall the buildings they had passed on their way to the bar. She opened her eyes again and pulled Bradley behind her across the street.

"Come on," she said, feeling him hesitate. "I know just where to go."

She ran down Broadway, feeling a stitch begin in her side

at about Tenth Street. Only two more blocks, she told herself, still tugging on Bradley's hand. She looked back to see how close their pursuers were, gasping to see that they'd closed the gap to less than half a block.

"Hurry," she urged. "We're dead if they catch us."

Chapter 24

You Can Leave Your Hat On

"Your son is a genius," Richard said, shaking his head with disbelief as he hung up his cell phone.

Harriet snuggled next to him in the big pink bed. "He gets it from me."

Richard laughed and kissed the top of her head. "Is that where he gets his modesty from, too?"

"I always found modesty to be overrated."

Thank God, Richard thought, looking down at the naked curve of Harriet's back. No, she wasn't stick thin like some starving supermodel, but she had smooth skin and the healthy glow of a woman who took care of herself. She was also, he had found, unashamedly sexual—whether from pent-up demand or otherwise, he was afraid to ask. Right now, he was too delighted with being the object of a woman's uncontrolled desire to question much of anything.

"So, what has my son done to garner your adulation?" Harriet asked, running her fingers lightly up and down his bare thigh, making it difficult for Richard to concentrate.

"He may have led us to El Corazon."

"Umm. And how did he do that?" Harriet all but purred.

Richard groaned and put his hand on top of hers to stop her teasing fingers. "If you don't stop that, I won't be able to form a coherent sentence. Now, do you want to know what Bradley discovered or not?"

Harriet gave him a sultry smile that told him she knew exactly how she was affecting him. Like a satisfied cat, she slipped out of bed and stretched her arms above her head with a yawn. Then, slowly, she slid her silk floral robe over her shoulders, hiding her creamy tanned skin from view. She turned at the doorway to look back at him and said, "Well, if all you want to do is talk, I might as well make us something to eat."

At that, Richard jumped out of bed, tugging his pants on as he hurried from the room. "No, no. Let me do it," he said, afraid of what he might be expected to ingest if he left it up to her.

Richard pulled a carton of eggs out of the fridge along with a bag of fresh spinach, a tomato, and some Swiss cheese. He'd insisted that they stop at the market earlier that day to stock up on food. Harriet was out of the basics like flour and milk, besides having virtually nothing healthy in her pantry. Richard set the food on the counter and went in search of a frying pan. As he whisked half a dozen eggs together for a perfect, made-for-two omelet, he turned back to Harriet, who was looking at him with such satisfaction that Richard knew he'd been had.

Ah well, nothing wrong with being had by an attractive woman.

He scooped a bit of butter out of the butter dish and let it melt around the bottom of his pan. Then he poured the egg mixture into the skillet and turned the heat to medium to let the eggs set.

"Bradley discovered that the cash collection program was sending coded messages to another computer outside the casino just as the collection manager closed the books. That's how El Corazon knew how much money to send over."

"How would this help you discover the drug kingpin's identity?" Harriet asked, pulling a chilled bottle of wine from the fridge. "Nothing like a romantic supper in bed," she said with a wink.

Richard turned the heat up to medium high. "Every computer is uniquely identified by something called an IP address. Bradley found the IP address of El Corazon's computer embedded in our cash collection program. With that information, our agents can go to the Internet service providers like AOL or Earthlink to see if they provide e-mail or Internet access to the computer with that IP address. If they do, we can get the billing information for that account, including name, address, and credit card number. It's just a matter of time before we catch this guy."

"That's great," Harriet said, pouring white wine into two glasses. When Richard turned his back to her in order to slice the tomato for their omelet, Harriet came up behind him, slid her arms around his waist, and pressed her hips to his. She let her hands glide lower until she was caressing his hardening penis. "I always love it when the good guys get their man."

Richard closed his eyes and let pleasurable sensation wash over him. "Yeah, me too," he murmured, turning the burner off as he let Harriet get her man.

Delphine pulled Bradley through the entrance of the cemetery they'd passed on their way through town earlier that day and let go of his hand.

"Hide," she ordered, taking off across the neatly manicured lawn.

The gang of youths burst through the entrance just a few short moments after Bradley and Delphine. When Delphine heard their shouts, she knew she had to stop running or she'd be caught. The moon peeked in and out of the fast-moving clouds, shining on and off like a strobe light. She crouched behind a concrete cross and plotted her next move, knowing she'd be visible the next time the clouds moved away.

Off to her right was a statue of a naked man, à la
Michelangelo's David. When the group of young men turned
their backs on her for a moment, she ran behind the statue,
clutching the warm marble for support as she tried to stay
hidden behind it.

It took her a moment to realize that she was grabbing the
statue's ass, but in hindsight, she realized it probably didn't
matter. Statues didn't sue for sexual harassment.

She remained motionless behind the David lookalike,
peering out between his waist and his forearm to keep an
eye on the group of young men as they fanned out among
the crypts and raised tombstones looking for her and Bradley.
When the clouds parted momentarily, Delphine scrunched
her eyes closed and buried her nose in the small of David's
back, hoping she'd go unnoticed. She heard the men's
voices coming closer and knew that if the clouds didn't
come back, she'd be discovered.

The sound of the voices came closer. And closer.

Delphine was just putting her weight on the balls of her
feet, getting ready to run, when the clouds whisked the night
back into darkness.

The men passed by the statue, not ten feet from her. As
they came into view, she hugged the statue's waist and slipped
around to David's front, trying to ignore the huge bulge that
was now pressed into her chest. She couldn't resist running
her hands up the statue's abs.

Not bad, she thought, realizing with a start that her dance
for Bradley earlier that evening seemed to have awakened a
sexual need in her that was making her blood run hot in her
veins. She stood looking up at the statue's taut muscles and
firm thighs and realized that she was turned on. Whether
from the adrenaline of being chased, or the way Bradley had
leaped on the younger man to protect her from harm, or the
feel of the hard naked statue that reminded her what it felt
like to touch a man, she wanted sex, she wanted it from
Bradley, and she wanted it now.

Delphine almost groaned with frustration as the young men's voices started to fade away.

Get out of here, she wanted to scream, but forced herself to remain silent.

After what seemed like hours, she finally heard nothing but the rustling of the wind in the trees. She closed her eyes, pressing her cheek against David's stomach.

"Delphine? What are you doing?" Bradley whispered from behind her.

Delphine swallowed and tried to take the edge off her desire, afraid that she'd scare Bradley away with the force of it. She opened her eyes and turned to him.

He blinked at her and stood still in the darkness, his bare chest rising and falling with each breath he took.

She knew then that she had to finish what she had started on that dance floor. This was her chance to show him that she wasn't afraid to expose herself to rejection. She had told him earlier to give everything of himself to his audience and she was going to do the same.

Delphine took a deep breath, trying to remember the words of the song Bradley had sung earlier. She fixed the melody in her head, the rhythm that had her hips swaying in time to the silent music.

With one hand, she grabbed the hem of the T-shirt Bradley had tossed at her earlier. Slowly, revealing her skin inch by inch, she lifted the material until it slid off her head. She shook out her hair and hung the shirt by its neck on one of David's fingers.

Delphine lifted her hands to her breasts, closing her eyes and tilting her head back as she touched herself. She slid her palms lower, down over her stomach, stopping at the button at the waistband of her jeans. Her hips gyrated in slow motion to the silent music as she eased her zipper down with one hand, leaning her head back on the statue's abdomen and sliding her other hand up its chest as she did so.

Bradley let his guitar slide soundlessly to the ground.

He had never . . . ever . . . in his entire life . . . seen anything as sexy as Delphine stripping for him in the moonlight.

She slipped off one sandal and then the other, hanging them by the straps on another of the statue's fingers.

Then she turned her back to Bradley, sliding her jeans down her hips one infinitesimal centimeter at a time. Bradley couldn't take it anymore. He couldn't stand here one second longer without touching her.

"Stop," he groaned.

Delphine whipped around to face him, her cheeks flaming with embarrassment. Her hands came up to cover her naked breasts, which suddenly seemed laughably small and inadequate. God, she felt like such an idiot.

Bradley took a step closer, pinning her against his warm body and the hard length of the statue. He buried his hands in her hair, holding her mouth in place while he ravaged her with his lips.

"I can't wait. My God, Delphine, I'm sorry. I . . . you . . . please tell me you don't want me to wait," he moaned against her neck.

Delphine let her hands fall from her breasts, running them up and down Bradley's firm back instead. She laughed, still a bit self-conscious. "If you stop now, I'd have to hunt you down and kill you," she said.

Bradley didn't waste time laughing. He got down on his knees in the grass and lifted his hands up to grasp the waistband of her jeans. "You are so sexy. Do that dance for me again," he begged.

Delphine delighted at the sight of his strong, tan fingers against the softer, whiter skin at her waist. She closed her eyes again, trying to get the music back. Then, she said softly, "Sing to me, Bradley. I want to hear that song you were singing back in the bar."

He started singing and the words washed over her until Delphine felt as if he had written the song just for her. Unconsciously, her hips swayed to the beat as she buried her hands in his thick, dark hair. She pushed his cowboy hat off his head, reveling in the sensation of his silky hair beneath her fingers.

Bradley slipped Delphine's jeans off slowly, slowly, watching as first her silky lavender panties came into view, then her soft thighs, her knees, her strong calves. He lifted her left foot, holding it gently as he helped her step out of her jeans, then did the same with her right. She had narrow feet, her toenails painted a surprisingly demure pink, and Bradley was tempted to kiss each toe in turn. Instead, he turned his attention to her stomach as the words of his song died away.

Delphine kept swaying to the beat of the song, her hips moving back and forth.

Bradley slid his hands down the outsides of her thighs, stopping to caress the soft skin behind her knees. Then he slid his fingers slowly up the inside of her thighs, higher and higher as she kept moving to the silent music, her hips pulsing toward his searching fingers.

When Bradley looked up, he saw that Delphine was watching him with heavy-lidded eyes.

He slipped his fingers inside her panties, rubbing her until she groaned.

But this time, it wasn't enough. He wanted her closer, more intimately joined to him.

He slid her panties down her legs, helping her to step out of them. Then he pulled her toward him, his tongue seeking her desire-engorged center. Delphine moaned when he touched her, sucked her inside his mouth. Bradley brought her to the edge and then pulled back, watching her throw her head back and push against him with frustrated desire.

Bradley laughed huskily, knowing that she both wanted him to end it and didn't want him to, at the same time.

Then she took him by surprise, pushing his shoulders until he toppled backward. Before he could gather his wits, she had his pants unzipped and had freed his erection, taking him in her mouth with greedy abandon.

"No," he said, trying to pull away. "Don't, Delphine. I can't last if you do that."

She let him slide slowly into her mouth, teasing the tip of his erection with her tongue as he slid out again. Then she pushed his pants down his hips, slipping them off his legs. She straddled his hips, and Bradley could feel himself pushing against her hot, wet opening. "Condom," he ground out, having a hard time thinking of anything besides the sight of Delphine naked in the moonlight.

"I'm safe," Delphine said, which Bradley took to mean that she was both disease-free and on birth control.

"Me, too," he groaned. Then he stopped thinking altogether and let emotion take over.

The grass tickled at his back as warm wind washed over them. Bradley raised his hands to touch Delphine's cheeks, to bring her soft mouth down to his. His tongue touched hers at the same moment she opened herself to him. She teased the sensitive tip of his penis, letting him slide in and out of her. When he tried to push farther into her, she laughed and scooted up his stomach, taunting him with the power she held over him.

Bradley knew he could stop her at any time. He could put his hands on her sexy derriere and hold her in place while he buried himself in her. But this torture was too exquisite to stop, no matter how much her teasing made him want to howl with frustration.

Delphine sucked his tongue into her mouth and slid back down on his erection with a satisfied "mmm" of pleasure.

Bradley pushed against her, loving the feel of her stomach against his, of their sweat-slicked bodies sliding over each other. He ran his hands lightly down Delphine's back, his fingers tracing circles in the dimples where her back and buttocks met. When she raised her head to look at him, Bradley smoothed Delphine's hair behind her ears. "I want all of you," he murmured, looking into her passion-glazed blue eyes.

She kept her gaze locked with his as she took him in, her eyelids lowering with desire. Bradley could feel her muscles tightening against him, holding him in.

He rocked his hips backward, and she moaned with pleasure as the friction between their bodies fed her desire. She tried to scoot down and recapture him, but Bradley stopped her with his hands at her waist. He was about to explode.

He pushed back into her with one tiny stroke.

And then pulled out again.

She nearly sobbed with frustration.

Bradley did it again. And then again. She was writhing against him now, and he groaned with the effort of holding himself back.

He pushed into her, harder and faster, and she started to moan, her head back, her long hair tickling his fingers as he held on to her hips and drove himself into her and out again.

As he felt the waves of her orgasm crashing against him from inside her body, Bradley let himself go, groaning her name with the force of his release.

And then there was silence.

Complete and utter silence, as if they had captured all of the forces of the night within themselves with the power of their lovemaking. Delphine collapsed on top of him and Bradley lay staring up at the darkened night sky, stroking her naked back while they both attempted to recover the use of their limbs.

Chapter 25
Believe Me

"I can't believe we had sex in a graveyard," Bradley said, picking his hat up off the ground near the statue's feet.

"Me, neither," Delphine said as she tugged up the zipper on her jeans and retrieved her sandals from David's grasp. "I've never done *that* before."

"You haven't, huh?"

Delphine rolled her eyes skyward at the self-satisfied tone of Bradley's voice. "Have you?"

He grinned at her. "Naw. It was great, though, wasn't it?"

Delphine laughed. "Yes, it was."

They left the cemetery and walked in silence toward the RV park, about fifteen minutes away. As they stopped at the front door of the darkened motor home, Bradley put out a hand to stop Delphine. Absently, she noticed that the RV next to them had every light burning, and she wondered if the owners had gone out and forgotten to turn out their lights. Then she shrugged. As long as they were hooked in to the RV park's electrical system, it didn't matter. If not, well, they were sure to have a dead battery the next morning. But surely they wouldn't be so foolish as to drain their own system? Besides, it wasn't any of her business, she thought as Bradley leaned his guitar up against the side of the RV and then turned to cup her cheek. "You know, Delphine, I think you're pretty special. You've been a real trouper about this whole mess with my mother, not to mention how great you've been at using your management experience to help my career."

Delphine felt her heart plummet at his words. Was this all he thought was special about her? That she was a "trouper" and helpful in his career? Those were not exactly words that made her heart go pitty-pat.

Then he bent down to kiss her, his lips warm and tender against hers. He put his arms around her waist and pulled her to him, softly dancing with her in the quiet moonlit night. When he raised his head, Delphine sighed and rested her cheek against his bare chest.

"Besides all that," he continued, swaying with her in the darkness, "I think you're smart and sexy as hell. Hell," he joked, "if you didn't hate country music, I might just fall in love with you."

Delphine tripped over his booted foot, nearly twisting her ankle when her foot came out of her sandal.

Bradley kept a hand on her arm, helping to steady her. "Are you okay?" he asked.

Delphine cleared her throat. "Um, yes, I'm fine. I guess I'm just a bit tired. Maybe we should call it a night?"

Bradley let her go. "Yeah, I guess we should go in. We've got an early morning. I'd like to make it to Nashville the day after tomorrow and we've got a stop to make along the way."

Delphine barely heard Bradley's words. She was still so stunned by his earlier comment about falling in love with her that she could hardly think about anything else. Why had he said that? Had he guessed that she had fallen for him? Wouldn't that be embarrassing?

She closed her eyes, lifting her face to the pale moonlight.

She would give anything—anything she could—if only the words he had spoken were true.

• • •

"Hurry up, they're leaving," Gus said, pounding on the bathroom door and raising his voice to be heard over the running water of the shower.

"Can't you drive this thing?" Jim yelled back.

Gus blinked. "Yeah, of course I can. But . . . but you're in the shower. Is it safe to drive it if you're not buckled in?"

Jim stuck his head outside, shampoo dripping off his head and onto the carpet. "Of course it's safe. That's the beauty of these things. The only person who has to be seated is the driver. Of course, try telling that to the idiot who sued an RV manufacturer because he put the cruise control on at seventy miles per hour on the freeway and went back to make himself a pot of coffee."

Gus snorted. "Dumbass."

"No kidding. So, get going. I'll be out of the shower in a few minutes."

"Okay," Gus said, hurrying to the front of the RV as Harriet's Winnebago disappeared out the exit of the park.

He turned the key in the ignition, expecting to hear the engine purr to life.

Instead, it just made a *rrr* sound and the lights inside the Jayco flickered. Then the lights went off. And then the shower stopped.

Gus cursed and hit the steering wheel with his palms. Couldn't anything go right on this trip?

Jim stuck his head out of the bathroom again. "What the hell is wrong? Why did the water stop?"

"How the hell should I know? What did you do to kill the battery?"

Jim frowned. "I didn't do anything. All I did was play around with that panel over there to get the water to turn on." He waved toward a panel of knobs and switches near the refrigerator.

"Well, now the battery's dead. I hope you're happy. I don't know why you had to have *another* fucking shower this morning. You took two last night already."

Jim stepped outside the bathroom, pushing his soapy hair out of his eyes as he stalked toward Gus. "Listen, I've had just about enough of your accusations and your bad temper. This hasn't exactly been a picnic for me, either. All I want is to get whatever pictures or evidence it is that El Corazon is looking for us to provide and get back to Reno. Can I help it if I don't know anything about this camping crap? I mean, it's not exactly your forte, either."

"Fine. I'll take care of this. I just hope that Dickie and Harriet will do something soon that we can get on film. Those two haven't come out of that damn Winnebago except to fuel up and get groceries since we started following them in New Mexico. I'll be damned if I'm going to spend the rest of my life trailing those two stiffs around the country."

"I agree. Now, if you'll call the gate guard, I'm sure he knows what we can do about fixing our battery. I'll bet that our pair will be getting right back on I-40 and heading east, just like they've been doing for days. They're nothing if not predictable."

"You're right about that," Gus said, turning in the driver's seat but not venturing back to get his cell phone, which was lying on the dining table. He waited for a moment, getting more uncomfortable as the seconds ticked by.

"Well, aren't you going to call the gate guard?" Jim finally asked.

Gus felt his face start to burn as he glanced from the windshield to the rear of the motor home and back. "Yeah, as soon as you get out of sight," he said.

Jim looked down at himself then, as if just now realizing that he was standing in the living room, completely naked. He raised his eyebrows at Gus. "What? You've never seen a naked man before?"

"Of course I have," Gus answered defensively. "I've seen plenty of naked guys. I'm just not used to having long conversations with them."

After what seemed an eternity, Jim finally turned back toward the bathroom and Gus could almost have sworn he heard the other man mutter, "Homophobe," as the bathroom door closed behind him.

Bradley grinned to himself as he spied the exit up ahead.

Poplar Bluff. Delphine's hometown.

He couldn't wait to see if it was as charming and quaint as she had made it out to be. He also couldn't wait to see the look on Delphine's face when she found out that he'd made a special detour so she could visit her sisters. He'd been surprised that she hadn't asked if they could stop—after all, it was only forty minutes out of their way and she said she hadn't been home in quite some time. He figured she was just too worried about inconveniencing them to ask, but they still had two days to get to Nashville in time for the awards show.

He hoped she'd missed seeing him take the turnoff. She had her nose buried so far in her music business books, Bradley doubted she'd notice much of anything right now. Hell, he could probably strip naked and dance in front of her and she wouldn't notice, he thought, glancing over at the woman sitting in the passenger seat of the motor home.

She had the seat reclined back as far as it would go, her long legs stretched out and her bare feet resting on the dashboard. The book she was reading was propped up on her chest, right below her breasts. Her hair spilled over the back of her chair, a blondish-brown curtain that was almost long enough for the ends to touch the carpet.

Bradley remembered her hair tickling his chest last night when they'd made love on the cool grass and he shook his head in wonderment.

She was some kind of woman.

Sexy as hell. Decidedly not shy about her body, but not flaunting herself at every guy around, either. Funny. Smart. Loyal. And she believed in him so much that she was willing to use her time, expertise, and contacts to help him in his career. Even when he'd hit rock bottom, she hadn't given up on him.

He looked over and frowned as she turned another page in her book, struck by a shocking thought.

Delphine was everything he'd ever wanted in a woman.

The revelation didn't seem to trouble him. Which was odd, since he couldn't settle down and be a good husband now. He refused to do what his own father had done and let his wife support him. He'd seen how that could destroy a marriage, and he wasn't about to let history repeat itself. But maybe . . . maybe if Delphine could stick it out with him for a while and not expect too much, they might have a chance to make a go of it someday.

Feeling oddly calm inside, Bradley turned his attention back to the road.

He'd never expected that falling in love would be so peaceful.

"Delphine, would you mind switching seats with me? I have something I need to talk to Bradley about." Richard Swanson's deep voice sliced through Bradley's sense of calm. Not that he felt any animosity toward the man his mother was so obviously attracted to, but there was something edgy about the other man, as if he knew things about people that others didn't see. For some reason, it made Bradley nervous to be around him.

But he hid it well, pasting a friendly smile on his face as Delphine got up and walked to the couch, barely looking up from her book. "What can I do for you, Richard?" Bradley asked.

Richard pulled the lever on the passenger seat to bring the seat back up to a normal level. He clipped the seatbelt into place before answering. "My boss was really impressed with your computer skills and how you discovered the electronic messaging imbedded in the casino's accounting system."

"Uh, thanks."

"As a matter of fact," Richard continued, as if Bradley hadn't spoken, "he's so grateful, he wanted me to offer you a job. You could start in two weeks. You'd have full benefits, of course. And the pay's pretty good." He named a salary that was more money than Bradley had earned from his singing in the entire decade since he'd graduated from college. "You'd be stationed in Albuquerque initially, but we have offices all over the country. If you decided you wanted to move in a few years, there are opportunities everywhere for people with your skills."

Bradley didn't know what to say. He was more stunned by this job opportunity that had landed right in his lap than the revelation that he had fallen in love with Delphine.

Then it hit him.

He had fallen in love with Delphine, but he couldn't do anything about it because his career as a singer was going nowhere. He had committed everything to it for ten long years, only he couldn't make a go of it. And now, because of the computer skills that had always come so easily to him, he was being given the chance to start over again and make something of himself.

On the salary Richard had quoted, Bradley could marry Delphine. They could buy a house. Start a family. Live a real life—not the nomadic existence he'd had since college, but something more permanent.

Bradley tipped his cowboy hat back on his head and looked out the window at the passing trees. Absently, he noticed that as they made their way out of the Midwest and headed toward Tennessee, the landscape was becoming greener, more lush than it had been since they left Reno.

Was he ready to surrender his dream? Had he given it enough time? Enough effort?

He remembered visiting his father shortly after he'd moved out on his own. He'd been angry and bitter about not achieving stardom after all he felt he'd sacrificed for it. Would Bradley feel the same if he gave up now? Would he forever look at successful musicians and say, "That could have been me, if only I had kept trying"? Or would he be satisfied in his new life, happy with the security and the family he could have with a regular job?

"You don't have to decide right now," Richard said, interrupting Bradley's thoughts. "But it is a good job for someone with your talents. I know it would be hard to give up on the music business, but as I told your mom a while back, sometimes the easy thing to do is also the right thing. Think about it."

Bradley nodded and watched as a green sign flashed past. POPLAR BLUFF, 5 MILES.

In five minutes, Delphine would be home.

But would Bradley be any closer to making a decision on what to do with the rest of his life?

He shook his head and sighed. Truth be told, he wasn't sure he knew exactly what he wanted anymore.

"Poplar Bluff? Why the hell are they going there? The place is hardly big enough to warrant its own dot on the map," Jim grumbled as he turned the Jayco down the same two-lane road Bradley had taken just a few minutes ago. Since the gate guard back in Little Rock had been speedy with a set of jumper cables and a battery charger, it hadn't taken much effort for them to catch up with the Winnebago. Apparently, they weren't the only campers who had ever run down their batteries and needed assistance.

"I dunno, but maybe we can finally get Dickie and Harriet to come out of that damn vehicle. What the hell have those two been doin' cooped up in there for days?" Gus wondered aloud.

Jim shot him a look that told him exactly what he thought the couple had been doing, and it was what Gus suspected, too.

"If they don't come out tonight, we're breaking in," Jim said. "I'm sick of driving this damn motor home across the country following these two like I was one of El Corazon's minions. I don't work for that asshole, and if it were up to me, I'd kill them all while they slept. As a matter of fact, I just might do that. What's El Corazon going to do? Kill me?"

Gus frowned. "That's exactly what he'll do to you. And to me, too. I ain't doin' nothing more than what we were told to do, and that was to follow Dickie and get pictures of what he was doing on this road trip. I got a wife and three kids back in Reno and I ain't gonna get killed because you want to think that El Corazon don't run our lives already. That asshole could ruin us if he wanted and you're stupid if you don't know that. These drug lords have more money than we do, and they aren't concerned about being seen as legitimate businessmen. They don't care who they have to buy off, or who they have to kill to get what they want. You may think you can take out Dickie anytime you want, but if you do, El Corazon will kill you and your little boyfriends—"

Jim shot him a shocked look.

"What? You think we don't all know you're gay?" Gus snorted. "I have files on all of you, and you can bet El Corazon does, too. You're gay and Dickie's so damn celibate I figured he couldn't get it up. And me? I cheat on my wife with any of the cocktail waitresses who'll have me. I'm not gonna risk my way of life so you can feel like a big shot. We'll drive this fucking motor home all the way to fucking Alaska if we have to, and we'll do exactly what El Corazon tells us to do. You got it?"

Jim's expression had changed from shock to admiration to resignation in the space of a few seconds. "Yeah, I got it," he grumbled.

"Good. Now follow that Winnebago," Gus ordered, unbuckling his seatbelt to go back to the fridge and get himself a beer. He was sick and tired of all this—

Shit.

Why was the carpet all wet?

Gus looked around to see if he could spot the problem but didn't see anything. Then he opened the bathroom door and a wave of water about three feet high came rushing out, soaking his pant legs.

"What the hell did you do back here?" he yelled.

Startled, Jim jerked on the steering wheel and the Jayco veered into the left-hand lane. Brakes squealed and horns honked as the oncoming traffic tried to get out of their way. Jim wrestled the RV back into his own lane, and then groaned when he saw the flashing lights in his side mirror.

Of all the rotten luck.

"I didn't do anything back there," he said, looking for a place to ease the motor home over to the side of the road. At least not on purpose, he added silently.

"You must have left the water valve on when the battery died. Then, when we got it recharged, the pump must have started working again," Gus accused.

"Well, I'm sorry. I didn't hear the water running over the sound of the engine. Obviously, neither did you. Now get up here and get buckled in while I take care of this police officer."

"What police officer?" Gus asked, slamming the bathroom door closed just in time to see the unmistakable flash of strobe lights behind them. He laid his head against the imitation-oak-paneled wall of the hallway. "Why is this happening to me?" he groaned into the paneling.

"Stop whining and come sit down," Jim said peevishly. "You're not the only one who's miserable here, you know."

"WELCOME TO POPLAR BLUFF'S PRESIDENTIAL DAYS CELEBRATION," a banner strung across two streetlights proclaimed.

Bradley winced as the Winnebago approached, worried that the banner might snag on the satellite dish his mother had mounted on the roof. He ducked in the driver's seat, as if that would make a difference, and then cringed when he looked first in the left side-view mirror and then in the right to see that his fears had been founded.

The Presidential Days banner trailed down the road behind them while people on the sidewalks gasped and pointed.

"Damn," Bradley cursed, looking for someplace to ease the motor home to the side of the road.

"What's wrong, dear?" his mother asked from her seat at the dining room table.

"We caught a banner with your satellite dish," Bradley answered.

"Pardon me?"

Bradley shook his head. "Never mind. I'll take care of it."

He saw a bank up ahead and pulled the unwieldy vehicle into the crowded parking lot. "Could you give me a hand?" he asked Delphine, who was still lying on the couch with her book. Richard had disappeared some time ago into the back bedroom and Bradley didn't want to disturb him if the older man was taking a nap or busy with something else. Besides, now that they were here, Bradley couldn't wait to see the look on Delphine's face when she realized they'd stopped in her hometown.

Delphine laid the book she'd been reading on the coffee table and stretched out her arms. "Sure, just let me get my shoes on," she said, after indulging in a giant yawn.

She slipped her Keds on over her bare feet, not bothering to put on socks or untie the shoelaces. Bradley held the door for her, holding back a grin as Delphine stepped out into the sunshine.

"What do you want me to do?" Delphine asked once she was outside, raising a hand to shield her eyes from the glare of the sun.

Bradley waited for her to do something—squeal with excitement, jump up and down and scream, or, his favorite choice, throw her arms around his neck and kiss him— anything to show that she was happy to be home. Instead, she just stood in the parking lot, looking up at him with a slight smile on her face.

It was as if she didn't even know where they were.

Bradley frowned. "Delphine, don't you notice something odd?"

Delphine lowered her hand and shook her head. Then she looked around. They were parked in front of a neat redbrick bank with white columns flanking the entrance. The parking lot was crowded with cars, but nobody gave them so much as a dirty look for taking up two spaces with their larger vehicle. Some sort of street fair was going on, with crowds of people walking by on the sidewalk. A vendor was giving away free hot dogs, and the smell of cooking food made Delphine's stomach grumble.

Across the street was a strip mall of the sort that had been around for decades. A two-story department store was flanked by a furniture store on one side and a row of smaller shops on the other. The names of the businesses were painted on the windows with white paint. Delphine looked farther down the street. A gas station. The ubiquitous 7-Eleven. A grocery store with balloons tied on every lamppost and a multicolored circus tent taking up one corner of the lot. A Greyhound bus station.

Still, none of this was so out of the ordinary as to make Bradley look at her as if she were missing something critical. Delphine looked around the parking lot again, feeling as if she were about to fail some sort of test.

And then she saw it.

A trail of fabric stretching out behind the Winnebago like a length of toilet paper caught on a woman's high-heeled shoe.

Delphine laughed. *That* must be what Bradley was talking about. "Oh, it looks like we snagged something."

Bradley gave her a strange look but didn't say anything, so Delphine walked around to the back of the RV and looked to see if she could see anything else out of place. She couldn't, so she just shrugged at Bradley's strange behavior and started up the ladder attached to the back of the Winnebago.

She got to the top of the roof and braced her feet on either side of the ladder. The metal roof was hot from having the sun beat down on it all morning, so Delphine did her best to lean over without touching it and having it burn her legs.

Bradley came around the back of the motor home and saw Delphine on the top of the ladder, reaching out to loosen the banner from where it was wrapped around the satellite dish. She was wearing her denim shorts today, and from where she was standing, he could see all the way up her long legs. She'd snagged one of his T-shirts again—this one from a Toby Keith concert he'd attended a few years ago. The slogan "How do you like me now?" was emblazoned across her back, and Bradley had to stay focused on his own puzzlement or he'd be tempted to climb up on that ladder and show Delphine just how much he liked her right now.

He cleared his throat.

"Why don't you climb down? I can get that."

Delphine looked down at him and grinned. "What? You think I'm too weak and helpless to do it?"

Bradley rolled his eyes heavenward. "Honey, I think you're about as weak and helpless as a fox in a henhouse."

Delphine squinted down at him. "I'm not up on my country sayings. Is that a compliment?"

Bradley laughed. "To tell the truth, I'm not sure. But I don't think you're the least bit helpless. I just wasn't sure you could get that banner without burning yourself."

"Well, that's very nice of you," Delphine said, tossing the banner in question down from the roof. "But I think I can manage."

She backed down the ladder and Bradley trapped her at the bottom with his arms on either side of the rails. "So, come on," he said. "Are you just teasing me? I can't believe you haven't said anything about where we are."

Delphine looked around, still baffled by his questions. "Well, where are we?" she asked, genuinely puzzled.

Bradley narrowed his eyes at her. Then he let go of the rails and kicked the edge of the banner out so she could read the words. "We're in Poplar Bluff. Your hometown. I thought you'd be surprised."

Delphine stood in the hot parking lot, looking down at the banner for a long, silent moment. Then she looked up at Bradley with a smile spreading across her face. "Oh, this is wonderful. I haven't been back in so long, I didn't recognize the place. Why, this whole block is completely different than when I left. My gosh. Who would believe that I didn't even know my own hometown?"

Chapter 26

Time for the Truth

"Bradley, are you sure we have time for this? I mean, we've got to be in Nashville the day after tomorrow."

"We'll be there in plenty of time for the Country Music Awards. Besides, I thought you'd be thrilled to see your sisters. I'm sorry I didn't call them, but I didn't have any of their names and I didn't want to spoil the surprise by asking. You are happy to be home, aren't you?"

Delphine didn't look at him as they walked down the quiet, tree-lined street. "I am. It's just . . . they didn't know I was coming and they might not even be home."

"Where would they be?" Bradley asked with a frown. "It's the weekend. Surely *someone* will be home."

"Yes, yes, of course. It's just that they might be at the fair. Or on vacation. They all take vacations together, you know. It's great. All the kids hang out together, going river-rafting or making forts. The adults stay up late and play cards. Everybody has a great time."

"Why don't you join them?" Bradley asked, reaching out to take her hand.

"Oh, I do. We go somewhere new almost every year. One time we rented houses on the beach in North Carolina. It was so beautiful there. Last year, we went to the Gulf Coast of Alabama. Did you know they call that the Redneck

Riviera? I just couldn't go this year because of my job."
Delphine laughed nervously. "I guess I shouldn't have let
that worry me."

Bradley pulled her to a stop on the sidewalk and Delphine
looked just beyond his shoulder at the neat row of houses on
the other side of the street. The lawns had gone brown in the
relentless heat of summer, but they were mostly kept trimmed
down to a respectable height. There was one house on the
block whose front yard was spotted with weeds and crab-
grass and Delphine wondered why there was always one
house like that on every street, a place that showed obvious
signs of neglect—a shingle or two missing from the roof, a
floorboard cracked on the porch, rusted toys lying abandoned in the too-tall grass.

"Delphine, something is wrong," Bradley said.

"Oh?" she asked, feeling an almost overwhelming sadness as she looked at the chipped paint of the house across
the street.

"I can feel it. Something is wrong here, but I don't know
what it is."

Delphine shook her head and said brightly, "Nothing's
wrong, Bradley. I don't know what you're talking about."

"Where do your sisters live?" he asked. Then, without
warning, he reached up and covered her eyes. "Give me their
addresses."

"They all live on the same street," Delphine answered,
her voice taking on a dreamy quality. "It's so nice because
when one of them runs out of something like sugar or eggs
or diapers, they just send one of the kids across the street to
get what they need. Do you know what that's like, Bradley?
To have everything you want so close?"

"What are their addresses, Delphine?" Bradley asked
again, feeling as if a fist were clenching his heart.

"They all get together for dinner sometimes, too. It's not
a formal thing at all. It's like one night someone will decide
to barbecue so they'll send out the word that everyone

should come over. My oldest sister—she's the town's dentist, you know—well, she has a swimming pool in her backyard. Not one of those plastic kinds, but one of the real ones that are buried in the ground. Most of the time, everyone meets up at her house. The kids all love to swim and she has the biggest kitchen. My little sister is the best cook of the bunch, though. She always brings over the best desserts. One time she made a banana cream pie with a filling that was the richest caramel you've ever tasted. I could only eat one piece because it was so rich, but it was the best pie I've ever eaten."

Bradley slowly lowered his hand, his eyes not leaving her face. "What are your sisters' names, Delphine? When were they born? Where did they go to college? What are their children's names and how old are they?"

Delphine smiled at him, but her eyes were bright with unshed tears. "I don't know, Bradley. Nobody's ever asked me before."

Bradley dropped her hand and took a step back on the hot sidewalk. "You've never been here before, have you?"

Two tears dripped down Delphine's cheeks when she blinked. "No."

"You didn't skin your knee when you lost control of your bike back there near the ditch?"

Delphine rubbed her suddenly chilled arms and shook her head.

"And you didn't break your arm when you fell from that tree over there?" He pointed to one of the trees that lined the street.

She shook her head again.

"And you didn't go to Sunday school at that church we just passed. And your best friend from kindergarten doesn't still live in the cute little blue and white house down the road. And you didn't go to your high school prom with your older sister's best friend's brother who lives on the other side of town."

Delphine remained silent, the tears running down her face giving him all the answers he needed.

"It was all a lie. I trusted you and you lied."

Delphine closed her eyes and nodded, the ends of her soft hair brushing against her chin.

"What else have you told me that wasn't the truth?" Bradley's eyes narrowed when the full force of what she had done hit him square in the chest. He grabbed Delphine by the arm. "You don't know anything about being a manager, do you? You've been making calls on my behalf for days and I let you because I thought you—Oh, my God. You've ruined my career."

"No," Delphine protested, sniffing and wiping her eyes with her hands. "I would never do anything to hurt you."

Bradley scowled down at her. "Perhaps not intentionally, Delphine. But don't you think the people you've been talking to know that you don't have a clue about the business?"

"*You* didn't."

Bradley took off his hat and shook out his hair. "Yeah, so what does that make me? The world's biggest fool?"

Delphine frowned. "No. I'm a quick learner. Nobody has any idea that I'm new to this business. I promise, I haven't done anything that would hurt your career. I know it's the most important thing in your life."

Bradley snorted and slammed his hat back down on his head. "It's the *only* thing in my life, Delphine."

"I know, but I had hoped that if I could help you become a success, you'd let me be part of your life, too. I love you, Bradley. Please, let me stay with you and help you. I believe in you, in your talent. I can help you. I can be everything you want me to be."

Delphine knew she was pleading now, but she couldn't stop herself. This scene reminded her too much of another time and another place in another life, being hauled away from yet another foster home because she wasn't young enough or smart enough or perfect enough for them to keep.

She had tried so hard, with family after family, to be what they wanted. The cheerleader, outgoing and bubbly and friendly. The brain, quiet and shy and obedient. The jock, athletic and driven and competitive. But it was never enough.

Something always gave her away. She didn't get asked to the prom, or she got a B in math, or she placed second in the track meet.

She tried so hard, but it was never enough.

No matter what personality she tried to fit herself into, it was always the slightest bit off, like a skirt that was just the tiniest bit too tight around the waist or just a fraction of an inch too short. The imperfection was virtually unnoticeable at first but it nagged and nagged at her until it was all she could focus on.

She wanted to throw herself to her knees on the dead brown grass at Bradley's feet and grab him by the legs and beg him not to let her go. She even felt herself starting to crumple to the ground like the first leaf falling under autumn's inevitable pull.

But she knew it would be useless, just as it had been useless when she was fourteen, howling and crying and clutching at her latest foster mother as if the woman might take pity on her and tell Child Protective Services to go away. Of course, since her foster mother had been the one who called CPS in the first place, it was doubtful she'd have a miraculous change of heart right there on the front stoop, where Delphine had fallen to her knees to beg for another chance.

And all because Delphine had thought that what this family wanted was a star athlete. She'd been exhausting herself at practices, trying to become what they wanted. Only, in the end, they hadn't wanted that at all. What they had really wanted was for her to keep up with the laundry. The Sokolskis fostered a total of four children that year—two of whom went through an enormous amount of diapers every day. Delphine's chore was to do laundry since it was something she could do late at night, when she got done with track practice and finished with her homework. She put a load of dirty clothes in the washing machine the minute she got home from practice, before she even changed out of her sweaty T-shirt and shorts. Then, by the time she'd heated herself up something for dinner and started on her homework, the next load was ready to go into the wash.

Only, after two months of trying to be the perfect student and the perfect athlete and the perfect daughter and the perfect baby-sitter for the three younger children, Delphine found herself falling asleep during her classes. Her grades started slipping and Mrs. Sokolski had frowned over Delphine's report card when she'd come home from work.

"You'll never amount to anything with grades like these," she'd said.

That was all that was said about the matter, but Delphine knew this was the first grain of sand in her newest foster family's sandals. She had to fix the problem before that grain of sand caused a blister.

So, she'd studied harder, only she couldn't skip track practice. Mr. Sokolski had even come to her last meet, so she knew how important that was to him.

But, like a balloon filled with water, whenever she squeezed one part it pooched out somewhere else. She had tightened down on her studies and track, and the only place left for the water to go was down the washing machine . . . or under her bed, as the case might be.

She took to hiding the laundry under her bed. Sometimes it was clean and just waiting to be folded, and sometimes it wasn't even washed. All she knew was that she had to get it out of sight so the Sokolskis wouldn't know that she wasn't good enough for them to keep.

It had been stupid of her to think they wouldn't notice, especially not with two babies in diapers.

Delphine would never forget the day she'd come home from practice to find all the clothes she'd stuffed under her bed yanked out in the middle of the bedroom she shared with the next-youngest foster child. Her dirty little secret, exposed to the world.

Her caseworker from CPS had shown up the next week, even though Delphine had washed, dried, and folded every stitch of laundry in the house since she'd been caught. She even stripped all the beds and cleaned all the sheets. She'd hung new towels in both of the bathrooms. She made sure the babies had stacks and stacks of freshly laundered diapers.

But it was too late.

She hadn't been able to be the daughter the Sokolskis wanted her to be and Delphine had gone to the next foster home. And the next one. And the next.

She looked at Bradley now, knowing she had disappointed him, too.

And he was right. She wanted to be the right person for him, but she wasn't. She didn't know how to be a musician's manager. She hadn't grown up with Faith Hill. She couldn't help make him a star, and as he had said, that was the one and only thing that was important in his life.

All her life, she had been trying to be the person others wanted her to be and every time—every single time—all she had managed to do was fail.

Chapter 27
An Honest Woman

My career is over.

The words played over and over in Bradley's head like a defective CD. Delphine's fictitious contacts with music-industry heavy hitters had been his last hope. Without them, he was finished.

He looked down the sun-baked street at the small houses with their fenced-in dying yards. Ten years of sacrifice and he had nothing to show for it. And now it was all over. His dreams were as dead as the brown grass under his boots.

Bradley was filled with a sudden calm.

He remembered Richard's words from earlier that day. Sometimes the easy thing to do was also the right thing to do.

Computers had always come easy to him. He understood them, knew how to make them do what he needed them to do. Music was so much harder because there were no rules. Everything you did was right—or wrong—depending on the outcome. With computers, there was no uncertainty. There might be different ways to arrive at the answer, but at least you knew when you had got it right.

Music had too many ambiguities. A song he loved was one the fans didn't much like. Or one the fans raved about got panned by the reviewers. One that the reviewers lauded as complex and interesting the fans found too "out there."

There were no such problems in the computer world. You were told to make the program do such and such and you did it. Problem solved.

He was tired of banging his head against the brick wall that was his music career, tired of fighting so hard for every step forward that he made. He couldn't ignore the signs any longer, and Delphine's pathetic—though well-meaning—attempt to help him was the final straw.

It was over.

He turned to Delphine, who was standing on the sidewalk, crying as though her world were coming to an end.

Bradley reached out a hand, cupping her cheek in his palm. "Why did you lie?" he asked softly.

"Because I'd rather dream about the life I wish I'd had than be crippled by what really happened. I never meant to hurt anyone."

Delphine closed her eyes and sniffled, and Bradley pulled her to him, pushing her head down on his shoulder. He murmured soothing words to her while she cried, wondering all the while why he wasn't angry with her. He stroked her back, holding her tighter when she started shaking with the force of her sobs.

He supposed then that he wasn't angry with her because she *hadn't* hurt him. It wasn't her fault that his music career was dead. She hadn't killed it. In fact, she had been trying her best to resurrect it.

No, Bradley knew that the blame for his failure lay, if not at his own doorstep, then with fate or destiny or karma or whatever name he could put to the fact that he had just never been in the right place at the right time to make things happen.

He was through trying to make those opportunities for himself. After a decade of struggling, he was giving up. No matter how much he had learned about the business or how many country music insiders he had met or how often he showed up at industry events, he just hadn't been able to make a go of it.

Now it was time to move on.

Bradley lifted Delphine's face off the shoulder of his now-soaked T-shirt. He could only guess at the awful truth she was trying to cover with her tales of the perfect family, but what did that really matter? Hell, he lived in his own fantasy world too, with his dreams of wealth and fame. The lies she had told were only to protect herself and to convince him to let her help him succeed—hardly something he could be angry for. He didn't know why she had tried to make him believe that she could help his career, but he did know that she hadn't done it for her own personal gain. He also knew that when he started his new life in New Mexico, he wanted Delphine at his side.

Delphine woke up alone in the bedroom of the Winnebago, feeling as if someone had stuffed her head full of cotton. She supposed that sobbing uncontrollably for over an hour would have that effect on a person.

She barely remembered Bradley leading her back to the motor home and getting her settled in bed. She had fallen asleep listening to the hushed whisper of voices outside, and she had no idea what Bradley had told Harriet and Richard about why she was in such a state. Of course, he couldn't have told them the truth, because he didn't know the truth.

She owed it to him to tell him why she had lied.

No matter how much the truth about her past hurt, she knew that Bradley deserved to hear it.

Delphine pushed herself up off the bed, willing her limbs to stop shaking. She stood staring at the doorknob for an inordinate amount of time. Why was facing the music always so hard?

She took a deep, calming breath and pushed the door open, only to be met with silence.

She was afraid her sigh of relief could have been heard two counties away when she discovered that she was alone.

Her notebook was lying open on the dining room table, and Delphine walked over to pick it up.

Bradley's note was written in uppercase letters and signed with just the letter *B*. He wrote that they were going to the fair and said that if she'd like to meet them, he'd be in the bank parking lot at seven. Delphine looked at her watch. It was six o'clock now.

She had an hour to decide what to do with her life.

She slid into the booth at the dining room table and sat staring at Bradley's neatly printed message.

If she were a stronger person, she would leave right now. She knew that Bradley would have a better chance of becoming a success in the music business with someone else— someone like Robyn who didn't have to lie about her industry contacts.

The problem was, she wasn't a stronger person. She loved Bradley and wanted to be with him. She truly believed that she could help him become a success, even though she would have to work hard to learn more about the industry. She wanted to be the one to help Bradley achieve his dream. And maybe, just maybe, if she could help make him a success, she could finally be *enough* for someone to love.

"You signed me up for what?" Bradley asked, looking at his mother with something akin to horror on his face.

"A talent competition. Why are you acting so strangely? You've been entering these things since you were a child." Harriet frowned at her son and looked as though she might reach up at any moment to take his temperature with the back of her hand.

Bradley started to tell his mother that he'd decided to quit the music business, but stopped when he saw Delphine coming toward them from half a block away. She had left her hair down around her shoulders and it swayed back and forth with each step she took. She was wearing a pair of skin-hugging blue jeans and the same filmy white and blue shirt she'd worn to the bar in Albuquerque. Her chin was tilted up at a defiant angle, as if daring the world to try to stop her, and Bradley found himself staring at her and wishing he knew all her secrets.

When she reached them, Bradley grabbed her hand. "Did you have a nice nap?" he asked.

She nodded, looking at him solemnly as Harriet and Richard joined hands and started walking down the sidewalk ahead of them.

"You didn't grow up in a small town, did you?" Bradley asked, doing his best to keep his tone light and conversational.

"No."

"Have you ever been to one of these local fairs?"

"No," she said again, making Bradley wonder if she was ever going to say more than one word at a time to him.

"They're really pretty fun. We didn't have them back in Jersey where I grew up, either, but as a country music singer, I've played quite a few of them in my time."

"I grew up in Chicago," Delphine offered, looking across the street at the strip mall that faced the bank.

"Hmm," Bradley said noncommittally.

"I was moved around from one foster home to another. I never stayed more than two years with any one family. I don't have any sisters. Or any brothers, either. My mother died when I was four and I never knew my father. My grandparents, whoever they were, didn't want me. I guess they weren't too pleased when my mom got pregnant when she was fifteen, and as far as they were concerned, she stopped being their daughter when she ran away to have me. I was lucky, though. I ended up in the more affluent part of town, so at least I didn't grow up poor."

Bradley stopped and turned her to face him. "I'm sorry, Delphine."

"There's nothing to be sorry about. I could have had it so much worse."

Bradley didn't say what he was thinking, which was, *Yes, but you should have had it so much better*. Instead, he sensed that she wanted him—no, needed him—to react unemotionally to what she was telling him, so he just squeezed her hand and started walking again.

"Because I moved around so much, I developed the, uh, skill, I guess you could call it, of pretending to be someone different wherever I went. To be honest, I think I've become addicted to the adventure of it. When you talked about country music when we first met, I just thought I'd try small-town life on for size. It sounds so wonderful, to grow up in one house all your life with the same friends all around you, never having to worry about being the new kid in school. When you asked me where I was from that first night when we left Reno, I just happened to see the name of this town on the map. So I said I was from here."

Bradley shook his head in disbelief. She'd been lying to him since the night they had met and he never once suspected. "Do you ever plan to settle down, Delphine? To stop pretending to be someone you're not?"

"We all pretend to be what we're not sometimes," she protested.

"That's not true. I don't see my mom or Richard trying to . . ." Bradley's voice trailed off when Delphine looked at him levelly.

"Your mother hid the fact that she was capable of sneaking nearly three million dollars out from under the noses of the Heart O'Reno's security force. Richard was posing as a casino owner who wanted to kill us. I will say it again, everyone pretends to be someone they're not when the situation calls for it."

"Not everyone. I mean, look at me."

Delphine did, taking in his black cowboy hat, his silver belt buckle in the shape of the state of Texas, and his snake-skin boots before she responded. "Yes, look at you. All dressed up, pretending to be a cowboy. But that's not who you really are."

"I just do it because it's what the fans expect," Bradley said, frowning.

"Exactly. That's why everyone does it. To be who others expect you to be. I guess the difference is, underneath it all, you *know* who you really are. I've been pretending so long that I'm not sure I can tell the real Delphine from all the ones I've made up."

Bradley stopped in front of a face-painting booth and put both hands on her shoulders. "I know the real Delphine. She's kind and caring and funny. She's smart and sexy as hell. And she's willing to lay it on the line for the people she loves. That's who you are inside. It has nothing to do with where you grew up or how often you moved or even who may or may not be related to you."

Delphine smiled sheepishly at that. "I'm sorry about that Faith Hill thing. I couldn't seem to stop myself."

"Did you even know who she was before you met me?" Bradley asked.

Delphine looked at the ground and shook her head. "Sorry."

Bradley sighed. "That's okay. I had already given up hope."

"What?" Delphine asked, jerking her gaze up to meet his. "You can't give up. Just because I may not be related to Faith Hill doesn't mean we can't get your career back on track."

Bradley took off his hat and raked his fingers through his hair. Then he went to put it back on, but hesitated. Delphine was right. This hat, these boots, this stupid bulky belt buckle—it was all a lie. He was no more a cowboy than Faith Hill was ugly. And Faith was damn sure not ugly.

It was time he stopped playing this part. He didn't need it anymore anyway. No computer programmers he knew wore hats and boots and dreamed of being country music stars.

Bradley turned to a little boy who was getting a Lone Ranger mask painted across his face. "Here, kid. You want this?" he asked, holding out his hat.

The boy looked skeptical, as if Bradley were offering him a tainted piece of candy.

"Look, I'll just leave it here. You can go ask your parents if it's okay for you to have it, all right?"

The boy nodded, looking hopeful as Bradley turned and steered Delphine away.

"My music career is over, Delphine. I gave it everything I had for ten years. Now I need to move on to something more stable. Something more lucrative. And I want you to come with me. As my wife. I know this isn't exactly the most romantic spot to do this, but—" Bradley stopped and hit the dirt with one knee, taking her left hand between both of his. "Will you marry me, Delphine? I'm going to take a job with the DEA as a computer specialist. We'll have to live in New Mexico for a few years at first, but if you don't like it, we can move when a transfer becomes available. What do you say, Delphine? Can I make an honest woman of you?"

Chapter 28
Face the Music

Delphine stared at Bradley, who was looking up at her expectantly, waiting for her answer.

He was offering her everything she had thought she wanted, only it was all wrong. She didn't want him at this price. Her happiness for his dreams. The thought of it made her feel sick all the way to her soul.

She stepped back, tugging her hand out of his grasp. "No, Bradley. This isn't right. You working with computers is as much a lie as me saying I grew up in a small town. That's not who you are. Don't you understand?"

Bradley slowly stood up, dusting off the knees of his jeans before he looked at her. "Are you telling me that I can't be whoever I choose to be because you don't like it?" he asked, his voice dripping ice.

"No. It's not that at all. It's just . . . you're too talented to give up your dream."

The muscles in Bradley's jaw tightened as he clenched his teeth. "Talent has nothing to do with it. In all the years that I've been trying to make something of myself, I've had talent. Don't you get it, Delphine? I've done everything right and it still hasn't worked. I'm giving up. And nothing you can say will change that. I'm going to attend the awards show the day after tomorrow because I want to face the end head-on and walk away with a clean slate. When the names of the debut male vocalist nominees are called, I'm going to applaud. And when the winner is announced, I'm going to give him a standing ovation. Then I'm going to walk away and never look back. My father made the mistake of holding on to his dream much too long and it made him a bitter and angry man. I am not going to make the same mistake."

Delphine shook her head, the hot sun blazing down on her head and turning the blond streaks in her hair to gold. "You can't compare your life to your father's. Maybe your problem isn't that you haven't tried hard enough. Maybe it's that you're trying *too* hard. When you sang to me on that stage in New Mexico, you didn't care who was listening because there was nobody there who could make a difference in your career. And I believed every word you said up there because you were singing from your heart and not from your head."

"That's just it. I'm tired of worrying about where the words come from. I want the success so badly that I can't forget about how much it means to me when I'm up on stage. I don't care about the computer stuff nearly as much, so whether I write the world's most awesome code or not doesn't really matter to me. There's something very freeing in that."

"That's a cop-out," Delphine said, feeling a sudden wave of anger wash over her. "Just because it's hard doesn't mean you should just give up."

"What do you know about it?" Bradley said, suddenly feeling pretty angry himself. "Tell me, have you ever stuck anything out long enough to see it succeed?"

Delphine narrowed her eyes to a squint. "I was going to stick it out with you, to help you make your music career a success."

"I don't want your help. I just want to start having a normal life."

Delphine looked at Bradley in silence for a long time

before she answered. "Then I'm afraid I can't marry you. I want more out of life than that."

And then she turned and walked away, fading into the crowd on the midway.

"Hand me that hose from the closet," Jim Josephs yelled to Gus through the open kitchen window of the Jayco. "Our holding tanks must have filled up. That's why it flooded."

Gus scowled at the top of the other man's head. When they were done with this miserable road trip, he was going to fly to Vegas, get the honeymoon suite at the Bellagio, find himself a willing cocktail waitress to snuggle up with, and order prime rib and lobster from room service.

Roughing it sucked.

He yanked open the closet door and rummaged around to find a hose. He spied a length of white tubing in a sealed plastic bag and picked it up off the floor, turning it around to see if there were any instructions or warnings included.

"You'd think this kinda shit would be easy," he muttered darkly to himself, not seeing any instructions with the hose. Then he shrugged. What could possibly be complicated about emptying out a couple of holding tanks?

He slid the white hose out the window toward Jim, who gave it the same inspection that Gus just had before unzipping the plastic bag to take the tubing out. Jim fiddled with getting the hose attached, making sure the tubing was fully inserted into the drain before he opened the valves to release the wastewater from the RV. That, at least, was one mistake he wasn't going to make. As bad as all their other mishaps had been, nothing would be worse than dumping raw sewage all over himself.

His nose crinkled with distaste as the smell of used wastewater reached his nostrils.

Ugh. If there had been someone at the near-deserted RV

park they could pay to do this vile task, Jim would have gladly forked over a thousand bucks to have it done. Unfortunately, the park seemed be without staff at the moment and Gus had used the fact that Jim had shot him in the foot to coerce him into taking on this distasteful job.

"Hey, I'm getting thirsty in here. Since you're already out there, why don't you try hooking up our water? How tough can it be?"

Jim looked at all the nozzles and plugs on the panel next to the concrete pad where the Jayco rested. He was getting a bit irritated with Gus's continuous comments about how easy this RV staff should be. It wasn't easy. As a matter of fact, it was damn difficult and he was kicking himself that they hadn't paid more attention to the rental agent's instructions before they set out on this journey.

Still, it rankled his pride to have Gus imply that he was stupid for not being able to just figure this all out. So, rather than refusing to hook up the water, he yelled back through the kitchen window. "Fine. There should be another hose in that closet somewhere."

He heard Gus rummaging around, banging things and tossing them out of the closet as if he expected maid service to come in at any moment and clean up after him. Jim frowned, knowing that *he* was the one who would be cleaning up after his slob of a motor home mate.

Gus shoved another plastic bag out the window, this one containing a black hose. Jim's eyebrows drew together as something niggled in the back of his brain. What had that rental agent said about the black hose? It seemed that it had been something important, but try as he might, Jim couldn't recall the agent's warning.

"Ah, hell. What in the world could he have said that was so important?" Jim said to himself, shaking his head in disgust. Gus was right. There was nothing difficult about connecting a hose to a water line.

Jim ripped open the plastic bag containing the black hose,

grimacing with disgust when a fresh whiff of sewage invaded his nostrils.

"You'd think the tank would be empty by now," he mumbled.

"What'd you say?" Gus hollered through the window.

"Nothing," Jim answered, wiping perspiration from his brow as he hooked up one end of the hose to the "Water Out" spigot on the panel before twisting the other end to the "Water In" connection on the motor home. Then he opened the valve on the panel and said, "We've got water."

He heard Gus turn on the faucet in the kitchen and felt an inordinate amount of pleasure at the fact that he had finally—for the first time during their trip—managed to do something right.

His sense of pride was shattered when Gus took a healthy swig from the tap and then, with no warning at all, spewed an entire mouthful of water through the kitchen window and all over Jim's shocked face.

Jim wiped a hand across his cheeks, unable to believe that Gus had just spit at him.

"Of all the childish, uncalled for—" Jim's rant was interrupted by the sound of Gus's retching. Jim watched with horror as his partner vomited into the kitchen sink . . . and over the kitchen counter . . . and into the carpet.

Jim raced around to the door of the Jayco, yanking it open just in time to see Gus fall to his knees in front of the closet, his stomach still heaving.

"What in the hell is wrong with you?" Jim hissed.

Gus retched one more time, then stared at the carpet as a shudder racked his body. Finally, he looked up at Jim with murder in his eyes.

Jim took a step backward, still holding the door. "What?"

"The water, you asshole," Gus answered, as if that explained everything.

"What about it? I got it hooked up and running. I thought that's what you wanted."

"It tastes like shit," Gus said, putting a hand on his stomach as the urge to throw up again passed.

"Well, excuse me, Mr. Potty Mouth. It's not like Perrier sent over a water purifier, you know."

"No." Gus pointed to the kitchen faucet. "I mean, it literally tastes like shit."

Then it hit him—what the rental agent had said. The black hose was for dumping black water, which was the polite term for sewage. And they didn't replace hoses between renters so that meant . . .

Jim felt his own stomach heave and turned away from the motor home just in time to lose his lunch.

Bradley shifted his weight from one booted foot to the other as he stood backstage and waited for his turn to perform. He had no idea why he was even going through with this stupid talent contest when none of it mattered anymore. Probably because, no matter what else he may or may not have done in his career, he had never missed an obligation. No matter how raunchy the venue, no matter how bad the pay, he played anywhere that he was booked to play.

Always the fucking good guy, he thought, glaring down at the tips of his boots.

Delphine was wrong about his decision to quit the business, but she was right about something else. He was sick of playing the part of the good ol' country boy.

Yeah, he liked country music but not the twangy stuff about pickup trucks and cattle drives and hound dogs.

If he had all the money he wanted, he'd buy himself a Mercedes and move to an apartment in Manhattan. Hell, he'd probably even get himself a cat. The last place he wanted to be was on some lonely ranch somewhere with nobody around for company but a bunch of smelly cows.

The spotlights mounted in front of the stage flashed, catching the silver of Bradley's belt buckle. He frowned at it, and then, in one smooth movement, he unbuckled the belt and tossed it aside. Then he sat down on the dusty floor and started tugging off his left boot.

"Excuse me, sir, but what are you doing? There are minors back here," a heavyset woman with a helmet of dyed red hair said, watching with horror etched on her face as Bradley exposed his naked foot to the children.

"I'm just taking off my shoes," Bradley said, yanking off his right boot and standing it up next to its mate.

The dusty floorboards felt cool beneath his feet, and Bradley curled his toes to get the full pleasure of the sensation. Then he scratched his stomach. He hadn't realized how annoying the panhandle of Texas had been. It had been digging into his gut for hours, but he'd just put up with it as a necessary evil.

The heavyset woman continued eyeing him suspiciously as she ushered her charge to the curtains leading on stage, as if she were afraid that Bradley wouldn't be satisfied with merely shedding his boots and belt.

Bradley stretched his arms above his head and grinned. This did feel pretty good. Maybe the woman had something to fear after all.

The woman pushed her little darling through the opening in the curtains and Bradley rolled his eyes heavenward as the tot started singing "I Wanna Talk About Me." The audience laughed and cheered, though, and the woman beamed at the boy, who seemed to delight in hamming it up in front of the audience.

Now there was someone who was just doing it for fun, Bradley thought, watching the five- or maybe six-year-old perform.

One corner of his mouth drew up in a mocking smile. When was the last time he had sung with such abandon, without worrying about who might be listening? He'd been thinking of music as a business for so long that he had stopped thinking of it as fun. When he went out there on that stage, he was never alone. There were always people on stage with him, watching over his shoulder to critique his performance.

His manager. His record label. His fans. The reviewers.

Even his father was there, asking why Bradley thought he could succeed when his own dad had failed.

Somewhere along the line, it had ceased being about the songs he sang and had started being about trying to please all those people up there on stage with him.

It was an impossible task.

There was no way he could please everyone with his music. Instead, he was tying himself in knots with every note, worried that he wasn't doing it right.

Bradley smacked his forehead with his palm. Delphine had been right all along. He kept looking for the right answer in his music—as if there were some sort of magic formula he was going to find that would tell him that a plus b equaled c. Only this wasn't algebra or accounting or computer programming, and what he should be doing was singing the songs that were right for him, because *he* was the a, the songs that resonated within him were the b and the right answer—not financial success or another recording contract or top billing on his next tour—would be the satisfaction he got from expressing what was in his heart and not the success he was continually seeking with his head.

And with that, he knew he couldn't give it up.

He loved the music, loved the songs, and he loved performing as much as that kid grinning on stage and taking his second bow did.

He had to find Delphine and tell her that he was not going to give up his dream.

Bradley turned and had started toward the exit when his name was announced. He looked from the curtain to the exit and back.

"You're on, mister," the kid who had just come backstage urged.

Bradley grinned. Yeah. He was definitely on.

He strode on stage, feeling the energy of this small-town crowd, out for a night of entertainment. Bradley finally got it—finally understood the debt he owed to each and every member of the audience, from the people sitting in the bleachers chatting with friends to the couples waiting on the makeshift dance floor for him to grab their attention and make this time they had given him as a gift count. He owed it to them to really and truly face the music when he performed.

When the song started, Bradley closed his eyes, pulling the microphone up to his lips.

And from the first note, the crowd quieted. The people chatting on the sidelines stopped talking and started tapping their feet. The couples on the hardwood dance floor started spinning, eyes closed, minds given over to the music.

And when it was over, they shouted for more.

Bradley looked at the emcee and raised one eyebrow questioningly. The older man smiled and said, "We can queue up something else if you want to sing another one."

Bradley nodded. "Okay. Just a second," he said, motioning for the little boy who had performed before him to come back on stage. The boy looked surprised, but didn't hesitate, coming out to stand next to Bradley. Then he thrilled the audience by looking from Bradley's bare feet to his uncomfortably booted ones and, with a flourish, whipping off his own boots.

Grinning down at the kid, Bradley asked, "Do you know 'The Truth About Men' by Tracy Byrd?"

The boy nodded. "I love that song."

"Good." Bradley pulled a stool over to center stage and helped the boy up onto the seat. Then he looked over at the emcee, who was fiddling with something in the wings. "Ready?" he asked.

The emcee nodded.

"Okay, hit it," Bradley said.

When the song was over, the kid held up his hand for a high five as the audience clapped and whistled.

"That was fun," the boy said.

"It sure was. Now I gotta go." Bradley handed the mike to the boy and started to walk offstage. After a few steps, he turned and smiled. "By the way, I hope you win," he said, then turned back toward the crowd, gave them a wave, and left to find the woman that he loved.

"Do you think Bradley will mind that we're getting married?" Harriet asked, rubbing her cheek on Richard's shoulder as they spun around the dance floor.

"I can't imagine why he would," Richard answered.

"Me, neither. I guess I'm just being paranoid."

"Yes, you are. Stop worrying. Everything is going to be just fine." Richard tilted her chin up and kissed her, letting the other dancers sway past them as they came to a halt in the center of the hardwood floor.

A flash came from the darkened sidelines of the dance floor, but neither Harriet nor Richard paid it any attention. Instead, Harriet looped her arms around Richard's neck and deepened their kiss. It was as if the outside world had ceased to exist.

Only it hadn't.

"We've got to get closer," Jim hissed.

Gus looked at the man who had been his traveling companion for almost a week now and was tempted to knock him over the head and take the camera out of his pale white hands. This, he decided, was why he had always refused his wife's constant nagging to take them on a family vacation. After five days of togetherness, he'd probably be tempted to kill his own children.

And the wastewater fiasco earlier that day had certainly done nothing to improve Gus's mood.

"Well, what do you suggest we do?" Gus asked, craning his neck for a better view of the couple out on the dance floor.

Jim looked around them on the half-empty bleachers. Suddenly, he spotted something. "I'll be back in just a second," he said. True to his word, he returned in just a moment with a woman's shawl and a white cowboy hat. He handed the shawl to Gus. "Tie this around your head," he ordered, plunking the cowboy hat on his own head.

Gus stared down at the piece of fabric in his hands. "This isn't going to fool anyone."

"Look, it's dark out there on the dance floor and we don't have another choice. I'm not sure what El Corazon is looking for in these pictures, but if we don't give him something soon, he's going to think we aren't doing our jobs. If you want to get back to Reno, we have to do this. Now, put the damn thing on."

Gus glared, but did as Jim suggested. He looked ridiculous, his brown eyes bulging out of his face like a Chihuahua's. Jim pulled the brim of his hat down over his forehead to cover his own eyes and grabbed Gus's hand. Gus automatically recoiled, and Jim shook his head with disgust.

"Come on. We've got to get closer to Dickie."

Gus let Jim lead him onto the dance floor, but when Jim pulled him into an embrace, he put his foot down. "If you don't leave six inches between us, I'm gonna kill you."

Jim's sigh was loud and long-suffering. "Despite what you think, I am not hitting on you. I don't even find you mildly attractive."

Gus frowned and relaxed against Jim's chest. "What do you mean? I'm an attractive guy. I've never had a problem getting dates."

Jim sighed again. "Just shut up and get ready to take the picture, will you?"

They whirled around, closer and closer to Dickie and Harriet, still smooching in the middle of the dance floor.

"Okay, get ready," Jim said when they were within flash bulb range.

Gus tightened his grip on the camera.

"A one, and a two, and dip." Jim gracefully twisted Gus so he was facing straight up, just a few feet from Dickie and Harriet. Gus snapped two quick pictures, the flash finally startling the lovebirds out of their embrace.

Jim tried to pull Gus back up to a standing position, but he underestimated the amount of strength it would take to haul a 220-pound man up from a half-prone position. He strained his back, trying to get some leverage, but then the heel of his shoe caught on something and they went down, flailing and cursing, on the hard dance floor.

"Get off me," Gus grunted.

"I'm trying," Jim said. "I slipped on your stupid scarf."

"It's a shawl, not a scarf," Gus corrected.

"Can I help you?"

Startled, Gus and Jim looked at each other, their eyes wide. It just figured that Dickie of all people decided to be a gentleman. Gus coughed and raised his voice to falsetto heights. "No, no. We're just fine, young man. Thank you anyway."

Then he shoved Jim off him and crawled across the dance floor on his hands and knees.

When he hit the dirt, he pushed himself off the ground and took off running, too humiliated to care whether or not Jim was following.

Chapter 29
Stick with Me

Have you ever stuck anything out long enough to see it succeed?

Delphine tossed another of her music business books into a plastic grocery bag and frowned. How dare he say that to her? In every foster home she'd been shuffled to, she stuck it out as long as they would let her.

Yeah, but this isn't a foster home, that annoying voice inside her head remarked.

Delphine slowly straightened, still clutching *This Business of Music.* Oh, no, she thought, the annoying voice was right. Had she really been living the same pattern laid out for her as a child? When something didn't work out exactly as she hoped, did she remove herself from the situation just as Child Protective Services had removed her growing up?

Delphine felt her knees give out and slid to the carpeted floor of the Winnebago.

Yes, that's what she'd been doing. It was why she'd never finished college, never stayed at a job longer than two years, and never had a long-term relationship with a man. She'd told herself it was because she craved adventure, but that wasn't the truth.

She never stuck with anything during the difficult parts, preferring instead to just walk away. Not because she wanted to move on to something more exciting, but because she was afraid that no matter how hard she tried, she'd never be able to meet other people's expectations.

And that's exactly what she was preparing to do now. Even though she professed to love Bradley, she was ready to give up because convincing Bradley to hold on to his dream would be hard and she feared she wasn't up to the task.

Delphine picked at a rough spot on the carpet.

She didn't know when she had become such an emotional coward, but it was time she stopped hiding behind the façade of someone she wasn't and dug in her heels for the person she really wanted to be. And the person she really wanted to be wasn't the type to run from a challenge. The person she really wanted to be would set goals and work her butt off to achieve them. She wouldn't let anything stand in her way.

Not even her own self-doubts.

Delphine pushed herself up off the floor and straightened her shoulders.

The person she wanted to be had too much to do to sit around feeling sorry for herself. That person—that woman— was going to go to Nashville and do whatever was necessary to give Bradley back his dream.

Delphine ripped a piece of paper out of her notebook and hurriedly scribbled a note to Bradley.

> *Dear Bradley,*
>   *I am not going to let you give up. I'm leaving for Nashville and I'm getting you another recording contract if it's the last thing I do.*
>   *I'll meet you at the Grand Ole Opry the day after tomorrow.*
>
>   *Love,*
>   *Delphine*

She looked down at the note, tempted to scratch through the "Love" bit and just say "Sincerely," but the new Delphine made her leave it just as it was. She set the salt and pepper shakers that were on the table on the corner of the note to hold it down, and then turned to pick up the plastic grocery bags she'd packed with the secondhand belongings she'd bought back in New Mexico.

Delphine felt a pang of insecurity when she wondered how a girl with nothing but two bags of possessions was going to help the man she loved become a star. But then she tossed away the thought. Talent and determination didn't care what you owned or where you came from. And in the end, it was those two qualities that were going to make her succeed. She didn't need fancy clothes or high-class connections or anything else.

Delphine picked up the bags and took one last look around the motor home. Despite everything, she was glad that she had been standing on that hot sidewalk in Reno on that fateful day a week ago. She had been swept up in the best adventure yet, and she knew her life would never be the same.

With a smile, she pushed open the front door and awkwardly made her way down the steps with a bag in each hand. She was sure there'd be a bus to Nashville. She knew she could have stayed in the Winnebago and gone to Nashville with Harriet and Bradley, but she didn't want to take the chance that Bradley would try to talk her out of it. He was so convinced that the right thing for him to do was to give up, but she didn't believe that. He had worked too hard for too long to give up now.

The first thing she was going to do—

Her thoughts were interrupted when she turned out of the entrance of the RV park and ran smack into the beefy chest of a swarthy man. She looked up and let out a gasp of surprise.

The man realized who she was at the same time she realized who he was. "Get her!" he shouted, unnecessarily, as it turned out, since he already had a viselike grip on her upper arm.

Delphine struggled and tried to pull her arm out of the man's grasp. She pulled her loose arm back, prepared to brain the guy with her bag of books, but the taller, thinner man at his side jerked her arm back before she could get in a good swing.

"Hurry up," the thin man ordered. "Let's get her into the motor home before anyone sees us."

Evie was on the phone with one of her most trusted employees when Jim Josephs's e-mail came through.

"She's been underreporting her drug sales for six months, J.R. You warned her once. Now kill her."

Evie double-clicked the first file Jim had attached, her eyes narrowing when she saw the picture. Her husband was kissing another woman. Very thoroughly, too, by the looks of it.

He used to kiss her like that.

Her heart felt as if someone had ripped it from her body and was squeezing it with an iron fist. She had known this day would come sometime, but she hadn't realized how much it would still hurt.

Her husband had betrayed her. And now he must die.

She interrupted the man on the other end of the line. "Do it, J.R. I don't care if she is the mother of your children. If you don't take care of her, I will be forced to have someone else do it. Someone who might want to make her death take a lot longer and be more painful than you might like. Do you understand me?"

Her employee sobbed into the phone and Evie found herself clenching her teeth. Didn't he realize that she was only doing what had to be done? If she let his girlfriend steal from El Corazon without being punished, others would think that they too could get away with it. As difficult as it was to harm those you loved, sometimes it was the only way.

"Yes, Corazon, I understand," the man said, after regaining his composure. "I'll take care of it."

"Good," Evie said. Then she hung up the phone and sent a response to Jim Josephs.

They could do whatever they wanted to with the other three, but she was going to kill Richard herself.

"I can't believe it," Bradley said, shaking his head.

"What? And where's Delphine? I expected her to be here waiting for us," his mother said.

Bradley picked up the note and read it again. Then he turned to his mother and smiled. "She's gone to Nashville."

"Oh. Then why are you smiling? I thought you had something you wanted to tell her."

"I do," Bradley said. "I wanted to tell her how much I love her, and that I want her by my side the day I finally get to stand up at the Grand Ole Opry and accept my award for top male vocalist. And when I do, I'm going to tell the whole world that I'm up there because of the love of my wife."

His mother looked at him as if he were losing his mind. "Your wife? But I thought you said that you and Delphine didn't go through with that ceremony."

Bradley laughed. "We didn't. But we're going to. Soon. Very soon."

Richard and Harriet exchanged looks and bemused shrugs that said they didn't quite understand these young people.

"She must have caught a bus back in town. Mom, Richard, I know it's late, but would you mind if we tried to catch up with her? I'll do the driving."

The other two shook their heads.

"Good," Bradley said, "because I can't wait to tell Delphine that I love her."

"I can't wait to get this over with," Gus said, shoving Delphine ahead of him with a hand between her shoulder blades.

"Me, too," Jim agreed.

Delphine wasn't quite as impatient, since she was beginning to get the idea that whatever it was they wanted to get over with wasn't going to be pleasant for her. Although being taken to the thugs' filthy motor home—which smelled sickeningly of a mixture of vomit and sewage and had curious stains all over the carpet—hadn't been very pleasant, either.

The trio trudged between motor homes, the dry grass crunching beneath their feet. Delphine waited for her opportunity to make a break for it, but with her hands tied behind her back and Gus holding the rope that bound her, she couldn't figure out a way to get far.

They turned just in front of a shiny new motor home and stopped.

The spot where the Winnebago had been parked was empty.

"Aargh." Jim's frustrated yowl was accompanied by a fit of stomping worthy of a two-year-old.

"Where the hell are they?" Gus growled, jerking on her tether.

"I don't know," Delphine answered truthfully, wincing when Gus jerked her arms again.

Jim lunged and grabbed the front of the Toby Keith T-shirt she had pilfered from Bradley's suitcase before she had set out for the bus station. He lowered his head until their noses were almost touching. "Where the hell do you *think* they are, then?"

Delphine wished she had a hand free to wipe the spittle off her face. Instead, she rolled her head to one side and wiped her cheek on her shoulder. "I think they're on their way to Nashville," she answered.

Jim hit her with the back of his hand. Hard. Instinctively, Delphine struck back, lashing out with a knee to his groin. He took a direct hit and collapsed on the ground, writhing in pain.

The bastard obviously hadn't expected her to fight back. Delphine got a sense of satisfaction out of knowing that she'd surprised him, but it didn't last long. Gus yanked the rope again, pulling her arms up until they felt as if they were going to pop right out of their sockets.

She wanted to scream "Uncle!" but she didn't. Her cheek throbbed where Jim had smacked her and her arms ached and she could taste blood in her mouth, but she didn't say a word.

Finally, the pressure on her arms eased, but then she felt the cold barrel of a gun against the back of her head.

Delphine closed her eyes.

He was going to kill her.

She heard a click, not sure if it was the safety or the gun being cocked or what. She had never much liked guns. Even just lying around, they frightened her. She supposed it was the potential they had of taking a person's life. An irreversible and grave act contained in such a small, cold package.

"Wait," Jim choked out from his position on the ground. "We may need her later."

Gus didn't move for a long moment and Delphine felt a bead of sweat trickle from her temple down her face. It dripped off her jaw and landed on her borrowed T-shirt, splattering on Toby's face.

Finally, Gus lowered the gun. Then he leaned over to help Jim up off the ground. "You're right. Let's get going."

And as he shoved her back the way they'd come, all Delphine could think was, *Music City, here we come.*

Chapter 30
Wish upon a Star

"Hello, Mr. Gamble. I'm sorry to be calling so late, but I just caught a performance by one of your artists and I wondered if you might be able to tell me how I can get in touch with him."

David Gamble, founder and president—for just two more weeks; once the triplets arrived, he was going to have his hands full trying to keep three babies and his exuberant wife Kylie in line—of Gamble Records in Seattle sat back in his chair and watched the rain pour down outside his window. "I'm sure I can get you his manager's contact information. And you would be?"

"You might say I'm Mr. Nelson's fairy godmother," the man replied with a smile in his voice.

"Oh?" David asked, frowning. Was this guy some kind of nutcase? If so, David certainly wasn't going to be the one to give him a way to get in touch with Bradley.

"Yes. My name is Emmett Randall and I'm a television producer for one of the major networks. We've got a fabulous new show lined up for the fall, but we've been struggling to find just the right lead. You see, the main character is an up-and-coming country music star so we need someone who not only looks good but can also carry a tune. I think your Mr. Nelson is perfect for the part."

"Really?" David asked, the gears in his brain churning. "Let me ask you, Mr. Randall, was it?"

"Yes. Emmett Randall. Senior vice president of production for ABA Studios in Hollywood, California."

"Mr. Randall, would you expect Bradley Nelson's record sales to increase as a result of this show?"

Emmett chuckled on the other end of the line. "Yes, Mr. Gamble," he answered. "I believe you might even say that I expect this show will make Mr. Nelson a star."

"Bradley, dear, there you are. I've been trying to call you for two days."

Bradley turned and frowned as Robyn Rogers slid the green convertible she was driving into the parking space next to the Winnebago. She got out of the car and walked toward him, holding out her hands as if she expected him to get down on his knees and kiss her fingers.

"My cell phone battery died and I left my charger back on your tour bus." Bradley crossed his arms across his chest and leaned back against the side of the motor home, the metal warm through the fabric of his shirt. Robyn looked somewhat taken aback by his cool response, but kept coming.

He had to admit that she looked beautiful in the sparkly green dress she was wearing. Yes, there was no doubt that Robyn Rogers looked every bit the star she claimed to be. Still, Bradley wished it had been Delphine in her blue jeans and Keds and his too-long T-shirt standing before him.

The Country Music Awards show was going to start in less than an hour. Where was she?

He looked down at his watch and then up at the building in the distance.

The Grand Ole Opry.

The holy grail of country music stars and star wanna-bes.

He was only going to be sitting in the audience tonight, but someday—someday soon—he was going to be up there on that stage. And when he was, it was going to be Delphine who was at his side. Not Robyn Rogers.

"What do you want, Robyn? You made it clear that you think I'm never going to be successful enough for you. Why don't you go see if the rumors about Garth Brooks are true? He might be available again."

"Bradley, honey, that's not fair. You know how much I care about you."

"I sure do," he said with feeling.

"Good," Robyn continued, obviously not catching Bradley's meaning. "Then you know how much I want you back. I made a mistake back in Reno. I should never have let you go. But it's not too late for us. All I care about is you. And me. Together."

Bradley's eyes narrowed suspiciously. "What's really going on, Robyn? You know you care about a hell of a lot more than that. You said it from the beginning—I'm Reno and you're Las Vegas. I don't want a wife who thinks I'm not good enough for her."

"I don't think that at all," Robyn protested, stepping closer and rubbing a hand up his arm.

"Look, Robyn, I don't know why you're here, but let's just be honest with each other for a minute. I have a long struggle ahead of me if I'm going to be successful. That's just the way my career is working out. Some musicians—like that kid Bobby Gorman—well, they have it easy right from the start. That's not how it's going to work for me, but I'm not giving up. You wouldn't be happy with that life, and you know it."

"Yes, I would. Really. I love the simple life." She pulled her hand back and the diamond and emerald bracelets she wore around her wrist clinked together merrily.

Bradley smiled and shook his head. "Sure you do. Look, Robyn, it's over between you and me. It's been over since you shoved me off your bus in Reno, but I just didn't realize it at the time. You wouldn't be happy with me and, to be honest, I wouldn't be happy with you, either. Besides, there's another reason we can't be together. I'm in l—"

Bradley choked on his words when Delphine stepped around the front of the Winnebago.

"Bradley," she gasped, her eyes wide.

"Delphine." He grinned, pushing himself off the side of the RV. "You're going to have to hurry to get changed. The awards show starts in forty-five minutes. My mom picked you out the most gorgeous dress. I think you're going to love it."

"I'm afraid she's not going to have time to change."

Bradley had just taken another step forward when Jim Josephs and Gus Palermo appeared, their guns drawn. "All of you, get in the Winnebago," Jim said, waving his pistol.

"I'm afraid I have to be going now," Robyn said, sidling toward her rental car.

Gus moved very quickly for someone with his girth, Bradley observed. Before Robyn could get two steps away, Gus had her by the arm and was pushing her toward the Winnebago. He waved his gun at Bradley while Jim moved his pistol to Delphine's temple. "Get inside," he ordered.

Bradley opened the door of the motor home and walked up the steps. His mother and Richard were playing poker at the dining table and Bradley tried to signal to them that something was up by rolling his eyes back in his head and flipping his head backward.

"Bradley, do you have a touch of heat stroke?" his mother asked, frowning with concern.

"No, Mom, I'm fine." Bradley stepped inside and made a gun out of his fingers, frantically waving it at Richard.

Richard caught on just a split second too late. He reached around to grab his gun from the back waistband of his jeans, but stopped when Gus pushed Bradley aside and leveled his own pistol at Harriet's forehead.

"Put your hands on the table, Dickie," Gus said, keeping his gun aimed at Harriet as he yanked Robyn into the motor home.

"I prefer to be called Richard," Richard said, doing as Gus instructed.

"How about I just call you dead meat?" Gus countered.

Richard squinted, as if giving the matter due consideration. "No, I think I still prefer Richard."

For that, Gus backhanded Harriet. She let out a cry of pain, and both Bradley and Richard lunged forward, only to be stopped in their tracks when Gus grabbed Harriet by the hair, tilted her head back, and stuck the barrel of the gun in her mouth. "One step closer and she dies right now," he said.

Bradley raised his hands in surrender and took a step back. Richard remained poised to strike, his weight resting on the balls of his feet and the heels of his hands. But, trapped behind the table as he was, he couldn't see any way to get to Gus before the other man got a shot off. And at such short range, there was no way Harriet would survive. Richard forced himself to relax, keeping his hands on the table as he slowly sat back down.

Jim Josephs entered the motor home then, pushing Delphine in front of him. "I'll take care of these three, Gus. You keep an eye on Dickie and Harriet."

Gus nodded, and Jim got to work tying Bradley's hands together. Then he tied Delphine's hands and shoved her over to stand in front of Bradley. With a length of nylon cord, he tied their bound hands together tightly. Then he did the same with Robyn, so they were all three tied together, facing each other. Next, Jim got to work on their feet, lashing them together like a human raft.

When he was done, he stood back to admire his handiwork. With a satisfied nod, he walked back to the bathroom, opened the door, and said, "Get in."

"This is ridiculous," Robyn said. "We can't even move."

"That's the point, baby doll."

Robyn tossed her head in Jim's direction, leaving Delphine

with a mouthful of blond hair, which she promptly spit out. "My name is Robyn, not *baby doll*."

"Whatever. Get in here before I shoot you."

"Why don't you just kill them and get it over with?" a voluptuous woman stepped into the Winnebago and asked, closing the front door behind her.

"Who are you?" Gus growled, keeping his gun aimed at Harriet.

"Evie? Evie Smith?" Richard asked, frowning. He knew the woman from his casino business—a former high roller's wife who frequented his place fairly often.

"Yes, that's me. Evie Smith. El Corazon. Evelyn Swanson. I'm all of these." She pulled a vicious-looking knife from her purse and walked over to stand behind Richard. Then she fisted her hands in his hair, yanked his head back, and lightly ran the blade from one ear to the other. "I think killing a man with a knife is so much more personal than doing it with a gun, don't you, Richard?"

Richard ignored her question. "I don't understand. What did you mean when you said you were Evelyn Swanson? My Evelyn died ten years ago."

"Yes, she did," Evie said, whispering the words in his ear. "She died because I killed her. She was weak, expecting her husband to give her the power and wealth she deserved. That was a mistake. When she died, I was reborn. Me, Evie, I know how to get what I want. I built a drug empire in Reno that is invincible. I'm rich beyond my wildest dreams. I finally have everything that poor Evelyn wanted but never had the guts to get for herself."

Richard turned his head, the tip of Evie's knife digging into the soft skin under his ear. "Everything except me," he said, looking into the woman's gray eyes.

Her eyes went cold and dead like a shark's. "You were mine for years. My hold on you was that strong. Even after my supposed death, you remained true to me. Until you met her," she hissed, flicking the knife so that it drew blood.

Richard felt his ear start to bleed but didn't move his hands from the table.

My God, he thought, looking around at the crowd in the Winnebago, *what have I dragged these people into?*

His wife, the woman he thought had committed suicide a decade ago, was alive and thriving on the evil she was harboring in her black soul.

"Evelyn," he said softly, "it's me you want, not them. Let them go."

"I'm not Evelyn anymore," Evie shrieked. "I'm not Evelyn. I'm not Evelyn."

"Evie, then," Richard said, trying to keep his voice low and soothing despite the madwoman holding a knife to his throat. "You want me, Evie? You can have me. Just let these innocent people go."

"Innocent? Innocent? I have pictures of this whore trying to seduce you. And you succeeded, didn't you? Didn't you, you whore?"

Evie pushed Gus out of the way, lunging at Harriet with her knife drawn.

Richard knew Evie intended to kill Harriet. While she had only been playing cat and mouse with him, at least temporarily, she wanted Harriet dead. He couldn't just sit by and watch his deranged wife kill an innocent person. Especially not an innocent person that Richard had come to love.

He stood up, prepared to throw himself in the way of Evie's blade, but stopped when a gunshot rang out in the confined space of the motor home. He waited to feel pain rip through his body. And waited. But it never came.

Instead, he looked up at Harriet, who was splattered with blood.

"No," he yelled, lurching out of his seat.

"Stop right there," Jim said from the back of the Winnebago, his voice deadly calm. "Gus, tie Dickie and

Harriet up and get them all out of sight. I've got to get us out of here before the authorities come to investigate."

With that, he shoved Bradley, Delphine, and Robyn into the bathroom and closed the door behind them. Then he stepped over Evie's motionless body and walked to the front of the motor home. The RV's engine purred to life and, within seconds, Jim had eased it out of the parking space and headed for the exit of the Grand Ole Opry's parking lot.

Chapter 31

Picture Perfect

"Get off me," Robyn said crossly from the bottom of the human heap that had landed on the floor of the bathroom.

"We're trying," Delphine said, her nose just inches from Robyn's. Being tied together face to face was awkward, even worse than being back to back would have been. She tried to roll over to get back on her feet, but all that did was bring Bradley down on top of her.

"Sorry about that," Bradley apologized, attempting to remove his knee from her groin.

"It's all right. If we tried to move together, it might help," Delphine suggested, spitting out another mouthful of Robyn's hair.

"Maybe if you would stop acting like you're in charge here, it might help."

"There's no need to be rude to Delphine," Bradley said.

"Who is this woman anyway? Ever since I left you in Reno, she keeps popping up wherever you are. Is there something going on here that I should know about?"

"Actually—" Bradley began, but was silenced when Delphine jabbed him in the gut.

"I don't think this is the time for explanations. Right now, we've got to find a way to escape and save Harriet and Richard. Now, I think we might be able to get up if Bradley rolls onto his back and pushes himself up using the wall for balance."

"Good idea," Bradley said.

"Good idea," Robyn mocked in a singsong voice.

Delphine shot the other woman a glare but didn't waste any more time on her. Instead, she rolled to her left, ending up lying facefirst on the floor of the shower. Bradley moved so that his back was against the wall as Delphine had suggested.

"Okay, are you two ready?" he asked.

"Yes," Delphine said, her voice muffled against the ground.

"Yes," Robyn answered grudgingly.

"All right. Here we go." After much struggling and a near miss or two, Bradley finally managed to pull himself and the two women to their feet.

The trio stood staring at each other for an uncomfortable moment, all of them wondering what to do next. Their hands and feet were still tied and, even if they managed to get themselves untied, there was only one small window near the ceiling from which they might be able to escape.

Still, it was their only hope.

Bradley braced his feet in an attempt to stay upright when the Winnebago lurched around a corner. Delphine swayed against him, while Robyn cursed as she banged against the shower controls.

Bradley smiled down at Delphine. "Do you think you can squeeze through that window?" he asked.

"I can try," she answered solemnly, holding her hands out in front of her.

Bradley nodded and tried to move his wrists to get the ropes loose enough to untie Delphine.

"Well, there's no way I'd make it through there. I don't have the chest of a ten-year-old girl like she does," Robyn said sourly.

Delphine looked down at her relatively flat chest and

frowned. Well, there was no lie in the world that would make those suckers grow and the thought of going under the knife to have some foreign material shoved under her skin just gave her the creeps, so she'd just be happy with what God gave her.

"Robyn?" Bradley said, not bothering to look up from his task of untying Delphine's hands.

"What?" Robyn asked warily.

"Why don't you make yourself useful and untie Delphine's ankles? She's our only hope right now and I think you might want to stop insulting her and get busy."

"Well," Robyn sputtered. "I don't know who she is that you can talk to me like that—"

"She's my fiancée," Bradley interrupted. "Now would you shut up and get to work, please?"

"She's your what?" Robyn screeched.

"My fiancée. The woman I'm going to marry. Really, Robyn, we could use some help here."

"No. She can't be your . . . You can't be engaged. I'm going to be your wife. I deserve to be married to a TV star, not her."

Bradley finally managed to work one knot free and started on another. "What are you talking about? Who's a TV star? Have you lost your mind?"

"You are. Or at least you're going to be. David called me yesterday because your manager told him that he'd quit and David didn't know how to reach you. There's a TV producer trying to get in touch with you. He wants you to star in a show next fall," Robyn blurted. "And I want to be your wife."

Bradley looked up then, his hands still busy working the knots free. "So that's why you showed up here. That's why you had a change of heart."

Robyn shook her head. "No, Bradley, I've always cared for you. You know that."

Bradley snorted. "Sure I do. Robyn, I want you to do yourself a favor. Close your eyes."

"What?"

"Close your eyes," Bradley repeated.

Robyn did so.

"Now, imagine your perfect day. Suppose that every dream you ever wanted had come true."

Robyn smiled.

"Now, tell me. Am I in that picture you have in your head?"

Robyn slowly opened her eyes and looked at him. Then, almost imperceptibly, she shook her head.

"That's what I thought. Don't you think I deserve to be the man of my wife's dreams?"

Robyn licked her lips and blinked several times. Then she turned to Delphine, whose eyes were closed. "Is Bradley there in your perfect day?" she asked.

Delphine opened her eyes and smiled. "Yes."

Bradley spared a second to kiss Delphine's nose. "Great. Now that we've got that settled, do you want to give me a hand, Robyn?"

Robyn didn't even grumble as she bent down to try to untie the ropes binding their feet together. The way she figured it, she had made her best attempt to get what she wanted. Now it was time to accept that she'd lost and move on.

"All right. I'm done here," Bradley announced.

Robyn tugged the final knot at their feet loose and kicked the rope out of the way. Then she cupped her hands together and looked up at the window. "Okay. Let's give it a try."

Bradley whipped off his shoe and used the heel to pound on the glass. "Let me break the window first."

He pushed the shards of glass aside with his shoe, and then bent down, giving Delphine a platform to try to escape from. Delphine put her right foot into Robyn's cupped hands, hoping that she could trust the other woman not to upend her in the shower.

Fortunately, Robyn held her steady as Delphine climbed up on Bradley's back.

She stuck her head out the window, yanking it back in when she saw Jim glance in the side-view mirror. When he looked away, she turned around with her back against the wall, whispered, "Here goes nothing," and popped back outside.

With her arms over her head, she reached up to find the railing that ran along the top of the motor home. Someone grabbed on to her legs and started pushing as she felt along for the metal bar she could use to pull herself up onto the roof. She found it just as her rear end slid off the windowsill.

Delphine gasped and tried to keep her legs inside the Winnebago. There was no way she could pull herself up and onto the roof without using her feet.

She looked down—mistake number one—and saw the pavement moving past at a good thirty-five miles an hour.

If she fell now, she'd be a goner.

Someone inside grabbed her legs just as she felt herself slipping, and Delphine heaved a sigh of relief. With the steadying hands on her legs, she was able to tighten her grip on the rail and move her feet to the windowsill.

Ducking to miss getting whacked by a passing tree, Delphine pushed herself up onto the roof. She let go of the railing for just a second to wipe her sweaty palms on her jeans, then screeched when Jim slammed on the brakes. She felt herself sliding toward the front of the Winnebago and desperately clutched at the smooth roof to stop herself from going over the top.

At the last second, she caught the railing, but not before the momentum of her slide pushed her over the edge. Her legs dangled weightlessly for a second over the front of the vehicle, like the coyote in a Road Runner cartoon who had just run out of cliff.

Then she slammed into the windshield with a muttered, "Oof." Still holding the railing, her body twisted until she was staring straight at the driver of the motor home.

She smiled sheepishly and dropped one hand to wave as Jim's eyes bugged out.

Delphine saw the gleam in his eyes a split second before he gunned the engine. Instinctively, she let go of the railing, rolling to the center of the lane as the Winnebago passed right over her.

As soon as the RV passed, she leaped up, screaming when a Honda hit its brakes and skidded to a stop, just inches from her knees.

She started running after the motor home, not exactly sure what she'd do if she caught it, but unwilling to let it out of her sight. That point became moot when Jim slammed on his brakes and jerked the RV around in a tight U-turn, coming back down the street against traffic, chasing her.

Delphine ran down the lane of cars, waving them out of her way. She spotted the Grand Ole Opry building up ahead and headed toward it, knowing that Jim and Gus wouldn't kill them in the middle of the crowd gathered for the show.

She turned her head, feeling the heat of the Winnebago's engine on her back like the hot breath of an angry bull. It was right behind her, with Jim leaning over the steering wheel, his eyes focused intently on her.

Delphine dodged between two cars and into the grassy median, with the Winnebago hot on her heels.

Half a block away from the Grand Ole Opry, she gathered the last of her waning strength and sprinted past the guard at the gate. She had hoped the security bar would slow Jim down, but he just barreled right through it, sending splinters of wood everywhere.

Delphine looked at the entrance of the building, with its red carpet laid out for all the hottest country music stars and their guests. The crowd had thinned, but a few reporters and film crews were still milling about outside. Delphine ran toward them, hoping to find help among the dwindling crowd.

When she heard the engine rev behind her, she twisted around and gasped.

Richard had Jim in a headlock and Harriet had thrown

some sort of white powder—flour, Delphine presumed—all over Gus. She saw the door of the bathroom burst open just as the Winnebago careened onto the red carpet, headed straight for the Grand Ole Opry.

"Get out of the way," Delphine yelled, waving her arms frantically as cameramen and reporters dove out of the way of the oncoming vehicle.

Delphine flew through the opening of the auditorium and tripped on the red carpet, rolling down the aisle as the Winnebago crashed into the building behind her. The crowd gasped and several women—and a few men—screamed and clawed over one another as the RV kept coming.

When the dust cleared, the Winnebago had finally come to a stop with its front wheels in midair, spinning ineffectually. "Call 911," she ordered, turning to a well-dressed man to her left, who obligingly pulled a cell phone from his tuxedo.

Delphine pushed herself up off the floor and ran back to the motor home.

She yanked open the passenger-side door and stepped back when Gus Palermo tumbled out, unconscious and covered with flour.

"You know," she heard Richard say, "for an accountant, you have a kick-ass left hook."

Harriet stepped out of the motor home and leveled Gus's own gun at the unmoving man's chest. "Thank you," she said. "I work out."

Jim emerged next, his hands awkwardly clasped behind his head and Richard's pistol between his shoulder blades. "On the ground," Richard ordered, not taking his eyes off the other man. "Bradley," he called, "do you have Evie tied up?"

Bradley popped his head out of the front door. "Yeah, she's not going anywhere. That bullet to the shoulder has to hurt, but Robyn's not one to cut her any slack. She's got her tied to the showerhead like a side of beef."

"That girl might have a promising career as a prison guard if this music gig doesn't pan out," Richard said dryly. Then he turned to Harriet. "I'm so sorry about this. For all these years I believed . . . I truly believed Evelyn was dead."

Harriet kept the gun trained on Gus's chest as she spared a glance at Richard. "This wasn't your fault. You don't need to apologize."

"I feel as if I should have known. I mean, I knew that my wife had some serious emotional problems, but I had no idea that she would have faked her own death."

"You couldn't have known, Richard. I think it's about time you and I both realized that we aren't—and never should have been—responsible for our spouses. If Bradley's father had wanted success as a singer, he should have worked as hard as Bradley's done. He shouldn't have expected me to support him forever, nor should he have expected it to be easy. It wasn't my fault he didn't get what he felt he should have had out of life."

Richard nodded, thinking of all the times Evelyn had looked at him with disappointment shining in her eyes. Disappointment because he wouldn't take bribes or steal drugs to give her what she wanted. Disappointment because she didn't feel she could tell him the truth about her awful childhood. Disappointment because he couldn't solve all of her problems for her.

And he realized that Harriet was right. He hadn't stayed true to Evelyn out of love. He'd done it because he blamed himself for not being able to provide his wife with what she wanted out of life.

It was time to let go of that guilt. If nothing else, Evelyn had proven today that the only person who could have made her happy was the twisted alter ego she had conjured up after faking her own suicide. No matter what Richard had done all those years ago, it wouldn't have been enough.

And now, Richard thought, looking at Harriet—strong, smart, capable, in-charge-of-her-own-life Harriet—he realized that it was his turn to go after what he wanted in his own life.

He wanted Harriet.

Delphine heard the sound of sirens in the distance and looked up to see Bradley watching her. She smiled and took a step toward him, then stopped when she heard loud sobbing next to her.

"My arm. My arm. I think I broke my arm."

Delphine looked over to see a boy of about nine or ten crying and holding his arm. She squatted down next to him. "I know it's got to hurt, but an ambulance will be here in just a minute. Do you think you can hold on?"

The boy nodded, his face streaked with tears.

Delphine squeezed the boy's uninjured shoulder and Bradley came to stand at her side. "Bobby Gorman, is that you?" he asked.

"Yes," the boy answered with a watery smile.

"Well, congratulations on your debut male vocalist nomination. I'm sure you worked very hard for it."

The boy frowned at him. "Do I know you?" he asked.

Bradley shook his head. "Probably not. Nobody else does. I'm Bradley Nelson. My first album came out this year, too."

"Oh, yeah. I bought it and I really liked it. Especially that one song. What was it? About sticking to your dreams? I listened to that one over and over again when I found out my record label wasn't going to pick me up for a second album. I almost gave up, but when I listened to that song, I felt like I wasn't alone, you know? Like you understood and were reaching out to tell me to stick with it."

"You're kidding?" Bradley asked, rocking back on his heels.

"No." The boy shook his head and winced with pain. "That song really meant something to me. Thank you."

Bradley blinked and reached a hand up to fiddle with the

cowboy hat that wasn't there. "Wow. I . . . uh, thank you," he said.

A cavalcade of police officers and emergency personnel swarmed in then, and Delphine motioned a medic over to help Bobby. The show's organizers hovered about, trying to keep everyone calm while the police hauled Jim, Gus, and Evie out to waiting patrol cars. Harriet and Richard followed the police outside to make arrangements to get the Winnebago towed and get a ride to the police station.

Robyn came out of the motor home looking as gorgeous and unruffled as though they had just spent the last hour having tea with the Queen Mother.

"Doesn't she ever get messy?" Delphine grumbled.

Bradley grinned but wisely didn't say a word.

"Mr. Nelson, may I have a word with you?" one of the event organizers asked, glowering at him and taking him by the arm as if he were a naughty child.

Bradley stopped on the red carpet and turned back to Delphine. "Wait for me," he said.

"For as long as it takes," she answered, stepping back into the shadows of the auditorium as she watched the man she loved walk away.

Chapter 32
Dream On

"The association would like to thank Bradley Nelson for agreeing to perform on such short notice. The, um, unfortunate incident that occurred half an hour ago necessitated a trip to the emergency room for both of the top debut male vocalists who could be here today. Since Mr. Nelson was a runner-up in this category himself this year, we're delighted to have him fill in."

The emcee stepped away from the microphone, leaving Bradley alone onstage.

Bradley looked out over the crowd of music-industry bigwigs and felt his palms start to sweat.

"Thank you," he said, then put a hand over the headset microphone he'd been equipped with as he cleared his throat. "I've dreamed of this moment since I was Bobby Gorman's age, when my dad brought me here to share his dream with me."

Bradley closed his eyes, feeling his mouth go dry.

God, he couldn't do this. The people in this auditorium were so much more talented, so much more wealthy, so much more connected than he was.

Bradley took a deep breath, imagining Delphine was standing before him. He knew what she would say if he told her what he was thinking.

She'd say, It's not about who has more talent, or money, or connections.

It's about the music.

It's about the stories you tell with your songs and what those songs mean to the people who listen to them.

Bradley opened his eyes and smiled. Then he picked up his guitar. He knew what song he wanted to sing. It was one he'd written a few years back about holding on to your dreams. Only, back when he'd written it, he'd been thinking that fame and fortune were the rewards of sticking with it. He hadn't been thinking about love at all.

Not the love of the music, or the love he might find with a woman who believed in him enough to come up with every lie in the book so that he wouldn't let her go. Now that he knew the truth, he would never let her go.

He started singing, and when he looked up, he saw Delphine emerge from the shadows at the back of the auditorium. Her hair was up in its usual messy ponytail, her borrowed T-shirt was two sizes too big, and somewhere along the line, she'd lost one of her tennis shoes.

To him, she was the most beautiful woman in the world.

Bradley started walking toward a set of steps at center stage. As he walked toward her, Delphine took one step and then another, coming closer to the stage as if in a trance. They met at the bottom of the stairs and Bradley set the guitar down, reaching out to take Delphine's hands as he continued to sing.

His voice rang out, clear and true, the words coming from deep within his heart. And when it was over, Bradley kissed her.

It was as if they were alone in the theater, up there on the stage with their mouths—their very souls—locked together. There was a silence in the auditorium such as Bradley had never experienced, a hush like none other he had ever heard.

Bradley lifted his lips from Delphine's and smiled down at the woman he loved.

And then there was pandemonium.

People stood up and cheered, clapping and howling and whistling. Bradley's smile turned to a grin, his face flushing with heat.

They were giving him—Bradley Nelson—a standing ovation.

Bradley bowed, closing his eyes and taking in the applause for all he was worth. After so long being in the shadows, he was going to milk this moment for every bit of pleasure it was worth. No, he wasn't going to win an award this year. But he would keep trying, keep putting his heart and soul into his music until every note, every word, resonated inside him. Then, and only then, would he know he deserved success.

The applause continued and Bradley laughed, reaching out to shake the hands that the front-row bigwigs were offering him. Bradley pushed Delphine in front of Faith Hill and said, "Ms. Hill, I'd like you to meet my fiancée, Delphine. She's a big fan."

Delphine blushed and stuttered and pumped Faith's hand.

And then Bradley pulled Delphine back into his arms and put his forehead on hers, drowning out the sound of the applause. He looked into her soft blue eyes and said, "Delphine, I love this." He waved his hands to indicate the cheering crowd.

"I love this," he repeated. "But I dream of you."

A slow smile spread across Delphine's face as she slid her arms around Bradley's neck. Her lips brushed his as the crowd continued to cheer. "Bradley?" she began, feeling tears well up behind her eyes.

"What, Delphine?"

"Dream on," she said, then smiled as the man she loved took another bow and led her backstage.

Turn the page for an excerpt
from Beverly Brandt's next book

The Tiara Club

Coming soon from
St. Martin's Paperbacks

Georgia Elliot raised the hood on her plastic poncho and pulled the elastic strap of her safety goggles to take up the slack at her temples. The rubber pulled out several strands of curly blond hair as it tightened around her head. Wincing, Georgia picked up the set of tongs next to the burner in front of her and gingerly poked at the can immersed in simmering water. With one gloved hand, she inched the flame up a notch and watched bubbles appear on the surface of the water.

She glanced at a timer as the seconds ticked by.

A blue-lined notebook lay open on the counter behind her. Georgia turned, picked up the pencil lying next to the pad of paper, and scribbled a note. *9:24 p.m., humidity 86%, raised heat to approx. 98° C. No sign of imminent explosion.*

Finally, after three months of experimentation, she was going to have her first success. Tonight, there would be no metal fragments to pick out of the ceiling, no oozing goo dribbling down the walls.

She glanced at the timer again. Only four minutes left to go.

"Georgia, come quick," a voice suddenly shouted from the living room. "We're going to be on TV."

Startled, Georgia poked her head out of the kitchen and into the parlor, where her fellow members of The Tiara Club were gathered, sipping frosty green margaritas and staring intently at Georgia's old thirty-eight-inch console television. Callie Walker Mitchell—Georgia's best friend since kindergarten when the Walkers moved from Birmingham, Alabama, to Ocean Sands, Mississippi, and bought the old Hiram Purdue place next door to the Elliots—aimed the remote control at the TV, pressing her right index finger on the volume button while shushing the occupants of the room.

"Shh, shh," Callie said, gleefully shifting her weight from one foot to the other in a perfect imitation of what Georgia termed the "tee-tee dance." Georgia had baby-sat Callie's four children enough to know that in anyone under ten years of age, the tee-tee dance required immediate action, but she assumed that her best friend's bladder was not what was causing her to jump up and down so frantically.

"What is it?" Georgia asked, glancing back at her timer to see that she had two more minutes left before her experiment could be deemed a complete success.

"Just listen," Callie answered, clicking the volume up another level.

Georgia peered at the television screen as a commercial ended and the cameras cut to a sterile studio kitchen. A granite-topped counter was artistically draped with gleaming produce and several woven baskets. An eight-burner gas cooktop that Georgia would give her Shrimp Festival Princess crown for was flanked by a built-in cutting board, a deep-fat fryer, and a professional grade KitchenAid mixer. Twin ovens, a microwave, and a Sub-Zero refrigerator were set in a wall lined with maple cabinets. It was the kind of setup every gourmet cook dreamed of. Georgia was so busy drooling over the equipment that she hadn't noticed the host of the show, who had entered the set and was looking into the cameras with a smile that didn't quite make it to his bright blue eyes.

"Welcome back to *Epicurean Explorer*. This is Daniel Rogers and today we're exploring products that promise to save you time and money . . . but do they deliver? I must admit that I think a good cook can get by with nothing more than a great set of knives and some decent pots and pans, but there are companies out there that manufacture gizmos that exist for something as simple as removing the seeds from lemon juice or separating an egg—both of which you can do just as easily with an ordinary sieve. On today's show, we went through our viewer mailbag and decided to put some of your favorite gadgets to the test. We were intrigued by a product mentioned in this letter from a Ms. Callie Mitchell in Ocean Sands, Mississippi."

Daniel Rogers picked up a folded sheet of white paper from the counter in front of him and started to read as a collective murmur of surprise went up among the group in the living room. They'd never had someone famous in their midst. "Ms. Mitchell writes, 'I love eating supper with my family because it gives us all a chance to catch up on what is happening in each others' lives. However, as a single mother of four young children, I was finding it impossible to make time for this nightly ritual. Impossible, that is, until my friend, Georgia Elliot, introduced me to a miraculous new product called the Miracle Chef. The Miracle Chef enables me to make a delicious, nutritious, four-course meal in under thirty minutes. Now I have time to not only make supper for my family, but to enjoy eating with them, as well. I'd love it if you would dedicate one show to showing me how to make even more meals in my Miracle Chef. Yours truly, Ms. Callie Walker Mitchell.'"

Daniel Rogers finished reading Callie's letter and stared at the piece of paper in his hand for a moment before turning his head to look right into the camera. Georgia watched as his lips curved up in a slight smile, his teeth white and even. Several strands of curly dark hair lay on his forehead, as artfully arranged as the waxy yellow squash and polished red apples on the counter in front of him.

"Well, Ms. Mitchell, the point of our show today is to prove that a good cook can whip up a four-course meal in under thirty minutes *without* wasting money on these so-called miracle gadgets. I would love to pit my cooking skills against this product but, unfortunately, our staff was unable to locate a Miracle Chef. My advice to anyone out there watching is to keep in mind that if a product seems too good to be true, it most often is." With that, he tossed Callie's letter back onto the counter and flashed his movie-star smile at the cameras before picking up another piece of paper.

Callie blinked at the TV screen, still holding the remote control tightly in her right hand.

Georgia's teeth snapped together as she drew up to her full five-feet-eight-inches and glared down at the television screen. "Why that arrogant son-of-a-Yankee. He has no idea what the Miracle Chef can—" she began, only to gasp when a loud *boom* sounded from the kitchen behind her.

Five of the six women gathered in Georgia's living room dove for cover. Having survived several of these disasters in the prior months, Georgia merely ducked, putting her arms over her head for protection.

"Oh, honey, you did it again," raven-haired Kelly Bremer said from beneath the coffee table, shaking her head.

Georgia turned and looked at the mess in her kitchen, at the light brown mess oozing down her normally clean white kitchen cupboards. With a heartfelt sigh, she walked to the stove and turned off the flame under her saucepan.

One of these days, she was going to get this right. One of these days, she'd find the perfect combination of timing and temperature that would produce the silky caramel that only a slowly simmered can of Eagle brand sweetened condensed milk could provide. She knew other women who could whip up the perfect treat without having can after can blow up in their faces, but, so far, success had eluded her.

A glob of sticky caramel dropped from the ceiling and onto the hood of Georgia's plastic poncho as she reached into the sink for a washrag.

"Want me to get the ladder?" Callie asked, peeking into the kitchen.

"I still have my rubber coat from last time. Want me to get it?" Deborah Lee Tallman offered.

"I brought some praline sauce from that gourmet shop on Main Street. You know, just in case this happened again," Kelly said, having come out from under the coffee table.

The other two members of The Tiara Club, Sierra Riley and Emma Rose Conover, made for the linen closet where Georgia kept her washrags and dishtowels. They'd experienced the fallout of enough of Georgia's experiments to know the drill.

"This is all that arrogant Daniel Rogers's fault," Georgia grumbled, swiping at another glob of caramel that dripped from the ceiling onto her head.

"He sure was rude," Callie agreed, gingerly stepping into the kitchen to help her friend clean up the mess. "But, really, what does it matter? So what if he thinks the Miracle Chef isn't up to his standards? You know that I appreciate it. I'm so glad you found it for me. I even tried to get one for my cousin but the shop on Main said they'd never heard of it. Are you sure you don't remember where you got it?"

Georgia pulled her safety goggles from her eyes and set them on the kitchen counter before rinsing out her washrag and tackling another smear of caramel. "No, I don't remember. I think I picked it up in Jackson the last time I was there with Mama, but I can't recall the name of the store. I'm real sorry."

"That's all right. My cousin turns pea-green with envy every time I use it. Since she's the one always braggin' about how *her* husband would never run off and leave her for another man, I'm actually kind of glad you can't recall where you bought it."

Georgia smiled at her friend.

Georgia and Callie were the founding members of The Tiara Club, a group they'd laughingly formed one night after a pitcher of margaritas. Their membership, they decided, giggling over the memory of putting glue on their behinds to keep their swimsuits from creeping and Scotch-taping their breasts together to create the illusion of cleavage, would consist of recovering beauty queens who had survived the pageant circuit. Both Georgia and Callie had been encouraged by their mothers to compete in pageants from an early age, but Callie's mother had taken her daughter's progress a lot less seriously than Georgia's had. Georgia and Callie decided to hold "recovery group" meetings the first Thursday of every month and opened their membership to their closest friends. Deborah Lee Tallman, Kelly Bremer, and Emma Rose Conover (who was also Georgia's cousin) had dabbled in the beauty pageant ring but hadn't gone all the way to the Miss Mississippi competition like Callie and Georgia had done in their prime. Sierra Riley, on the other hand, was a relative newcomer to the South who had tagged along with her fiancé when he'd been transferred to Ocean Sands three years ago. Three years later, he and Sierra still hadn't tied the knot, and she was still teaching first grade at the school where Callie's twin boys were currently enrolled. Callie had figured any woman who could cheerfully handle thirty hyperactive six-year-olds every day ought to qualify for Tiara Club membership, whether or not she'd ever set foot on a runway. Georgia agreed, and Sierra was invited to join their little group.

So far, The Tiara Club had been through one birth, four divorces (one each for Callie and Georgia, and two for Kelly, who insisted that there was a vast difference between getting a man and actually *keeping* him for any length of time), fourteen funerals, forty-three weddings (none starring a member of The Tiara Club, but since the average Southern wedding included at least nine bridesmaids, the six Tiara Club members had been tapped quite often to put in an appearance at the altar), and countless church potlucks.

Oh, yes, and four explosions while Georgia continued trying to perfect her caramel-making process.

"The viewers are clamoring for a cook-off. They don't believe you can beat the Miracle Chef's claims of a four-course meal in under thirty minutes."

When his boss said those words, Daniel Rogers should have made a joke and let it go at that. Instead, he did what he always did when his abilities were questioned—he weighed his chances for success and, because he believed winning was a sure thing, he said, "I'll take that bet." Which was why, two hours later, Daniel pointed his Internet browser to the site of the United States Patent and Trademark Office and began to perform a patent search on the mysteriously unavailable Miracle Chef. He refused to win this challenge by default.

"What sort of company makes a product that isn't

available anywhere?" he grumbled when the information popped up. The patent was held by one Georgia Marie Elliot in Ocean Sands, Mississippi.

Isn't the Internet grand?

Daniel swiveled around in his chair and picked up a manila folder that had been lying on the corner of his desk. The letters he'd read on last week's show were neatly clipped together under a series of notes he'd used during taping. He pulled out the missive that had started him on this sleuthing mission and reread it. It was obvious from the letter that Ms. Mitchell didn't know that her friend Georgia Elliot had invented the Miracle Chef, and Daniel couldn't help but wonder why there was so much secrecy surrounding the thing.

Whatever the reason, it wasn't going to be kept secret much longer. Daniel had no intention of letting his viewers think he was afraid to pit his skills against this wonder gadget.

He planned to win, no matter what.

"Genteel poverty is not what it's cracked up to be," Georgia muttered under her breath, looking from the bill in her hand to her computer screen and back. She was spared having to tackle her finances when her front doorbell sounded. She wasn't expecting company, but she welcomed the interruption. Before coming upstairs to pay bills, she had taken a pitcher of tea off her sunny back porch and put it in the icebox. Now, with the sun nearly set, a glass of chilled iced tea with company would be a nice start to her evening.

Georgia padded down the hall in her socks, being

careful not to slip on the smooth hardwood floor. She knew her well-bred Southern mother would admonish her for not changing into "proper" shoes before opening the door, but Georgia figured that whoever was arriving unannounced would just have to take her as she was.

When she opened the door, she had a split second to wish she had a whiff of her mother's smelling salts, because the sight of the movie star-handsome man standing outside on her front porch nearly made her fall to the floor in an old-fashioned swoon. She recognized him immediately as Daniel Rogers, the insulting host of that Food TV show Callie had been watching the other night. She had heard somewhere that most celebrities were less better-looking in person, but that was certainly not the case with Daniel Rogers. His dark hair looked softer and shinier, his blue eyes nearly aquamarine in the fading sunlight. His face was all strong angles, like Rock Hudson or Cary Grant back in their glory days. He wore a pair of off-white linen slacks topped with a silvery-blue silk shirt, and on his feet were a pair of the softest, buttery-tan leather loafers that Georgia had ever seen.

If this guy wasn't gay, he'd taken his makeover from the Fab Five of *Queer Eye for the Straight Guy* fame very seriously. No heterosexual male she knew could pull off the linen trousers/loafers with no socks look like this.

Georgia swallowed, trying to get some saliva back into her suddenly dry mouth, and said the first thing that came to her mind, "Mr. Rogers, I presume?"

The corners of his perfect, not-too-thin and not-too-thick mouth curved up in a slight smile and he held out a hand by way of greeting. "Yes. And you're Georgia Elliot, friend of Ms. Callie Walker Mitchell, and inventor of the Miracle Chef."

Georgia's still-dry mouth dropped open with surprise, an expression her mother would have frowned upon with her usual "Are you trying to catch flies, dear?" comment. Recovering as quickly as possible, she blinked her own brown eyes and cocked her head, smiling up at her handsome visitor. "Well, you've got one part of that right. Callie Mitchell has been my best friend since we were five years old. But I'm afraid you're mistaken about me inventing anything. Why, I'm a member of the Junior League, I work at a little gift shop over on the corner of Park and Main, and I've got my hands full takin' care of my ailing mama. Even if I had the inclination to be an inventor, I surely don't have the time."

She fluttered her eyelashes up at Daniel Rogers and put one pink-fingernail-polish-tipped hand on his forearm. She felt his muscles tighten under her fingertips as he narrowed his eyes at her in disbelief. However, before he could say anything further, they were interrupted by the sound of a man clearing his throat.

Daniel stepped to one side and turned toward the sound. A young man stood on the porch steps, wearing a ragged blue uniform with tarnished gold buttons and wielding a musket that was nearly as tall as he was.

"Excuse me," the young man said, taking his hat off and shifting his weight sheepishly from one foot to the next. "I think I'm lost."

"I believe you're looking for 118 *South* Oak Street.

This is 118 *North* Oak Street," Georgia said, stepping around Daniel and walking to the edge of the porch. "The street changes from North to South at Main, so if you'll just go back to Main and continue on for about a block, you'll find the Hall House there on the left."

"Thank you, ma'am," the young man said, doffing his navy blue cap as he turned to leave.

"You're welcome. Tell Miss Beale that Georgia Elliot says hey, would you?"

"Yes, ma'am," the young man said.

"What was that all about?" Daniel asked, his gaze sliding from the retreating faux-soldier to Georgia and back.

Georgia looked at him for a moment, considering the idea that had just come to her. She needed Daniel to believe that she was a simple girl; a simple girl incapable of anything more than being able to serve tea to her guests without spilling it in their laps or knowing how to cut the crusts off her tomato sandwiches without written instructions. A simple girl who could *not* be the inventor of a product he had exposed on national television last week.

Daniel Rogers was just about to discover the lengths she would go to in order to keep her secret from getting out.

Room Service
Beverly Brandt

When jet-setter Katya Morgan's father disinherits her,
Katya must get her money and her cushy life back. Having
no way to pay the enormous bill she racked up at the Royal
Palmetto Hotel in Scottsdale, Arizona, poses a slight problem—and the manager has the gall to suggest the unthink-
able: that she pay off her debt by working at the hotel—as
a maid. Alex Sheridan, the hard-working general manager
of the sumptuous Royal Palmetto Hotel, doesn't much care
for the spoiled Ms. Morgan—at first. But when she dons the
uniform and proves her mettle as a housekeeper who cares
about more than cold, hard cash, he starts falling in love for
the once-spoiled brat who's acting more and more like a
real woman every day . . .

"Another lighthearted office romance touched with humor
and suspense . . . fun, breezy beach reading."
— *Publishers Weekly* on *Room Service*

"Using a storytelling style that blends humor and pathos . . .
Brandt takes a spoiled brat and turns her into a giving indi-
vidual. *Room Service* typifies the warmth and humor of a
Brandt book."
— *Romantic Times* on *Room Service*

ISBN: 0-312-98422-7

**Available wherever books are sold
from St. Martin's Paperbacks**

Record Time

Beverly Brandt

Music mogul David Gamble figured he'd never again see Kylie Rogers so what was the harm if he kissed her? When he discovers that Kylie is a new employee working for his company Gamble Records, he's shocked—and secretly delighted—even if he can't quite admit it yet. David's orderly world turns upside down with disaster-magnet Kylie spreading chaos and skewed publicity in her wake. But when someone sets out to sabotage Gamble Records, David joins forces with Kylie to catch the culprit as they find themselves falling in love in record time . . .

"A playful blend of romance, humor, and light suspense . . . this fun, feel-good romance is the perfect pick-me-up for rainy days."
> —*Publishers Weekly* on *Record Time*

"A wonderfully entertaining book, even more fast-paced than the music-business world it brings to life . . . [will] keep you turning the pages."
> —Elizabeth Bevarly, author of *Take Me, I'm Yours*

"*Record Time* is a sparkling, fast-paced romantic romp. Witty and entertaining to the satisfying end."
> —Stephanie Bond, author of *I Think I Love You*

ISBN: 0-312-98184-8

True North
Beverly Brandt

Rustic Colorado is hardly Claire Brown's idea of a *primo* vacation spot, but the week-long getaway at a romantic mountain lodge promises to heal a rift with her increasingly detached fiancé. Claire decides to give this vacation thing a try. She can't help sensing, though, that her fiancé might not be as committed to their relationship as she is. The dead giveaway: he's brought another woman along on their romantic holiday . . . As proprietor of Hunter's Lodge, John McBride is duty-bound to find suitable accommodations under his sold-out roof for the cell phone-addicted, just-jilted guest. He's determined to steer clear of the suddenly single dynamo who's just checked in for the next nine days. Unfortunately, the annoying, yet very alluring, Claire has a way of popping up when he least expects it—and as John soon discovers, so does true love . . .

"Sassy and sexy with a touch of suspense! Beverly Brandt makes sparks fly in *True North*."
> —Julie Ortolon, bestselling author of *Dear Cupid*

"Filled with great characterization, humor, and excitement, this is a book to relish."
> —*Romantic Times*

ISBN: 0-312-97985-1